THE MONSTERS WE FORGOT

VOLUME 2

REED BEEBE   K. M. BENNETT   R. H. BERRY

VASHTI BOWLAH   R. C. BOWMAN   N. M. BROWN

KENNETH BYKERK   DAVID CLÈMENCEAU

CARYS CROSSEN   JOSEPH CUSUMANO   VICTORIA DALPE

TARA A. DEVLIN   MALINA DOUGLAS

MODUPEH DUNCAN   GINA EASTON   TONY EVANS

MARC G. FERRIS   REBECCA FISHER   DOUGLAS FORD

DAVID GWYN   SAM HAYSOM   GRANT HINTON

J. S. KIERLAND   C. M. LANNING   CONNIE TODD LILA

THAMIRES LUPPI   JAMES D. MABE   DAWN NAPIER

STEPHEN NEWTON   PETER NINNES   MAUREEN O'LEARY

BEKKI PATE   CHARLOTTE PLATT

ALANNA ROBERTSON-WEBB   LIAM RONAN   E. SENECA

J. L. SMITH   TAMIKA THOMPSON   STANLEY B. WEBB

SOTEIRA
PRESS

CONTENTS

THE MONSTERS WE FORGOT

VOLUME 2

RED DEVIL

J. L. SMITH

The sun hangs low in the west and shines in shimmering golden bands through the dense foliage of the swamp. An orchestra of frogs, birds, and insects greets the approaching evening as they either begin or end their respective daily cycles. Still it is peaceful, and what typically passes for *quiet* in such areas.

Ted Beaumont creeps as quietly as possible through the grass along the swamp's edge as only a well-seasoned hunter can. He listens closely, picking out every sound: frogs, bugs, birds. In the distance there comes a heavy splash. His eyes scan the foliage, skillfully breaking up nature's camouflage and searching for any minute movement. He sniffs the air and at first smells only swamp. He has only the barest moment to pick out something else—something *sour* riding on the gentle breeze—when the *SNAP* of a twig breaks his concentration. With a low, exasperated sigh, he glances over his shoulder to his son Ted Jr., standing stone-still and looking guiltily down at the small, broken branch peeking from beneath his boot.

"Boy, *watch* where yer *walkin'*," Ted quietly scolds.

"Sorry," the young man sighs.

Ted returns to scanning the distance, and momentarily thinks he sees movement. Wordlessly he raises his rifle, loosely shouldering it to peer through the scope. He searches, using the simple crosshairs to separate trees from bushes.

There seems to be something out of place. Ted focuses, patiently picking out a patch of reddish-brown fur amid the foliage. It's barely visible, and he doesn't know what it is. What he *does* know is that it has no reason being there. As he watches, he can't help but think that whatever it is seems to be *hiding* from him.

He licks his lips, breathing slow and shallow, not moving a single muscle.

"Somethin' wrong?" Ted Jr. asks.

The barely-there patch of red instantly disappears from Ted's view. He sighs heavily in annoyance. Lowering the rifle, he turns to look at his son and steps aside. With a toss of his head, he gestures for Ted Jr. to go on ahead of him.

With a bit of reluctance—and feeling as though all his father sees in him is failure—Ted Jr. starts into motion, moving along the swamp's edge. After a few steps, he realizes that he is the only one walking. He stops and turns. "You comin'?" he asks.

"Go on." Ted nods up toward the foliage where he saw the patch of red fur. "You get it out in the open."

Ted Jr. swallows hard, nodding and hoping he doesn't screw up again.

As his son moves cautiously upland, Ted raises his rifle and once more finds the spot he'd been watching. He sees no sign of the patch of fur, nor any further movement. Briefly, Ted Jr. moves through his line of sight—his line of *fire*—and Ted Sr. waits impatiently for him to pass. Once the boy is clear, Father goes back to task, hoping Son doesn't screw up—*again.*

Ted Jr. steps as carefully and cautiously as he can, trying not to make too much noise. He knows he is meant to scare whatever animal his father has spotted out into the open, but knows also that if he spooks it too soon, he may not be able to spur it into the proper direction. He's unsure of exactly what he's looking for, so he keeps an eye open for anything out of the ordinary. As he moves, he monitors the swamp's edge. If he's not careful, he could end up *becoming* dinner, rather than "scaring it up."

The thought of dinner distracts him briefly, reminding him of the pain in his belly; ever-present now, after a good three days without a proper meal. He used to ask his father why they didn't just move out of the swamp, into even a *small* town, where there might be food to buy and work to earn the money for it. But Ted had grown up in the swamp—lived there all his life—and insisted that he'd die there if he had any say in the matter.

Suddenly Ted Jr. stops, and food becomes the farthest thing from his mind. There is an overpowering stench, and he is sure that there must be a gas pocket nearby. Covering his nose and mouth, he tries not to retch. Then a rustling from the foliage just up ahead catches his attention.

Keeping his nose and mouth covered, he starts cautiously forward. He isn't totally sure when the rustling is coming from his movements and when they're coming from ahead, but he is sure that the animal is close. As if to confirm this, he sees a shift among the flora.

Then suddenly the smell on the air doesn't matter, because Ted Jr. can't even breathe.

Ted Sr. catches movement in the scope, but his son partially obscures his line of sight. He holds back an expletive, hoping the boy will smarten up on his own and move. At the same moment, the red-furred animal that he'd glimpsed before darts out into the open. He can't tell what it is, but at this point doesn't care; they need to *eat*. He gets it in the crosshairs, anxiously waiting for it to get far enough away from his son for him to take the shot, but the angle keeps Ted Jr. too near the scope's field of view.

Dammit! he thinks, then yells, "*Move*, boy!"

Behind him, Ted Jr. can hear his father. He understands the command. But astonishment keeps him rooted to the spot like a sapling.

"MOVE, dammit!"

Ted Sr.'s jaw tightens, anxiously watching the low-loping animal as it moves farther away.

Dammit boy…

He does his best to keep the thin black lines of the crosshairs on the moving patch of red, making a last-second decision to take the shot—despite the fact that his son is still dangerously positioned. For half a heartbeat he thinks it would serve the boy right. He squeezes the trigger.

Ted Jr. flinches at the rifle's report. The streaking blur of red drops still about twenty yards from him. His heart pounds hard, and blood rushes in his ears. He still can't believe what he saw hiding in the bushes just moments before, and can't believe that his father just *shot* it.

We can't eat that, he thinks.

"Did I get 'im?" Ted calls.

Ted Jr. can't even nod, still transfixed on the tall grass where the thing fell.

What is it? he wonders.

His father slings the rifle over his shoulder with a perturbed sigh and grumbles, "You'd think the boy never seen a dead animal." With no further need for caution or quiet, he starts toward his son—and their dinner.

As he approaches, he notices that the sour smell has returned. It becomes more potent with every step. He grimaces against it as it grows, and hopes that whatever he's killed wasn't sick.

Ted Jr. doesn't budge, and doesn't look away from the kill. Ted Sr. bites back a barb as he comes up behind his *precious* son, and follows the boy's gaze. Suddenly, he is devoid of any anger as his mind tries to desperately wrap itself around the *thing* that lies on the ground before them.

"What the hell...?" he manages. He hands the rifle off to his son. The boy doesn't take it right away, his attention still held rapt by the creature.

"Take this," Ted Sr. instructs. Ted Jr. obeys without shifting his unblinking gaze. On his periphery, he sees his father take two steps toward the small, red-furred beast and kneel.

"Pa, *don't*—!" he says as his father reaches for the carcass. Ted Sr. shoots him a look that he knows all too well, one that says *shut yer mouth or else!*

Then his father turns back to the small form and touches it.

Ted can scarcely keep from gagging on the animal's stink, and nearly cringes at the stiff, dirty feel of its fur. The still-warm body lies facedown, so Ted gives it a careless shove to turn it over onto its back, expecting to see something foxlike.

What he sees instead is a small, *monkey-like* face with a short snout and a mouth that hangs slack, exposing four long, dangerous fangs.

He swallows hard, trying to find his voice. Instead he gives the creature another nudge, just on the small chance that it's playing possum. It stays still.

"Pa..." Ted Jr. says softly.

"Hush, boy." Ted's tone is soft but irritable.

He cautiously moves his trembling hand near the thing's face, and uses his thumb to push one eyelid up, exposing a large amber-colored iris centered with an inky-black slitted pupil.

Believing the thing to be truly dead, Ted sits back on his heel. He lets out a short chuckle.

"Hell, boy... d'you got any idea what this is?"

Ted Jr. shakes his head, then realizes his father isn't looking at him, but at the strange, red-furred animal. He is about to answer, but Ted Sr. goes on.

"Way back when I was a boy, 'bout yer age or younger, my pa used to tell me 'bout the *Red Devil*."

"What is it?" Ted Jr. manages.

His father just shakes his head. "Don't really know, son. Hell, I never thought it was *real*. Some say it come from the swamp. Some say it ain't natural… an' I'll agree to that."

"You mean…" Ted Jr. swallows, his mouth feeling very dry. "You mean it's been around all these years, all this time…"

Ted hears something like panic in his son's voice, and whips his head around to see a sight that truly disgusts him. "Boy, wipe yer face an' be a man. It's just an animal. An' now…" He stands, smirking down at the small bag of bones and fur. "It's *supper*."

Ted Jr. wipes the single tear from his cheek, and when he hears the word *supper* can't help but cringe.

"Pa, we can't—"

"Boy, if the next words out o' yer mouth ain't 'waste this perfectly good meat' then you best just shut it."

Ted Jr. does as instructed, as his next words were not what his father wanted to hear. He looks down at the creature, thinking he doesn't even want to touch it, let alone eat it. Then, as if reading his thoughts and wanting to punish him for what he sees, Ted Sr. tells his son *he* can carry it back home. Ted Jr. wants to protest, but fears what reprisal might come if he does.

With a pit of dread in his stomach and his gorge nearly in his throat, he hands the rifle back to his father, then moves tentatively toward the beast and kneels beside it. He looks it over, desperately wanting *not* to touch it, but knowing he must. With a quiet sigh he wraps one bony hand around the thing's wrists, cringing as he does though trying not to show it, and awkwardly wraps the other around its ankles. He stands, hoisting the creature up and noting that it isn't very heavy. Holding it out from his body, he turns to his father.

Ted Sr. observes the awkward way that his son holds the dead animal and shakes his head.

"Hell, boy," he says, taking a handful of the thick red fur and lifting the animal up and over his son's head and onto his shoulders, "ye gonna go through yer whole *life* the hard way?"

Again, Ted Jr. cringes, nearly sick at just the sensation of the bloody, still-warm body draped around his neck. He watches as his father starts back the way they came, and in the back of his mind wonders just why he seems to hate him so.

. . .

Ted Sr. enters the small cabin silently, without even a backward glance at his son. He was quiet the entire walk back, and Ted Jr. had to put forth pained effort to keep from sniffling and to control the hitching in his chest. He is about to drop the now-cool body onto the cabin's small stoop when his father calls from inside for him to "Bring it." He reaches up to swipe a nearly-dry tear on his cheek but instead feels fur. He jerks his head away in disgust before entering the cabin.

He spends the next half-hour watching his father skin and gut the small animal. He would prefer not to, but knows that he will only bring more of his father's scorn upon himself if he doesn't.

"Y'know," Ted Sr. says, "I'd have thought this thing'd be the size of a bear from the stories my pa told." He studies the carcass with furrowed brow as he cuts skin away from flesh. "I doubt this'll last more'n a few days."

Ted Jr. chokes back bile as his father separates pelt from meat. Once finished, he sets the dirty, smelly fur aside and goes about butchering. He looks a bit awkward at first, as the animal's shape isn't one that he's used to, but soon enough seems comfortable with it.

"We're gonna eat good tonight, boy," he says with a satisfied grin. "Meat's good & lean."

Ted Jr. swallows thickly.

"I'm not really hungry, Pa."

Ted Sr. quits his task and sets the knife down with a *clunk*.

"Boy, what the hell is *wrong* with you? I swear, sometimes it's like you ain't even my son."

Ted Jr. just stares at his father, unsurprised by the man's words.

When the boy says nothing, Ted Sr. continues to butcher the animal, shaking his head irritably as he lets out an exasperated sigh, "Fine," he says gruffly. "Ye ain't hungry—don't eat. But do me a favor *if it ain't too much trouble* an' toss *this* out, will ye?" He carelessly hands over the bloody pelt. "Ain't worth nothin' no how."

Ted Jr. reluctantly accepts the remains, not at all certain if his father's disparaging remark was aimed at the pelt or at Ted Jr. himself. Wordlessly, he takes the hunk of fur and bloody skin outside and gets to work digging a small hole to bury it in. He gazes warily down at his handiwork, and recalls his father's reprimand—trying his best to ignore the hunger-pain that wracks him.

You ain't hungry—don't eat.

And he doesn't.

While Ted Sr. eats greedily, slurping down spoonful after spoonful of the stew he's made with the leanest meat and a few nearly-spoiled vegetables, Ted Jr. just watches, unable to imagine bringing even a single bite of the strange meat to his lips. He'd scrubbed for all he was worth after burying the skin, wanting desperately to be rid of any essence of it.

His father looks over at him countless times, practically sneering with contempt and grumbling under his breath. He spoons out the last bit of stew in his bowl, then stands and wordlessly moves over to the still-simmering pot, ladling out another helping while pointedly glaring at his son. With a scoff, he goes back to the small dining table and digs in.

Going to bed without supper wasn't necessarily a new thing in the Beaumont cabin, but usually it was due to a *lack* of food. Never before had Ted Jr. willingly missed a meal when food was available. But as he lays there, only half covered by a thin sheet and boiling in humidity, he can't help but wonder if what his father ate really was "food." Again and again he replays the image of the animal as it fled, sees it darting out from the mess of grass and plants where it had been hiding. He hadn't told his father, but the animal had first looked up at him, and there was a discernible look of fear. Then it had run.

It had *run*.

It was only for a second, maybe two steps, but it had taken them while being nearly fully upright before falling to all fours to try and escape. And when the bullet struck, leaving the briefest cloud of red mist hanging in the air, it had let out the most pathetic *mewling* sound. Like a newborn baby.

Ted Jr. tosses and turns, throws off the sheet, then quickly pulls it back on despite the cloistering heat, feeling suddenly exposed.

Despite the discomfort—physical as well as mental—he soon starts to drift. But he fights it, worried that he'll see it again. Not just the creature, but its eyes. He fears that he will dream of the almost human expressiveness, of the small body falling dead, and finally of his father butchering and devouring its meat.

Eventually, however, exhaustion takes its toll, and Ted Jr. begins to drift again. He's almost out, slipping over the precipice of consciousness, when an unfamiliar howl lets out in the distance.

He shoots straight up in his saggy bed and freezes, shrouded in darkness and listening intently to the usual sounds of insects and night birds, and hoping that *other* sound was all in his head; just a nightmare he was lucky enough to wake from before it really started. And in his tired state he's already forgetting what it sounded like, remembering only that it was like nothing he'd ever heard before.

Soon Ted Jr. realizes that he is no longer too warm, as he is covered in a cold sweat and nearly shivering. He swallows dryly and keeps listening. He hears only the usual swampy nightlife. Again he pulls the cover up and closes his eyes.

Then the howl comes again, sending a spike of fear right into his heart and locking his air in tight. This time he can't even sit up; he's frozen in his bed, straining to listen through the sudden deathly silence of the swamp. Raising his head off the pillow just enough to glance toward his father's bed, he sees that the man still sleeps soundly.

Though fairly sure his father could sleep through just about anything, how he can still be softly snoring after two such horrific shrieks, Ted Jr. can't figure. After all, the second seemed to be just a bit louder, a little bit closer, and carried less of an echo.

Again, Ted Jr. can't help but notice the quiet that replaces the usually lively outdoors of the nighttime swamp. Quietly, he lets out a slow, steady breath, realizing that his lungs have begun to ever so subtly throb. Then he freezes again, sure that in the stillness he can hear something approaching the cabin, rustling the surrounding foliage as it nears. He listens for what feels like several minutes, but is in reality only agonizing seconds. His heart throbs in his throat, which feels dry as a wad of cotton balls, leaving him unable to swallow. For a moment all is deathly quiet.

Then the sound of a creaky board on the cabin's front porch turns his blood to sludgy ice-water in his veins.

For several moments, the only sounds are Ted Sr.'s snoring and Ted Jr.'s thunderous heart, threatening to burst forth from his chest. Then comes another creak. And one more.

Ted Jr. wants to call out to his father, wants to get up himself, grab the rifle and point it at the front door, poised to blow a hole in whoever—or whatever—waits on the other side.

Bedsprings squeak, and his head snaps toward his father's direction, eyes wide and unblinking, cold and dry.

Ted Sr. looks at his son and slowly swings one bare foot down onto the dusty wood floor. He brings one finger to his lips in a silent *shush*. He doesn't realize the boy couldn't make a sound if his life depended on it. And when there is one final groan of shifting wood, the faintest sound of some animal breathing huskily from just outside, Ted Jr.'s eyes twitch uneasily to the cabin's front door where a large shadow shifts, blacking out the thin crack of moonlight that bleeds through the frame.

His bladder lets go, soaking his bed and his pants in the warmth of his fear. He's glad his pa won't notice, and truthfully, even *he* barely notices through the terror he feels at what waits just outside the cabin.

There is another light, springy creak from the bed. From the corner of his eye Ted Jr. sees his pa easing the other leg down over the edge of the bed.

Ted Sr. stands—as quietly as possible, though not without some complaint from both the bed and old floorboards—and reaches for his rifle. His eyes never leave the cabin door as he takes the weapon up and shoulders it.

With a sudden *CRASH* of splintering wood, the cabin door bursts inward. A humid gust of swampy night air wafts into the room, carrying the same rancid stench from before. Neither Ted can help but retch and gag as they gaze through watery eyes at a large, beastly shape standing just inside the cabin, silhouetted by the moonlight.

At first, Ted Jr. has no clue what he's looking at. His mind stops working altogether, leaving him unable to comprehend the large, hunched figure, or the red-tinged aura that borders the silhouette in wild tufts. But when his own eyes lock onto two dimly lit pinpoints of color, he feels every last bit of air evacuate his lungs, every clammy bead of sweat that coats his entire body, every hair that stands on end and every muscle in him that threatens to give and send him collapsing to the dirty floor.

He looks over suddenly at the sound of the bolt on his father's rifle, but he can tell right off that the report isn't right. In the dim he can see that his pa is toiling with the jammed bolt. Ted Sr.'s breath hitches with effort as he strains to push the bolt forward and back down, but the steel seems frozen in place. All is quiet save for the harsh sound of the creature's breathing and Ted Sr. struggling to unjam the rifle.

Then the creature begins to lumber slowly forward. As it nears, both father and son realize that it holds something in its long-clawed hands. What they see there is all that's left of the night's dinner: the smaller Red Devil's dirty, ragged, bloody pelt.

Ted Jr. immediately realizes that if the thing his father shot and killed was *a* Red Devil, it wasn't the *only* Red Devil; it was a child, and now the parent had come looking for it.

Ted Jr. can hear his father grunting in effort. The rifle's bolt won't budge, and the creature—the *real* Red Devil—grows closer by the second, until it stands mere inches before them.

Only then do Ted Sr.'s efforts come to a stop, the rifle dead in his hands. Ted Jr. thinks he will faint as the beast—head and shoulders taller than he, and a head still taller than his father—leans in and begins to scent him. With a guttural exhalation, it settles back momentarily before bringing up the skin of its offspring and turning to look to Ted Sr.

The Red Devil leans in again and scents.

Ted Sr. knows then that it knows.

It knows that he is the one that killed and devoured its young.

The creature straightens itself as its chest expands. Then, within the confines of the small Beaumont cabin, it lets out with that blood-curdling howl.

Ted Jr. faintly hears as his father releases a fearful shriek. His mind races. He wishes he'd never even laid eyes on the little Red Devil, wishes his father had never shot it, wishes he'd never even seen a swamp, let alone been raised in one. And with a final anguished sob, Ted Jr. knows beyond a shadow of a doubt that his short, unhappy, unfair life is nearly over.

Ted Sr. drops the jammed rifle. He grabs hold of his son's arm, jerking the boy to stand between him and the beast as he begins to blabber.

"Take 'im!" Ted Sr. sobs, giving his son a shove. Ted Jr. instinctively plants his feet, resisting his father's strength.

"Take *him*!" Ted Sr. begs again, keeping his son at arm's length like a shield.

All goes quiet save for Ted Jr.'s short, shallow, wincing breaths, his father's hoarse, labored panting, and the low, animal purring sound emanating the hulking beast. In the darkness its eyes are dully reflective. The stench that emanates from it fills the cabin with cloying acridity. The stench fills Ted Jr.'s throat, and he feels he is on the verge of retching. Fear alone keeps him standing.

Once again, the Red Devil leans in and sniffs the boy. In his mind's eye he can see it snatching him up in some horrid version of eye for an eye and taking him away, off into the night and into the swamp, tearing him apart and devouring him, just as his father had the Devil's young. As it releases another piercing howl, Ted Jr. covers his ears, closes his eyes, and waits for the agony of teeth and claws tearing into his raw, sweaty flesh.

When it doesn't come, he opens his eyes and peers into the dim.

Then the Devil's long-fingered, clawed hands wrap around his shoulders.

He's especially glad to have forgone dinner, as he's sure his bowels would've let go. Effortlessly the Devil lifts Ted Jr. into the air, so close that it is practically *nuzzling* the boy, and deeply scents its scant quarry.

"Yeah," Ted Sr. quavers. "He's all yours."

The creature turns its gaze to the man with a single quick jerk of its head, and Ted Jr. is suddenly tossed aside, his head knocking into the wall with a painful, sickening *thump.*

The Devil leans in toward Ted Sr. and the man almost chokes on the stench of the beast. When the monster shrieks again, Ted Sr. responds in kind, screaming in terror. The Devil takes in a long, deep whiff of the man and snarls, baring its many fangs in the dim.

Still dazed and crumpled on the floor in pain, Ted Jr. doesn't see the Red Devil wrap its long, bony fingers around his father's head, easily *palming* it, and drag the man from the cabin. In his semi-conscious state, he is barely aware of the man's steadily distancing screams. Within moments the boy's fear, stress and fatigue take him over, sending him into full unconsciousness.

When Ted Jr. comes to, he is greeted by the usual early morning sounds of the swamp. He groggily eases himself up onto one elbow, then moves up to a sitting position. His head aches and his stomach feels tied in knots of hunger. For just a moment he wonders why he is on the floor. Then, as his sleepy eyes rove over to the cabin's front door—which hangs ajar on one hinge, letting the morning light spill in to highlight ghostly motes of dust—he remembers: *The Red Devil.*

Cold fear rushes over Ted Jr. at once, causing him to shiver. His eyes shoot down to the rifle nearby, the bolt still jammed, then over to his father's empty bed.

Pa... he mouths.

Despite the sudden tremor that overtakes him, he gets to his feet. He walks cautiously over to the door, certain he'll see the gory remains of his father torn and spread across the porch, all bits of bone and puddles of blood, maybe even his skin tossed carelessly aside, just as he'd done to the little Red Devil.

Cold sweat trickles down every inch of Ted Jr.'s body as he nears the door. Each of his small, timid steps cover hardly any distance. The warm morning breeze drifts in, carrying with it the faintest trace of the horrible stench from the night before. For just a moment, Ted Jr. stops. He swallows dryly, attempting to wet his lips, and forces himself forward.

At first the sunlight is too bright. He squints, shielding his eyes with his free hand. As his vision adjusts, he takes in the sight.

The swamp is just as it would be any other morning. There is no visible trace of the creature or Ted's father anywhere to be seen.

BLACK MUMMY

REED BEEBE

"Robert stood at the crossroads with his offering. Because he hated the sight of blood and it was almost midnight, he slaughtered the chicken quickly, offering silent thanks to the bird for its sacrifice."

— *UNWRAPPING "BLACK MUMMY": A HISTORY*

Film historian Cameron Tyler opens his 800-page panegyric to the film *Black Mummy* by imagining the movie's director, Robert Labrecque, at a Louisiana crossroads, summoning the devil in order to trade his soul for a cinematic masterpiece. While previous scholarly works have ignored the dark stories surrounding the film, Tyler's book makes the movie's legend and tragedies its centerpiece. The result is a chilling read just as spooky as the movie it examines.

Black Mummy is arguably the scariest movie of the 1970s. Critically and commercially successful (it beat out that other 1973 horror movie, *The Exorcist*, by about $10 million at the box office, an impressive feat for a low-budget "blaxploitation" film produced primarily for distribution to an urban African-American market), the film benefits from its creative triangle—Labrecque, the writer/director, who wanted to create not just another blaxploitation film in the mold of *Blacula*, but an enduring horror film; Seabury Lyme, an acclaimed British stage actor appearing in his first American movie; and Denise Page, a beautiful young actress starring in her debut film.

The film's success—and tragedies—inspired the legend that Labrecque sold his soul to Satan. Tyler finds that Labrecque contributed to this myth; Labrecque boasted to his colleagues that his grandmother was a New Orleans voodoo priestess, and that he practiced witchcraft. While Tyler interviews several contemporaries who recall Labrecque's claims, there are no eyewitnesses to Labrecque's proclaimed occultism.

Some point to Labrecque's previous mediocre work—two uninspired blaxploitation gangster films—as further evidence that something diabolical was involved in the creation of *Black Mummy*. But Tyler believes that the director was shrewd to cast Lyme and Page in the movie, as their performances are largely responsible for the movie's success.

Tyler examines the party scene so central to the film's occult legend: Yvonne Carter (Page), an archaeologist, visits the mansion of Lazarus Duke (Lyme), who shows Carter his prize possession, an Egyptian mummy he would like her to study. Significantly, Duke is hosting a Halloween party; the scene has background actors wearing macabre costumes. Among this gruesome group, two actors stand out: a decomposed man and woman with horrid facial expressions shamble in the background. The two are so horrific that they distract from Lyme and Page's performances; the actors also bear an uncanny resemblance to Lyme's wife and Page's father, both dead.

Tyler finds that no one has been able to identify these actors; indeed, none of the other actors or crew recall seeing them during filming. Because the two steal the scene, it is puzzling why Labrecque would include them in the final cut. And the resemblance to the deceased is eerie, given later events.

One week after filming wrapped, police found Lyme dead in his Los Angeles apartment, a suicide. The police were there to arrest him for the murder of his wife; British authorities had found her decomposed body buried at Lyme's countryside home. Neighbors reported that the couple had been feuding for months; the public commotion ceased just days before Lyme's departure to America.

Page's body was discovered days later, her throat slit. Her father was murdered a year before in the same fashion. Local police suspected Page was responsible for her father's death, but small-town community sympathy hindered the investigation; Page's father was an unliked, abusive drunk, and when Page left for Hollywood, the investigation was quietly closed. The actress' murder remains unsolved.

Labrecque disappeared three days after the movie's premiere. His whereabouts are a mystery and, along with the other tragedies, fuel the myth that supernatural forces had a hand in the creation of *Black Mummy*. Tyler concludes the book noting that multiple fans swear they have seen an elusive, haunted-looking figure resembling Labrecque at various screenings of *Black Mummy*; these sightings are a fitting indicator that the folklore surrounding the film persists.

* * *

The veteran police detective noticed the book on the floor, a thick tome with a title he found humorous: *Unwrapping "Black Mummy": A History*. It was the only bit of humor at the grim crime scene, a party turned bad. The host had invited his friends over to watch a movie—*That movie*, thought the detective—and had decided to blow his brains out, after he shot and killed his guests.

The apartment was hot. The detective thought the place smelled weird, the odor an odd mix of blood, gunpowder, and something else… brimstone? An image of actress Denise Page, a look of horror on her face, was frozen on the television screen.

The CSI took pictures of the deceased. "You think there's any truth to that urban legend?" she asked the detective. "About *Black Mummy*?"

"Nah," he responded. "It's a popular movie. It's watched by a lot of people, so of course you find it at a lot of crime scenes. That's all it is. No devil voodoo shit."

The detective wished he was as certain as he sounded. Over the course of his career, the movie had turned up at the locations of so many violent incidents, suicides, and murders, it was strange. The detective turned to look at the television and the captured terror of a long-dead actress. Looking at her eyes, he felt a chill.

ANGRY SLASH OF BLOOD

TAMIKA THOMPSON

Even in her liquored-up state, Shareefa didn't believe in monsters. When the fellas at the bar had brought up "Skinned Alive" and offered the legendary beast as an explanation for the local slayings, Shareefa figured that was just the half-pint of Johnnie Walker talking. "This is Medford," she'd argued. "The killer is probably some cracker who wandered here from the suburbs, high off smack."

But, as she wobbled up the porch steps, stood at her front door, and held up her chain to the light of the half-moon—*Which shiny piece of nickel silver was the correct damn key?*—a chill crept up her neck. She swayed on those creaky wooden planks, slid the key in the lock, and waited for the goosebumps to pass. She was pissed as hell that talk of the shape-shifting creature had actually gotten to her. The home where tonight's murders took place was two blocks from hers. Shareefa wanted to make sure Maisoon was okay.

The key fit perfectly in the hole, but the lock seemed stuck. Maisoon wasn't expecting her this early in the night. Shareefa couldn't be sure whether the door was jammed or Maisoon had gotten hold of her Gorilla Epoxy and poured the glue in the slot, locking her out. Maisoon had done that several times before.

A leaf crunched across the street. Shareefa glanced over her right shoulder, but no one was there, just a row of one- and two-story homes with facades of brick or aluminum siding. She and Maisoon lived in one of the better 'hoods Medford had to offer. The sound of gunshots was always far away, and their neighbors usually sat out front having a drink and watching their kids play basketball in the street until it was too dark and cold to continue. But not tonight. Folks were scared. The street was bathed in dim, orange streetlight but empty. All porch lights were out. The road was slick with untouched dew since cars probably hadn't driven down the asphalt in hours.

She yanked the collar of her leather jacket up to cover her neck. The previous day, she'd gotten a fresh shave on her Mohawk. Her scalp felt every October breeze, and the bitter air was killing her whiskey-buzz. She twisted her key the other way. The lock still didn't budge.

"Ain't this some shit?" Shareefa's pick-up had given out on her ten blocks from home. Police had shut down three streets near hers, which forced her— debauched and with leaden feet—to trudge a quarter mile around her neighborhood. To top off this shit-sandwich of a day, Maisoon also hadn't picked up the freakin' phone, probably still mad about their fight the previous night.

Wind whistled in the trees that lined the curb, shaking more leaves from the branches and littering the ground. When Shareefa stared at her home, the brick seemed paler than it had seconds ago. They'd hung two signs outside the front door when Maisoon had moved in. Maisoon's read, "Sharp-tongued. Butch-proud. Enter at your own risk." Shareefa's read, "To kill me, you have to die with me." No one ever knocked on their door. Not FedEx, not UPS, not even the Jehovah's Witnesses. The signs usually made Shareefa chuckle, but tonight they reminded her of how she and Maisoon had insulated themselves from friends, family, and neighbors with bold displays of anger. Other than the fellas, whom she only talked sports and killer mythical beasts with, Shareefa spoke to Maisoon and no one else, making the days and sometimes weeks of Maisoon's silent treatment all the more disorienting and lonely.

It was the first night they'd met. A decade ago. At a nightclub. Shareefa had saved Maisoon from an ass-whooping. Maisoon had picked a fight with some heifer over the use of a spare chair. That first night, Shareefa watched the quiet, potty-lipped brunette in the corner go from innocent and calm to raging lunatic, and the transformation had turned Shareefa on in a way that nothing had before. Shareefa took Maisoon—petite frame and dressed in a floral skirt—back home that night. Maisoon never left, and Shareefa never wanted her to.

She jiggled the key in the slot. The lock still didn't give. Her whiskey-buzz was gone completely, replaced by an ache that pounded her head. She rubbed her temples as if to blot out her shame. After all her promises to Maisoon, after spending three months regaining Maisoon's trust, and several more pretending to be in AA, Shareefa still woke this morning on the hallway floor, head throbbing, dripping cut on her arm, and no memory of the evening beyond her fifth shot of tequila. What she did remember, she wanted to forget. She could remember an argument, or more like Maisoon shouting at her and Shareefa stonewalling Maisoon, which was really just a silent shout.

She glanced down at her forearm. But how had she gotten the wound? What had she done? After the morning she'd had, she should have been over the taste of alcohol forever. But she'd be lying if she said she wasn't still longing for another sip of scotch.

Feeling like a damn fool, Shareefa knocked on her own front door. No answer. This scenario was familiar. Maisoon regularly stopped speaking to her, or destroyed necklaces and bracelets that Shareefa had given her, or made Shareefa beg and scratch to get into the squat one-bedroom she'd bought with the only savings she'd probably ever have. This time, Maisoon had screamed at her about, "The lies. The filthy fucking lies!" Maisoon had said she'd tailed Shareefa for a day. Had seen Shareefa skip AA to meet the fellas near the abandoned auto plant for an early-morning drink. Had seen Shareefa on her lunch break from the body shop grabbing a beer and burger at the pub around the corner. Had seen Shareefa meet the fellas again at a bar after work instead of putting in overtime, like she'd said she would. In response, Shareefa had chastised Maisoon for spying on her, but that hadn't gone over well. The circumstances of the fight didn't really matter. Every argument they had was about the same thing—trust, or the lack thereof.

It was their first wedding anniversary. Just as Maisoon said, "I'll never let you go," a cloud passed over the sun, a shadow covered the left side of Maisoon's face, and Shareefa's wife glared at her—a fiendish glare that contained a threat of iniquity. Shareefa should have known then that their future together would be troubled.

Sirens wailed the next street over. The police lights strobed between the homes. Just before her truck had died, the radio reports had said that within a five-block radius, four people were strangled in their beds, one with his neck snapped. The reporters said that in each home, from the master bedrooms to the beams of the front doors, all that the suspect had left behind was "an angry slash of blood," shaped like a fingertip dragged along the wall.

"Signature Skinned Alive," the fellas had said at the bar. "No obvious motive. He offs happily married couples. Then leaves his mark just before trans-forming back to a regular simp."

Two witnesses had said the killer was naked and covered in so much blood that it looked as if he'd skinned himself head to toe. The evidence backed up the "skinned himself" theory because the blood on the wall didn't match that of the victims. That was the part of the story that messed with Shareefa the most. Imag-ining all that blood.

The killings had come in waves—four earlier in the year, in March, then two the previous night, and two tonight. "Beast must be ticked off about something," the fellas had said. All Shareefa wanted to do was make sure Maisoon was okay. *Was that so bad?* Maybe the news reports had frightened Maisoon enough to be relieved to see her and open the jammed—or purposely locked—door.

Leaving the key still hanging out of the lock, Shareefa grabbed the knob and shook the door in its frame.

"Babe? You home? Open up!" The slider stayed put. "Shit."

Another breeze grazed her cheeks and ears. A dog barked on the next street. It was a persistent bark, as if the mutt had spotted a squirrel or skunk in its yard.

She took out her phone and tried Maisoon one more time. The line trilled in her ear. She imagined Maisoon, with that dark edge that appeared in her eyes when she was angry, glaring at the phone in her hands, perhaps cursing Shareefa the way she had the previous night, threatening to leave, threatening to tell Shareefa's probation officer that she was drinking again, threatening to cut Shareefa if she didn't keep her "dirty, deceitful hands" to herself.

Maisoon's suppressed anger always drew Shareefa in, made it so that even in the heat of their disagreement, Shareefa couldn't keep her hands off of Maisoon's thick thighs, dainty neck, juicy lips, long tresses. But whenever Maisoon erupted, it repelled Shareefa. Made Shareefa worried for what her wife might really be capable of. Shareefa glanced again at the bandage covering the slice on her arm and wondered whether Maisoon had, in fact, slashed her with that razor blade she'd pulled from the medicine cabinet.

A familiar buzzing sound sprang up from inside the house. The low hum coincided with the line still ringing in Shareefa's ear. Maisoon's phone was vibrating on the other side of the door. The tiny device was probably gliding across the wooden entry table, its light blinking in the dark of their living room. But where was Maisoon? Was she just on the other side of that door, peering into the screen's glow, ignoring Shareefa's knocks and calls?

The dog's barks came to an abrupt stop. The animal whimpered once and then grew quiet. A thump came from inside the house. She pressed her ear against the cold wood. Another thud from behind the door was followed by a muffled scream. *What the hell?*

"Maisoon?" She looked around the desolate street in the hopes that someone would have been brave enough to venture out. No luck. She had no one to help her, short of calling the police. And the last time she'd dialed 911 for help with one of Maisoon's angry episodes, the mofos arrived, took one look at Shareefa—six feet tall, muscular as hell, with "bad bitch" tatted on her neck—and threw her black ass in the squad car.

A surge of adrenaline shot through Shareefa's gut. She stepped back, kicked the wood near the knob three times to loosen it, and, using the left side of her body, slammed her weight into the door. The slider dislodged. The door banged open. She snatched her keys from the lock. Warm air from the radiator rushed out to meet her.

In the living room, she flipped on the light. Maisoon's phone lay on the floor at the head of the dark hallway. Shareefa's head pounded harder as she edged toward the darkness and clicked on the hall light. She wanted to shout to Maisoon, but she kept quiet. Cautious.

Droplets of blood dotted the wooden floor. Shareefa's ears rang when Maisoon's t-shirt and jeans, blood-soaked and scattered near their bedroom door, came into view. The fighter inside of her, who usually emerged in bar brawls and acts of road rage, woke up and readied her for a physical struggle. Careful not to make any noise, she eased open her blade. If someone had laid a hand on Maisoon, Shareefa would cut out his heart and feed it to him.

The only sound in their home was Shareefa's steel-toed boots squeaking as she crept down the hall. If the killer had gotten in, how had he gained entry? Had Maisoon let him in thinking it was Shareefa? Had the killer jammed the lock?

With the blade in front of her, she, sensing a presence inside the bedroom, stood just outside the door. Jagged breaths on the other side of that wood told her that someone was hurt. She prayed to God to have mercy on her even though she didn't deserve it. Maisoon was obviously injured, but Shareefa prayed that when she entered, Maisoon wouldn't be dying.

Shareefa flung open the door and flicked on the light. The knob crashed against the wall. Doubled over in a trembling ball between the bed and the dresser, Maisoon was on her knees, her body covered in blood. Shareefa blinked.

Was the skin on Maisoon's back really drawing up like a shade? Had that shade of skin really disappeared into a bloody mass? Had her wife's hair really shrunk back into her scalp and vanished? Shareefa blinked again, trying to clear the image, but the blood-covered skeleton that was Maisoon remained. There was no longer any skin on Maisoon, no strands of hair, just that oozing red fluid. Shareefa should have stayed on guard, checked under the bed or in the closet for the killer, but Maisoon seemed on the brink of death. Shareefa dropped the knife and shouted her wife's name. She dashed across the room to Maisoon's side.

Maisoon's torso jerked up and she pounced on Shareefa, knocking them both to the floor. Maisoon, who was half Shareefa's size and only a quarter as strong, straddled Shareefa, pinning Shareefa to the floor, their faces inches apart. Warm blood dripped from Maisoon's chin into Shareefa's mouth. Maisoon's dark brown eyes were the same, but the eyelids seemed to have been sliced away. Who had done this to Maisoon? Or had Maisoon done this to herself?

Maisoon hissed, spewing saliva into Shareefa's eyes. Shareefa should have fought against Maisoon, who had pinned Shareefa's arms and legs to the floor with growing pressure from her body. It was as if Maisoon was becoming heavier the longer she was on Shareefa.

"What are you doing? Maisoon? It's me!"

Maisoon hissed again and Shareefa closed her eyes. She loved this woman. This was Maisoon on top of her. This was Maisoon crushing her body. Even if Shareefa could reach her knife several feet away on the floor, could she really raise it to Maisoon? It was messed up, but if Shareefa would be killed, Maisoon was the only one she'd let do it.

It was their wedding day, with Maisoon's ivory gown and the fresh tattoo of a red demon on Maisoon's deltoid. The Turkish sun had made Maisoon's smile seem a part of the atmosphere. This could be Shareefa's last thought before dying.

Maisoon's body felt like a car had fallen on Shareefa, like she was being crushed. Wet blood landed on Shareefa's cheeks. Sour breath seeped into her nostrils. Then, as suddenly as it had come, the weight was gone. When Shareefa opened her eyes, Maisoon sprang through the air and came down on her hands and feet in the hallway, landing the way a panther would. Maisoon's bloody back turned the corner, her feet pounding along the wooden floor and out of the house.

Shareefa shot to her feet, stepped over the knife, and made it back into the hallway. From the master bedroom to the frame of the front door, all that

Maisoon had left behind was an angry slash of blood shaped like a fingertip dragged along the wall. Shareefa tore down the hall and out of the house. She raced down the front steps, following the trail of blood in the middle of the drizzle-slicked road.

Maisoon could have killed her. She could have crushed Shareefa or strangled her there on the floor, breaking her neck even, but she hadn't. Shareefa had seen the real Maisoon, had learned all of her secrets, and still wanted her, even if it put Shareefa in danger. That was what Maisoon had been doing for Shareefa and her drinking, and now Shareefa would return the favor. Find her. Protect her. Love her in spite of. Love her, perhaps, because of. Shareefa sprinted in the direction of her wife, trust and hope growing with each step. Her headache had left her, and brisk, liberating air burned her nose and chest as she drew it in.

BETTER TO CURSE THE DARKNESS THAN LIGHT A CANDLE

JOSEPH CUSUMANO

They mockingly call me "Diogenes," believing I carry my lantern merely to illuminate my path each night through the dark streets of Philadelphia as I search for an honest man. Yet it is not an honest man for whom I search, but a scoundrel, a liar, an adulterer, a thief, a murderer—ideally someone who has been all of these —for I must find a soul darker than my own.

This quest resulted from an earlier and more innocent one, first undertaken while I was a young man blissfully wed to Patience, who brimmed with optimism over what heaven had apparently planned for us. Not content with the considerable success I enjoyed as the proprietor of Silsbury Shipping Company, I sought more wealth, the respect of Philadelphia's business and merchant class, and especially the adoration which Patience showered upon me with each step my growing business took. On the occasion of my boasting to her that I now employed upwards of fifty men who labored on my behalf, moving goods from our warehouses to multiple sites hundreds of miles west, she swelled with pride in my accomplishment, and even her passions were aroused.

I achieved my success before the opening of the Erie Canal in 1825. When the canal first opened, there was no appreciable loss of business, merely a slowing in our rate of growth. However, by 1829, the volume of goods shipped through the canal, at lower cost than any land route could hope to provide, had a disastrous effect on my personal economy and, to a lesser extent, on all of Philadelphia. Even the powerful textile manufacturers were adversely affected. If my business had suffered only a loss of revenue, not all would be lost, but I had taken substantial loans from banks to further my seemingly unending profits, loans based upon the value of my business and personal property, including our home. As the city's fortunes declined, other borrowers faced the same issues as I, and the banks to which I was indebted ignored my entreaties to renegotiate the terms of the loans that might well be my ruin.

A man raised in a devout Calvinist community should never have resorted to what I did next, but had I not been taught that a man's eternal fate could be ascertained by the material success and wealth he amassed on earth? If I lost everything, would it not be proof that I had no place among the chosen? How would my community judge me? Worst of all, how would Patience judge me? Thus did I begin a life of deceit, a series of mounting lies to everyone, especially my beloved.

"Charles," she asked one September morning as I prepared to leave for work, "have not the city's declining fortunes affected your business?"

"Hardly at all," I responded. "By letting part of our work force go, I've saved enough in labor costs to allow us to weather a moderate decline indefinitely. There is no need to trouble yourself over this."

"But what of the men and their families whom you no longer employ? What is to happen to them?"

"I have pledged to each and every one of them three-fourths of their salary until they find new employment. They were immensely grateful."

"Charles! What a lovely thing to do! But I shouldn't be surprised; it's the right thing to do, and you are a righteous man." She completely accepted this fabrication and bestowed a passionate kiss upon me. A righteous man would be consumed with guilt, but I was already preparing my next lie.

"Patience, my darling, I won't be home for supper tonight. I have an important business meeting to attend and will return very late. You could visit your mother tonight, if you wish." She happily agreed to this suggestion.

We believe work to be virtuous, but where is virtue when one can find so little to do? Incoming orders to transport goods to points west had plunged. The warehouse, greatly enlarged and refurbished with borrowed money, was less than a third occupied with goods for transport. Thus, I spent the day on the edge of despair, reading the increasingly insistent letters from the banks. These I answered with deceitful replies, claiming that the number of new orders had risen over the previous month and that my debt would be paid with only slight additional delay.

At the end of this disheartening day, I rode to an inn at the outskirts of the city, being of no mind to feign merriment with the merchants and professional people who frequented the establishments in the business district. However, once I reached the inn, a glass of wine and a hearty stew of boar raised my spirits considerably and prepared me for what lay ahead. I then resumed a westward course, thankful for pleasant autumnal weather and a dry road free of ruts. The change in the color of the trees was as beautiful as any I could remember, providing welcome distraction from my growing unease regarding the two sisters I sought. I had known of these two since childhood and had been warned to shun them. Almost never did they venture into the city, and I had not seen them for years. All details now forgotten, I remembered them only as middle-aged spinsters.

More quickly than I wanted, the cabin reputed to be the home of the two sisters became visible as I surmounted the crest of a hill and gazed down into a shallow valley. The cabin appeared in a rather poor state of repair, and might have been uninhabited but for the smoke drifting from its chimney. After dismounting and securing the reins of my horse to an odd piece of pagan statuary in front of the cabin, I approached the door and knocked hesitantly. There was no response of any kind, and a part of me began to hope that none was forthcoming. I knocked a second time with still no sign of any stirring within. When I turned to remount my horse, a woman's voice broke the silence. "Whom do you seek?"

A glance back at the cabin door showed it still shut, but a dark-haired woman now stood at the left side of the cabin, some ten yards away. She appeared more vigorous than I expected, likely at the transition from her third decade to her fourth, a youthfulness still lingering. Then a second woman appeared at her side, appearing of similar age and visage although slightly smaller in stature. Neither showed any hint of apprehension at the arrival of a stranger. As they approached, it took some effort to stand my ground.

"Who are you, and how may we be of service?" the second woman asked.

"I am Charles Silsbury, a businessman in Philadelphia. I... my business has fallen upon hard times," I replied, reluctant to admit my misfortune even to these two strangers.

"Pray come inside and have tea," the taller sister responded.

The inside of the cabin, a single room, was clean and orderly, and they bade me to sit at a small round table near the hearth. In one corner of the room stood an old spinning wheel. In another, two cupboards with multiple shelves held uncountable bottles, jars, and tins. There was only one bed, placed against the wall opposite the front door and adjacent to a partially opened window. Four tall posts of polished mahogany supported the bed, and the remainder of the wooden furniture appeared to be equally well-fashioned.

The tea they served was highly aromatic, extremely hot, and flavored with a variety of herbs which gradually settled into the bottom of my cup. Instead of arousing me, the tea had a calming effect, perhaps taking me off my guard. After several swallows, life itself seemed to slow. My mind latched upon one thing at a time, no longer racing from one conjecture to another. I found myself able to focus on individual sounds in the room, including the ticking of a single-handed clock atop the fireplace mantle. This mindfulness was most queer, yet pleasant. With the two of them seated expectantly at the table, I began my story, unable now to withhold anything.

They had offered no introduction of themselves and I chose not to ask, suspecting there would be no meaningful response. But in my own mind did I name them. The taller would be Smirk, for the sneer that wrestled constantly with her otherwise welcoming smile. The shorter, who smiled not at all, became Malice; her eerie stare unnerved me until the tea had completely taken hold. Both women listened intently and never once interrupted, simply nodding with understanding as I explained my situation. In my confession, I acknowledged my godless ambitions and the unyielding pride that had engendered so many fabrications. The closest either of them came to making any rebuke occurred when Smirk said, "You wish us to help you out of the pit you've dug," but fortunately, neither sister inquired as to why I believed they could do so. Had they asked, I would have felt compelled to answer.

"Yes, I entreat you. I see no way to help myself." After a moment's silence, the two women glanced at each other. Malice gave her sister the merest of nods. Smirk rose and approached one of the cupboards, whereupon she chose a short, wide, cylindrical candle. She placed it within an open-top glass container almost twice its height, then brought it to the table and reseated herself.

"This candle will enable you to harness a power which cannot be exhausted; its source is eternal," Smirk said. The candle was brown, the brown of old blood, but I made no inquiry regarding its origin.

"While the soul resides within the body," Malice continued, "even a body ravaged by disease, it is safe. And when the body dies and the soul has neared its heavenly destination, also is it safe, provided the individual led a virtuous life. Yet there is a time during which every soul is vulnerable to those bold enough to entrap and harness it for their own purposes. This occurs just as the soul emerges from its corpse. For only a moment, it is as helpless as a newborn baby emerging from its mother."

"Take this candle and place it at the bedside of one who is at death's door," Smirk said, pushing it toward me. "The dying individual must be of good moral character, and the candle must be lit just before the moment of death. Do not light the candle too soon, lest it melt completely and lose its flame. At the instant at which the soul departs its body, the candle will flare with a bright blue light. Thus will you know that you have succeeded."

"Succeeded?" I asked.

"In capturing the soul and imprisoning it within the flame," Malice answered. "Once trapped, the soul becomes unable to ascend to its destination, and the energy it expends in vain is yours to harness until the candle is willfully snuffed and the soul set free." A shudder took me, for in that moment, I fully believed they possessed the power to bring about such an abomination. But how was I ever to bring myself to interdict the baptized and consecrated soul of a fellow Christian and withhold from it the beatific vision? All this merely to escape a financial calamity of my own making?

Smirk saw my incertitude take hold and said, "Once the flame has captured the soul, no harm will come to it, and the candle will burn indefinitely without further consumption of its substance. When your affairs have been set to rights, snuff the candle to release the soul so it may continue its journey. Resist the temptation to keep the soul beyond a restoration to what you once had. Contain your greed and seek nothing more." Still uncertain, yet unwilling to display any further lack of resolve, I accepted the candle, deciding I would later choose whether or not to employ it.

"What of my payment to you?" I asked.

"You are in no position to pay us now," Malice answered. "We will name a price once you are restored." With that, our meeting concluded, and I remounted my steed to return home.

Weeks passed with no interruption of the downward spiral of my fortunes, weeks during which I came to chastise myself for foolishly believing that the sisters could provide me with a solution. Yet, a debate continued to rage within me as to whether I would execute their plan if the opportunity presented itself, but time was running out. I had received a writ of lien and eviction concerning my warehouse and all its contents. My creditors intended to sell everything at a time of severely depressed market prices and would not obtain sufficient funds to satisfy their claims against me. They would subsequently investigate my personal holdings and assets to make themselves whole.

Heretofore, the thought of actually creating the precise opportunity to entrap a departing soul had not occurred to me, but spurred by the writ of eviction, I devised an ingenious plan to find an elderly and righteous citizen near his or her natural death. And my church would be the vehicle for executing this plan. Showered with praise from Patience, I volunteered to become one of those who visited the sick and dying. The church itself would supply me with the information and the pretext I needed to enter the homes of the most vulnerable, and if this plan failed and I was eventually forced to rely upon the charity of the church to mitigate the effects of my impending ruin, there would likely be a reservoir of good will upon which to draw. So occupied was I in lauding myself for this clever solution, I scarcely considered its predatory and heinous nature.

Within days, my sights were narrowed on an excellent prospect. The Widow Huxford, age sixty-seven, was in a pitiful state of physical ruin. Blind and ravaged by lockjaw and dropsy, she would welcome her imminent death as a merciful event. Her daughter, Anne Crofton, was exhausted from caring for her mother and a family of her own, and she accepted with alacrity and gratitude my offer as a fellow church member to spend two nights a week with her infirm parent.

My vigil began on a Sunday night at the Widow Huxford's two story freshly painted home on Canal Street where I was warmly greeted by Anne. Many hurricane lamps illuminated the first floor of the home, and the absence of the unpleasant odor associated with the cheaper varieties of whale oil further attested to the widow's affluence. Upstairs in her room, she lay in bed, propped upright with three pillows, her dropsy and shortness of breath having progressed. Both her eyes were a milky opaque, and gangrenous bedsores on her backside produced a truly wretched odor. Anne informed me that the bedsores had worsened rapidly when her mother's failing respirations no longer permitted her to assume a recumbent position on her side, but she did not apologize for her mother's condition and tended to her with great affection. My task seemed simple. I could hasten the widow's suffocation merely by removing the pillows which kept her upright and thus be assured that her death would transpire while I was present with the candle afire.

Having determined to carry out my plan on returning three nights later, I arrived promptly at nine o'clock, assured Anne that I would not stray from her mother's bedside, and bade her goodnight from the front door as she descended the stoop to return to her own dwelling. Inside, I climbed the sturdy but creaking staircase and entered the widow's bedroom, finding her immobile with eyes closed. Had she already died? Was I too late? I strode to her bedside and placed my palm against her forehead, finding her feverish and damp. After observing her intently for several additional moments, I detected the gentlest undulation of the nightgown that covered her chest, yet the movement lacked the regular cadence of normal respiration. I had witnessed this pattern previously at the death of my own mother, in which progressively deeper and more rapid respirations were followed by a brief period during which respiration ceased entirely. This was repeated every forty to sixty seconds, always leaving an observer wondering if the last breath had been taken.

I removed the unholy candle from my valise and placed it on the nightstand beside an oil lamp, then procured a long match to transfer the flame from the oil lamp to the candle. When the match flamed brightly, I withdrew it from the lamp and moved it to the glass in which the candle sat. But with the flaming match only an inch away from the candle wick, my arm froze in hesitation.

As my determination wavered, the widow entered an episode of apnea more prolonged than its predecessors. My own breathing ceased as I wondered if she had taken her last breath before the brown candle was lit. Yet she began again, and when I glanced back at the candle, it was aflame! This could only have occurred by means of a force beckoning from within the candle rather than by my own volition.

The candle burned with a shuddering glow, throwing prancing silhouettes about the room. I thought of extinguishing the oil lamp, but decided that it best not contain a full measure of oil on the morrow, and thus my vigil continued. Carriages passed in the street below, and I watched as a nearly full moon was first shrouded and then unveiled by the passage of clouds. And still she breathed. I checked the candle and found to my alarm that less than a third of its brown substance remained. Was this frail old woman defying me?

Thus far, I had done nothing that could be construed as harmful, but with the candle shrinking seemingly quicker than before, I snatched her pillows away and left her completely supine. Now I had truly crossed a bridge and burnt it. The minutes passed, and still she breathed.

She was defying me, somehow mindful of my impending ruin and waiting for the candle to extinguish itself before drawing her final breath. Another glance at the candle revealed mere moments remaining!

Panic ignited a fury within me, rage at her willful defiance. Grasping a pillow with both hands, I pressed it over her slack face and dropped a knee upon her small bony chest to make respiration twice impossible. Another glimpse at the candle assured that it still burned. Increasing the pressure of my knee against her chest suddenly caused her breastbone to snap, and a moment later, the candle flared just as Smirk and Malice had promised. Her soul was trapped, and it was mine.

Despair! All is lost, all has been taken, even my beautiful Patience. Everyone thinks ill of her, certain that she callously chose to abandon me as we plummeted toward financial ruin. In truth, financial ruin was not the cause of her flight to her parents. I discovered this the moment I returned home on the morning after the Widow Huxford's demise. Hearing me enter our home, Patience rushed from the kitchen to greet me, but the moment our eyes met, all joy left her and she halted several feet away. She stared at me as if I were a stranger. Or an intruder. All that she could utter was "Oh…"

"Patience, what is it? What is wrong?" I asked as I approached her with extended arms to embrace her. She took several steps back, covered her mouth with her hand, and regarded me in uneasy silence and confusion. Had the stain of murder descended upon me? A stain that was all too apparent to her? She turned her back on me and quickly ascended the staircase, whereupon I rushed to the large mirror in our foyer to search for what had repulsed her. Exhaustion from a lack of sleep, something which normally evoked her solicitous nature, was evident, but an unmistakable darkness had also crept into my countenance, and I liked it not. Not at all.

My entreaties to her were as futile as those directed to my creditors; she simply was no longer mine to cherish. I soon found myself possessing little more than my personal items, a small sum of money that I had disclosed to no one, and the mysterious candle that continued to burn day after day after day. Those who observed my protective and covetous manner regarding the candle thought me deranged, and I did little to discourage this attitude since it caused them to leave me in peace.

Left to my own devices and living alone in a cheaply furnished, poorly-lit room for rent, I examined the events of the preceding weeks, focusing primarily on my encounter with the two witches. How else to regard them? The candle was no less enchanted than a goose which lays golden eggs, but it had brought me nothing but ruin. Had it not flared brightly at the very moment of the widow Huxford's death, as promised by Smirk and Malice? And do I not flinch when a twig snaps underfoot, the echo of a cracking breastbone scolding me?

Presently, I came upon a frightful realization. The candle was no talisman or channel of good fortune, but rather a cursed object or a weapon, and that I was nothing more than the sisters' means of procurement. They must have known full well of the candle's ruinous effect and that I must return to them seeking redress, with the evil instrument in my possession.

How had I have become sufficiently gullible to believe that a scheme requiring the death of a God-fearing and righteous woman, a member of my own congregation, could bring me anything but despair? My murderous rage at an imagined defiance on the widow's part arose from nothing more than her innocent grasping at the last tendrils of God-given life. What to do? What to do, indeed!

If the sisters' plan was to obtain this wretched candle, I might yet thwart them. By extinguishing the candle, the widow's soul could be freed, and this cursed object need never fall into their hands. Their possession and use of it would only bring misery to others. Thus might I redeem myself and vow to live righteously until the end of my days. But the appeal of this plan began to fade when I considered that I may have blundered in some way while capturing the widow's soul. But how?

Whipsawed by this conundrum, I paced my small dark room in search of a resolute plan. If I extinguished the candle before seeking the sisters' counsel, I would surely spend the rest of my life wondering if I had discarded an opportunity for great wealth, perhaps even regaining the love and admiration of my dear Patience. This propelled me to a decision. I would return to Smirk and Malice with the candle, but carry a weapon of my own.

·　·　·

With a borrowed steed, I retraced my previous journey westward, stopping around midday at the same small establishment where I had supped four weeks prior. Emerging from the inn after a satisfying meal, I was tempted by light rain and distant thunder to remain there, perhaps overnight, but ultimately chose to continue my journey to conserve what little money remained. Before long, I regretted this decision, a storm soaking and chilling me, its thunder pummeling my ears and terrifying my steed. The road became enveloped in mud, slowing my progress and causing my trek to seem interminable. Yet I knew there was no risk that the ensorcelled candle would be extinguished.

Upon finally arriving at the sisters' cabin, I thumped the front door impatiently with my entire forearm and demanded entrance. The door abruptly swung inward, and Malice beckoned me to enter. Smirk took my coat and hung it on a hook attached to the inside surface of the door. Had they expected me? On so wretched a day?

"Please be—" Malice began, but halted as I extracted the candle and its glass enclosure from a leather sack and lay it upon their table. Both women took a step back from it, then stared at me.

"What have you done?" Smirk demanded.

"I have followed your every instruction and entrapped a soul, the soul of a righteous woman, a member of my own congregation, but disaster and despair have become my daily lot," I answered, accusatory. "Everything has been taken from me, and my wife has fled to her parents."

Wordlessly, both sisters slowly approached the candle for a closer inspection. I thought they wished to determine precisely how little of the brown substance remained. But I was mistaken.

"How do you perceive the flame?" Smirk asked, turning to me with eyes blazing.

"As you can plainly see, it is bright crimson," I replied. "And it flared at the instant the emerging soul of an old woman was entrapped."

In a slow, threatening tone, Malice uttered "You... must take that candle away at once and never return. It poses a grievous threat. You killed her, didn't you?"

"I had to! The candle was near to extinguishing, yet on she lingered."

"Simple instructions were you given," Malice continued, penetrating me with that eerie stare. "You were to be in attendance at the moment of death, not cause it. Worse, the soul entrapped in the flame is no more virtuous than your own. Its destiny is eternal punishment."

"How is that possible? Everyone knew her to be a saintly and pious woman!"

"She most likely murdered her husband, no saint himself, I'd wager," Smirk answered. "'Tis such a simple thing to poison a man's porridge."

"But what threat does the candle pose?" I continued in a voice that both demanded and pleaded.

"If the candle is willfully extinguished, the widow's soul, inexorably pulled to the pit, will drag with it a soul like itself, one to delight the demons, one with which to bargain with them," Smirk said. I was about to ask whose soul will it choose? when the answer leapt upon me. I would be its victim, for I had murdered the Widow Huxford. These two witches were no paragons of virtue, but I gathered that neither had committed that most heinous of crimes. Yet they wanted me gone quickly and with the flame at my side.

"But what am I to do?" I begged unabashedly, my pride now smothered in desperation.

"You must search for another," Malice answered. "One whose crimes are darker than your own. Only in his company may you smother the flame, for the widow's soul would reward the demons with one more hideous than your own."

Accepting this admonition, I took my leave, never to see either of them again. I knew I must rid myself of this accursed candle. Only then might my fortunes be restored and the redemption of my soul achieved.

Months have passed, and I have been unable to rebuild my life. The ill fortune of the red-flamed candle thwarts me at every turn. There is nothing for it but to live in penury and continue my quest for someone more deserving of damnation than I. Surely such an individual can be found among a population of eighty thousand, for is there anything more certain than the reprobate nature of man?

Charity from my congregation and an occasional stint of manual labor enable me to keep body and soul together, and each night I renew my search for a monster in the City of Brotherly Love. The crimson flame is now enclosed within a brass lantern. Its metal handle creaks in a regular cadence as it sways by my side. Some of the regulars on the streets and in the alleys jeer at me. "Diogenes, if you haven't found an honest man by now, give up!" Others, more perceptive, remain silent and avoid me.

My inability to assess character, evidenced by my foolhardy selection of the Widow Huxford months ago, means that I must witness a crime so heartless that the widow will be compelled to drag someone other than myself into the pit. Only then will I extinguish the flame. I believe my quest to be right-minded, for surely it is no sin to ensnare the damned.

CURSE OF THE SAAPIN

VASHTI BOWLAH

She was the type of girl a man would want to marry—ripe young age, long flowing black hair, cocoa-brown skin, and a body every woman craved. There was no shortage of proposals, yet she was still unmarried at nineteen. That was quite old for a girl living under her parents' roof in the small village of Sugarcane Valley. Her friends and former classmates were already married… with children.

On each occasion when the potential groom's family came to make it official, they suddenly refused. One boy's parents even sent a message the next day with a distant relative, informing them that their son was in love with someone else so they gave in to his wishes. Another stated that they could not go through with the marriage because they had received a larger dowry from another girl's family.

Maya was disappointed, but not as much as her mother. Her younger sister already had a family of her own. Their little house seemed crammed with her three brothers, their wives and children all vying for space under the same roof. It wasn't until she returned from the vegetable market one morning that she heard the murmurs coming from the kitchen.

"Ent, I tell all you she have a snake in she back," said her eldest sister-in-law to the other two.

"How you know that?" asked the youngest. "Maybe she just bad lucky."

"I know because my mother first cousin was a *saapin* and she had a V-shape point coming down she forehead just like Maya. You ever see how she hair does make a perfect V when she comb it back?"

"You think that is why nobody want she to get married to their son?" asked the other.

"Them old people does know these things. I sure they take one look at she and run for they life. Nobody in their right mind go want a saapin to kill their son," stated the eldest.

Having heard enough, Maya strolled in and placed the two bags on the makeshift counter, keeping her back to the women as they renewed their interest on cleaning the *chataigne* they had picked from the tree earlier. The silence was deafening as she unpacked the fresh vegetables, storing them in their respective places. Then she left.

It wasn't until a week after her twenty-first birthday that a proposal bore fruit. She had stumbled upon a former classmate at the market one Saturday morning. Amit approached her as she started her mile-and-a-half walk home. She did not recognize him at first, since he was no longer the boy she remembered him to be. His overgrown disheveled hair was now shorter and combed back in a neat style, his hand-me-down clothing now replaced with modern trousers and shirt. Handmade leather sandals adorned his feet instead of the rubber slippers he always wore. He wasted no time asking for her hand in marriage.

Her mother was much too anxious that something might go wrong, and arranged for them to be married by the end of the month. Since losing her father to a heart attack eleven years ago, Maya's mother had been burdened with financial responsibilities, taking his place at the cocoa estate where he worked. As for her brothers' wives, they were silently relieved that they would no longer receive curious stares or be questioned about their unmarried sister-in-law, though they continued to eye her suspiciously.

Maya settled into her husband's home, growing more comfortable each day. They were getting to know each other, and were able to share their most intimate thoughts. She was happy to care for his bedridden mother who had suffered a stroke earlier that year, and happy to share the home with his family; his two brothers also shared sections of the house with their own families.

One day, in the midst of hanging the hand-washed laundry on the backyard lines under the midmorning sun, she heard a frantic voice calling in the front yard. She dropped the trousers into the bucket and rushed to see what the commotion was about.

She recognized the person on the bicycle as one of Amit's coworkers. She had seen Kishore while dropping off her husband's lunch after he forgot it on the kitchen table. Kishore's face was pale, and he avoided looking directly at her. But he mustered the courage to inform her that the truck her husband had been driving ran off the big bridge and plunged into the Aatma River. By the time a few nearby cane cutters pulled him out of the water, it was too late.

He offered to help in any way he could, and promised to return after work.

That night during the wake, Maya lay coiled up in the corner of her bed with her knees drawn up and arms circling her legs. His brothers made all the funeral arrangements, and Kishore returned as promised to assist them over the next few nights. Her mother-in-law was grief-stricken, and succumbed to her illness two days after her son's funeral.

Maya's mother checked in on her for weeks after the two funerals, ensuring she had her meals as she seemed to be withering away. When Maya became weak and ill, she took her home.

It was only months later that Maya went out in public again. She was shocked and distressed to hear the whispers behind her back whenever she walked by.

"You can't see she is a saapin?" said the butcher's wife to the market vendor as she selected some tomatoes. "Why else she husband go dead so sudden? And a nice-nice good-looking fella like that."

"You sure? Suppose she do him something so she could get a share in the property?" replied the market vendor.

"Nah, you must watch she face good and see how she eyes does shine like a snake," stated the butcher's wife with an animated nod of her head.

Maya studied her reflection in the bureau mirror when she returned home. She pulled back her hair with both hands as she had several times before. Certainly, there must be other women with such a hairline. Did that make her a saapin? How could a snake be embedded in her back? It made no sense to her. She thought of confiding in her mother, but did not want to cause her unnecessary worries since she was always so tired after work.

Maya straightened her shoulders and lifted her chin, deciding there was no room in her life for idle gossip. There was no way she could have been responsible for her husband's accident.

Her eldest brother helped her secure a job at the tailor's shop sewing on buttons and pressing finished pants and shirt-jacs. The shopkeeper's son was a regular customer, and they grew attached over the following weeks. Their nine-year age difference created no barrier for their blooming romance, though she was somewhat surprised when Suresh asked her to be his wife. They were married in a small ceremony at the village temple in the presence of their closest family and friends. Even Kishore attended. The pundit was a middle-aged man, of average height and slim build. Maya was taken aback by his close scrutiny and the eerie way she felt around him. She later found out that the pundit was his father and he sometimes accompanied him to the temple.

Soon, Maya forgot the pundit. She was happy; she and Suresh occupied a small section of the house shared by his parents, grandparents, a sister, an older brother and his wife. She hummed the words to popular film songs playing on the radio while she cleaned the windows or tended to her small vegetable garden.

But a few months after celebrating her twenty-third birthday, grief struck Maya for the second time. Suresh was helping a neighbor construct a shed when he slipped and fell off the roof. He died five days later at the district hospital.

This created quite a stir throughout the small village. How could a young and vibrant woman lose two husbands in such a short time? No one addressed her personally, but eyed each other whenever they spotted her. Maya stayed indoors as much as possible to avoid the piercing eyes of the villagers. Everyone soon noticed that dirt smeared her windows and her vegetable garden remained untended. Maya was broken. Again, her mother tried to save her from herself. She made regular visits until she finally persuaded her to return home where she could be cared for.

Maya's three sisters-in-law feigned sympathy in the presence of their husbands, reserving their thoughts and comments for their private discussions.

"I don't know why she mother keep bringing she back here for," complained the eldest sister-in-law. "She born with that curse and nothing could help she."

"But I still don't understand how she coulda cause that," said the youngest.

"Let me tell you how because you young and naïve just like she. When she go to bed with she husband, the image of the cobra from she back does come alive and bite him on the tip of he tongue, especially on a full moon night," she continued with an air of authority, "but he don't die right away or even from the snake bite, he does die from some kind of accident or sickness."

"My *aajee* was telling me that you could do a prayers for a woman like she," commented the other. "All you ever hear about that?"

"Well," said the eldest. "They say if a husband suspect he wife is a saapin, then he could get a pundit to perform a *naag puja,* but them two husbands she had didn't stand a chance because they didn't even know what hit them."

Maya remained hidden behind the thin wooden wall separating the kitchen from the small drawing room. Why was this happening to her? Could they be right? Did her husbands die because of her? If so, then she still didn't understand. Accidents happened to people all the time, but that didn't mean they happened because of her. None of this made any sense. She felt more confused now than before.

She returned to the tailor's shop, working from a secluded area adjoining his sewing room. Although she did not expect to receive further proposals, she decided that she would never marry again. She buried herself in her work, agreeing to stay longer hours before the new school term began, or when there was a wedding or funeral in the area; that's when the workload was heaviest. When at home, she remained in the bedroom she shared with her mother.

It was a pleasant surprise late one evening when Kishore entered the shop as she prepared to leave. He wanted to alter a *kurta* for a puja they were having in the Shiva temple the next Thursday evening. He offered to walk her home and invited her to attend. She politely refused.

"I always admire you since the first time I see you two years ago, and think about you all the time." He smiled. "I was real sorry about what happen to Amit, but never had the nerve to tell you how I feel."

"Well is a good thing you didn't, because… is just good that you didn't."

No more words were exchanged until they arrived at her front door.

"At least think about coming, it go be nice to see you." His smile deepened as he tried to persuade her.

The tailor gave Maya permission to leave early the next Thursday after all the extra hours she had put in. It was a spontaneous decision, but she felt a strong force drawing her towards the temple. She removed her slippers at the entrance and placed it with the others lined up against the wall. She slipped into a vacant space on one of the sheets spread on the ground for devotees. Kishore was at the front with a woman she believed to be his mother, along with a younger boy that bore a close resemblance to his father. His father was being assisted by another pundit as the puja drew to an end.

Her eyes were drawn to the majestic Shiva murti to her left: the likeness of a black cobra wrapped around the Lord's graceful neck. That eerie feeling crept up inside her, again unexplainable, yet she could not turn away from the glowing eyes of the cobra.

Kishore greeted her with a warm smile at the end of the puja. She later volunteered to help share the food to devotees who sat in rows against the walls on crocus bags topped with white cotton sheets. They served *channa* and *aloo*, pumpkin, *chataigne*, mango *talkari* and *paratha roti* served on hand-picked *suhari* leaves. White enamel cups were filled and served to devotees with their choice of freshly made juice or water. When Maya announced that she was leaving, Kishore took hold of her wrist and led her over to his parents. He proceeded to introduce her.

"Have nothing to do with this woman!" bellowed his father.

"She's my friend! How you could say that?" Kishore's confusion was evident, but he did his best to defend her.

"I know what I saying and why I saying it!" replied his father.

Nothing more was said. Kishore knew better than to argue with his father, especially in public. He accompanied Maya to her home. She insisted they go their separate ways.

They next saw each other three weeks later, when Kishore waited for her at the tailor's shop. After work, they walked to the nearby savannah and sat on a wooden bleacher under the pavilion. They watched as young boys played wind-ball cricket.

"Leh, we get married at the temple tomorrow," said Kishore. "Then everybody will have to accept the marriage."

Maya sat wide-eyed, startled. "You don't care that my last two husbands die right after we get married? You not worried?"

"About what? They had some kind of accident, is not like you kill them."

"You don't understand! They get kill because of me! Because something wrong with me and I don't know how to fix it, or if it could fix!"

He studied her for a moment, the hurt and pain reflected in her eyes. "You talking nonsense. It have nothing wrong with you; you can't control what happen to somebody else. Just agree to meet me at the temple tomorrow and I will get a pundit to do the ceremony. Please Maya, and you go see how everything go work out," he insisted stubbornly. "Unless you don't feel the same way about me, like I feel about you."

He refused to take no for an answer, so Maya gave in with great reluctance and a heavy heart. That night, after her mother had fallen asleep, she searched through the cardboard box under her bed for something appropriate to wear. She settled on a yellow *garara* with a touch of blue, and highlighted with heavy gold trimmings. Then she took out the small brown paper bag hidden at the bottom of the box, containing a gold necklace with matching earrings and a pair of gold bangles. They were wedding gifts presented to her by her former in-laws.

All the while, she wondered if she was making the right decision. What if she *was* cursed? She realized then how deeply she cared for Kishore; if something were to happen to him, she will not be able to live with herself… not this time.

She left the house the next morning under the pretense of going to work. She informed the tailor that her mother had asked her to assist with an urgent family matter. She hurried to the temple carrying a large paper bag with her wedding attire. Kishore was already there with the pundit when she arrived. She emptied the contents from the bag and changed in a secluded area. The ceremony was brief with the pundit and caretaker standing as witnesses. The ceremony had already ended when Kishore's parents turned up on their bull cart.

"I warn you about she and look what you gone and do." Kishore's father shook his head in despair. "The only way to save you now is for me to perform a naag puja. But you cannot think about she as your wife until after that."

He went on to explain her curse, which occurred at birth, and said the only way to placate the snake was to perform a special worship ceremony on the fifth day of the bright fortnight; the day of *naag panchami*. He informed them that the festival fell on the seventh day of August, so they were to stay apart for the next four weeks. He instructed Maya to meet them at the Shiva temple at six o'clock in the evening on the day of the ceremony. She must bring offerings of milk, sweets, turmeric, saffron, rice, honey, flowers, deyas and a new *taria*. She also needed to make the image of a snake from flour. It was important for her to seek the blessings and protection of the naag devata with her offerings and prayers. She must also observe a fast on that day so her body would be pure.

"And one more thing." He paused, wary eyes dancing from groom to bride. "If you care about this stubborn son of mine and want to keep him alive, you will stay away from him."

Maya clasped her hands around her husband's, her voice tender. "He right you know, so we should do what he say and maybe it will be okay this time."

On the seventh day of August she returned to the Shiva temple at the specified time, her arms wrapped around a small cardboard box. A growing number of women were also making offerings on the auspicious day of naag panchami. Some prayed for protection from snake bites, while others prayed for the long lives of their husbands. The resident pundit led the chants and presided over the worship and offerings.

She spotted Kishore and his father, and made her way toward them. Wasting no time, his father led her to a special prayer room in another area of the temple. He asked Kishore to wait outside while he performed the ritual.

When they finally emerged after what seemed like a lifetime, Kishore was pacing the floor like an expectant father. She understood his confusion. She couldn't say with confidence that nothing bad was going to happen again, but she felt like a different woman; one who was just granted a second chance... or maybe a third. She could now attempt some kind of explanation, which Kishore deserved so much.

They were making their way through the gathering when she saw the familiar figure leaning forward with a red *orhni* covering her head. She recognized the woman's flowing red garara with multicolored beads and trimmings. Maya watched as she fed the snake images with milk from a silver spoon, after which she offered fruit. Maya waited until the woman had completed her offerings before confronting her.

"What you doing here, Ma?" she asked, confused.

Her mother mirrored the same facial expression. "What *you* doing here? You tell me you working late today."

"And you never mention anything about coming here."

They retreated to a quiet space away from prying eyes and ears. Maya felt compelled to explain what she had been going through—her doubts about being a saapin; her grief after losing her husbands; the guilt of knowing that she might be responsible for their untimely deaths; and the gossip flowing through the village.

She told her about Kishore, and of his father's intervention when he found out about their elopement. She apologized for not confiding in her, and recounted every detail of the just-completed rituals performed by her father-in-law. She described the powerful forces she experienced while repeating the various chants, and admitted that she had no control over her body while carrying out the worship and offerings. She had collapsed on the floor when all was done, and the pundit revived her with one touch of her forehead and a brief chant.

"I'm so sorry, Ma. I didn't tell you about all this because you wouldn't understand. Nobody will."

Her mother looked at her with knowing eyes. "I've been sneaking away here for the past thirty-one years since I married your father. I *do* understand." She let her orhni drop to her shoulders and pressed her greying hair back with both palms to reveal the v-shaped hairline on her forehead. "You see Maya, nobody besides my parents—your *nani* and *nana*—know that your father was my fifth husband."

THE ORIGIN OF MY FAVORITE FRUIT

THAMIRES LUPPI

You probably know guaraná as one of the ingredients on energy drinks.

It's a fruit that grows on the Amazon rainforest in South America. Here in Brazil it's very popular, and a lot of our soft drinks are based on guaraná. The fruit is delicious, naturally sweet, with exotic and rich flavor. It's an important part of our culture.

The fruit is usually light red when ripe, yellowish when unripe, with white pulp and a very black seed in the middle, resembling an eye. The pulp and seed shows when the fruit is mellow and ready to be consumed.

Have I told you the legend of guaraná? my grandmother would ask.

Yes, she's told me many times, but I loved to hear my old lady talking about her people.

In the Mawé tribe, there was a lovely couple that the whole community held very dear. They had been together for many years, but weren't able to conceive a child.

Both of them prayed for Tupã every night. The couple only wanted a healthy and happy child for themselves. Tupã, you see, is the messenger of the main indigenous divinity—Nhamandú—and the sender of thunders. Nhamandú is incorporeal, so he manifests through Tupã.

After a time, Tupã finally blessed them with a baby boy.

From the moment he was born, the little boy was special. Everyone loved him. He was beautiful, smart, and a very good child.

His birth bought good fortunes to the tribe. Soon, there were more fish in the river, the trees were more bountiful with fruit, and even the war between the Mawé and the rival tribe ceased.

As if that weren't enough, the boy was an accomplished hunter, tagging along with his father and other adults from a very young age. The boy was full of energy, and taking him to the hunt always assured the tribe would have plenty of food for days.

In other words, he was a blessing.

It was during one of his hunts that he met his tragic fate.

You see, no good in this world can last forever. The bad gods are not always bringers of chaos. Everything has a deeper meaning. Sometimes these gods must restore the balance when there's too much peace, so that we can keep learning from our struggles.

The good gods, on the other hand, maintain the balance in the other direction, intervening when things get too bad.

That is the will of Nhamandú, an energy older than the universe itself, something that will outlive the very concept of existence.

First, Nhamandú created Añã'gwea, or Anhangüera—the old soul. Right after that he created, Anhandeci, the matter.

He then created three guardians: Iara, a beautiful mermaid that protects the waters, singing a siren song to attract those who mean to harm it; Caaporã, the protector of the forests and of all the beings; and Tupã, the guardian of the skies.

Understanding the creation of Nhamandú is crucial in accepting the fate he reserved for the poor little boy, Grandma always said.

She only told me this story on rainy nights, and at this point, when rain lashed and thunder roared, she interrupted herself to pray that Tupã would have mercy on the less fortunate, those who were homeless or in precarious houses, and wouldn't allow their lives to be taken by the floods and intense rain.

I would smile complacently. She had told me this story since I was a little girl, probably about the same age as the doomed boy from the tale. I never believed it, but I loved to entertain her. It was the culture of her people—my people too—and I knew I would tell this folklore to my children and grandchildren, even though they wouldn't believe me either.

So what happens next? I asked without fail, even though I knew the answer almost word for word.

The little boy attracted the fury and envy of Jurupari, the god of the darkness. Jurupari decided to reap the boy's life and restore the conflict in the Mawé tribe. To accomplish this task, the evil entity became a snake.

Tupã, observing from above the clouds, sent deafening thunder to warn the boy's father, but it was too late. The snake bit the boy and almost instantly took his life.

The elders prayed to the good gods, that they might provide an explanation for this tragedy. Tupã, instructed by Nhamandú, told the grieving tribe to bury the eyes of the boy apart from the body. He then sent a heavy, persisting rain.

When the sun finally rose again, above the place where the parents buried the boy's eyes was a plant. Its sweet fruits provide energy for whoever eats it.

The boy's legacy still lives.

So ended the tale.

But baby.

I perked up. This was new; this time, there would be more to the tale.

All the light disappeared from my Grandma's gentle face when she spoke. *This is the legend as we tell it to most people, but there's one last thing that almost nobody knows. I must pass it along to you now that my time is coming.*

I listened closely.

For his goodness, Nhamandú decided to transform the boy into one of his guardians too. What the tale doesn't say is that the boy had to become omniscient and eternal for this. His consciousness is still and forever contained in every fruit. That's how he watches over his beloved forest—with millions and millions of eyes.

HESTER'S BLIGHT

JAMES D. MABE

The sky was an ever-darkening bruise.

A Chevy engine rumbled into a higher gear.

The wind lashed.

"What have you done, boy?"

Duane "Buster" Kellogg glanced down at the child blubbering in his passenger seat, and then turned back to the road. His skin prickled and his heart beat dangerously fast. His mouth went sour. He knew what the boy had done, or close enough. He, and probably others, had gone somewhere that they were not supposed to go. And when they got there, they had done something they couldn't take back. He could tell that much just by where the car had been parked. Only the trunk and rear bumper were visible from the main road, obscured by bushes at the mouth of a path that was barely a path. He passed that black hole in the forest every day. He knew it well enough.

"Never mind," he said. "Forget it. You live near here?"

The boy shook his head, sucking snot, tears streaming. "They just went away... like just, they were gone and I tried to look for them and shout for Erica, but she wasn't there and I didn't know what to do and I thought maybe she and Randall were playing a trick on me but..."

"Hey!" Duane swallowed hard. "I need you to focus, boy. Tell me where you live. Now."

"Listen to me," the boy pleaded. "They disappeared!" He was no more than seven, and his composure had long cracked. He slid ever closer to outright, ugly hysteria.

"Yeah. Yeah, and your daddy, or somebody, needs to know about it! So where do you live?"

The boy's voice climbed in pitch, "1712 Creek Burn Road!" He cried harder, shaking.

Duane clenched his jaw and nodded. It wasn't too far, fifteen minutes, maybe. "All right. I'll get you home. What's your name, boy?"

Duane thought about simply dropping the kid off and going about his own business. He didn't want to get sucked into the hole this was about to open. But he didn't. He couldn't, not in good conscience. So he walked with the boy to his front door and knocked. There was a muffled yell from inside, and the door opened. A disheveled, tired-looking man stood in the doorway.

"Hello?" The man glanced down. "Raymond?"

"Mr. Ogilvie?" Duane tried to sound formal, put something straight and impersonal in his voice. He barely stopped himself from trembling.

"Yeah… Raymond, what's going on, where's your sister?" He stifled a yawn.

The boy sucked in air and his lips contorted into a soft wail. He nearly fell forward onto his father's waist, hugging.

"Uh, Mr. Ogilvie, that's why I'm here." He shifted slightly, tilting his weight to a different foot. "You see, I found your son, Raymond, here out by Number 11. I was on my way home and saw him running up the road, crying. Bawling. He was running away from a dirt road where a grey Focus was parked." He cleared his throat. "He tells me that he went with your daughter and her boyfriend to a place out in the woods, and that something happened to them. He thinks that they got lost, or he did, somehow."

"Oh, all right. Thanks, I guess, for bringing him home." He looked down at his son. "Ray, you all right? Where are Erica and Randall?"

"They went over the wall…"

"The wall?" He blinked at something, then wiped at the corner of his eye with his ring finger.

The boy nodded.

Ogilvie looked up at Duane and raised an eyebrow. "Do you know what he's talking about?"

"I might." He cleared his throat. "There's an old… structure out in the woods. If I had to guess, that's probably where they went to."

"A structure?"

"Ah, yeah. The old Hester garden. It's like a farm, of sorts. Or it used to be, a long time ago."

"Great," Ogilvie said, scratching the top of his son's head. "So I ask your sister to watch you for a bit and she takes you to some spooky old farmhouse, huh? Super."

The boy said nothing, only hugged his father's waist tighter.

An empty beat passed. A gust of wind howled along the eaves of their home. Ogilvie squinted and turned his head slightly, wondering at his son's silence. "Ray?"

"I don't know," was the muffled reply.

"Okay…" Mr. Ogilvie muttered. He sighed. "Well, where is this place?"

Duane nodded. "You can follow me, if you want. I live back that way."

"All right, that works. Let me get my keys. Ray, we're going to go get your sister and Randall, so go ahead and strap in the car, okay?"

The boy shook his head furiously and began to sob again. "No, I don't want to go back…"

"Hey, we're not going to be there long, and you'll be with me this time, okay? Besides, I need you to show which way they went. All right?"

"No!" The boy cried harder, his face reddening from the effort.

"Raymond! What is wrong with you?"

"I don't want to disappear!"

"Ray, you're not going to disappear." He put his hand on the boy's shoulder and squeezed. "Nobody is. It's okay. We're going to go find your sister, and everything is going to be fine. I'm sure they were just messing with you and it got out of hand. Right, Duane?"

Duane caught Ogilvie's eye and then quickly averted his attention, looking down at Ray. "Ah, right. That's probably what happened."

Raymond let go of his father and wiped his nose on the back of his hand. He looked back and forth between the two adults. "You promise?"

Ogilvie sighed. "I promise. Now will you get in the car? I'd like to get back before your mom gets home. Okay?"

The boy sniffed and seemed to weigh his options before finally giving a resigned, "Okay." He took a tentative step away, and began the slow walk to the car.

"Jeez. They certainly put a scare into him, huh? Oh," Ogilvie added, "It's Mark, by the way." He proffered his hand. "Sorry about all this, and thanks again for bringing Ray home."

Duane absently shook his hand, sucking at his cheek to fight off a grimace. "Yeah. It's no problem."

Mark pressed down on the brake when he saw Duane's turn signal blink on. Ahead of him, the truck slowed and eased into the tall grass on the side of the road. He followed, slowing and merging onto the shoulder as weeds belted the front fender and undercarriage. On the opposite side of the road, largely hidden along the tree line, he saw the rear of a grey Focus.

"Looks like this is the place."

Behind him, Raymond began to sniffle again, the reservoir of tears filling.

"Hey, hey, hey now." Mark looked in the rearview mirror at his son. "None of that. We're going to get your sister and her idiot boyfriend, and then I'm going to yell at them. A lot. And then we're going to go home. No fuss, no muss. And I think your mom want to make tacos tonight. Sound good?"

The boy sniffed, swallowed, and nodded.

"Great. So come on, let's go get them."

Mark unbuckled, opened his door, and stepped out into the windy, overcast day. He watched as Duane did the same, his shirt now untucked, the tails flapping idly. Ahead of them was the Focus, inert and somehow unsettling, as though a thing that should be animated, alive, had crawled into the woods to die. Leaves swayed around it, branches screeching against metal and glass. Gesturing.

A car door slammed behind him. Mark jumped and bit his tongue as the wave of nervous adrenaline ran its length across him. Nearly cursing at the boy, he felt himself unclench. He exhaled and glanced over his shoulder. "Let's go, Raymonster."

The two walked to where Duane was standing. He nodded toward the Focus. "Come on, there's a path behind where the car's parked. I'll walk you back there." The man gave a cursory look up the road for traffic and then started across. Mark and Raymond followed.

"How far is it to this place?" Mark asked.

"Less than a mile. The path has mostly been left to the woods, but there's still enough of it to find your way. Hester and his people, they appreciated their privacy."

"And who was this Hester person? He own the farm?"

"Ah, essentially, yeah. I believe that Hester was the one that owned the land."

"Mmm. So what'd they grow out there?"

"Hmm?"

"What kind of farm was it? Cows, chickens, corn? Hooch?"

"Well... it wasn't that kind of farm, exactly. They didn't grow nothing you could eat. It was more of a big botanical garden. Apparently they used to have all kinds of exotic plants and such. Not that anyone around here knows all that much for sure. The whole group kept to themselves. Didn't much mingle in the local social circles."

"Huh."

Duane paused at the Focus and lifted his hand toward the forest. "Right down here. Careful not to get caught on any stickers." He started to ease between the weeds and the car's fender. A moment later he stood in front of the car in a narrow clearing. He waited for Mark and Raymond to make it through, and then turned down the path.

Behind him, the boy whispered something to his father.

"Just relax, Ray. It's fine. Nothing but stories."

"It's true," Raymond affirmed in a low, sullen tone.

"Fine. Duane?"

"Yeah?"

"Raymond tells me this place is supposed to be haunted. Are there any ghosts that we need to look out for?"

Duane let out a rough laugh. "Huh. That's one of the stories, yeah. But there's all kinds of stories. Don't mean they're all true."

"See?"

Raymond shook his head. "Randall said if you look through the wall, then you can see a ghost. There's a big crack and he and Erica looked, but they said they couldn't tell what they saw. I didn't get to look because I couldn't reach, and they told me to wait while they went inside, and that they'd let me look before they left if I didn't go anywhere. But they didn't come back out and I waited and shouted and they never came back..."

"Okay, okay, calm down." He motioned with his palms. "If they went in, then they're probably still in there."

"They disappeared!" The boy balled his fists, resolute.

"Raymond," Mark said with more of an edge. "Did you see them get hurt?"

"… No."

"Did they act like anything was wrong? Did you hear them yelling?"

"No."

"Then stop worrying. They obviously haven't left yet, so I'm willing to bet they're out in the woods looking for you, scared half to death that they lost you. Hopefully," he said to himself. "You don't see me or Duane panicking, do you?" he added.

"No."

"No. So you shouldn't, either. Right Duane?"

Mark turned look at Duane, expecting a reply. The man stared back, his face blank. "Nope," he said, finally. "No point in panicking."

Mark raised an eyebrow. "Great. Thanks." He turned back to Raymond. "So get moving, unless you want to get left behind. Again."

The boy looked down at the dirt path and began walking. He said nothing as he caught up to, and then passed, his father. Sighing, Mark rolled his eyes and followed. Ahead of them, Duane clipped along at his own pace.

Around them, the forest slowly overtook the path. Trees reclaimed the land, as though closing the wound of civilized intrusion. The canopy enveloped them gradually, almost unnoticed, until they were fully beneath its shadow. The line of dirt they had been following gave way to a mere indentation in the leaves. Dark, unbroken clouds drained the world of vibrancy and contrast, so that the woods exuded a uniform gloom. It was a place unto only itself.

Though he didn't mention it, Mark was surprised that Raymond had even made it to the road at all. He could have easily gotten turned around and stumbled even deeper into the forest. Erica would have hell to pay when he found her.

They walked in silence for several minutes. Leaves crunched underfoot as cicadas hummed somewhere overhead. Heavy branches swayed in the wind, a collective wave that gave the impression of being in the belly of a single, immense thing.

"Built this place pretty far out, didn't they?" Mark said.

"Yeah. As I said, they weren't a sociable bunch. Not that they needed to be, I reckon. Whole mess of folks lived out here. If they'd built it in the 60's, people would have sworn it was some kind of hippy commune."

"Is that right? When did they build it?"

"1920s or thereabout. Stories vary."

"Huh." Mark nodded and let his eyes wander among the trees. "So what's the real story?"

"I'm sorry?"

"These old places, they've always got some kind of supposed dark past to ramp up the creepiness, right? Something to give the teenagers a thrill? And I guess this one has ghosts? So what's behind the ghost story?"

"Ah. Well, nobody knows for sure." He exhaled though pursed lips, considering his reply. "But that don't stop them from making things up. I suppose ghosts are just easier to understand. Of course, you don't really need ghosts for a place to be haunted, do you?"

"I, ah…"

"There it is, dad! That's where Erica and Randall are!" Raymond exclaimed, cutting off his father.

"Yep," Duane said. "We're here."

Ahead of them, the trees opened up, just a bit. The path widened again and they walked into something of a clearing. There were still trees, but they were younger, more sparsely distributed. Weeds and kudzu fought for real estate.

"Holy shit," Mark whispered.

In the center of the clearing was an immense stone wall, punctuated only by a wooden gate, so thick that it might have been constructed from rail ties. The wall stood roughly seven feet high, and surrounded at least an acre of land. Towering from inside the wall was a large wooden building, long stripped of any color except a faded grey. It was three stories high and, to Mark, looked more like an antiquated hotel than any farmhouse. Near the building, in what he supposed was the front yard, the tip of another structure was visible, though he could not get a sense of what it might be.

"Yeah," Duane said. "It's something, ain't it?"

Mark stopped and stared, taking in the magnitude of the place. "It certainly is."

Duane stopped as well and turned to the boy. "Raymond, why don't you have a seat on one of those big rocks over there?" He pointed toward a line of small boulders that framed the entrance to the path. "Me and your daddy are going to have a look around."

Mark opened his mouth to speak up, but Duane looked sharply in his direction, catching his eyes. He looked gravely at the man and gave a subtle shake of his head. Mark furrowed his brow, but said nothing.

"But," Raymond began.

"It's all right, Ray," Mark said. "Have a seat and rest for a minute. We aren't going anywhere."

"Fine," the boy said through a sullen sigh. He walked toward the most comfortable looking-boulder, kicking leaves as he went.

"You know," Duane said, looking over to Raymond, "those rocks used to line this whole property. Used to circle the yard, supposedly, with some others squiggling about until they reached the wall. Over time, I reckon people grabbed them all up as souvenirs, 'cept those that was too big to carry."

"Hmmph," Raymond said as he picked up a stick and began poking around in the leaves, scratching at the dirt.

"Well," Duane said, turning back to Mark. "Let's have a look see." He motioned for the man to follow and started walking toward the nearest edge of the wall.

Mark did as he was asked. He paused only to glance back at his son with a reassuring, if forced, smile. The boy didn't notice, instead busying himself by gouging a line in the earth. The smile settled naturally into a grimace, and he left the boy to his devices.

"Erica," Mark yelled as he stepped onto the property. "It's your dad! Get the hell out here! Randall! It's Erica's dad! You can stay!" Then he caught up to Duane a few feet from the wall. "The hell was that about?" he asked.

"Nothing. Didn't want to scare your boy any more than he already is."

"Huh," he said, not sure that he wholly trusted this man. "Well, this place certainly isn't lacking in the creep factor, I'll give you that."

He inspected the wall, amazed that such a place could exist, simply forgotten in the woods. Kudzu snaked up and across much of the surface, but beneath it he could see that the stone work was impressive. The bricks were each roughly the size of a cinder block, but undoubtedly more solid, and polished to a smooth finish—with the exception, he noted, of a line of symbols etched into the uppermost area, just beneath the lip. The symbols were evenly spaced, only appearing every third stone, and he assumed that they stretched across the entire perimeter.

"What are those?"

"Can't rightly say. There's a whole lot that folks don't know about this place. Nobody knows for sure what they were all doing out here, and nobody knows for sure what happened to them. Or if they intended it. My granddaddy always claimed that they was devil worshippers."

"Devil worshippers?"

"Yeah. Another story. Might have some truth to it, might not. But." He paused, emphasizing the point. "Whatever they were, something went wrong here."

A tree limb cracked in the distance.

"How's that?"

Duane started walking, tracing the line of the wall. "Fall of 1934. One night the neighbors claimed they heard all kinds of strange noises in the distance, almost like a big machine surging to life, then tearing itself apart. Said there were lights fading in and out of the sky up here. The air that night had something foul, syrupy in it. I never found nothing about it in the local papers from back then, but that don't mean much, either."

"Well that's… fucking freaky as shit." He made a nervous sound masked inside a laugh. "Nobody just came over and asked what happened?"

"They did. Eventually. But there wasn't anyone to ask. As far as folks could tell, it was abandoned. Not that they could get inside to check," he added, almost under his breath.

"They never opened the gate?"

"Barred from the inside. Thankfully."

"Lovely," he said with a dry gravity. "And my kid's in there somewhere?"

Duane cast a sidelong glance at Mark. "If your son's right about what he saw. Which I have no reason to doubt."

"So how do we get inside?"

"This way," he replied, gesturing down the length of the wall.

Mark clicked his tongue against his teeth. "All right, then." He continued on. "Erica," he shouted again, louder, more forcefully than before. "Get out here, now! You two scared the shit out of your brother!"

There was only silence from the other side of the wall.

Duane slowed to match the other man's pace. "Mark…"

"I know they can hear me in there; it isn't that far. You think they left? Maybe went looking for Ray?"

Duane shook his head. "I don't think so. Just… just come with me.

"Duane," he began cautiously, "I'm going to be completely honest here. I get the impression that there's something you aren't telling me."

Duane let out a sour laugh. "That right? Well, that's fair. But I'm no expert on this place. I just happen to live down the road. So most anything I can tell you would just be something I was told, myself."

"Which means?"

"It means I don't know anything for a fact. Not about this godforsaken shit-hole. But what I have heard, what I grew up hearing… and somebody should have told you. Somebody should have warned you not to let your kids go snooping up here. That Randall boy, too. And I'm sorry that they didn't."

They came to the end of the wall and turned the corner. The trees were closer on that side, their shadows intimating the true depth of the forest. Duane pointed ahead. "You see that pile of rocks down yonder? At the base of the wall?"

"Yes," Mark said, almost whispering.

"Story goes that, back in '34, some folks did come and try to find out what happened to old Hester. Couple of weeks after that night, once the word got around, group of local boys got curious. And, when they couldn't get that gate open, they piled some of them rocks from the yard up by the wall. Figured they'd just climb over and have a look. First one was Mitchell Peaks. Bit later, when they didn't hear anything from Mitchell, Francis McLaren went in looking. Same thing happened."

"Them other boys waited, tried to get a handle on what was going on, but they couldn't figure it. They even looked over the wall, but couldn't see a damn thing. Just the garden. Supposedly, it looked like parts of it was moving on their own. Leaves shaking. Branches bending. But no Mitchell, and no Francis. Understandably, they got spooked. They didn't wait much longer, and they didn't try going in themselves.

"But they weren't the last. Town lost a deputy after that, though from what I've heard, it wasn't much of a loss. A few others, scattered over the years. Folks will get brave after time gives them some space from fear."

Mark looked over at the man as they came closer to the rock pile. "What the hell are you telling me right now?"

"I'm telling you that this place has a history. And your little girl's gotten caught up in it."

"Duane, what happened to those people who went inside?"

Duane cocked his head. "Well. That is the question." He took a step back, nodding. "You climb up on those rocks there and peek over the wall. Don't try to get inside yet. I just want you to look. Tell me what you see."

Mark stared at the man for a heartbeat, narrowing his eyes, chewing at the corner of his bottom lip. An errant gust of wind funneled by, tousling his hair. A moment later, he turned toward the wall and carefully climbed up onto the rocks. He gripped the upper edge and, straining, pulled himself up to look over into the garden. "The fuck?" he whispered.

Inside were plants he did not recognize, strange root structures that spiraled and twisted with their own secret logic, flowers he could not hope to identify. They rustled, here and there, in unnatural ways. The plants grew wild and tall, and he could just make out more of the Hester house over their canopy. The house was ruined by age and weather, the front porch sagging, the windows shattered, revealing only darkness.

In the center of the garden was a haze of some kind, as though that spot alone was kissed by early morning sunlight. Within it stood an object. He could not tell if it was a statue or a machine of some sort, but to look upon it twisted his stomach into a knot of fire and sent needles of anxiety across the back of his neck. The object was smooth, pale, with dark filaments running its length where pieces slipped together. Seeing it, he wanted only to unsee it, and the thought suddenly consumed him.

Mark pushed away from the wall and, before realizing what he had done, lost his balance and fell. He crashed back to the ground, grunting, and reflexively kicked himself back farther. "What... what is that thing?"

"I don't know. People have guesses, but that's all they are. I reckon it's part of what scared them boys so bad back in '34."

"Yeah... yeah... Jesus Christ, Erica's in there with that thing!" He scrambled to his feet and moved closer to the wall, intent on climbing it again.

"Mark!" Duane shouted. "Stop right there!"

Mark turned to face him, eyes wide. "Stop? Are you out of your fucking mind? I don't care what kind of backwoods hoodoo you believe in, but my daughter is in there, and I'm going to get her out."

Duane gritted his teeth and took a deep breath. He seemed to consider something and sucked at his teeth. "Mark, I'm sorry you're going through this. But I brought you out here to show you something. I have to show you, because it's the only way you'll believe it."

"What?" He spread his arms wide. "What? I saw your garden, and I don't care. I'm going after my daughter."

"Not the garden. Not like that, anyway. Turn around and look over to your left. A little over halfway up the wall."

"Duane, I don't have any more time for this bullshit. I—"

"Just do it, goddamn it!"

Mark scowled at the man, sneering slightly. "Fine," he sighed. "What am I looking for?"

"Good." He exhaled a sigh of his own. "Thank you. You'll find a crack, a big one. Big enough to see through."

"Uh huh."

"When you looked over into the garden, I reckon you noticed all those exotic plants. And you might have noticed how all their roots seemed... off, somehow. Vines that looked like they was coiled around nothing but air. Trunks bent for no reason."

"Mmhm."

"Well, you were only getting part of the picture."

Mark found the opening and peered through, squinting. His eyebrows knotted. "The fuck?" he muttered again.

And then he gasped.

He recoiled, stepping back quickly, stumbling, and almost falling.

"Through there, that's the whole picture," Duane said. His voice was emotionless, save a faint tremor. "You can see what shares that space."

"Oh my God, oh my fucking God!" He blinked wildly, mouth hanging open. "Randall, that was Randall and... and it was in him! It was inside him!"

"Yeah. Yeah, that's about what I figured."

"He... he's still moving, he's... it, it, what the fuck? What the fuck is in there?"

Duane only shook his head.

"Oh my God, Erica," Mark said suddenly. He scrambled forward, slipping on leaves, and bolted for the pile of rocks.

"Hey!" Duane raced after him. He caught up at the base of the wall and grabbed the back of Mark's shirt, yanking violently. The man fell back, flailing, and landed on his side.

Mark rolled over and quickly got to his feet. He balled his fists and twisted his features into a vicious sneer. "Are you out of your fucking mind?"

"Are you? You can't go in there! Did you listen to a goddamned word I said?"

"Bullshit," Mark shouted, pointing. "Bullshit! My fucking daughter is in there, man!"

"And she's dead! She's gone, Mark! Not coming back! And you won't either, not from there!"

"Fuck you! Fuck you, I don't believe it!"

"You believe it," Duane said, shaking his head and swallowing hard. "I see it on you. You believe it."

"Fuck. You." He accented each word with a job of his finger. "I'm calling the cops, and I'm going over that wall."

"Dad," came a faint shout from the other side of the property, muffled by the wall.

"Shit," Duane muttered. He fumbled at the back of his shirt, not taking his eyes off of Mark, and pulled his hand free a moment later. It held a revolver, which he promptly pointed in Mark's direction. "Tell him to stay over there," he hissed. "Tell him everything's all right, and to wait over there where he was."

"What the fuck, put the fucking gun down! Are you—"

"Now," he growled. "Now, before this gets out of hand!"

Mark glanced between the gun and Duane's face, breathing shallowly. "Ray," he yelled, trying his best not to sound terrified. "Ray, everything's fine, stay over there!"

"Dad?" Raymond was closer now, and they could hear rustling leaves.

"Go sit back down Ray, we'll be back in a minute!"

"Dad, what are you doing?" The boy had stopped, but sounded scared. "Did you find Erica?"

"Raymond," Mark nearly screamed, in a voice that could have been filtered through gravel. "Go wait for us where you were! Now!"

The boy said nothing. A moment passed. Again they heard the faint shuffling of leaves, growing steadily softer.

"Good. That's good, Mark. Now I want you to listen. Listen to what I am going to tell you, and you believe it." He licked his lips, tried to calm his breathing. "If you go inside that plot of nightmares, you will die. You'll die, and that garden will make use of whatever's left of your corpse. That will be the end of you, and your boy won't have a daddy no more. You and his sister, half his family, gone in one day."

"You piece of shit."

"Fine. Yeah. That's fine. But you think about what I'm saying. Really consider it. And hell, you go ahead and call the police. They'll come. But most of them will know. If they grew up here, which they probably did, then they'll know. So they'll do what you expect them to do, and they'll tell you that they're searching, and you'll wait. And you won't stop waiting, because they aren't searching. Not in there." He sucked at his cheek and gestured toward the garden. "They've heard the stories. They've heard the names the old timers have for this place."

Mark glared ahead, his eyes burning through his captor.

"File a missing person's report," Duane said. "Get rid of that boy's car, and file a report. That's my advice for you."

"Or," Mark countered, "I could take a sledgehammer to that fucking wall. Torch everything inside."

The color drained from Duane's face and he took a step back. He blinked, dumbfounded. "It don't burn," he said, almost to himself. He shook his head and pointed the gun directly at Mark, centered it on his chest. "We can't have nobody tearing down that wall." He shook his head again, eyes wider. "No sir. No, that garden, it exists in two places. It's in between. And whatever's in that other place, it cannot be allowed to get out of those walls. Ever. Do you understand me?"

Mark said nothing.

"Do you fucking understand me?" Duane took a step closer, shaking now. "If I even think you're going to let that abomination out, I will end you right now! Do. You. Understand?"

"Dad?" Raymond's voice was nearer, his approach masked by the wind's steady howl.

"Goddamn it," Duane said through gritted teeth.

Worry spread across Mark's face as the leaves softly rustled; Raymond was running now.

Duane brought his free hand to the back of his head, ran his fingers nervously through his hair.

"Mr. Ogilvie, your son is on his way." He cocked the hammer back. "And one of us has a decision to make."

HALLOWED INK

LIAM RONAN

Maggie and the teenager stared at one another across the desk, drowning in the late afternoon heat as they waited to see whose mask would slip first. Andrew was still wearing his in, and while it was tempered with youthful arrogance, its sullen glower was not yet fully dry.

I can break it, Maggie thought, resisting the urge to pat at the perspiration gathering upon her brow. *It's not too late.*

The boy was kidding himself if he believed there would be any other kind of outcome. Maggie wasn't old, but she was still a dinosaur compared to the children and teenagers she cared for. The mask she wore here at the youth center was fully matured, if not too badly weathered. She had bitter experience on her side, having taken more than her fair share of scalps in matters such as this. Andrew's mask would falter and slide to reveal his true face long before hers ever would.

We all wear them, she liked to tell the older kids. *Like characters in a story that exists only in our minds. But we have to remember to take them off occasionally. If we forget... Well, some masks fit more snugly than others. I just have to help you find one that you can live with when the story is over.*

"So are you going to tell me about it?" she asked.

The teenager held her gaze and shrugged.

"If you know where Josh is, Andrew, speak up. Let me help him."

Another leaden shrug.

"Who were those boys I saw chasing you?"

Andrew blinked and glanced to the side, his lips parting in a short sigh.

There it is, Maggie thought as he turned back towards her. *The first crack.*

"They were waiting when you left that night, weren't they? Tell me who they were."

"Just forget about them, Maggie. Forget about Josh."

"Why?"

"It's safer."

"Is that some kind of threat?" she said sharply. Like every good mother, substitute or otherwise, Maggie knew how to play the boy. Andrew's brow furrowed.

"No… But you can't help him. Not now."

"Sounds like you've given up on him."

"It's not like that. You don't understand."

"I never thought you were the sort to abandon a mate. Josh hasn't been seen for days."

Andrew looked up at the ceiling, tired eyes coated in a slick sheen of duress.

Almost there, now.

"I know Josh has been dealing again," Maggie said. "That's why Carl threw him out. Maybe I can help him with whatever mess he's ended up in."

Andrew snorted and gave her a derisive look. "You and Carl think you both know what's going on around here, but you don't."

"Here's your chance to enlighten me, then."

He was silent for a long beat, and Maggie could almost taste how badly he wanted to unburden himself.

"You really want to know?" he asked quietly.

"Of course I do."

"You won't tell anyone?"

She lied and shook her head. The boy swallowed hard, his mask sagging with misery.

"There's a new crew on the estate," he said. "Everybody's scared of them."

"I hadn't heard that."

Andrew gestured at the office door. The communal hall was on the other side, and apart from Carl and a couple of younger children who were waiting for their parents to come and collect them, it was empty.

"Open your eyes," Andrew said. "This place is deserted. Haven't you wondered why?"

Of course she had. It was high summer, and up until a fortnight ago, the youth center had been crammed with kids. But their numbers had thinned out recently to the point where Maggie had only seen four or five all day. Whatever the reason was for the sudden change, Maggie hadn't expected it to be linked to what happened last weekend, when Josh had been ejected in tears and Andrew had followed him out. She had gone after them in time to see the pair running away beneath the glow of the street lights, two older boys wearing hoodies at their heels. Now Josh was missing, and she had coerced Andrew into meeting her so she could find out why.

"So what are you saying—that everyone's joined this new gang?"

Andrew nodded.

"Some have. Others are just scared, and won't come out."

"Why? What are they doing?"

"Stuff."

"Drugs, you mean."

Andrew nodded.

It always comes down to bloody drugs.

"It's not normal gear," he continued. "It changes you, makes you different from who you used to be."

"That's what drugs do, Andrew."

"No, this is something new, something... I don't know. Something *more*. They call it ink... Hallowed Ink."

He shook his head sadly as Maggie raised an eyebrow.

"I knew you wouldn't understand."

Maggie felt a phantom prickling from the old scar tissue running along her forearms, and thought: *Kid, if you only knew.* But that was her business, and whether it was wearing long sleeves on warm days or convincing herself that part of her life had been one of many masks she learned to cast aside, Maggie kept those memories locked up tight.

"And that's where Josh is now, is it?" she asked. "With this gang?"

"Yeah, I think so."

"Who else is involved?"

"Uh... Marie, John, Bethan... Dave, Tony... Chris. Loads of them."

Maggie studied Andrew for any sign that he might be holding back, but knew he was telling the truth—the names tallied with some of those the council's safe-guarding team had already given her that afternoon.

"Well, that lot have certainly been keeping their heads down. Where are they hanging out now?"

"Don't know," the boy said as he studied his feet.

Maggie thought he might actually cry. She leaned across the desk and placed a hand on his arm. "Andrew, I can't change any of this unless you tell me every-thing. You do want it to change, don't you?"

He nodded slowly. "I don't know where they go. But they're all part of his crew now. They're with him."

"Who, Andrew? Give me a name."

The teenager hesitated for a beat, then responded in a tone that made him sound far younger than his years.

"Carver," he said quietly. "Leon Carver."

"He's playing you, Mags," Carl said after Andrew left. "Leon Carver doesn't exist."

They'd decided to shut the doors early and were clearing up for the evening. Maggie swept the floor while Carl switched off the row of computers lining one side of the communal hall.

"What do you mean?"

"Carver's a myth, a council estate legend. They told tales about him when I was a boy—how he robbed grannies, beat up a teacher, cut up rival dealers. Where did you say you grew up again?"

"Newport."

"You must have heard similar stories there."

Maggie thought about it for a moment. "Bomber Reggae," she smiled. "God, I haven't thought about him in years. Poor sod was just a harmless old drunk, really. We didn't even know his real name. But any time someone went missing or got beaten up, we used to say that Bomber Reggae had got them."

"Well, there you go. Every town has got one."

"So Carver's not real?"

"Nope. He was supposedly writing everything he did into some kind of book, some On-The-Road-with-switchblades type of thing. If it happened now, the kids would probably say he was uploading footage to the net."

Maggie paused and leaned on her broom. "What's Andrew so scared of, then?"

Carl looked across at her and raised his eyebrows. "You're not blind, Maggie. We've been losing Josh ever since his brother got out of jail. That scrote has probably got the kid out there pushing for him right now, and I'll bet you twenty quid that the guys chasing him were part of that scene."

"Like a turf war?"

"Exactly. Andrew didn't want to grass on his mate, so he gave you the town's favorite bogeyman instead."

Maggie thought about that. If it was true, where were all the other teenagers who had stopped coming to the youth center?

"What about this new gang? Andrew said the kids are all joining up."

Carl finished with the computers and leaned against one of the tables.

"I've heard whispers, but you know how the kids embellish things. Remember what I told you about the PVM?"

She nodded. The Pro-Violence Mob was long gone, its members all settled into middle age now. But the local teenagers still talked up their exploits. Carl had grown up with the PVM crowd, and would laugh at some of the stories that the kids swore were true.

"What time is it, anyway?" he asked as Maggie checked her watch.

"Almost eight."

"I promised Karen I'd be home early tonight. Are you okay to lock up?"

"Sure."

"I'll see you tomorrow. And I'll ask around about this gang, okay?"

Maggie nodded and watched him leave, knowing that he was on his way to see his girlfriend, not his wife.

Just another mask that's on too tight, she thought, and turned to finish sweeping up.

Maggie lived on a new housing development built on reclaimed land at the edge of Port Hafoc. It was all saplings and modern homes, and had little in common with the estate where the youth center was based. But Maggie had come up hard in Newport, harder than even Carl knew. Everything she had now, she had earned.

On her way out of the estate, she pulled in at an off-license which sold milk, bread, and newspapers. Older kids usually hung around the entrance, but tonight there was only a boy and a girl who looked to be of primary school age. The boy carried a sheaf of loose pages, and the girl held a staple gun. They spared Maggie a glance as she got out of her car. She thought she recognized them from somewhere. The center, probably, although they weren't regulars.

As the pair approached a tree near the off-license and prepared to fix one of the pages to it, the shop's door was thrown open. A sallow-faced teenager burst out and sprinted down the street, a bottle in his hand. The shopkeeper—she knew him only as Mr. Mehta—appeared in the doorway and yelled after the fleeing youth. "Don't come back, you little shit! You're barred, hear me?"

"What's happened?" Maggie asked.

"Ah, just a druggie shoplifter," he replied. "Gave me a false name when I asked for ID."

"Have you called the police?"

"No point. He'd only get a slap on the wrist."

"Yeah, but you can't let him wander around the estate with alcohol. He might share it with other children."

"Rotten bastards can choke on it for all I care."

"Oh, come on. They're not all like that."

Mr. Mehta looked at her curiously.

"What would you know? Do you even live on this estate?"

"No, but—"

"Spare me the bleeding heart, then. I've had this shop for thirty years, and I've never had to close up this early before. If you had any sense, you'd get off home, too. You don't belong around here."

"Wow. Do you speak to all your customers like this?"

"I mean it's not safe anymore—just ask them."

He gestured at the boy and girl by the tree. As Maggie followed his gaze, Mr. Mehta retreated into the shop and shut its door. "Bloody kids think I came down in the last shower," he muttered. "Carver, indeed."

Maggie snapped round at that, but he was already drawing the bolts. As she cursed under her breath, she noticed that the boy and girl were staring at her.

"Hello," she said, stepping towards them. "I've seen you at the youth center, haven't I? I'm Maggie."

They eyed her suspiciously.

"We don't go there anymore," the girl said.

Maggie looked at what they had fixed to the tree. It was a poster. Beneath the word 'Missing' was a poorly printed photograph of a smiling teenager. His name was in block capitals below: "Kyle Bannister."

"Is this your big brother?"

"Yeah," the boy said. "Have you seen him?"

Maggie shook her head.

"The grown-ups think he's run away," the girl told her.

"And what do you think?"

"He's been taken," the boy replied. The girl punched him on the shoulder.

"Shut up, idiot," she hissed.

"Why do you say that?" Maggie asked.

The boy glanced at his sister, then back at Maggie.

"We're not supposed to talk about it."

Maggie sighed. "Don't tell me—Leon Carver, right?"

The children didn't reply.

"You do know he's not real, don't you?"

"Yes, he is!" the girl said indignantly. "We've seen him."

"Where?"

"Everywhere," her brother answered. "This is his estate."

"It's getting dark." The girl tugged on the boy's sleeve. "We have to go."

They turned to leave. "If you see Kyle, will you tell him to come home?" the boy asked.

Maggie smiled and nodded. "Of course I will."

She watched as the children stepped around an older girl hurrying along the pavement, checking her phone and not looking where she was going. She was nineteen or so, and as she passed, Maggie saw her glance at her watch and frown.

"Excuse me, love," Maggie called out impulsively.

The girl looked up, eyes wide. "What you want?" She didn't slow down as her gaze moved from Maggie to the streetlights overhead, which were flickering to life. Another frown creased her face.

"I was wondering, do you know anyone called—"

"Piss off, will you!" The girl broke into a trot and hurried past.

The shop grew dark as Mr. Mehta switched off its lights. Maggie turned in a slow circle, suddenly aware of how empty the street was despite the warm weather and earliness of the hour. She was alone on the pavement, and there was nothing to hear—no voices, no laughter, no music drifting out from an open window... No open windows.

This doesn't feel right.

This doesn't feel right at all.

Maggie drove to an all-night petrol station on the edge of town in a troubled mood, and picked up her groceries there. When she got home, there was a message on her answer machine.

"It's Carl," the recording said. "There may be more to this Carver business than I thought. Give me a ring on my mobile, will you?"

Maggie set about making a cup of tea and dialed his number while she waited for the kettle to boil. Her call went straight to voicemail.

Probably doesn't want his wife to interrupt him while he's with his girlfriend.

She settled down on the sofa and switched the television on, and tried Carl again an hour later. This time, she got through.

"Carl, it's me," she said. "What's up?"

There was no response, but she could hear him breathing against the receiver.

"Hello?" she asked again. "Can you hear me?"

"I can hear you," a voice answered, its soft tone unfamiliar.

"Carl?"

"No."

"Oh... Sorry, I must have dialed the wrong number."

"Shit happens," the voice said, and the line went dead.

Maggie dialed again, this time using the number stored in the phone's memory. The call was answered almost immediately.

"Carl?"

"Afraid not."

It was the same voice as before. Maggie checked the phone's display, then put it back to her ear.

"Who is that?"

"Who do you think I am?"

"Where's Carl? Why have you got his phone?"

"He's careless like that."

There was a burst of background noise that sounded like laughter.

"Is Carl with you?"

"Yes."

"Put him on."

"I don't think so."

"What's your name?"

"You already know it."

Maggie felt a stab of trepidation.

"Why don't you tell me anyway?" she asked quietly.

There was a long pause.

"I will," the voice said. "Soon enough."

There was another rush of background laughter before the line went dead. Maggie thought about it a moment, then dialed a different number.

"Yeah?" a woman's voice demanded.

"Karen? It's Maggie from the youth center. Sorry to call so late, but I was wondering if Carl was home?"

"He's in the pub. Try his mobile."

"I did, but I can't get through. Can you ask him to call me please? It's just work stuff, but it's pretty urgent."

Karen laughed bitterly. Maggie instinctively knew that the woman was well aware of what her husband was up to.

"Yeah, I'll bet," Karen replied. "Don't phone here again, Maggie."

She cut the call before Maggie could respond.

Great, she thought. *She thinks her husband is knocking me off, too.*

But it was her conversation with whoever had answered Carl's mobile that was of most concern. Had they lifted it from the bar when he wasn't looking, perhaps? Or had it been taken from him more forcefully?

Her doorbell chimed. Maggie jumped off the sofa and stared down the short corridor to her front door. It was a quarter to eleven, far too late for any casual callers, and the recent conversation had left her feeling jumpy.

Get a grip, she told herself. *It's probably Carl—he's come around in person because his phone is gone.*

She moved to the door, checking that the key was turned in the lock and that the chain was on.

"Who is it?" she called out. But there was no answer.

Maggie was debating what to say next when the door shook with a violent blow. She leapt back, startled.

"Who's there?" she said more forcefully.

Again, there was only silence.

Maggie walked into the living room and stepped across to the curtains. She peered through the gap, but the doorstep was empty. Whoever had been there was already gone.

Movement across the road caught her eye. In the glow of a streetlight, she could see three figures gathered on the pavement. Two of them were standing, and the third was sitting on the curb. They all wore hoodies despite the warm evening air, and were staring at her house.

Maggie jumped as the mobile in her hand suddenly rang out. She checked the display and saw the name 'Carl.'

But was it really him this time?

She raised the phone to her ear, not wanting to take her eyes off the figures on the road outside.

"Hello?" she said, unable to keep a tremor out of her voice.

"Why don't you answer your door... Maggie?"

Maggie tore the phone away from her ear and killed the call in fright. She stared at it for a moment, then dialed the police. When she looked back up, the figures on the pavement were gone.

"I don't know why his name has come up now after all these years, but Leon Carver is definitely dead," the inspector said. "He died back in 1972."

The policeman's name was Coyle, and he was sitting on Maggie's sofa holding a cup of tea.

"So he was real, after all."

"Oh, yes. All the Carvers were well-known around here at one time, and I hauled Leon in on more than one occasion. He was cut from some pretty rough cloth, but he did have a bit of depth. Literary aspirations, mainly—he thought he was going to be the honest-to-goodness voice of his generation, although I think his ambition outweighed whatever talent he might have had on that front."

"Is it true that he was writing about his crimes?"

Coyle shook his head.

"No, he had too much native cunning to be that stupid. He did carry a notebook around with him, but all I ever saw was weird, hard-boiled, speed-freak gibberish. Leon had quite a habit."

"How did he die?"

"Someone stabbed him in the chest, then dumped him in the canal. It was down near where the old slaughterhouse used to be. Where they've built that new grill restaurant?"

Maggie knew the spot.

"We never found out who did it, but then most people thought it was a case of rough justice—those-who-live-by-the-sword and all that. I suppose in Leon's case, the sword turned out to be mightier than the pen."

Coyle smiled at his own joke before continuing.

"We put it down to a deal gone wrong. His family weren't too happy, and we had quite a few months of trouble while they roamed all over town looking for his killer. But it spelled the beginning of the end for them around here, too."

"How so?"

"Leon's death demonstrated that the Carvers weren't invulnerable after all. It damaged them, you see? People stopped being so scared."

"Do they still live in town?"

"No, they're long gone. Until tonight, we hadn't heard a peep about the Carvers for over forty years."

Coyle had sent someone round to Carl's house after Maggie's call, but found only Karen at home. She had given the police her own interpretation of her husband's whereabouts, and although he hadn't said it, Maggie knew that Coyle now thought her concern for Carl was inspired by more than just fears for his welfare.

"What about this new gang?" she asked.

"I'll look into it, but that's a new one to me, too. It's actually been quiet these last few weeks. Some of the lads at the station are joking that crime has taken a holiday."

"And the Hallowed Ink?"

"Could be anything—the dealers invent new slang for their wares all the time. Ever heard of an A-Bomb?"

Maggie shook her head.

"It's a joint made with marijuana and heroin. Quite the fashion, if you're into that sort of thing." Coyle put his cup down on her coffee table and stood up. "Look, it's late. We'll keep an eye on things tonight. I think those kids were just bobby-knocking, but call us if anything happens. Quote the incident number we've given you, and someone will come around straight away."

Maggie nodded. "And Carl's phone?"

"Probably stolen, but we'll look into it. Try not to worry, yeah? Let's give him a chance to turn up first."

Coyle smiled again, and Maggie fought down a sudden surge of anger. *That's the mask he wears most of all,* she thought. *And it's as fake as the rest of them.*

The policeman could try and placate her all he wanted, but it didn't alter Maggie's growing sense of apprehension. Something strange was happening in Port Hafoc. Whatever it was, the authorities were blind to it. But she could feel it, creeping steadily closer, moving through the youth of the town.

She locked up after Coyle left, then went to bed. Maggie lay beneath the covers, sweating in the heat but unwilling to open a window, and thought about everything with her mobile in one hand and a kitchen knife in the other.

Her scars were itching badly, yet she refused to acknowledge them. They were part of the old life she had cast off, a period which had no connections with the mask she now chose to present to the world. But she couldn't forget about them tonight, not when it appeared that someone was steering the kids she cared for down a familiar dark path.

Something needed to be done. When dawn finally broke, Maggie knew what it was. She stepped out of bed, climbed into the shower, dressed, then left the house early to find Leon Carver.

Given the earliness of the hour, the streets and parks were mostly empty. Maggie had more luck down by the canal. It was pleasant and clean these days, but even she had heard the stories about how it had once been a place to avoid. The old slaughterhouse had disgorged all manner of muck and offal into its waters, and the canal had been filthy and overridden with rats.

Now the slaughterhouse was gone, replaced by a car wash and a restaurant, and strict environmental laws governed what ended up in the water. Although the paths running alongside the canal's overgrown banks were popular with dog walkers and joggers, Maggie had them all to herself this morning. It struck her as odd, but didn't sway her mind. She parked close to the spot where she thought Carver had died and walked the rest of the way there, feeling the sun warming the back of her neck. It was going to be another hot day; in a few hours, the heat would be coiled and heavy once more.

Maggie walked for a few minutes before turning a bend in the path. Someone sat on the bank a few feet in front of her, staring across the canal at a dark sewer entrance on the opposite side. He seemed oblivious to the dank smell seeping out of the opening, and she recognized him immediately.

Josh...

The teenager turned sluggishly at her approach, but did not get up. Josh looked like he might have been sleeping rough—he was wearing dirty jeans and an unwashed hoodie, and beneath it, his eyes were ringed with deep shadows. He looked terrible, and as she drew closer, Maggie noted a pattern of small, shallow cuts all around his mouth.

Another mask, she thought. *But this is one that he will never be able to take off.*

"Hello, Maggie," Josh slurred. "Have you come to tell me one of your stories? You always did have the best ones."

He was mocking her. Maggie remembered what Carl told her about how they had been losing Josh for some time, and realized he was right. The teenager reminded her of how her own brother had looked, shortly before the overdose which had served as her own wake-up call.

"Where is he?" she asked flatly.

"Who?"

"This faker, the one running around telling everyone he's Leon Carver."

Josh only smiled. The cuts around his mouth widened horribly. They made Maggie think of tribal scars, and she had to force herself to look past them.

"That is what's happening, isn't it?" Maggie said. "Someone is taking over. They're pushing this Hallowed Ink shit, and they've decided to make the legend real to help it along."

"You're the storyteller, Maggie. What do you think?"

"Grow up, Josh. You're no tough guy."

"And you'd know all about pretending to be something you're not."

"What the hell does that mean?"

Josh smirked and scratched at the dirt on his jeans. "How's my old mate Andrew holding up? I keep meaning to catch up with him."

The rotten smell suddenly intensified. The teenager nodded as Maggie wrinkled her nose.

"The slaughterhouse left its mark," he said. "They're never going to get that stink out of the water."

"I can see why you like it down here."

"Oldest part of town. Didn't know that, did you?"

"I meant it's about your level."

"I know what you meant, you stuck-up cow. I just don't care."

"I'll have to up my game, then."

"I'm sure you'll run into someone with a sharper tongue soon enough."

This wasn't the teenager Maggie remembered. The Josh she knew was cowed and untrustworthy, more likely to flip two fingers up at your back than say anything to your face. *It's the drugs*, she thought. *Somewhere beneath the bluster, he's still a lost kid.*

"They used to slaughter more than animals here," Josh said, gesturing with a grubby hand at land beyond the opposite bank. It was a wild, wooded plain that served as a barrier of sorts between the town and the distant Port Hafoc steelworks. "Iron Age tribe, the Silure-something-or-other, they were in charge then. They dragged prisoners out here and cut their throats. The trees and the ground soaked up all the blood. It's still in the air. You can taste it."

"Stop living on your brother's reputation, Josh. He's the tough one in your family. I've seen you cry, remember?"

"My brother?"

Josh pointed at the sewer opening on the opposite bank. It was fashioned from old blocks of rough stone and crumbling mortar. A steel grid had been added across its mouth. The lower half was a tangle of weeds and rubbish.

"That's a drain from the old slaughterhouse vats. See the gap in the bars? It would take a special kind of tough guy to climb through there, don't you think? No, you'd only go into a horrible place like that if you were looking for something." He smiled again, revealing teeth that were stained black. "And maybe if a tough guy did that, they might find out they weren't so tough. Maybe the tough guy would cry a bit too, eh? But not for very long, I think."

His ugly grin was wider than ever, and Maggie noticed that there was a milky opaqueness about the teenager's eyes. Whatever this Hallowed Ink was, it was bad news, and she was wasting time listening to him.

"I feel sorry for you, Josh," she said. "I tried my best to help. I really did. But I know a lost cause when I see one." Maggie leaned in towards him. The old Josh would have flinched, but the stranger before her barely blinked. "I won't lose any more, do you hear? You tell that faker to come and see me. I want to see him, tonight."

"Well, he's a very busy man, Maggie. But he might make some time for you."

Maggie straightened and turned around. As she walked away, Josh giggled sickly, and Maggie knew for sure that not a trace of the boy she had known was left in him.

Maggie spent the rest of the day at the youth center, alone. Not a single child or teenager walked through its doors. Neither did Carl. She called Inspector Coyle, but he was off duty. She left a message outlining her plan, made her preparations, and locked the center's entrance before retiring to her office to catch up with reports and funding applications.

At some point the silence, heat, and weariness from her lack of sleep caught up with her. Maggie dozed off. When she awoke, dusk had fallen, and someone was pounding on the front door. She left her office, recognizing Andrew's terrified voice before she was even halfway across the hall.

"Let me in, Maggie! They're after me! Let me in!"

Maggie unbolted the door. Andrew all but fell across the threshold. As she bent to pick him up, the open door was viciously kicked into her thigh. She cried out and staggered back as a group of youths poured into the center, all wearing hoodies. Josh stood at their head.

He gave her a feral grin. The cuts around his mouth opened to form a bloody star. "Hello again, Mags," he slurred. "So how do you think this story is going to end, eh?"

The teenagers dragged Maggie and Andrew into the communal hall. Dumping them onto the floor, they gathered around in a circle that soon became three rows deep as more figures entered the center.

My God, Maggie thought. *How many of them are there?*

Some of their hooded faces were recognizable, and wore the same opaque eyes and tell-tale scars that Maggie had seen on Josh.

"What the hell do you—" she began, but Kyle Bannister, missing no more, leaned in and backhanded her across the face. There were sniggers at this, but if they'd expected Maggie to cower beneath the blow, she quickly disappointed them. Maggie swung around with a haymaker and punched Kyle as hard as she could, sending the boy crashing into his peers even as she rounded on the rest of them.

"Come on, then!" She bared her teeth. Andrew whimpered beside her, still desperately looking for a way to escape. But as a rich, charismatic voice rang out, he dropped his gaze to the floor, too frightened to do anything but kneel.

"I knew you wouldn't disappoint, Maggie," the voice said from outside of the circle. "You've still got it, haven't you? It's locked away somewhere deep, but it's there."

Maggie turned, looking for the speaker. There was a noise from the front doors as someone slid the bolts into place.

"A touch of the wild," the voice continued. "A streak not yet fully broken by the domesticity which you have forced yourself to accept."

Maggie had vague impressions of someone walking slowly around the circle of youths. She heard another whimper from Andrew, and knew that the faker had arrived.

"That's what society is, after all. Just a confederation of tamed savages, carefully trained in the art of bow-and-give instead of rise-up-and-take. Utterly submissive, a boring failure. An abject lesson in stalled potential."

"Come out here," Maggie called. "Let me see what you look like."

"How quickly we forget our true nature," the voice continued, ignoring her. "The play starts out well enough, but somewhere along the way we become mired in the middle, and lose sight of the third act."

The figure came to a halt.

"And when that happens, our only option if we want to feel truly alive once more is to inject it with fresh life."

The circle parted as he strode forward, and Maggie finally got her first clear glimpse of the imposter.

Unlike the casual sportswear of the teenagers, he was dressed in a vintage leather box jacket and faded denim jeans, the bottoms slightly flared. He looked to be in his mid-twenties, and wore his dark hair long and pushed back from an unusually high forehead. When he grinned, the corners of his lips curled to reveal both rows of teeth. But the smile never touched his burning indigo eyes.

All of this paled by comparison when Maggie saw his skin.

Her initial thought was that he was black until the color altered and swirled beneath the pale surface, like oil upon water. It was fascinating to behold, a terrible kind of beauty that constantly alternated between light and darkness.

"Maggie," he said, a Rorschach test made flesh. "At last we meet."

"Your face..." she whispered, unable to look away from the dizzying, shifting patterns.

"Tells a tale, doesn't it?" He stepped closer. "What's written up there, Maggie? What do you see?"

Maggie's vision swam. For the briefest moment, a flurry of long-suppressed memories surged to the forefront of her mind, and she saw a mattress in a dirty squat as her brother pocketed a handful of notes. She heard him telling her to be nice to his friends, and felt the burning, all-consuming need for chemical oblivion. The pain that accompanied the memories was intense, and Maggie forced herself to look away.

That is not me... I am not that person!

She swallowed and glanced back, careful to focus only on his eyes.

"Nothing," Maggie said. "I see nothing but a fake."

He smiled.

"Very well, Maggie. Say your piece. We will bear witness."

"Leon Carver is dead," Maggie announced to the teenagers. "The police confirmed it. This idiot stole his name to trick you and get what he wants. I don't know what's wrong with his skin, but he's just a faker using a dead man's name."

The teenagers didn't react. Maggie knew she was preaching to the converted, but that hadn't been why she'd demanded this meeting take place.

She looked back at him. "If you're Leon Carver, prove it," she said. "It's going to take more than dressing up like some druggie hipster to convince me you're the real deal."

"I'm no plagiarist, Maggie. I've been away, but now I'm back where I belong."

He started to unbutton his shirt. An excited murmur rippled among the teenagers. As they watched their leader, Maggie stole a glance at the computers.

I hope this works. I never expected there'd be so many.

"I *am* Leon Carver," he continued. "The night I died, something climbed out of the canal, something very old, and changed me forever. The morticians had their way with my flesh, but could not prevent what was happening on a molecular level."

As he parted his shirt, Maggie felt her legs go weak, all thoughts of the computers forgotten. From the floor beside her, Andrew released another high-pitched whine.

Carver's pale torso swirled with the same unnatural darkness as his face, a living shadow that swam beneath the surface of his skin. But its ebbs and flows could not hide the autopsy scar that ran down the center of his chest.

That was not the worst of it. The changes he had boasted of lay on either side of the scar—six short, stubby appendages, spaced out like teats on the belly of a sow. Each of them tapered to a gaping, moistened slit, and their edges were rimmed with thin hooked barbs. Maggie watched in slack-jawed shock as a dark, viscous liquid dribbled from the slits. It fell in irregular drips, puddling on the floor where it sizzled with heat.

Carver raised his arms and closed his eyes as the appendages coiled and recoiled in a series of obscene, darkly sensual pulses. They began to thicken and stretch, curling and wavering like the tentacles of a sea anemone, searching for prey. Once the appendages were extended a full three feet out from Carver's torso, the last of the pulses shivered down their engorged lengths. The barbs at the tips of each member opened and closed as more dark liquid oozed forth.

Carver opened his indigo eyes and smiled.

"Taste of me," he said.

Maggie's nerve finally broke. She lashed out at the teenagers closest to her and scrambled over them as they dropped, desperate to escape the monstrosity before her. But there were too many of them to fight. The others grabbed her, hauled her upright and held fast. Andrew remained on the floor, tears on his face, watching as six of the teenagers stepped out of the circle to stand before Carver.

The barbs on the ends of the swaying tentacles began to clack in an agitated manner. The hooded youths knelt and leaned in towards their leader. Maggie could only observe, aghast, as the fleshy tubes drifted eagerly towards their mouths. Fastening themselves around the teenagers' lips, the hooked barbs sank into their flesh. Finding purchase, the appendages clamped onto Carver's acolytes like a set of awful enteral feeding tubes. The unnatural organs began to pulsate, and the youths greedily guzzled Carver's foul fluid.

"The Hallowed Ink," he purred. "It is me, and I am it. Print is dead, Maggie. Digital is passé. I am the architect of a new genre, and the pages I write upon are bound in flesh and blood."

One of the appendages unhooked itself as a freshly-anointed teenager staggered backwards. He turned as he retreated, milky eyes rolling upwards in ecstatic communion even as droplets of black matter trickled down his chin. Behind him, others were released, their places claimed immediately as more teenagers surged forwards for their turn.

Carver looked across at her, his face a constantly changing mask. "We are the papyrus and the vellum, the parchment and the copperplate," he said. "My books live and breathe, and the stories I weave are limitless."

Carver looked down at Andrew and gave a slight smile. The boy was immediately hauled to his feet. He wailed in fright as Josh pushed him forward. Andrew resisted as best he could, but the serpentine barbs quickly found him, and Maggie saw for herself how they reached out and sliced into his face, anchoring him in place. He cried out shrilly. Then the tube pulsed, and his captors released his arms.

Andrew didn't struggle for long. Within seconds, he too was a willing supplicant.

"The old have always feared the young, for we remind them of what they have lost," Carver continued. "Their anxiety is well-founded. I am going to rewrite their town."

Another wave of engorged youths fell back. Maggie felt herself being forced forward alongside a violently quivering Andrew. Josh and the others pushed her down onto her knees, and as she looked up at Carver, he flashed her another chiaroscuro smile. "I need you, Maggie," he said, gently stroking the side of her head. "I need your center. Revolution requires youth, and from here, my library can grow. So join with me—be my bibliotheca."

"I'll fight it," Maggie hissed. "I've done it before."

Carver shook his head. "The ink will not be denied an audience. Up until this moment, your whole life has been a bland fiction. But the living word embraces all. Drink deeply, now; let yourself be rewritten."

Maggie did her best to resist as the appendage drifted languidly towards her face. She tore her head out of Josh's grasp and turned to the row of computers. The small lights of their webcams shone, assuring her that they were filming everything, sending it to a dozen different sites in a bid to provide Coyle with hard evidence he would be forced to act upon.

Coyle won't get here in time, Maggie thought. *But whatever Carver is, whatever he's planning, there'll be no pseudonyms to hide behind, no anonymity—not anymore.*

I've taken all of his masks away.

She laughed bitterly as her head was twisted back towards Carver. The nauseating teat was upon her. There was a brief, sweet pain as its needle-teeth sank into her flesh, quickly joined by a hot, wet pressure against her lips. The extremity started to pulse.

As Maggie tasted the first drops of the Hallowed Ink, she had just enough time to wonder what her new mask might look like. Then dark electricity flooded her veins, and she gasped as a brand-new chapter began to unfold.

The End

R.I.P. SKINNY

MAUREEN O'LEARY

This was my brain on drugs: I didn't know whose hands were on the steering wheel and when I moved my fingers to see if they were mine, I was not relieved to find that they were. I drove hunched over the wheel like an old guy while my best friend Erik snored and the road moved in the headlights like a snake. Those were my hands, though. I was in charge.

Then what happened was:

I closed my eyes just for a second and when I opened them again, I was headed for a bunch of fallen wooden crates toppled onto the highway shoulder like a pile of broken bones.

Broken bones was my last thought before we hit and hard pillows blasted out the dashboard and we flipped through the smashing and crashing of metal and glass.

We landed upright and the car rocked a little as if it was thinking about one last go.

"You okay, man?" I asked.

Erik didn't answer. His head rested at a wrong angle. He'd been too high to fasten his seatbelt and I'd been too high to do it for him.

The engine hissed and I worried about a fire starting because in the movies that's what tended to happen. I brushed the glass windshield pebbles from Erik's shirt, sober enough to see that if he was still alive, pulling him clear would kill him.

I settled back in my seat and gave up trying to fix the problem. If the engine blew, Erik and I would die in flames together and in my aching foggy brain I hoped we would.

A siren wailed from so far away I doubted it was for us.

Above the ragged beat of my own heart, I thought I heard somebody laughing.

I woke under fluorescent lights in the hospital with my neck in a plastic brace and my body strapped to a board.

"Erik?" I called to no one because I was in the room alone, except for the tall man wearing a hooded sweatshirt leaning against the wall almost out of my sight line. Maybe the guy was in the wrong room, or just maybe the alcohol and Oxy in my system played tricks on my brain.

An alarm rang from across the hall and there was the burst of a defibrillator and someone yelling orders in doctor talk. The hooded man lifted his arm to point at me, his finger curling unnaturally long like a paper blower from a kid's birthday party.

"Hell no." My voice cracked as he whispered inside his hood. I thrashed on the board like a fish on a line and yelled for someone to help me.

The hooded man chuckled in a voice so deep the sound rumbled in my bones. He approached me with leisure, his finger leading the way until he reached me and probed my side where the doctors had ripped my shirt open. The cold finger buried into the space between my ribs and pushed through the skin until my bones moved apart in popping bursts of bright blue pain. He poked through my ribcage and pressed that long finger into the muscle of my heart.

I arched on the board in impossible pain. The monitors attached to me shrieked and the hooded man stepped aside as the doctors jumbled in.

He pantomimed a gun with long white fingers.

Aimed at me.

Pulled the trigger.

. . .

Twitter rumors spread that my best friend and I were dead on arrival. R.I.P. Erik and Colin.

#RestInPeace
#Bros4Life.
#R.I.P. Skinny.

Erik's nickname was natural for a kid who was six feet tall and beanpole lean, but people were wrong about us. We didn't die in the wreck I caused driving drunk and high. One doctor saved me from the freak seizure that stopped my heart while another doctor across the hall inserted breathing tubes down Erik's throat. His brain wasn't damaged, but the nerves of his neck were severed at C-7 and everything below his waist was a ghost town.

Erik and I both lived and there was no resting and there was no peace.

I lay awake my first night in the state Juvenile Detention Center with a hard cry fluttering in my mouth like a moth in a net I could not let out. I had Googled everything I could find about going to kid prison, basically getting an online PhD on how to get through ten months of lockup without getting the shit kicked out of me. I didn't know if the information was any good, but it was all I had.

Online wisdom suggested that nights were supposed to be the worst. For example, it was important not to think about the fact that the door to my room locked on the outside. Also, it was a bad idea to think about what I'd done to get to JD. I had to put my crime out of my mind.

The only problem was that the image of Erik covered in glass and looking dead played in my head on an endless loop every time I closed my eyes. Until I learned to sleep with my eyes open, I'd be thinking about what I'd done to Erik every night of my life.

Something rustled in the air vent.

"Hey, did you hear that?" I asked the guy in the next bed. George was his name.

"Just be cool," he said.

George was giving good advice, but there was something in the vent and I couldn't breathe very well.

Claws scratched against thin metal. At least that's what it sounded like. I made myself still as a dead kid, thinking if I was already dead then nothing could get me.

I closed my eyes and there they were, pieces of glass like diamond pebbles sparkling on my friend's chest. I opened them again, too scared to even blink, and from a deep place in the air vent someone was laughing. My brain turned somersaults of denial. It was kids in another room. It was a guard playing a prank. It was a trick in my brain caused by a summer spent snorting Oxycontin through the nose.

"*One two, buckle your shoe.*" The voice crackled like fire.

I tightened the blanket around my neck.

"*Seven, eight, get your neck on straight.*"

The vent banged as though something inside needed to get out.

"*Colin,*" the crackling man crooned. "*I waaant yooou.*"

The pajama pants issued me that day by the state of California warmed and just as quickly cooled as I wet them.

It's a myth that boys don't like to talk about their feelings. In JD there were boys who never stopped talking about their feelings. There was the boy who talked with his arms wound around his body as if he were holding a wild animal inside his rib cage. There was the boy who talked while staring at the floor, and there was the boy who talked while staring at the ceiling.

One of my old crew broke into my house and held a gun to my little sister's head.

My mother beat me with an extension cord. A wooden spoon. A hammer.

My stepfather did worse. You don't want to know what he did.

During the first few group sessions, I made the mistake of thinking that the guys were making shit up until I realized that the most interesting thing about the stories was that the dudes telling them survived. Yeah, they were in JD. Not great. But I had to admire them for being alive when it seemed like the whole world wanted them dead.

It was my cellmate's turn to talk. George had been riding in the backseat of his cousin's car on the way to a house party when they took a detour for a drive-by. George wasn't a gang member, which meant he hadn't known what was going down, but it didn't matter. Under new anti-gang laws, George faced twenty-five to life and in five years was heading for adult prison.

"I'll be forty when I get out," George said.

I examined my palms to avoid looking at anybody because I could not imagine a lifetime in prison for George. He was a quiet guy who loved to read, and besides that, he didn't even do the thing that landed him in lockup. My best friend was paralyzed for life because of me, and the judge only gave me one year. I wouldn't have blamed George for hating me for the fact I was getting out by the next Christmas, but he didn't. We weren't friends, but he never acted mad. I examined my palms and wondered if I would have been as cool as George was if our stories were switched around.

"What about you, Colin?" Counselor Dave asked.

Dave was kind of young and not as bad as the guards or the teachers. It would have been nice to make him happy by talking in group, but it just wasn't going to happen.

"I've got nothing, Dave. Seriously. I'm just an asshole."

"Nobody believes that, Colin," Dave said.

A big guy so fat that everybody called him Baby Huey raised his hand.

"I believe it," Baby Huey said. This comment earned him laughs. Huey looked around with a half-smile on his round face. "You all are laughing," he said. "But none of you are talking about the man with the hood, and I know you've heard of him."

"Let's not change the subject," Dave said.

"No, let's." I sat up.

"Mr. Hood's always there." Huey warmed to his audience. "He sees everything you did to get here. He's like Santa Claus, only Satan Claus. Do you feel me? I hear him at night."

"Me too," I said.

"Don't get Baby Huey started." Good advice from George that I knew I couldn't follow.

Huey leaned forward with his elbows on his knees. "Oh, now the asshole wants to talk. You hear Mr. Hood through the walls?"

So I hadn't broken my brain with pills and alcohol. The thing haunting me even had a name.

"I hear him every night through the vents," I said. "He tried to kill me in the hospital."

"Mr. Hood can't kill you."

"Are you sure?" I asked, rubbing my chest where his finger broke my ribs and plunged into my heart.

"Let's talk about what this story symbolizes for you," Dave said.

Huey and I both turned to look at our poor dumb counselor.

"Seriously, guys." Dave let out a little laugh. "You're talking about your own subconscious. There isn't an actual boogeyman talking to you through the vents."

"Not the boogeyman," I said.

"The boogeyman is a different thing," Huey said.

"Mr. Hood then." Dave nodded like he understood. "A Satan Claus or whatever."

Huey turned back to me. "Just because he can't kill you don't mean he's not coming for you."

"What can he do?" I waited for the other guys to shut the conversation down with calls of bullshit, but everyone sat straight as rods. Even the guards standing along the walls were paying attention.

Huey shook out his shoulders like he was getting ready to wrestle. "Mr. Hood can't kill you, but he can make you wish you were dead."

"How?" I asked.

"He can hurt you so bad that you give him your soul yourself and then thank him for taking it."

At this, the other guys finally erupted. A couple of the boys rushed Huey, their chairs flying backward. George rocked back and forth, crossing himself over and over while another kid hugged himself and moaned. Dave just pressed against the wall in terror as the rest of us took a knee like we were supposed to during a fight. I got down in time to avoid a face full of pepper spray but my eyes were burned almost blind anyway, and my nose was a running mess. I would never get used to the pepper spray.

Later, in the cell, George lay on his bed with wet paper over his face. "You got Huey riled up," he said.

"Do you know what he was talking about?" I blew my nose but it didn't help.

"Maybe. I don't know." George pressed the heels of his hands into his eyes. "Everybody's got a story about this and that. Huey's crazy."

"He may be crazy, but he wasn't lying," I said. I clung to this piece of truth as if it would save my life in a flood.

George didn't answer for a while. Finally, he sighed like he was tired and removed the paper towel from his eyes. "Huey doesn't know everything he thinks he does."

"Like what? What was he wrong about?"

George shook his head. "Talking about the man with the hood makes him come around. And by the way, quit drawing his picture. The more you do that shit, the more you bring him to life."

George crossed himself in an elaborate dance of hand to forehead, lips, heart, shoulders, back to heart and lips. I wished I had a magical protection like that. All I had was drawing and George was right about my sketches. Every page was filled with a hooded man, and I wore my pencils flat from shading in the black where the face should have been.

Later in the night, when our noses finally stopped flowing and George fell asleep, I stayed awake and let myself think about Erik. The first time I met him was at the skate park one night when I was hanging out and he was in the bowl, practicing flips on his board. He caught air and slapped down before joining the other skaters, all gliding back and forth like planets in separate orbits. Sometimes a board would slip out in a jumble of elbows and skidding wheels, but even though Erik was a tall gangly kid, he never fell. He moved like water.

I smoked a joint and drew in my sketchbook for a while until I felt like entering the bowl myself. I skated through until my mind went blank and clean.

Once the crowd thinned some, Erik kicked a 180 with serious air. He made flying look easy, so I tried the same and fell hard.

"Put your back foot more on the edge," he said.

I hadn't meant to try again. I'd meant to go home rather than look like an idiot at the skate park. But I got back on my board because Erik thought I should, and I fell even harder the second time.

Erik laughed but not in a mean way. "Open your shoulders. Lead with your heart chakra, man."

"My heart chakra. What the hell?"

He grinned. "The board wants what you want. One more time."

I don't know why I decided to trust this kid who said the word chakra, but I put my foot close to the edge and stopped thinking. I opened my upper body on the jump and landed facing the other way without a wobble, like I'd been doing it that way my whole life.

We skated together until the moon rose and when it was time to go, I ripped out the drawing I had made of Erik on his board and handed it over.

"You did this," Erik said. I couldn't tell if he liked it or not.

"Yeah. Whatever. You can keep it."

"This is so cool."

"See you around." I waved as I headed across the grass towards my own neighborhood, feeling light and okay.

And from that point on until the night of the wreck, Erik was always the one who kept me steady.

I blinked at the ceiling of the cell I shared with George, and for the first time really let it sink in what I had done to my best friend. On the night of the wreck, Erik's broken vertebrae sliced through the nerves in his spine and the skinny, white-haired boy scooping the skate park bowl in the moonlight broke into pieces in an explosion of metal, glass and bone.

When the strange voice began chuckling from inside the wall. I forced myself to listen, lying still with my ears tuned to the tangle of noises like static going in and out, until one line strung out clear as a song, deep and full of a slow, bubbling gladness.

Shame on youuuuu

My last night in JD, I tried lying perfectly still staring at the ceiling. I thought about what being paralyzed would feel like. It could be peaceful. Or maybe a person's brain still held memories of movement and paralysis was just a prison sentence that never ended.

"Why so quiet?" George asked. He was refolding his extra t-shirts.

"Shit on my mind," I said. Mr. Hood was watching me all the time now. The gaze of his non-eyes burned into the back of my head.

George messed around with the stuff on his desk for a while until finally, when there was nothing left to clean, he sat on his bed and let out a long breath.

"All right, man," he said. "You've been okay. You stayed on your side. Didn't make a mess. I'll tell you a few things. About—you know."

I sat up, already full of questions, but George wasn't having it.

"Nope. Just listen." He put up his hand. "Huey led you astray, Homes. The hooded man *can* kill you. People always think they can make dudes like Mr. Hood follow rules. But the Devil does what he wants and he doesn't follow men's rules."

"What can I do about it?" I asked.

"Go to church. Pray for forgiveness. Then maybe you'll live."

"That's it? Which church?"

"What do you mean, *which church?* What the fuck does it matter?" He ran two hands through his hair. "Just listen, Jesus."

I sat on my hands to keep them from shaking while my roommate crossed himself twice. He took a deep breath. "Think of it this way," he said. "He lives off your bad feelings about what you did. The Hood is like a vampire but not for blood. He gets off on your shame."

"That doesn't make sense."

George gestured to the door. "Why do you think he's so large in here? Everybody has something they wish they could take back. We all have somebody at home crying because of what we did."

There were so many people I had made cry. Erik and his family. My mother. Probably my father too, at least on the inside.

"Church won't be enough by itself." George rubbed his perfectly shaved chin. "You'll have to do good works. Tip the scales. Try to get more deeds on the good side than the bad, feel me?"

"It's too late," I said. Good works wouldn't help Erik walk.

George pointed at me. "You're wrong about that too. There's a bunch of stuff you can do on the outside. I can't make up for nothing stuck in a cell for my whole life."

My throat got tight. George had been helping me since day one. He didn't deserve prison.

"It was your cousin that did that guy," I said. "I heard you tell your story in group, man. You don't have any mark on you."

George looked at his hands. "I can still see that kid's face. He was shot down just standing there with his friend."

"But it wasn't you," I said.

"When the bullet went through his head, the blood came out the other side like a flower. I think about that a lot." He splayed his fingers. "Splash. A tiny red flower."

"It wasn't you that shot him."

He wasn't listening. "I didn't say stop when my cousin pointed his gun. I didn't get out and help the kid after it was done. It wasn't *not* me."

I bowed my head.

"Listen to me," George said. "Get the Hood's name out your mouth. Stop talking about him. And stop drawing him." He crossed himself again.

"Thanks, man," I said. "For everything. Not just this."

"Just be better than you were before out there. Tip the scales." He tried to smile but his eyes weren't in it.

At lights out, George ran through his nightly prayers. I would miss the sound of his urgent Hail Marys whispered in Spanish. I wished so badly that George was getting out with me. He would have been a solid partner in tilting the balance for good.

In my dream, my head whipped back against the headrest of the car I drove the night of the wreck. There was a shot, the sharp scent of gunpowder, and a red lily bursting from Erik's head beside me.

I woke up to the sound of someone choking, but it wasn't me who was dying. Across the cell George was wheezing like he was trying to get oxygen through a straw. He was on his back, reaching across the space between our beds, and it was then that I saw a dark form huddled on his chest. The shadow turned its head in the half darkness, its face hidden in a shadow as thick as oil. George's opened his mouth wide as if to scream, but nothing came out but a tight hiss.

I rushed to George's bed and the shadow man leapt at me like some kind of fucked up cat. He hit me in the face and a hard black film sealed my nose and mouth. My heart muscle seized and I couldn't even yell, but what could the guards do anyway? This was pure chaos smashing against my face and getting somehow *inside* me. I gagged while shame expanded against my ribcage like a living, pulsating organ that wanted only to feed and grow.

Guards hollered outside. The shadow man slithered off me and tapped along the floor as if on a million insect legs, oozing between the slats of the air vent and vanishing into the ducts.

George wasn't breathing and with purple spots bursting in my vision, I pounded on his chest like I thought you were supposed to until the guards busted in and pushed me out of the way. I hugged my knees as one guard called for a medic through his radio and the other tilted George's head back and put a plastic thing over his face so he could do mouth to mouth.

When they remembered me, the guards smashed me to the floor. I lay with my cheek on the cold tile with my face turned to the wall. Eyes like shiny black coins blinked at me from between the slats of the vent.

The guards clicked handcuffs around my wrists and pulled me to standing. As they pushed me down the hall, I whispered aloud the parts I could remember from George's prayers. *Hail Mary please save George. Help him be free.*

Now and in the hour of our death amen.

THOSE UNDERNEATH

VICTORIA DALPE

It was raining. Great sheets of heavy cold rain, and the thunder pounded overhead, those things I can remember very clearly.

It was on account of the rain and that unimaginably loud thunder that I didn't hear them until it was too late. Didn't hear them until they were on top of us, and all I could do was call out. I remember Dolly looking up, and our eyes met, and then her head exploded like an overripe melon. The shotgun at close range rendering her into so much meat in a blink. A split second.

I wanted to scream, but clamped a hand over my mouth and ducked down low, knowing if they saw me, I was as good as dead too. I buried myself in the mud, more like swimming than digging, it felt like, as I burrowed down, low and fast. I was a good digger, much faster than Dolly. I felt a bullet strike mere inches from my shoulder, but the thick earth stopped it.

Heart hammering in my chest, muscles burning, I dug, faster and harder than I ever had before. I'd never dug to survive, after all. If I didn't get away, I'd be dead as Dolly up there. Dolly. My sweet Dolly. My heart ached with a loss I had yet to process.

More bullets, but between the dark, the mud, the ceaseless rain, and my desire to be as far away from them as possible, I got away.

I made it deep enough they couldn't follow. I kept moving and digging, the weight of the earth, its coolness, its silence, all slowly calming me. I kept seeing

Dolly's eyes meeting mine in that last moment, her face curious, innocent. She never saw them coming, had no idea that she was going to die. Perhaps it was better that way in the end, cleaner.

Deep down in that earth, with no one to see or judge, I wept for my sister, and for myself. For if the hunters had come, then they knew about us, and we would have to move on. I needed to get to my family, we needed to arrange to get Dolly's body if we could. We don't leave our dead alone to rot. We take them with us.

I barely remember digging my way back to the more familiar trails and tunnels running beneath Shady Pines. But somehow I made it, exhausted, and it was a sweet relief to crawl along instead of dig. When I reached the main burrow, Mother was there, as was my older sister Cora, nursing her two babies.

"Where's your sister?" my mother said. I feel to my knees in a sob, not wanting to appear weak to the elder women, but too sad and tired to hide my grief.

My great-grandfather used to tell me stories as a child. He must have chosen me because I'd always been a good listener. He told me about the hunters. About all of it. He was a huge man, though greatly diminished with age, deflated and bent. His claws were still longer than my forearms though, and I could imagine what a specimen he must have been in his youth. But he was very frail. It's why he no longer hunted, and instead stayed in the main burrow and had the younger members bring him his food. He couldn't remember the last time he'd even seen the sky.

"It's overrated up there," was something he would always say.

He liked to tell stories of the old days, when bodies were buried in a flimsy pine box, or better yet, with nothing at all save a shroud. "You'd come right up underneath, and no one up top ever had to know. They mourned from above, put their flowers, talked about heaven, and down below we could feast, as nature intended. Not like now, with the chemicals, the locked metal boxes, the cremation urns. Starving us all out."

And it was. The way he told it, we'd once been a mighty clan with highways of tunnels running all over the country. Huge burrows that could house hundreds of us. He loved to tell stories of the old wars, wars on American soil, where the bodies were left where they fell.

"We'd come up at night, and they would just be laid out for us, like a beautiful buffet. We were never hungry then. We were strong, had big families, were so fat we could barely fit in our burrows." He'd always chuckle then.

"Now we are nothing but scavengers, like a rabbit bothering the farmer's garden. Bah—we used to be a great race, powerful and important. *Worshipped* in the old country."

Worshipped. I often thought about the time before his time, the time in the old country where our kind were worshipped as an important part of the ecosystem. To be chosen by us for consumption was a blessing. We absorbed their lives and lived on through them, making them truly immortal. Or something like that. He wasn't totally sure, as they were the stories told to him by his grandmother.

I wondered why we would have left the old country if it was so great, especially if we were gods there. Seemed a bit foolish to give all of that up. I mentioned that to Dolly once, lovely Dolly, the prettiest of the sisters, and the smartest, the best of us.

"It's because it's not *true,* Una. We were just as feared and hated there too. The only safe place for us is down here underground, living like vermin." She crossed her arms and sighed. "I would love the stories to be true. I would love to be seen as a goddess, a valuable goddess."

"I think you're valuable," I replied and she rolled her eyes.

"You're my sister, it's different. I love our family, I love you the most, but don't you find it depressing that this may be all there is for us? Digging and eating, hiding, and telling old tales? Until eventually we die?"

"When you put it that way, it doesn't sound like much, but what else is there? What do you want?"

She pointed a long finger up toward the earthen roof. "I want to go up and explore their world. I want to learn, I want to see the sun, I want to feel the ocean, experience the topside."

I was shocked and scandalized by Dolly's wants. All forbidden things, things that would get us killed, that would bring the hunters looking for us. But it was Dolly, and she was the bravest of the three of us. Cora was like mother, cautious, a little cold, but always thinking family first. I was the coward, and Dolly was the dreamer.

"You aren't a coward Una." Dolly pushed my arm, gently. "You just didn't want to go off with Clive and have a bunch of his babies and live with his horrible clan. And you don't like to go topside feeding with me because it's more dangerous. That's not cowardice, that's caution. Give yourself a little credit. I think you'll be running this clan someday."

I thought that was absurd when she said it, but sometimes I wonder if she wasn't a little clairvoyant.

Occasionally we had "wars" for territory with other clans, though that becomes less and less of an issue as the clans become smaller, or are hunted to near extinction. Our territory was good. The cemetery had sections for a few religious sects that didn't believe in embalming. The meat was untainted and cleaner than most, and because of that it was a valuable area. We'd been settled there for almost as long as I remembered.

It was only a few days after Dolly had been killed. And we were all reeling at the fact we couldn't get her body back. That the hunters had dragged her remains away as some sort of trophy. My heart was heavy with her loss. As a custom, we always ate our dead, bringing their flesh and blood into our own, so they become part of us. But not Dolly.

Cora, ever the aggressive den mother, and grief-stricken over Dolly, wanted to go to war to defend our territory. I thought she just yearned for someone's blood. Her mate, Doon, had seen another clan sniffing around our main cemetery —a scout looking to see if it was claimed. Doon had confronted the other man, they had a little scuffle, and he sent him off limping. But the outsider threatened to be back, with reinforcements.

"He said at least ten in his clan were warriors. *Ten*, Cora."

My mother looked up from the bundle of offal she'd been eating, "Ten? Do you believe him?"

Doon shrugged, but looked scared. *Ten.* We were only myself, mother, Cora, and Doon now. And the babies needed to be protected. Dolly was gone. Everyone was gone, it seemed. Just the last vestiges of a clan about to disappear from the world. Our names lost under the crush of the earth.

"Grandfather said we were once worshipped as gods. Is that true?" I said aloud.

"Una! Get your head out of the clouds. This is serious. I have my children to think about," Cora snapped. "We need to protect our territory."

"There is no territory anymore, Cora. The hunters know we're here. They killed Dolly, they took her from us, remember?"

Cora plodded on as if she didn't hear me, "We can't fight ten. If I stayed home with the twins, it would be three against ten, and none of you are great fighters. Maybe if we still had Dolly…"

Mother shut her eyes tight, the pain too fresh. "But we don't have her, and the odds are bad, and Una is right. It's not safe here. I used to be a warrior, but no longer. We move on. Leave the fools to be hunted."

We spent the rest of that night planning our departure. I would have to be the scout now. This was normally Dolly's job, one she had always enjoyed. Dolly loved the topsiders, found their world complex and strange, utterly fascinating.

The next night I was aboveground.

Unlike Dolly, I felt far too exposed up top. Walking the streets, sticking to shadows, hugging buildings and cowering in alleys. I found the rush of cars and the scores of living bodies to be overwhelming and unwelcome. All around me was the hum of electricity, always buzzing and humming. The bright neon burned my sensitive eyes, the myriad smells made me nose blind. I missed the cool darkness, the press of earth, the safety of being surrounded so close.

I needed a map, some sort of tool to see further than I could with my own eyes. I knew the topsiders had all manner of technology. Tiny computers in their pockets, larger ones in their homes. Big glowing screens that could transport you anywhere, tell any type of story.

Dolly would be so jealous that I was topside, venturing further than she had ever been allowed to go. And while fear choked me, and the urge to flee back into the safe earth was nearly all-consuming, it was her voice, her jealousy, that kept me on my mission.

I wore a large man's overcoat, big enough to cover my entire body and even my feet. The sleeves were long enough to hide my claws, and with the collar flipped up and the knit cap on my head, I could almost pass as a topsider. I wore sunglasses even though it was night because my eyes couldn't bear all the neon. We were below creatures, long adapted to the dark, our senses razor sharp to hear the subtlest vibration in the earth. Topside all of that was useless, and my poor body was battered on all sides by the buzz of machines, even the wind.

I hugged the buildings, using the brick and glass as a support, for it was hard to stay upright, and my spine screamed. I'd seen dogs before, and imagined they would be as uncomfortable walking on their hind legs as I was.

Didn't matter. I needed maps. I needed information. We were diminished and would never survive a clan war. Even with Dolly, we'd be no match. But if she'd been here at least I wouldn't be alone. We could plan together. Hell, there would even be a chance she'd be excited by the prospect.

The city stretched up and ahead, the buildings tall and threatening, I wasn't sure how far I'd walked, or even how I would get home when the time came. I put on topsider clothes, I wandered out of the cemetery, and that was all. Fool.

Maybe we didn't belong in this world anymore. I hated to think that, but it was hard not to as I looked up at towers that pierced the clouds, and way above even those, flying machines skimming along the surface of the sky like water bugs. How could our clan, our species be a match for humans? We were simple creatures and I couldn't imagine this era of humans ever worshipping us as gods.

We were little more than scavengers, the last few of a dying race, that when gone would dissolve into the earth, easily forgotten.

"Hey! Hey you!" a voice called, pulling me from my reverie, I flinched, trying to make myself small. But the voice drew nearer, and soon there was a man next to me. Closer than any human had ever been.

"You! Yeah, you, all okay?"

I looked at the man, trying to keep my face hidden by my collar, trusting that the hat and glasses concealed more than showed. The man was middle-aged, I guessed, though I'm never quite sure with topsiders. He had a ruddy complexion and black hair. He wore a uniform, but not a police one.

"You all right? Been watching you from the station across the street, looks like you are having a hard time walking. You need help?"

I shook my head, wondering how best to make this man leave.

"You sure? I'm an EMT. You in trouble, you need to go someplace? You're safe with me."

Why wouldn't this man go? I shook my head no again, and finally said: "No thanks, please leave me be."

The man's face shifted from concern to surprise. "You're a girl? How old are you?" he said, squinting as he tried to see past my disguise.

"I'm fine. Leave me be. Please."

The man raised his hands up to show he meant no danger. My back hurt, and

I just wanted to be free of all of this. My natural defenses begged me to get away from this topsider, from any topsider. But he had offered help.

"I need a map."

"A map? Like a subway map?" The man's eyebrows were up to his hairline.

"A map that shows cemeteries."

He frowned. "Cemeteries huh? Come with me into the station, we may have some old maps in the office. Now we all use GPS on our phones." He looked me up and down. "I'm guessing you don't have a phone."

"No."

"Okay, yeah. That's cool, come on in with me, and I'll look for you." As we started across the street, the man was careful not to touch me, though I was aware of his guiding hand near my back. Could feel the heat of his skin. I tried to understand his motives. While I knew I was young and relatively attractive in my clan—nowhere near Dolly of course—I knew that couldn't be the reason. I was hidden entirely, hunched and hobbling, and besides that, topsiders would find me to be grotesque. A monster, even.

Was it kindness? He said he was an EMT. I didn't know what that meant, but he was wearing a uniform of some sort and taking me to "the station," which wasn't home, so must be his work. Perhaps his job was to help those that needed help.

We reached a lit parking lot with vans and large red trucks. A few other men milled around, big and watchful. They all stopped and stared as I approached.

"What you find, Miguel?" a large older man said.

"Young lady needs a map," he responded.

The older man smirked. "Young lady? A map?"

"That shows where the nearest cemeteries are," Miguel said flatly.

The older man chuckled now, not hiding his amusement. "Ah, Miguel you sure do love catching strays, don't you? Well, lemme go check in my desk. I may have some old street maps kicking around. Wait here."

I looked between the men, painfully aware they found me strange. But they were still willing to help. I knew if a stranger came to my clan for help, they would most likely be attacked. It caused a little bloom of shame. Especially if we found the creature to be odd or unnatural, there was no way my mother would let them into the den to explain. No, such things weren't in our nature. Perhaps we were too much like animals in that regard.

"That's the chief. He's all right when you get to know him. You hungry or thirsty? Want to sit down?" Miguel said. Another man had emerged from the open garage door, dark-skinned and very tall. He watched me suspiciously.

I shook my head no, eyes on the tall man, wary.

"Why do you need a map of cemeteries? You a freak?" he asked.

"C'mon. Back off, Daryl."

I shook my head no, dropping my eyes and head to stare at the pavement. A bare toe, long-clawed like a bird of prey, peaked out from the hem. I edged it back under, hoping no one noticed. "My... sister is buried in a cemetery in the city. But I don't know which one, or where."

My answer seemed to leave him curious. "So you don't know where your sister is buried? Didn't you go to the funeral?"

Funerals. That was a topsider ritual I knew very well, and had witnessed peeping from grate drains and bushes many times. The art of interring the dead with prayers and flowers, with handfuls of dirt. Then down, down, down into my world. "I wasn't able to come."

"Okay, I got one, Miss." The Captain emerged with a crumbled piece of paper held high. He opened it up near me and pointed a thick finger. "Here's us here. And we got Shady Pines here." He stabbed again.

"Yes, that is where I came from," I said quietly. "She's not there."

"Okay, well, you got a few other options. Got Northside here. And Sacred Blood over here."

"Can I have this? Your map?" I could feel the captain, Miguel, and the Tall Man staring at me, trying to see past the glasses, the knit cap, the flipped up collar. Too close, in too bright a room. They would see my hands, or the milk white pallor of my skin. My pink eyes.

"Sure, sure." The Captain raised an eyebrow. He held the map to me and I reached out, fingers trembling. I had my thumb and forefinger on it when a sudden alarm screamed through the space. I cried out. The sound—an alarm, I would later learn—was louder than anything I had ever heard. Even with my hands clapped over my ears, it was deafening.

"Okay, boys, let's get back to work," the captain hollered. "Miguel, get her the hell out of here, now."

I felt Miguel's hand on my arm and fought the urge to yank it back. "Come on. Let me help you."

The men were running around, frantic, and it took a moment to find my feet. The map was on the ground. Miguel fetched it and walked me out as a huge red truck backed out of the garage. Lights flashed and sirens wailed. "Here. What's your name?"

I took the map and stuffed it in my pocket, afraid he would take it back. "Una."

"Una. That's pretty. Can I drive you someplace? You shouldn't be walking around out here alone."

I wanted to go back to my family. I wanted to get underground. "People are waiting for me at Shady Grove."

Miguel offered to drive me, said it was only a few blocks. So I allowed him to lead me to his van, in part because this would probably be my only opportunity to ever ride in a human vehicle. The seat was soft, though difficult to sit comfortably with my spine. I gritted my teeth and breathed shallowly to make it bearable.

Miguel started the car and began to drive. I marveled at the ease with which he turned the wheel and blended into traffic, the cars around us a herd of large metal beasts in a row.

In mere minutes, we pulled into Shady Grove. "Easier than walking, right?" he said.

I nodded. "Thank you for your kindness. You have saved my family." I regretted saying it as soon as it was out.

"What do you mean, saved your family?" He looked out at the cemetery and back to me. When I didn't answer, he said, "Heard some weird shit has been going on in this cemetery. Groundskeeper said some weird animals have been eating the bodies."

I scrabbled with the door, realizing too late that he could see my hand with its long white fingers, and even longer talons.

He sucked in a breath.

"Thank you again, Miguel." The door opened, and I threw myself out of it. He called out but I was already running, half up right, half on all fours. I managed to get the map out, and put it between my teeth as I stripped off the coat. He was close enough behind he surely saw me, my pale body adapted to run on all fours. I wove between the graves and tombs until I could no longer hear him. Only then did I make my way to the tomb my family used to come up from beneath.

. . .

Down in the tunnels I breathed a sigh of relief. I could almost hear Dolly laugh-ing. Enjoying the thrill of duping the topsiders, of riding in cars! I just felt tired. I made my way along the path, imagining how impressed my mother and sister would be when I brought them the map. We would move on, to a new cemetery. I let myself have the slightest smile, knowing Miguel would never be the same. He would think about me running in the moonlight, and he would question everything he knew. He would question the world. We may never be worshipped as gods, we may be quietly succumbing to extinction, but knowing that Miguel getting back into his car, looking out at the mounds of tombstones, and feeling afraid and curious that his world was not entirely his after all, made me feel a little better.

KEEPING THE FAITH

CONNIE TODD LILA

The star gathering that formed the Plough wheeled across the night. Once frozen furrows below held their shape as their blanket of snow melted into the soil. From high above, the subtle energy of Polaris softly reached into a small burrow revealed by snow melt.

It opened its eyes, blinking away soil. Winter dreams of sun-warmed fields and barns filled with potatoes and soft baby mice ceased. It clawed away the rest of the burrow's comforting nest and stood. The tangle of hair and bristles on its head brushed the ceiling of roots and earth. With short, quick strides, it reached the mouth of its burrow and crawled up to stand atop a thawing row. Milky eyes raised to the Plough constellation flickered a sharp, blueflash spark, a moonstone spark. Sliding its hands over the front of its squat shape, it found maggots stuck to the damp soil clinging there. These it picked off, stuffed into its mouth, then trotted toward the dark outline of the barn.

"They were called 'coffin ships.'"

Gran closed her eyes to better see the memory she shared with Rylie and Keira. In the early Spring sun, the porch looking onto the North field warmed enough for the girls to sit with Gran after tea.

"Tell us a story," they would beg.

Stories she told, always stories of the land her own Gramma Maeve loved and left, weeping, hunger forcing her family into the unknown.

"I was young like you, but sickly and small. We had only the food we carried on board, no untainted potatoes to bring. What little water there was stank. My Gramma, my Da, Mama and I shared one filthy pallet for us all."

Keira reached to tuck Gran's lap shawl closer around her knees.

"At our deck level, filth seeped through, and all around us lay sickness and death. I was so weak with hunger that I fell with the ship fever, too. I recall little, so deep in fever dreams."

She quirked one brow above eyes drifting into the fog of memory...

Young Maeve lay in her Mama's lap, weak with hunger. The ship fever took her and she floated between darkness and light.

Mama's trembling hand smoothed away the perspiration relentlessly dripping into her eyes. Fluttering her eyelids, she briefly watched with blurred vision as her Gramma Maeve raised her one piece of dry oat bread for the day to her lips. Kissing it, she returned her hand to her lap, next to the soiled roll of rags she clutched there. A small, brown hand darted from the rag ball, snatched the bread, then disappeared into the rags again. The image blended into another fever dream, in fitful sleep.

Gran wiped her eyes, clearing the picture from her memory.

"I remember such a stench... likely the dying around us and my own unwashed body."

She shuddered, let her head rest against her rocker. Wearied from reliving that horrid ocean crossing, Gran closed her eyes. Her breathing deepened. Rylie and Keira gathered the tea cups and left her to nap.

"Sweeter dreams, Gran," Keira whispered.

Connor forked up another half-eaten potato. None had been planted in the kitchen garden. These came from the barn stores, from what precious food they had to keep them whole until harvest. Had to be rats, or something big enough to steal and then carry them here to bury. Cursing, Connor threw down the fork, pulled his kerchief to mop his sweating brow, shoved it back in his pocket.

"Brian!"

Hearing his father's roar, Brian latched the pig pen gate and ran to the garden.

"Fork through this mess. Might be potatoes here still sound." Connor spat on the ground in disgust, turned and stomped to the barn.

The workshop of the barn was a cool respite. Spaces between the boards dappled sunlight across Connor's tool bench. He reached to hooks on a beam and brought down two steel jaw traps. Rasp in hand, he filed with short, angry strokes, sharpening the rusty teeth to deadly shine. Breathing harder with exertion, he spat to rid his mouth and nose of the overwhelming stink of rat droppings.

He filed harder.

It watched Connor from between barn boards, quietly chewing on a piece of potato. Connor slammed down the file, pulled the stained kerchief from his hip pocket, wiped his upper lip, mouth, and hands. He gathered the traps, then jammed the kerchief at his pocket. He never noticed when it fell out behind him.

When Connor left the barn, it trotted forward from the shadowy edges. It snatched up the kerchief and disappeared into a fresh hole against a wall. It quickly traveled along this new tunnel, hopping over piles of dried apples, potatoes, tangles of half-bitten earthworms. By a nest of newborn field mice, it paused to take one and crunch it, biting off the tail. This it pressed onto its body, the sticky, earthen surface holding it fast.

"My Gramma taught me how to make our bannock before she passed. Now, it is my blessing to teach you."

Rylie dropped handfuls of oats into the mortar for Keira to rub into flour with the heavy pestle.

"Look, Mama. We are making the oat buns today."

Kathleen smiled at her girls from the doorway. Setting her egg basket on the counter, she went to the table to circle her mother's waist with a hug and praise her girls, dropping a kiss on top of one russet head and one dark one.

"Did your Gramma live to come to this new farm with your Da and Mama? Did she get to see it?"

Gran held her bowl for Keira to pour in her ground oats. She added the salt pork grease and hot water, began stirring before speaking.

"Only just. She recovered only a little. She did get to walk out to the new fields, to see where the new potatoes would grow without threat of blight."

The oat bun dough was ready to turn out onto the table for kneading. The girls enjoyed this part.

"When she passed, all she owned was that bundle of rags she brought with her. She even carried it when she walked to the new fields for her first look at them. Gramma said it held naught but an old woman's lifetime dreams. In a way, it did. Her bond to the land was her whole life. She kept the old country ways as her health allowed, showed me how to make the spirit candles at Summer's End, and such. I grew up learning to keep the faith at her side. That's what she called it, keeping the faith."

"What is Summer's End, Gran?" Keira scattered flour onto the tabletop, raising a soft cloud that dusted her hair and made Rylie sneeze.

Gran used a corner of her apron to smooth the top of Keira's dark head.

"Summer's End is when the harvest comes in, and the land is put to sleep so it can rest from giving forth our food, our very life." Gran looked into the eyes of both girls in turn, underlining her story lesson. "The land is a living thing, my dears. It has a living spirit. It feeds us, and we must feed and care for it in return."

"Is there a Summer's Beginning?" Keira asked, while Rylie drew circles in the flour with her fingers.

"Ah, my dear, Summer does, indeed, have a beginning, a glorious one. A lucky lass will go to the fields on a fine, Spring night." Gran's eyebrow was quirked again, as she described the memory she was lost in at that moment. The unanswered questions in Keira's wide, innocent eyes sobered Gran back from the past, and she hastily spoke a more fit reply.

"Yes, this faithful lass and her chosen lad will go to the fields and bless them with clear, sweet water and prayers for a safe and good growing season, in the old way. That makes Summer begin." Gran wiped her hands together and turned out the dough onto the floury table.

"Did you bless the fields, too, Gran?"

Reverie threatened to wash Gran back in time. Focusing on the girls' hands poking into the bread dough, she governed herself.

"Sometimes, my dear."

"Did your Gramma bless them, too?"

"Yes, faithfully. She lived her life keeping the faith."

"Did your Mama keep the faith?"

"Da didn't hold with it, so Mama wouldn't speak of it around him. To him, those rags Gramma Maeve carried all the way from the old country just held a bit of soil from home, nothing more. All that fell out when he unrolled it was soil." Gran quirked an eyebrow in the way that meant she was seeing into the past again. Rylie and Keira smiled at each other and squashed the oat bun dough around the flour dusted table.

Leaving the barn through one of its tunnels, it darted from tree to tree, making its way to the woods beyond. When it squatted inside a fox den, it opened its hand and shook out Connor's kerchief. It squeezed the soiled cloth in the middle and plucked the baby mouse tail stuck to its body. Using this to tie around the kerchief, it twisted and rolled the rest of the rag into crude arm and leg shapes. It scratched a handful of earth, spat into it, worked it into clay texture. This it pressed around one of the leg shapes of the kerchief. The filthy poppet was left to dry, and it retreated to the warren of tunnels beneath the farm.

A warm, oat bread scent filled the kitchen with comfort. Gran nodded approval, smiling at the girls and their tray of golden bannocks cooling on the table.

"You must take this one and leave it at the edge of the north field, the big one." She wrapped the warm oat bun in a kitchen cloth.

"Why? We made these for supper."

"My Gramma told me the old ways bade us to always give due to the land you revere... the land and what lives there."

Rylie and Keira looked at one another.

"Oats and corn? Rabbits?"

Gran pressed her lips in the firm line that signaled she'd had her say. That eyebrow lifted again.

"I don't want that ancient biddy filling my girls' heads with her spooks and nonsense!"

From a mousehole in the skirting board, a blue spark flashed and went dark, like a small light blown out in a wind. A faint scuffling sound went unnoticed beneath the shouting.

Kathleen closed their bedroom door, pressed herself against it, another fight brewing.

"The girls will hear you, and so will Mama."

"Let them! It's my back that breaks to see them fed. It is well for them to hear and respect me!" Connor seized Kathleen's arms in a bruising clench, breathing whiskey in her face.

"And you, woman, you will respect me, too."

He hurled her at the bed. Kathleen landed hard, slid across to fall onto the floor. Connor staggered to that side of the bed and reached for her. His drunken grasp caught only her chemise, ripping it down the front. She clutched it to her bared breast, choked back her sobs that her children wouldn't hear, and pulled Connor's leg from beneath him. He reeled to the floor.

Kathleen pushed herself up and ran from the room. At the kitchen door, she paused to open it and kept running, barefoot, bare chested, into the darkness.

Connor caught up with her at the edge of the north field. Wrapping her in a brute's embrace, he dragged her onto the cold, rough soil. Kathleen flailed her hands into the ground, squeezing handfuls of soil to throw in Connor's face. He pressed a beefy forearm across her chest and shoulders, pinning her beneath him. With his free hand, he opened his trousers, yanked the rag of her chemise up over her hips. He forced her legs open with his knees. Engorged with rage and triumph, he rammed her into the cold field.

A hard, blueflash gaze peered from a tunnel the size of a rat hole. It watched the big man savage the screaming woman, then collapse on top of her. She lay sobbing, trying to shove him off. After a while, the man stumbled to his feet, the last of his fury dripping onto the soil. He shuffled toward the farmhouse. The woman lay weeping a while longer. She sat up at last, used the ruin of her chemise to wipe humiliation and soil from between her bruised thighs. When she could stand, she limped to the well and washed herself.

Connor rose before dawn, wanting to get the drag across the north field before the sun made such work miserable. He swallowed a cup of bitter coffee, scowled at Kathleen. He put a bannock in his pocket with a hunk of cheese and headed to the barn.

The traps he'd set by the walls were empty, dried apples missing, honed teeth closed, pin sprung. Cursing, he kicked one out of his way and went to the stall side of the barn. The heavy drag waited in the field. Connor led his draft team out to where they last stopped smoothing the soil. From habit, the big horses backed into place easily and stood still while the chains were fastened to their harness.

From one of its tunnels, it reached the fox den without coming above ground. The hideous poppet lay where it left the thing to dry. It picked up the poppet, stared at it with a blueflash glow in its milky, rheumy eyes. Opening a brown hand, it grasped the leg of dried clay and squeezed, stained teeth clenched, crushing the leg shape into a handful of rag and dust.

Shoulders and flanks glistening, the team dug hooves into the soft earth, pulling the heavy drag to level it. Connor sat behind them on the narrow bench seat. He reached for his kerchief to wipe his sweaty brow, looked behind himself to his empty pocket. At that moment, on the lead horse's side, a small, brown face popped up from a hole just where the next hoof step would fall. Sunlight struck a hot blue spark from its milky stare and it bared its sharp teeth in a wicked grin.

With a shrill scream, the horse reared, pulling his harness mate off balance toward him. Connor slid toward that side, harness straps useless in his hands. The horses jerked forward together in panic just as Connor hit the ground where the heavy drag was pulled across his leg, shattering the bones. Screaming until shock took him into oblivion, Connor watched his fallen bannock and cheese disappear into the field.

"It's nothing, Mama. Twisted my ankle taking laundry to the line, is all."

Gran noted the bruises on Kathleen's arms and cheek, pressed her lips together to hold in her words.

"Here, I'll take your tea out to the porch for you. Go enjoy this pretty day." Avoiding her mother's eyes, Kathleen poured tea.

Settled in her rocker, cup and saucer in her lap, Gran watched Brian forking hay from the loft.

"Growing into a fine and strong man, this first born," she spoke to no one in particular.

Gran finished her tea, carefully moved her bite of wild honeycomb to the edge of her saucer. Easing herself out of the rocker, she walked across the door-yard to the kitchen garden. At a clump of lamb's quarter, she tipped her honey-comb out onto the ground. Nodding once toward the north field, she turned and walked back to the house. Keira opened the door and skipped down the steps. Rylie followed, rag dolly tucked beneath her arm. The girls encircled their Gran, wrapping her in a loving hug. Gran kissed them both and left them to play in the sun.

Keira ran to the rope swing hanging from a large oak and sat on the weath-ered board seat.

Rylie carried her dolly to the kitchen garden. Mama's flowers were bloom-ing, and she wanted a daisy crown for dolly and herself. She sat on the grass, little legs tucked beneath her skirt, humming. Dolly lay beside her so she could pick daisies with both hands. Rylie braided stems the way Mama showed her, faint russet brows drawn together over her nose in concentration. All the daisies in front of her plucked, she rose on hands and knees and scooted to the next clump. She noticed something in the grass that glistened in the sun. Crawling closer, she found the bite of wild honeycomb Gran left there. Rylie knew this. This was the sweetness her big brother Brian found in the woods when he hunted rabbits. Daisy chain forgotten, Rylie reached for the melting honeycomb and stuffed the bite into her mouth. Her hands too sticky to hold her dolly, Rylie left her in the grass and ran inside to find Mama.

From behind the stone foundation of the well, it watched Rylie steal the food the old woman put out. The hard, blue glint struck from its eyes by sunlight disappeared in an angry squint. It withdrew into the tunnel beside the well to wait for darkfall.

The last lamp went out, leaving all the farmhouse windows dark. It crawled from its tunnel beside the well and trotted to the kitchen garden. A waxing moon showed glistening grass where the honeycomb had lain. It reached out to touch the sticky grass, brought the drops of shiny honey to its mouth, and smacked wide, shapeless lips around the faint sweetness. A sound like a growl rumbled from somewhere inside it, and it shot a gaze to the farmhouse that blistered blue-white in the moonlight. Scanning the ground, it spotted the little rag doll forgotten in the grass. It grabbed the dolly, then reached for the daisy crown Rylie had been weaving. It wound the flower chain around Rylie's dolly, then trotted back toward its tunnel. Before disappearing down the hole, it tossed Rylie's daisy-wrapped dolly into the well.

Kathleen carried Connor's untouched side pork and coffee to the sink. She brushed a tendril of hair up and off her forehead, wiped her reddened eyes. Nights were sleepless, trying not to move and pain his broken leg. The wooden strips and wrappings shifted and itched, making him rage constantly.

Brian came through the kitchen door, already exhausted before his breakfast. He'd shouldered the chores he could manage by himself while the call for a farm hand was told around the county and at church. Kathleen sniffed and carried her son's first coffee to the table. She'd left the rest of the house asleep and rose in the pre-dawn darkness to make breakfast for her son. A bellow from the bedroom made her hand shake, spilling the coffee.

"Mama, how can you go on!?" Brian wiped his own weary eyes. "He will be the death of you, of this farm, and us all." He swallowed coffee, breathed deeply, looked at Kathleen. "Mama, you must sell up, take Gran and the girls and go from here. I will manage things and follow you."

Kathleen pressed her aching head between trembling hands.

"My mother almost died on the ship that brought her family here. All they had went into this land, into this very soil we stand on. I was born here. Your Da came as a hand, stayed to husband me and help us keep it. Our blood is in this land!"

Kathleen gave in to the flood of despair and frustration exploding in her center. She turned and ran through the door, blinded by tears. Her flight brought her against the stone circle of the farm well. Cool water was what she needed. She reached for the bucket rope, looked into the well.

And screamed.

And screamed.

And fell to the ground, screaming blindly.

Gran pressed a fresh, cool cloth to Kathleen's forehead, drew the quilt closer. In her mother's bed, Kathleen could sleep. She drifted between seeing her sweet, russet-haired baby floating in the well and the rage of her invalid, cruel husband. Gran left the room, closed the door softly.

The casseroles and baked goods from the church still sat on the table and countertop. Keira leaned close against the kitchen doorframe, face pale beneath her dark hair. She twisted the front of her smock in her hands. Gran sat at the table, speaking to herself, or, no one.

"…keeping the faith… not keeping it…"

"What, Gran? What's keeping?" Keira whispered, afraid to speak aloud.

Gran snapped her vision back to present time and place, staring both at and through Keira.

"Faith, child! Keeping the faith!"

Keira stepped back, closer to the doorframe again.

"But…we just took Rylie to church. Mama says she has to stay with the angels now." Keira's vision blurred.

Gran didn't hear Keira. She was away again, back with her own grand-mother, potatoes rusting in the field.

Connor's bellow made Keira cry out, startled, and yanked Gran back to the kitchen table.

"Where is your big brother, child? Where is Brian?"

"Closing up the chickens for dark."

Thin chest rising with a heavy sigh, Gran stood to answer Connor.

He lay in a sweat, leg swollen tight against the wood lath and stained wrap-pings. Infection streaked up his thigh, burned him with fever.

"Where's my wife?"

"She sleeps, near perished from giving her baby to the angels."

"Angels quit this farm long ago," Connor growled. His bloodshot eyes burned into Gran's. "And it's you turned them from us!" His rage having a focus, he unleashed it at her. "You poison my family with your nonsense and fairy tales. You make them believe it's dancing under the moon that will get the farming done. Always, it's 'the old ways' with you! Old ways won't get corn in the barn and potatoes out of the ground!"

Spittle frothed in the corners of his mouth. He spat as he raged on.

"You'll put none of the food off my table out in the dirt to play at your old ways, you hag!"

Gran listened in stony silence. Turning, she walked back to the kitchen. Keira still clung to the doorframe, cheeks streaked with tears from what she'd heard. Gran looked at the plate she'd made to take to Connor. There was half a roast hen, boiled potatoes and butter. She picked up the plate, called to Keira.

"Come with me, child. I want to show you something important."

Keira followed her Gran outside, to the edge of the north field.

Exhausted, Connor slumped back into his stained pillow.

"God, it stinks in here," he swore to himself. "Brian! Brian!" Bring a trap!"

Soft, sliding sounds came from a hole in the skirting board beneath the bed. Connor saw a shadow on the wall across from him, moving down along the floor. Rats! Connor leaned forward, as far as his throbbing leg allowed, to see the shadow more clearly.

A horrible vision popped up from the foot of the bed. Connor fell back, breath held. He saw a wizened, grotesque face with long, matted hair. The eyes burning in that face were milky pale and blazing blue at the same time. It opened its impossible mouth, thrust crusted, pointed teeth at Connor.

His own eyes wide, Connor clutched at his pounding chest, lost his hold on his final breath, and died in a spreading puddle in his bedclothes.

Brian and Cassidy finished the butchering, washed down the pen with bucket after bucket from the well. Grateful for a hired hand to help with the bloody work, Brian set aside meat for the smokehouse. A basin of side pork he carried to the house for Kathleen and Gran to get salted.

A decent harvest put corn enough in the crib to keep a sow over the winter. The sow would farrow come Spring, and there would be piglets enough to sell and to fatten.

Cassidy looked upon Kathleen with more and more favor. Her cheeks, once so pale and thin, took on a rosy fullness. She smiled more, started making sure that her hair was washed again and her dress pressed. Gran approved.

When the last potato was dug, the last cornstalks bundled and tied, Gran asked Keira to fetch a big turnip from the cold pantry. She brought this to the table, where Gran sat, holding the potato knife.

"Thank you, child. Now, this is how we do it." Carefully, Gran began carving a hole in the top of the turnip. She pared until she had a roomy hollow. Rising, she lifted the wood stove tongs and reached into the firebox. She brought out a small, glowing coal. When she carefully placed it inside the hollow turnip, the root warmed and gave off a spicy scent.

Tongs back on their hook, Gran picked up the coal-filled turnip and beckoned for Keira to follow her. Together, they set the turnip on the porch. In the autumn twilight, the ember-filled spirit lantern glowed, golden and fragrant.

"Summer's End, right, Gran?"

Hugging Keira to her side, Gran whispered, "You'll do just fine, child, just fine."

There was not so much green noise now. It could hear the Call...the time of Not Growing was making the Call. Dream Time was coming. Dream Time was good.

It sought the best burrow, the one with worms and dried apples and bitten potatoes, buttons, string, torn laces, a dropped tobacco plug, a pearl from a broken necklace, a wooden spoon, a sock dropped from the line. Standing at the burrow entrance, it lifted its milky gaze skyward. The star gathering that formed the shape of the Archer walked overhead. His belt of three bright stars sent subtle energy to strike a final moonstone flash from its rheumy eyes.

Sleep now. The star Plough would come, at the time of Spring lambs and, with them, the fresh, fat milk. The women would leave bowls filled with it in the field. There would be piglets, soft first and then crunchy.

Yes, Dream Time was good.

It settled comfortably into its earthen nest, and closed its lids on a faint spark of blue.

End

THE PALE RIDER

C.M. LANNING

I was thirty-three years old when my life came to an end. The year was 1877, and I'd taken one risk too many, pushing my luck to its breaking point.

When I was alive, my name was Jacob Thompson. My momma named me after a favored brother who conned his hungry sibling out of his birthright for stew. I spent a few years conning people out of their money before they became wise to my act. Then I got a gun and started taking their money without consent. Sheriff called that robbery and ran me out of Habus County, Kansas.

I spent my living years taking what I needed to survive. Never more than that. But I guess it doesn't matter why you break the law or how much of it you break. When it's broke, there's consequences all the same. Least, that's how judges, juries, and the Devil look at it.

The funny thing about my death is that it wasn't supposed to happen, at least not at that time. When Death showed up to claim me, he produced a large red book with more pages than I could count and flipped through them until he found my name.

Death takes many forms, but to me he appeared as a large man with graying hair and a beard. He carried with him a long, gnarled branch of a stick. At the end of that lengthy piece of bark sat a smooth metal blade that curved downward toward the ground. His clothing was simple, tattered robes stitched together, all in shades of gray and black like the hair on his head.

What really stuck out about Death was his eyes. They were the color of murky water, like the pond I fell into and died.

"Jacob Thompson, outlaw and thief. Your time came sooner than expected," the older man spoke in a raspy voice that felt like sand scraping the inside of my ears.

We had this conversation in a vast desert devoid of heat and color. Nothing around but dust and boulders. No sun shined, but a pale light filled this land all the same.

"Watcha mean early? Do men that live my kind of life really last that long?" I asked, scratching my thick black beard.

Before Death could I answer, I took off my brown wide brimmed hat and spat on the mix of dirt and ash I stood upon.

"I sense a lack of respect from you, Jacob," Death said.

I sniffed deep and spat again, draining my nose. Then I put my hat back on and said, "Respect is earned where I come from."

At this, Death cocked his head and said, "My being a timeless immortal who reaps the souls of men isn't enough to earn your respect?"

I looked Death square in his faded eyes and said, "Man can be lots of things. A priest, a bartender, a bank robber. People are someone every day. It requires no effort. Deeds earn my respect. Offering me a drink of water after a hot day, popping my shoulder back into place after I get tossed out a train car, giving me the peace to lay my head and close my eyes at night. Those are things that earn my respect."

Death smiled. It was an eerie look. I expected a spider to crawl out of one ear and across his face or a snake to slither from his tattered clothes, but neither happened.

The deity's laugh was even more unsettling; his lips parted to reveal four rows of perfectly white teeth while his belly bellowed without seeming to draw a breath.

"All men have two reactions upon meeting me, Jacob. They beg for more life or they welcome my embrace into the eternal. Mostly it's the former. But you… you haven't done either. Why is that?" Death asked.

I shrugged, growing weary of our conversation. I felt like he was postponing the inevitable. And so those two desires clashed inside, my craving to stop beating around the bush and get it over with and my inclination to avoid rushing unnecessarily into fiery damnation.

"I have a theory," Death said.

"Congratulations," I said, and there went the laugh that sent shivers down my spine.

"I think you've spent your life drifting through good days and bad, taking what you need to survive by force without so much as a thought for the eternal. *Damn the consequences* might as well have been your motto. You killed men, took money that wasn't yours, and moved on, restless and without a place to call home," Death said.

I found a nearby boulder and sat down. As long as Death was giving me a lecture on the life I'd lived, I might as well take a load off.

"And when you dove into that pond to avoid the bounty hunters instead of shooting them as Fate originally intended, you died before your time. So here we sit with a cosmic accident, the likes of which I've never dealt with before."

I thought back to the five men who had tracked me just south of the Missouri border. They'd shot my horse, and I was running through the woods full steam ahead. Out of breath, I came to the top of a mountain and realized I was surrounded by dead trees everywhere. For July, it was odd to see such a ring of decaying wood.

But gunshots rang out behind me, one bullet flying into that dead wood near my shoulder. The five men were seeking to cash in on a $300 bounty if I was taken dead. The extra $20 wasn't worth the trouble of taking me alive.

Seeing as I didn't have an inclination of dying that day… or any day really, I considered my options. I could fight, take a couple out before likely being shot in the back by someone who flanked me, or I could find a hiding spot and wait for them to leave. I chose the latter option and saw this pond of murky water.

With the men about thirty feet behind me, I dove in, intending to hold my breath as long as I could. Then I woke up here in this colorless desert.

"I don't remember drowning or anything violent," I said.

"No, you didn't drown," Death said.

"Was I shot underwater? Did a poison snake bite me?" I asked, trying to remember how I died. Of course, nothing came; I blacked out upon hitting the water.

Death put his book away, sliding it into his robes and stood before me.

"The pond you found is called the Death Spring. It only fills with rain once a year and acts as a portal into the afterlife. I figured the dead trees surrounding the water would have been an obvious enough sign to keep out of the water," Death said.

"Huh… so I was dead right when I jumped in?"

Death nodded, and I thought back upon my actions in life for the very first time. I had no crazy thoughts about redemption at this point. I knew what was ahead, and I accepted it. I'd drift forward as I had for the last thirty-three years of my life. And at last, the desire to stop beating around the bush and get it over with declared victory.

"So, you going to drop me in a lake of fire?" I asked, wishing I had one last smoke.

"Can't," Death said simply and without explanation.

"Why not?" I asked.

"There's no place prepared for you yet. Weren't you listening when I said you died before your time? You were supposed to win that shootout and die at the age of sixty-two by the noose," Death said.

"You mean I was supposed to hang an old man?" I said, furrowing my brow.

"Yes. You were supposed to swing until dead outside of Denver for crimes committed against the great state of Colorado," Death said.

"Okay… so what happens now?" I asked.

Death sighed, again without inhaling, and it continued to spook me. He sat down on the rock next to me and thought for a moment.

"We're usually very organized, you know. For something like this to happen, well… it's unheard of," Death said.

"Sorry to throw a wrench into your plans," I said, mindlessly.

"No, you're not. You don't give a damn one way or another," Death said.

"Got me there," I said.

We sat there for… hours? Days? Months? Eons? Who knows? Time just didn't seem to flow there.

After about my fifteenth sigh, Death stood up and said, "I think I'm going to let you keep drifting for now."

"You're going to send me back to life?" I asked, raising an eyebrow.

"Not quite. I don't have a place for you in the afterlife, but you are surely dead. I think I might be able to get some use out of you," Death said.

I threw my arms up in the air and said, "What are ya thinkin'?"

"There are people who cheat me once in a while, Jacob. Just as you died before your time, there are some souls out there who don't die when it is their time. Sometimes they use extraordinary means to keep drawing breath long after they should have stopped," Death said.

"So?"

"So I want you to go back and kill them for me," he said.

Death pulled out a long scroll and unraveled it before me. The scroll fell to the dust and kept rolling past my feet. I couldn't count the number of names on it. The edges of the scroll were bound by a gnarled wood similar to his stick.

"What's in it for me?" I asked, immediately realizing even in the afterlife, my habits stuck with me like a tick.

The antithesis of life seemed to anticipate this. Death knew he was dealing with a lifelong outlaw who was nothing if not selfish. If there was nothing to gain, I wasn't interested. An eternal drifter, the cattle rustler, bank robber, and survivalist like myself wasn't interested in wasting time. There was always somewhere new to be, mountains to hide in, and grass to lay in watching the clouds.

And while the average person might call all those activities "wasting time," I would argue it simply depended on one's priorities in life. A drifter's priority was to keep moving before life got stale. Any activity that kept someone in one place for long was a "waste of time."

Settling down, building a home, falling in love, having children? Those were all wasting time to me.

Death knew all of this. Since the beginning of time and until the end of time, he carried souls to their final resting place. Good men, bad men, everything in between, he witnessed them all. In life, a man could be many things. But in death, a man could only be his true self. There were no personas in the afterlife.

"Surely avoiding eternal damnation for decades if not centuries is payment enough?" Death said.

Without a moment's hesitation, I said, "You'd think, wouldn't ya? But if you want my services, I want a permanent way out of the darkness and gnashing of teeth."

Death shrugged and looked to the… west? East? Was there any direction in this wasteland?

"What you do in between hunting down names on that list is of no concern to me. Should you find some way to redeem yourself, I care not. Just hunt those souls down and send them to me. And don't waste too much time, or I'll come find you myself," Death said, tapping twice on the scroll as it rolled up tightly and bound itself with a brown snakeskin cord.

I walked over and held out my hand to take the scroll, but Death shook my hand instead. And I felt all the warmth and goodness drain from me if that makes sense. My skin became pale as Death, and my stomach flopped and floundered.

Looking up, I saw a blanched appaloosa form from the dust and ash. It stood tall behind Death with glowing purple eyes that seemed to pierce my very soul.

"Do not mistake yourself for one of the living, Jacob. You are dead, and nothing will change that. You will dwell in the land of the living, but you will see it's no longer your home. You're just passing through as you hunt down those on my list," Death said.

He finally let go, and I looked at my black fingernails.

"I'd get some gloves," Death said, chuckling breathlessly.

"I'm sure the ladies will love my new look," I said, looking over my now-tattered buckskin jacket and wool trousers.

"You're not going back for the ladies. You're going back to serve as my pale rider to hunt down those who have unjustly escaped my grasp," Death said, his gaze sending a warning.

I crossed my arms and raised an eyebrow, shivering. I still wasn't used to the lack of warmth on my insides. "I thought you said you didn't care what I did in my free time?"

Death pointed a finger at my face and said, "You don't have free time. You're on Death's time now. If between hunts you sleep with a whore or shoot a bear, fine. But remember my warning. Don't linger long on the trails and towns, or I will come for you."

I nodded, then walked over to my new steed and climbed on her back. She made no indication as to whether she enjoyed carrying my corpse or considered it a burden.

"Which way do I ride?" I asked.

Death pointed to a rocky ridge in the distance and said, "Just past that rock you'll find the Death Spring entrance. Leap into the water with your steed, and you'll find yourself back in the land of the living."

I nodded and scratched my shoulder-length black hair. The afterlife was itchy.

Lightly clicking my tongue and tapping the horse with my boots, we set off. I decided to name the horse Moon Snow on account of how she looked like snow-fall under the pale full moon.

After another few hours, days, months, years, and decades, I at last came to the rocky ridge. It rose about two hundred feet into the sky of the afterlife, worn with scars and corrosion. And past it, there was a spring full of murky water.

I had Moon Snow speed up, and we leapt from the shore into the water. Any worry I had the water would be too shallow was obliterated when we sank immediately without a single splash. It was as though we simply faded into the middle of the Death Spring.

My skin barely registered the water's touch, and I assumed much in the living world would feel different now that I was Death's Pale Rider.

Things went black for a moment, and then we were rising out of the water under a half moon with the sound of cicadas around us. It wasn't until now I realized how dead silent the afterlife had been.

At this moment I also realized that although I was back in the same woods as earlier, and there was indeed some color coming from fireflies around, things felt different.

I was wet, but only for a moment. The water droplets themselves seemed to flee my presence. And I wasn't breathing, either. Air wasn't a priority anymore, what with my lack of a beating heart.

Landing gently on the muddy shore, I looked back and saw the Death Spring drain like a bath with a hole shot in it.

Breathlessly sighing, I pulled out the scroll and untied the snakeskin cord. The first name was Albert Jameson. As I read it, I could picture his face and crimes in my mind's eye. He liked to watch prairie houses and wait for men to leave. Then, when they were gone, he broke in and took the women and children by force before slitting their throats.

He was being kept alive by some tribal shaman paid with lots of gold. I saw how he should have died and how he cheated Death.

"Well, can't have that. Boss says that ain't right," I muttered wrapping the scroll up and tucking it back in my inside left jacket pocket. "Let's go, Moon Snow." I directed the horse west toward Indian territory. "I know exactly where he'll be."

THE WATER MAIDEN

MODUPEH DUNCAN

Six men had died in the past six months and each full moon took another. More fresh holes to dig, more cold bodies to fill them. My village was slowly running out of men and I knew at eighteen, I could be next.

An oppressive cloud settled over the village. Everyone grew more watchful and cautious with each passing day. Someone or something was taking innocent lives and no one knew who or why. Many of the jobs in the village had been paused to keep people out of the forest. Men traveled to the fields in groups and women stayed by their huts and kept their children close. Jobs for younger men and women, like wood and water retrieval, were done in large groups and only during the morning hours. But despite all the caution, men continued to turn up bloated and purple at the village entrance.

The sixth victim was found at the same spot the other five had been found, on the boundary between the forest and the village entrance. Only the trees knew who had placed them there. Once, those wooden giants had been a protective barrier around the village, but now they increased the seclusion, the claustrophobia.

So far, the youngest victim had been eighteen, like me, and the oldest twenty-seven. But in all the chaos, all I cared about was seeing Number Six.

"Anu, this is a bad idea," Yousef said, his light brown face set in a scowl. As his best friend, I always succeeded in dragging him into all my adventures. I waited as he went through his obligatory refusal, his dark braided hair moving as he explained all the reasons we shouldn't. We walked through the center of the village square crowned by large rectangular huts topped in heavy thatched roofs, all blending together like a giant umbrella. Three women hastened by, watchful, as though a monster would jump out at any second, the hems of their dresses flapping. The square was quieter these days, lacking the sounds of children playing, teenagers yelling, and smoking men arguing. I grabbed Yousef's hand and dragged him behind the nearest hut.

"We need to do this. Don't you want to see a drowned corpse?" I walked towards the village boundary. Five huts down was the one that housed the dead man. I tuned out Yousef's protests, planning what to do if someone saw us. We would need a good excuse.

"No, I don't. What if—"

"This way," I interrupted and turned into the thin space between two homes. The guard was nowhere to be found. I climbed the two steps and pushed. The door moved and we slid into the dim room.

"Someone will find us," Yousef said, walking close behind me. The one-room hut had been emptied of everything except the man under the straw mat. I looked at Yousef. One of us had to move the mat. Yousef stopped at the center of the room, rooted in place. I sighed and moved towards the mound in the corner. One step at a time. I looked back at Yousef, who urged me forward with his hands. I stopped a few feet away and heard Yousef's voice, "Hurry up, Anu."

"Don't rush me." I knelt down and followed the pattern on the woven mat. My hands hovering over the edge closest to me. When my fingers touched the mat, the figure moved. My scream joined with Yousef's as I scrambled away, panicked.

"Anu, Yousef, what are you doing here?" a man's voice said.

We bolted from that room like wild animals being chased. I ran for the forest with Yousef behind me, my ears pounding as blood raced through my body. We ran breathless until the underbrush of the forest covered us, although no one followed. We stopped, fighting to breathe, and then I started laughing and Yousef joined. Our laughter rang into the trees, mixing in with the wind.

The next day, I watched the crowd gather, bodies shifting against the setting sun. Yousef nudged me as Laili walked by. Her beautiful dark skin shone luminous against the orange and green pattern of her dress. She waved to someone further down my row and I ducked, afraid she might see me. All my bravado died when she was nearby; even words became my enemy. By now she probably thought I was a fool. I heard the timbre of Yousef's laugh.

"Wow!" was all he could say.

"Leave me alone. I'll talk to her one day."

"When you're both using canes to walk?"

A drum pounded in the clearing at the center. Different tones of dark faces on logs encircled the clearing; it looked like everyone in the village was present. Three rows down I saw my mother talking to my little sister as she fought to sit still. My father's head bobbed as he dozed on and off, having spent the day in the fields.

The center of the clearing started to glow as the sun hid further. Multicolored lines and swirls formed on the ground, highlighting Story Man where he stood. His cloak glowed too, matching his stage. He raised his thick wooden staff and the crowd grew silent. Everyone waited to learn why six men were dead, and how they might stop Death's toll. The half-moon watched from the sky, also waiting.

Story Man's staff landed in time with the boom of the drum.

"Hundreds and hundreds of years ago, another village stood here. In this village lived a maiden so fair that men far and wide came only to look at her beauty. Her parents knew she could marry anyone—kings, princes, chiefs. As much as she was fair, she was also kind and good-natured. She was always happy and laughing, filled with life's joy, an angel on Earth. When she reached the age of sixteen, it was time for her to marry. Men lined up before her father's hut with gifts to win her favor, but she accepted none."

"Sounds like Laili," Yousef whispered.

"Shush," I said.

"On the third day, a man approached that none could compare to. He was as handsome as the maiden was fair, with eyes of greenish-blue, the color of lakes and rivers. As soon as the maiden saw him, he was all that mattered. The only gift he brought was a golden bracelet, which he placed on her wrist. He told her he would return again and vanished. Her parents did everything to remove the bracelet, but nothing worked. Terrified, they warned their daughter against seeing that man again. The maiden only smiled. The next day, she packed her clothes. When asked where she was going, she said she was preparing to leave with her husband. Her parents didn't know what to do, so they drugged her and took her to another village far away, hoping the man would not be able to find her. Each night, she tried to escape, but they stopped her."

Story Man's shadow grew, ominous and dark, towering over the crowd. His voice rose and fell in time with the story, like a pulse, giving it life. Eyes fixed on him, everyone swayed to his movements, hypnotized.

"Eventually, she stopped eating and grew too weak to run away. Her parents knew she was dying, so they decided to bring her back to their village. On the way back, the oxen were caught in a fast-moving river. By the time they got them to shore, their daughter was gone. They searched and searched and on the seventh day, she came back, drenched. Green and blue silks clung to her skin, and upon her head was a golden crown set with emeralds and sapphires. She told her parents she had returned to say good-bye. Her parents were happy to see her, but refused to let her go again to the Land of Deep Waters. So, they made a plan with the jealous men that still wished to have her. The parents told their daughter to ask her husband to come to a Wedding Feast, as they now had no reason to fight their love. The daughter was thrilled and used a bowl of water to ask her husband to come."

Story Man grew quiet. The crowd leaned towards him like plants to the sun.

"After three days of preparation, the King of the Water Spirits came for his bride and their Wedding Festival. The celebration lasted five days and nights. When the couple was finally at ease and believed all was well, the parents sprang their trap. A Medicine Man cast a spell to sever the King from his water magic. Because he was now mortal, the jealous suitors held him down and stabbed him with knives until he lay still. The maiden was mad with grief, but they held her and made her watch. She clawed, gnashed, and kicked herself to freedom. Falling on her dying husband, she took the last of his spirit into her hands and jumped into the closest puddle she could find, vanishing from the village. Months passed. No one could find her, but they all heard stories of a woman seen every full moon, wailing by the river in the forest.

"One full moon they found a man, drowned. At first, no one connected the death to the presence of the wailing woman. But on the next full moon, another drowned. After two more met the same fate, the Medicine Man called to the Maiden, begging her for forgiveness. She took three more men before she appeared at the village again. She told them each month she would take one man in his prime, until she was given a male vessel in which to place the essence of her murdered husband. She gave them the purifying rites that the vessel must undergo before being taken to the rushing river in the forest. The village complied and the deaths stopped. Every hundred years, these rites must be followed to prevent the monthly deaths."

The drums banged and Story Man was quiet. I watched as the crowd digested this information before realization struck. Someone else had to die. Who would sacrifice their son for the good of everyone? Yousef sucked in air beside me, his hands trembling. I looked down at mine. They too were shaking.

Silence hung as crickets' song filled the air. The Chief moved into the clearing as Story Man took his seat.

"We have all heard the story that so many of us have forgotten or never knew. Now we must decide who will be the Water Maiden's next husband. We will cast lots. It is the only fair way."

The crowd rumbled to life as people turned to their neighbors. The fear was palpable in families with young sons. No one wanted to lose their child or friend. I looked at Yousef, who still sat frozen, his hands squeezing each other.

"Anu, what if it's one of us?" he asked in a terrified whisper. I had no answer and I always had answers. My mind ran through all the ways to escape this. Nothing.

"It probably won't be one of us." I hoped my voice sounded calm, carefree. Yousef looked at me. Even in the dim, his pupils were needle pricks. "We'll be fine. And if it's one of us, we can fight a Water Spirit. How tough can she be?" I asked, patting my friend on the back. One of us had to be brave.

In the five days that passed before the selection of the Chosen, as everyone called the sacrifice—I think it made them feel better about what was to come— the village buzzed, restless and scared. People moved about like the undead. Mothers held their children closer. A curfew was passed and even Yousef and I obeyed it. We all waited to see who was doomed and with about ten days to the next full moon, time was running away from us.

Then it was here, the day of the choosing. With the noon sun mercilessly beating down, we all shuffled back to the clearing to hear who the Chosen would be. Each family had been given a number for each male under thirty years in their home.

We all went, our numbers carved into our minds. In the short space of three days, most of us could recite each other's numbers. I, Number Twenty-Two, was once more walking with Yousef, Number Twenty-Seven, to the clearing. This time the air was suffocating and I was terrified. My bravery had melted, and I felt no shame in this. My mother's tears had been the hardest to bear. I could no longer look at her without more flowing. Ayo, Number Seventeen, bounced off me without even feeling it. I moved away and sat towards the back with Yousef next to Zalme, Number Twenty-Five, an acquaintance.

The Chief entered the clearing. This time, no drums were needed to call for silence; you could hear the wings of a fly. Salim, a child of twelve, brought the giant gourd filled with our numbers. The Chief approached it. His weathered face reflected the feelings of his tribe.

This was it.

"We have all agreed to the results of this ceremony. I will take one number, and there will be no fighting this." He reached into the gourd. His hand returned and the crowd stopped breathing. Salim took the gourd away. The Chief looked at the number, grimaced, held it up. The row closest to the center read it. Some people in the back stood to get a clear view. There were mixed reactions: gasps, sighs, tears. My heart stopped. I looked towards my parents, who were closer, to read their reaction. Anything. But I could not see them as more people stood up.

"Number Twenty-Four," the Chief read aloud.

And I could breathe again. I grabbed Yousef's hand. The relief was shared. He gave me a small smile. We bottled our happiness for now. We may not have been chosen, but someone had been.

My mind searched. Who was Number Twenty-Four? Dayo... Malik...? No.

"Everyone, please, sit down. Dele Sabode, please come forward," the Chief's voice rang. People took their seats, one at a time, until the clearing appeared again. I heard Dele's family crying. He stood and walked to the front, head held high. He was a muscular hunter of approximately twenty-two years of age. I had once seen Laili talking to him and giggling. At the time I was filled with jealousy, but now all I felt was pity. Dele kept his eyes fixed on the Chief as he took steady steps towards the clearing. The chief patted his firm, bare shoulders before rubbing white chalk paint across his chest.

"We thank you for your sacrifice. You and your family's." At this, his mother and aunts yelled in misery. Most looked away, ashamed to share their pain because they were happy their sons and loved ones were not chosen. "We will start the purification ceremony tomorrow," the Chief finished.

My eyes landed on Laili, who was crying, and I looked away. The apathetic sun shone on us as everyone shuffled soundlessly back to their jobs and homes.

Ten days passed, and it was time for Dele to give up his life. No one knew what to expect. Would the Water Maiden take his body whole into the river, never to return? Or would she leave a corpse behind? The village was given clear instructions: Dele would be the only one to take the long walk through the forest to meet his fate at the river. But I had a better plan and after two days of convincing, Yousef agreed to join me. We would follow Dele and see this Water Maiden. I promised Yousef that we would remain as far away from Dele and the river as we could and to make sure of this, we did a trial walk earlier that day.

That night as the full moon lit the sky, Dele took his final purifying bath. Then, with his legs, arms, chest, and forehead smeared with sheep's blood, he began his solitary walk to the rushing river. And Yousef and I followed with the stealth of panthers. Yousef had decided to bring a cutlass and I didn't argue. We followed, keeping to the denser part of the forest, away from the trail. The trees shifted in the darkness, and the moon played with their shadows.

"*Ow!*" Yousef banged into a tree that seemed to come from nowhere. The forest was denser than I remembered, even though we had been running through it all our lives. This forest was not ours; it grew and shrunk, alive. The underbrush tangled and grabbed at our arms and feet as we moved, leaving deep scratches on our arms and legs.

"Can you see Dele?" I hissed. Yousef, busy using the cutlass on a vine tangled around his ankle, didn't answer.

A snap to the left made us jump. something else was in that place with us, and I knew somehow that it was not human. We scrambled, slipping and sliding downhill towards the trail, all thoughts of the solitude of Dele forgotten.

Dele gasped as we burst from the cover of the trees. "What are you doing here?"

"We thought you could use the company," I said.

"I'm supposed to do this alone." But there was something in his voice that was thankful.

Together, we three continued the march, our feet the only sound in this eerie forest. Yousef clung to his cutlass even more tightly than before. Things moved on both sides of the trail: wisps of light flaring and fading, casting larger shadows. Why had I thought this was a good idea? I wanted to go back, but when I turned around, I saw only a thick, breathing darkness. The trail now only existed before us.

I nudged Yousef, who jumped. "What?!" His panic was raw. Dele looked at us.

"The... the trail behind us is gone..." I said, looking over my shoulder. Both turned to confirm and didn't like what they found. The darkness rolled towards us, eating the trail faster than before. I grabbed Yousef's hand and ran. The darkness gave chase, emitting thunderous crunching noise as it consumed the very fabric of reality.

Dele, being taller and more fit, was ahead of us. Yousef tripped. I felt his fingers slip from mine. His throaty scream exploded as the darkness ate him. I watched as my best friend vanished from existence.

And then the crunching, devouring darkness resumed its chase. I could barely make out Dele as he sped further and further away into the night.

I was next.

Up ahead, water glimmered through the thick forest.

"The river. The river!" I panted. There it was before us. Dele had already stopped on the bank. I put on a final burst of speed. As I crossed some unseen threshold, the darkness halted and reared back, somehow repelled. Of course; this place was sacred, untouchable. I could feel it.

Dele was looking at something and I followed his gaze. On a large rock downriver stood a woman bathed in moonlight. Her clothes and long, white hair floated around her like one submerged. Her skin was the color of onyx, her eyes a glowing blue. She turned towards Dele and smiled. In a flash, she was in front of him.

"You remind me of him," her ghostly voice thrilled. Her slender fingers grazed his cheek and he smiled, transfixed. I held my breath, afraid she would notice me. I shifted my weight and that was all it took. She was behind me.

"You don't belong here," she said. She ran her finger across my bare shoulder blades. It burned like hot coals. I screamed. The beautiful woman was gone; in her place were shrunken ice-blue eyes, scaly skin of green and grey, and large sharp teeth.

I turned and ran. Her laughter rang out behind me, high and crackling. All at once she was on me, tearing and ripping at my body. My hands flailed and fought to defend my body and face, but she shredded through them easily. I fell to the ground and tried to crawl. Every movement flooded my nerves with fire, but I had to get away.

"You don't belong here," was the last thing I heard. I felt the sharp pressure of her claws as they pushed through my back and grabbed my heart.

The End

THE BASEMENT

REBECCA FISHER

Five boys and a man sit around a campfire. They're all in matching t-shirts, shorts, with little red bandanas tied around their necks. Earlier they wore matching wide-brimmed hats, but those have been abandoned, are now lying carelessly on the floors of tents and atop sleeping mats some miles away.

It's dark out and there are no stars. The mosquitoes are biting through layer upon sticky layer of bug spray. No one seems to mind, however—they have marshmallows to set aflame and ghost stories to tell.

"All right, boys," calls the older man, their counselor and squad leader. He looks tired—as tired as someone who's been watching a group of ten-year-old boys for three weeks straight should look. But he is not unhappy. "Who's next?"

The boys go into a frenzy, scrambling over each other, pushing and shoving, stretching to see whose hand raises the highest.

"Me!"

"Me!"

"Pick me, Mr. Harker!"

"No, me!"

"That's not fair! You just went!"

"So? *I* tell the *best* ghost stories."

"Do *not*!"

"Do *too*!"

"*Boys!*" calls the counselor. The sharpness in his tone has lost some of its edge, worn down by days out in the wilderness. "Settle down now. *Everyone* will get a turn."

Mr. Harker notices how the smallest and quietest of the boys didn't participate in the jumping and fighting. This boy is sitting with his hands tucked under his thighs, looking into the fire with a thoughtful expression on his face.

Mr. Harker wonders if the boy even heard him. "Marvin," he calls to the boy, "how about you?"

Marvin looks up from the fire with a jerk. His eyes widen as he realizes they're all looking at him. He quickly turns away from his peers, who are grinning at him viciously. The flickering light of the fire makes them all appear to have hollow eyes and flashing sharp teeth.

Marvin represses a shudder. "I… I don't know, sir," he answers, trying to keep his focus on their counselor. He silently pleads for Mr. Harker to realize what's been happening right under his nose these last few weeks. "I don't really know any ghost stories."

But Mr. Harker only smiles, oblivious as ever. "Come on," he says gently. "You've been so quiet tonight. Tell us your *best scary ghost story.*"

"Don't force him, Mr. Harker," says one of the boys.

"Yeah, if he says he doesn't know any, then pick on someone else."

"Marvin's quiet because he's *dumb.* Let him speak, and we'll be here all night listening to his *stu-stu-stuttering* and *sta-sta-stammering.*"

"I know a great one! It's about the girl and her boyfriend who go off in the woods to—"

"*Boys!*" Mr. Harker rounds on them. These four have become quite the thorn in his side. He's looking forward to sending them all home tomorrow. "That's *enough.* Keep it appropriate or we'll close the circle and all go back to our tents for the night. And you've already told your story, John. I was talking to *Marvin* and *Marvin only.*"

When he turns back to Marvin, he is sure to keep his expression soft and open. He'd been so busy trying to wrangle the others all these weeks, he's had little time to get to know this odd, quiet child. He regrets that now, and wants to make it up to him. "So, how 'bout it, Marvin? Wanna give it a go?"

Marvin looks back and forth between the boys and Mr. Harker. He then takes a deep breath, preparing himself. "All… all right," he says. He's refusing to give the others the satisfaction of cowing him. Tonight, he will be brave—even if there is a chance they'll give him hell for it later.

Hopefully, it would be a slim one. "I do know… one story that might be good. It's from my hometown."

One of the other boys made a gagging noise. "*Bor-ring.*"

"Lame!"

"I can already *tell* this is going to put me to sleep!"

"*Yeah*, John's story sounds *way* better."

"Marvin, just pass up on your turn—we don't want to hear about your *stupid hometown.*"

"*Boys, that's enough!*" Mr. Harker shouts, loud enough to make all four of them jump. "One more peep out of you and you're marching right back to your tents. Is *that* what you want?"

They all give him that sheepish look. "No, Mr. Harker," they mumble in unison.

Mr. Harker sighs, perhaps a little too heavily. "All right, *then be quiet*. Go ahead, Marvin. Whenever you're ready."

Marvin takes another deep breath. Then, he begins:

"Okay. I heard about this one from our neighbors. They come over for dinner sometimes and like to talk about what our street was like when it was first built."

Mr. Harker's face is open and interested, but the other boys are enjoying all the ways they can tease him with their hands—index fingers going down throats and turning to guns pointed at temples with waggling thumbs as the trigger. For one vengeful moment, Marvin finds himself wishing they actually *were* holding guns.

He focuses on the gathering shadows behind the heads of his fellow campers. He's trying to place one word after another despite how they threaten to rush out all at once. "Anyway, in the fifties, there was this woman who lived across the street from our house. It wasn't our house yet, obviously, but it would be later."

"Anyway," he says again, swallowing nervously. He shoots a pleading glance at Mr. Harker, who only nods encouragingly. Marvin gives up and continues: "She lived there with her son, and after her husband died of cancer or whatever, she went a little… crazy. Apparently, the whole street used to be able to hear her yelling and screaming at her son through all hours of the night. The police were called a lot, but it never seemed to do much good and no one ever really did anything else to try and stop it.

"The son was kind of a bad kid. He was known for skipping school, pick-pocketing—he even stole a car once, or so they say. As he got older, he started to fight back more, and then it was the two of them screaming at one another all the time. They hit each other, too. Our neighbors said it was really rough for a while. There were some people who were even starting to consider *moving* because they just couldn't stand the noise and the violence anymore.

"And the one day, Mrs. Anderson—that was the woman's name, the crazy one. The family were the Andersons."

"Hey, my last name is Anderson!" shouts one of the boys, appearing offended but only for Mr. Harker's sake. Marvin knows he's just playing it up for attention.

"*We know*, Billy," Mr. Harker says, sounding exasperated. "It's a common last name. *Please* don't interrupt someone when they're speaking. Go ahead and continue, Marvin."

Marvin watches Billy's expression turn sour as his feeble plot to get Marvin in trouble falls through. Small victories.

He continues, feeling more confident the longer he speaks. "Well, one day, Mrs. Anderson came home from shopping and found her son on the couch with another boy. They were kissing."

The shouts that erupt from the four small boys across the fire could have woken the dead.

"Eeewwww!"

"Gross!"

"That's *disgusting*, Marvin!"

"Leave it to you to tell a story about a bunch of *fags*."

"Yeah, Marvin—I bet this is actually a story about you. We *all* know *you* like kissing boys," says Billy, to a chorus of prepubescent laughter.

"*BOYS!*" shouts Mr. Harker, but they're out of control this time, cackling wildly and high-fiving each other. Marvin is half inclined to tell the older man to give up, too. He's red in the face and no closer to gaining control over the four than he had been when camp first started. "This is your *last warning*! No more profanity, no more insults, and if I hear you use that word to describe someone again, I'm going to call your mother to come pick you up, *tonight*. Is *that* what you want?"

The laughter ceases. "No, Mr. Harker," mutters Billy, hanging his head in a mockery of shame. "I'm sorry."

"Yeah," says John. "We're *sorry*."

But when Mr. Harker turns around to swat at a particularly nasty mosquito and dig a can of bug spray from his bag, John leans in across the logs and shoves Marvin as hard as he can. Marvin falls, landing on the pile of backpacks that had been thrown down unceremoniously after their hike. One of the boys left their swiss army knife open—probably in anticipation for this very thing—and Marvin slices his palm open on the sharp edge. He hisses in pain, clenching his fist around the wound to hide the blood.

Glaring at John and the others, who are snickering softly to themselves and mouthing "gay" and "fag" over and over, Marvin scrambles to his feet and resumes his seat on the log before Mr. Harker can see him on the ground. One of the boys freezes, his eyes growing huge at the sight of the blood trickling between Marvin's fingers. For a moment, he looks like he is about to say something, perhaps even tell the others to stop laughing, that Marvin might have seriously hurt himself. But then Mr. Harker turns back around. The boy shrinks back into the shadow of his friends, leaving Marvin alone and defenseless once more.

"All right," says Mr. Harker, completely unaware of the events that have just transpired. Marvin sets his jaw, clenching his fist harder. The cut stings. He hopes it isn't too deep. "Sorry about all the interruptions, Marvin. Please continue."

"Thanks, Mr. Harker," Marvin says, careful to keep his voice calm, neutral. His tone is almost conversational despite the persistent throbbing in his hand: "So anyway, Mrs. Anderson came home to find her son kissing another boy. This is the part where the story is a little different depending on who's telling it. Some say an argument broke out. Some say the two boys tried to make a break for it. But everyone agrees that at some point after she got home, Mrs. Anderson went to her dead husband's old safe, pulled out a gun, and shot her own child dead—straight through the heart. Still holding the smoking shotgun, she screamed at the other boy to *get out*, and he did.

"A neighbor heard the shot and called the police. When they got there, they found crazy old Mrs. Anderson in the basement, trying to stuff her son's blood-soaked body into the icebox. No one knows why the icebox. There was no hiding the murder—everyone had heard the gunshot, there had been a witness, and there was blood *everywhere*. But she never told them why she went for the icebox, even when she was sentenced to the electric chair.

"Her son—Malcolm was his name—was buried next to his father in the family plot. The whole neighborhood showed up to watch him be put in the ground, for the satisfaction of knowing that their nightmare was finally over if nothing else.

"But after that, the house sat empty for a few years. They say no one could scrub the blood stains out of the floor, and anyone who came to look at the house wouldn't set one foot in there after finding out what happened to the previous family.

"Rumors started to pop up: people saw lights on, movement behind curtains. Someone said they even heard the TV click on at one point. They figured it was just teenagers breaking in for a laugh, but whenever they went to investigate, they would find the house still, quiet, and empty.

"People avoided that house all together after that, believing it was haunted by the ghost of Malcolm, or his crazy mother, or *both.*

"More time passed. In the late sixties, a young couple bought the house, fixed it up all nice and settled in. The neighbors were happy to have some new faces around. They thought, finally, they could forget the Andersons once and for all.

"But then the husband of this couple started drinking. It just got worse and worse, and then they started to fight a lot. They say the guy would beat up his wife real bad. She did her best to hide the bruises from the neighbors, her family and friends, but everyone knew what was *really* going on.

"And again, the police were called all the time to investigate and break up the fighting, but they eventually stopped coming. You see, the wife—Lucy was her name—just kept saying everything was fine, she could handle her husband, there was no need to worry.

"But one night, she realized that everything *wasn't* fine, that she *couldn't* handle him. He'd been out drinking with his buddies, and stumbled home *real* angry and drunk. He went after Lucy, and Lucy grabbed one of the cast iron pans she used to cook dinner and whacked him in the head. Cracked his skull, killed him.

"They say Lucy stood over the body, horrified by what she'd done. She knew she'd probably go to jail and get sentenced to death, just like Mrs. Anderson.

"So, what did she do? She drags her husband's still-warm corpse down to the basement and shoves his body in the icebox, closing the lid and bolding it shut. They had a refrigerator by that point, so the icebox mostly went unused. It was the best place to hide the body until Lucy could figure out what to do next.

"They say she was on her hands and knees, scrubbing at the bloodstains on the floor, when she noticed someone had come into the room, was now *standing in front of her*.

"When she looked up, she forgot to scream. There was a boy there, a boy wearing fifties-style clothes and slicked back hair. His handsome face was as white as a sheet, with blue veins showing his in neck, jaw, and cheeks. What stopped her breathing was the sight of the bullet hole in his chest, how his shirt was torn and stained and soaked through with blood.

"Lucy was smart. She knew the stories about what had happened in her house a decade earlier, knew what the neighbors all murmured when they thought she couldn't hear them.

"'What do you want?' she asked the ghost of Malcolm.

"But Malcolm only put a finger to his lips. Then he started to help her clean the floors."

"Wait, hang on!" shouts one of the boys.

Marvin huffs in irritation. He was into the story now, and the interruptions were starting to get annoying. "How does a ghost scrub floors?!"

"Yeah, aren't they supposed to like, *be able to walk through walls*?" another one chides.

"This story *sucks*," says a third.

The last one, the boy who continues to stare at Marvin's bloody hand, says nothing.

"Seriously, boys," Mr. Harker growls. "This is your last warning. Another interruption, and you're all going back to your tents. Is that *really* how you want to spend your last night at camp?"

"*No*," they answer as one.

"Sorry, Mr. Harker."

"Don't apologize to me, apologize to Marvin. He's the one you're being rude to."

One of the boys—John—turns to Marvin, smirking. "Sorry, *Marvin*," he spits.

Inwardly, Marvin winces at his own name being hurled at him like an insult. As he wipes spittle from his face with his good hand, he thinks about stopping the story, about telling Mr. Harker he is tired and wants to go to bed. But it would be a lie, and he knows the safest place for him right now is within sight of the only adult here. He dreads to think what could happen to him out in the tent or the woods, alone in the dark with no witnesses.

Besides, he wants to keep telling the story. It feels too much like home.

When Mr. Harker inclines his head, Marvin continues. "Anyhow, the two were cleaning the floors, getting rid of all the evidence. Malcolm never said a word to Lucy, but the more time the two of them spent together, the less afraid she felt. Somehow, she knew he wasn't going to hurt her.

"So when the house was clean, Lucy slowly got to her feet. Her back was aching, and her knuckles were raw from all the chemicals. Malcolm was still there, just watching her.

"'What am I going to do with the body?' Lucy asked, and started to cry again. The guilt for what she had done had set in, but she knew she'd had no other choice. Had she not grabbed for that pan, *she* would probably be the one in the icebox right now.

"Lucy felt something cold on her shoulder. She looked up from her crying to see Malcolm, still pale as death with his front totally stained in blood. The sight of it made her think of her husband's body again, lying just below their feet, and her lip trembled. But Malcolm only smiled at her and shook his head. Then, he vanished—right before her eyes, as if he'd never been there at all. Lucy fainted, and when she woke up, she convinced herself it was all a dream.

"A few days later, Lucy dared to go down to the basement to check on the body. But there wasn't a body—the icebox was empty. She stared and stared, but couldn't make sense of it. The body, the blood—all of it was just… gone. There was no evidence pointing to her as her husband's murderer. She was *free*.

"Happier than she'd been in a long, long time, Lucy lived in that house for a few more years. She told any curious neighbors that her husband had decided to leave her and skip town. No one questioned it; people were just relieved to finally have peace and quiet return to their neighborhood.

"Eventually, Lucy met another man and left. Not too long after, a new family moved in to the Andersons' old home. This was an older couple with two teenage children, a boy and a girl.

"They say the girl, their daughter, was a straight A student. She was beautiful, she was popular, she got accepted into every college she applied to after she graduated. She could do no wrong in her parents' eyes, and she made it easy for them and everyone else to play favorites.

"The boy, her brother, was… less fortunate. His grades weren't up to par with his sister's, and his parents were constantly comparing her successes to his failure.

"The boy was depressed, angry, and quickly grew to be filled with hatred towards his parents and especially his sister, who did little to stand up for him when he became the unwilling target of their parents' disappointment. He got so angry one day that he moved all his stuff from the bedroom he had next to his sister down to the basement. He was still too young to move out on his own, but he wanted to be as far away from the rest of the house as he could.

"After all, it wasn't *his* fault his grades were bad. The teachers laughed at him when he asked for help, and doing homework was difficult enough without all the letters and numbers moving around before his eyes. No matter how hard he tried, he was falling further and further behind in school, and was getting close to flunking out altogether.

"But it wasn't too long after the boy moved into the basement that his sister, the brainy one, the pride and joy of the family, *disappeared*. They say she went into her bedroom one night and just *never came out*. She wasn't anywhere in the house, the backyard, down the street. She wasn't at any of her friends' houses, at the school, in any of the parks.

"Her parents, distraught, called the police and filed a missing person's report. Whole search parties went out looking for her, every night for months and months. The brother was taken in for questioning numerous times, since everyone believed he had done something to her out of jealousy. But he was just as clueless as the rest of them, and knew nothing about where his sister had gone. Eventually, they had to let him go.

"Several years went by, and the parents, grief-stricken at the loss of their daughter, decided to move out and start fresh somewhere else. During that time, the boy had somehow been able to turn his grades around. He finished school early, and they say he picked a college all the way out in California, as far away from his parents as he could get.

"To this day, no one knows what happened to that girl. She was just *gone*, and everyone assumed that, at this point, she was either dead or did simply not want to be found.

"From then on, one strange thing after another went on in that house. Then, weird things started happening in the neighbor's houses. Then, it spread to the whole street, and finally the whole neighborhood. People who were mean or stuck up or hurt others, people no one liked or that almost *everyone* liked, were just suddenly gone one day, without a trace. I heard there was a guy living three blocks over who had trained his dog to go after neighborhood children. He was old and bitter, and the last time anyone saw him, he'd been drinking whiskey on his front porch. Some people assumed he'd been put in a nursing home or died in his house from old age. Others weren't so sure.

"And then, the mayor of the town retired and moved into one of the bigger houses in that neighborhood. He was known for throwing lavish parties, but would then turn around and make his poorer neighbors clean up after his messes. He went and vanished one day, too, without a trace.

"Many believe it's Malcolm, delivering justice to those who need it most, trying to give people like him a second chance at a better life. They say he protects the neighborhood and everyone who lives in it. Being born there leaves a mark on you, and they say he'll come help someone in need wherever they are, as long as they're from that part of town."

Marvin sits back, careful to wipe his still-bleeding hand on his shorts in a way Mr. Harker won't notice. Everyone is looking at him, expecting more.

Marvin shrugs. "That's it," he says. "That's the end of my story." He's looking past the boys now, past Mr. Harker into the woods beyond. He's wondering if he just saw a shadow move, or if it had merely been a trick of the firelight.

"That was *boring*," says Billy, throwing his head back dramatically.

"Yeah, there should have been more blood and guts," remarks John. He's seen Marvin looking around behind them but doesn't turn around. He figures it's just Marvin's attempting to scare them. *Pathetic*.

"I wanted someone's head to get cut off."

"You wouldn't know a good ghost story from a hole in the ground, *Marvin*."

"Yeah, ghosts are *mean* and *scary*—they don't help people. That's what superheroes are for!"

"Dummy."

"*Stupid Marvin*."

"You couldn't tell a good ghost story to *save your life*."

"Yeah, this is why *no one likes you*."

"It's why you don't have any friends at school!"

"How do we even know you didn't just make that all up?"

"Yeah, there wasn't really a ghost, was there? Freak."

Marvin clenches his fists. He glares at the boys. "Shut up," he says through gritted teeth. He's been putting up with this torment for weeks now, and he's starting to get sick of it.

John, the biggest of the four, stands up from his log and puts his hands on his hips. "*Make me*," he taunts.

Something inside him snaps—*finally, blissfully* snaps—and Marvin goes flying off his log, knocking the bigger boy off-balance. The two wrestle to the ground, narrowly missing the flames. The shouts and jeers from the other boys are drowned out by the fight and the sound of the crackling flame. Perhaps Mr. Harker is shouting at them, too, but Marvin can't hear it. He feels only the punches and kicks from John, and the satisfaction on seeing that he has, some-how, managed to make the other boy's nose bleed.

Then, suddenly, the roaring fire goes out, and the whole circle is plunged into darkness. The boys all shout in shock and surprise.

Just as quickly as it went out, the fire roars to life again. John looks around, down where Marvin is pinned underneath him. He's ready to swing another punch, but Marvin's not there.

Wiping his nose, he gets up and looks around. "Where'd he go?" he shouts to the others. But they're looking around, too, just as confused as he is. Somehow, in that split second, the smaller boy managed to escape.

"Marvin? Come back here, you coward!"

"Marvin! *Marvin!*"

They've all gotten to their feet, are now walking around the fire. The peer into the shadows of the trees beyond, but none of them dare stray too far from the light.

Billy gives a shout, and points to Mr. Harker—or rather, the spot where Mr. Harker *should* have been. His pack is there, but his log is empty. Their camp counselor is nowhere in sight.

"Mr. Harker? Where are you?"

"Mr. Harker? *Marvin?*"

"Where *are* you guys?"

Their voices rise octave by octave as panic sets in. They keep calling into the silence, no sure what else to do. They never meant to be left alone out here, in the woods, in the dark.

At that moment, the roaring campfire extinguishes again. The second time they're thrown into blackness, the boys all scream. It lasts longer this time, and they're fumbling around in the dark in sheer terror.

"Who did that?! Who the *hell* did that?!"

"It wasn't me!"

"Wasn't me either!"

"What's going on? I can't see anything!"

"Marvin?! Mr. Harker?! Someone, help!"

"This isn't funny anymore!"

"*Help!*"

And suddenly, the fire comes *whooshing* back to life. Marvin and Mr. Harker's seats are still empty. The four remaining boys whip their heads around, wide-eyed and terrified. They huddle together on their log, shaking, whimpering with fear.

One of them squeaks when a shadow across the fire *moves*. They all watch as the figure slowly, *slowly* steps out of the woods to stand on the other side of the firepit. The newcomer is still shrouded in darkness, with only their outline visible.

"M-Mr. Harker?" a boy whimpers, even though they all know it isn't Mr. Harker standing there. None of them recognize the figure, who watches them with a casual ease that sends goosebumps up and down their limbs.

A boy feels his bladder let go. He hopes the others don't notice even as the wet stain grows to soak his shorts and the log beneath. He glances over to the other side of the fire pit, where something glitters on the ground: the swiss army knife, still lying atop the pile of backpacks. It's red and shinning with Marvin's blood. Dark stains have bled into the canvas of the backpacks. There are handprints where Marvin sat just a moment before.

The stranger in the shadows steps forward, and at the sight of him, Marvin and their missing counselor vanish from their minds.

Their throats close. They cannot scream.

A boy stands on the other side of the roaring flames. A boy perhaps a few years older than them. His dark hair is slicked back from his face, deathly pale and yellowish in the warm glow. The stranger's eyes are hidden in shadow, nothing but two black hollows.

As one, the boys realize who is standing there. One of them utters a strangled, screeching sound. Unnecessarily, the boy points a small, shaking finger again, this time at the older kid's shirt. It's soaked with blood, the red so dark it appears almost as black the shadows surrounding them.

Darkness presses in like walls. They cannot run. There is nowhere to go.

Trembling, whimpering, crying, they forget about Marvin. Forget about Mr. Harker. Forget about trying to act tough and strong and invincible. All they can do now is sit in their own filth, clutching each other desperately.

The boys watch as Malcolm gives a wide, black smile that nearly splits his face in two. He raises a long, pale finger to his lips.

Shhh.

When the fire goes out a third time, it stays that way. Not a single glowing ember can be found. The woods are quiet and dark once more.

WARMTH

DAVID GWYN

When Cara reached over in the middle of the night, she expected to feel her son in bed next to her. Since they moved into this house a few weeks ago, she'd been obsessed with ensuring he was there, feeling the boy's warmth in the bed they shared. What she didn't expect was for the sheets to be cold and wet. He hadn't had an accident at night in years.

She leaned over and flicked on the light. When she turned to see what was wet in the bed, she saw that the sheets were red with blood. In an instant, she threw the covers off herself and backed away. She looked down to see her hands covered in blood, too. Her fingers trembled, blood dripping from them. She looked from one corner of the room to the other. Her heart raced and it took her a second to compose herself.

"Eric!" she called out to him. Then she was silent, hoping for a response. The house shifted and shuttered, creaking endlessly the way old houses in the Midwest do. She couldn't stop her mind racing. Had her fears become reality? Had the bastard finally found her and Eric the way he said he would?

She ran to the bathroom, hoping he'd be there, a simple bloody nose to explain away her fear. But her panic only increased when she swung the door open, revealing an empty bathroom.

Cara thought about screaming, but who would hear her? She was nearly a mile from the Hendersons' house to the east. The Hunts to the north were even farther. She grabbed a towel from the rack and wiped the blood from her hands, running every possible terrible outcome through her mind. Maybe he was just getting a glass of water downstairs? But something didn't feel right. As she continued to panic, she saw something out the bathroom window. She could make out a tiny figure standing in the backyard, staring out across the wild wheat fields.

She flung the window open. It thudded angrily at being pushed up with such force. Chilled air swept into the house. She leaned out of the window so far that half her body hung outside. She called to Eric, but he didn't turn. He continued to stare at the tall stalks while they pushed each other one way and then the next.

In a moment she was downstairs then out the back door, sprinting towards him. When she was close, she dashed to her knees, grabbing him with two hands on the shoulders to turn him around. His arms felt so cold. The moon was full and shed enough light that she was able to see the blank look on his face. She shook him slightly, hoping to wake him up. His head lolled from one side to the other before it jolted up and he seemed to come alive all at once.

He shivered and reached out, grabbing his mother's arms and saying, "What happened?"

She remembered the blood. "Honey, are you okay?" She searched him. "Are you cut?"

"Cut?" he asked. "I don't think so."

Frantically, Cara checked his arms and legs in the moonlight, hoping for some indication of where the blood had come from. After a thorough check, she found nothing.

"Were you sleepwalking?"

"I'm really cold, Mommy," he said, hugging himself.

She rubbed his arms briskly, trying to force some warmth into his body. His skin felt like he'd been outside for hours. "Why are you outside?"

"The tall lady brought me."

"Who?" Then, feeling silly for asking, she said, "It must have been a dream. You were sleepwalking. Let's go inside. It's too cold out here."

Cara was about to stand up when she felt something behind her. Whatever it was radiated an icy chill. Had it gotten darker? Was she in the shadow of something now, where she hadn't been before? Had a cloud blocked the moon? Something had cast a shadow over both her and her son. Her breath came out in shaky sputters. Still on her knees, she turned her head quickly.

But there was nothing there except an empty lawn and the yellow glow from the bathroom window upstairs. She turned back to her son. Eric looked up above her face. "Don't you see her?" he asked.

Again, the feeling emerged that something loomed behind her. The hairs on her neck rose. "Let's go inside," she said, trying to ignore the way her son eyed something behind her. She took his arm and dragged him, taking a wide berth around the place Eric continued to look. When they got inside, she closed the door behind her and locked it. Then she led her son to the bottom of the stairs.

"Go up," she said, "I'll be right there. And don't be afraid of the blood on the sheets. Mommy had a bloody nose," she lied, "but she's fine now. I'll change the sheets in a minute. Now, up you go."

He hesitated for only a moment before bounding up the stairs. She wanted to see for herself if something really was there. She leaned over the kitchen sink, glaring out into the darkness. Everything seemed quiet. Just the yard, swing set, and wheat field, same as always.

When Cara was satisfied that they were alone, she started to go upstairs. When she reached the bottom, she heard her son's voice. She walked slowly at first, trying to hear that he was saying.

"I can't go with you," the boy said. "What about Mommy?"

She froze and clutched her chest. Had he finally found them? Had every fear she'd had when she left finally come true? How could she have been so foolish? Of course he'd find them. It was only a matter of time. She'd gone to such lengths to disappear, though. Not a single person from their old life knew where they went. She'd even let her son pick the spot on the map, eyes closed, middle of the country, one, two, three, finger down and that's where we're going.

"I'd miss her too much," Eric said from their room.

Her son's voice shook her to life. She'd kill the asshole this time. She was sure of it. She'd crept slowly down the stairs again, using the banister to guide her. Once at the bottom, she'd grabbed the golf club she'd hid in the umbrella holder. It was a trick she'd learned, living with that asshole. Keep weapons hidden in places only you can find them. Places he wouldn't notice.

When she got to the top of the stairs, golf club perched and ready on her shoulder, her son said, "I want to stay. I don't want to go with you."

She stormed into the room but there was nothing. Golf club still at the ready, she looked around but didn't see her son either.

"Eric," she called out. "Honey, where are you?"

"Here, Mommy," he said, poking his head up from the other side of the bed. Then he ducked his head back down and disappeared again behind the bed.

Cara put a hand to her chest and breathed. "Who were you talking to?" She looked down at the blood. This was definitely something she would have to investigate tomorrow, but Eric seemed fine and it was late. So she leaned the golf club against the wall.

"The tall lady," he said.

She shook her head, saying a silent prayer that a clean set of sheets was in the closet. She decided to indulge him. "So who is this tall lady?" she asked, opening the closet.

"The kids at school told me about her. Said she lives in this town."

She released a heavy sigh and her shoulders relaxed. So that's what all this was. The neighborhood kids had told her son all about some urban legend from the town and it had stuck in his head. "Okay, I see," she said. "Tell me about her." It was always best to let him get it out. He would tell her whatever he was afraid of, and she would explain it away.

She opened the closet. There were no sheets. That was odd. She would have sworn there were extras.

"She comes for new kids."

She fought a smile from coming to her face. *Clever bastards*, she thought. She supposed she should be mad at the kids from his school. They'd made up a story to scare her son. But she didn't have the energy right now.

She turned and, surprised, saw the extra set of sheets on the floor beside the bed. She looked at them, puzzling over how they got there. "And why do they come for the new kids?"

A voice crept up from the other side of the bed. "Because they won't be missed." It didn't sound like her son's. But when she turned her face, he was still there, staring up at her. She must be more tired than she thought.

She sat on the end of the bed and rubbed her eyes. "Do you think she's after you? Because you know I won't let anything bad happen to you." She yawned and lay back, hands behind her head, staring up at the ceiling.

A long pause hung in the air. Again, she heard the old house settle.

"But what if it already has?" Eric asked.

Cara knew what he meant. Their lives hadn't been easy up to this point. Her six-year-old grew up in a home that was unstable, loud, and violent. And now, he'd moved to a new place, been at school for only one month before it let out.

And now they had a whole summer in a place so new they had to use directions to get to town. She couldn't deny that she felt it, too—that these bad things had been piling up, weighing them down.

"Weren't you afraid of her?" she asked.

"I was," he said in his small voice, "but she told me if I didn't, she'd hurt you."

"You're very brave. I appreciate you keeping me safe," she said. Then she rolled to the side and closed her eyes. She'd started getting tired again and knew she needed to sleep if she would be able to make it through the day tomorrow. "How about you tell me what she looks like, so I know who to be on the lookout for?"

"She's *really* tall. She's wearing a black dress and her hair is really, really dark. Oh, and she has a white face."

Cara rolled to her other side and looked at her son. He sat on the floor with his hands on the bed peeking up at her. "Like she's pale?" she asked.

"No," he said, "not really. More like, well, here, come see." He pointed underneath their bed. "She's here."

He ducked again behind the bed where she couldn't see him. She climbed to her feet and moved, hesitantly, toward the spot where he lay.

When she got there, her son was gone. There was no trace of him anywhere. She looked under the bed frantically, unsure of what she would find.

But he wasn't there either.

Suddenly, all the doors in the house closed at once. Cara jumped back and slammed into the wall. Then, slowly, with a creak and moan, the door to her bedroom opened.

From downstairs, she heard Eric's voice. "Mommy." It was faint at first, like a child checking the kitchen for a mother he expected to find there. But then his voice came again, hysterical, like a child lost in the wilderness surrounded by things hoping to harm him. "Mommy!"

She sprinted down the stairs, golf club in hand, nearly falling on the bottom step. Then she stopped and called to him, listening for his reply. Her breath wheezed in and out of her while she fought back a sob. Shadows moved in every room and she eyed them carefully.

"Mommy!" Again his call came, a manic scream piercing the wooden floorboards.

The basement door opened slowly and a light flicked on. Without thinking, she bounded down the stairs and careened into the basement, golf club at the ready.

"Mommy, help!" her son cried. Cara looked but didn't see Eric.

What she *did* see froze her to the core.

In the corner of the basement, the tall lady turned. Pale, moon-white face, clothes black with dirt and grime. She gave off an ancient and moldy stench. Cara fought the urge to cover her nose. Instead, she kept both hands on the golf club. That face, porcelain white with black eyes glittering beneath wet, stringy hair. The tall lady crouched slightly, being too tall for the basement ceiling.

"He's mine." Her voice raised the hair on Cara's neck and sent goose bumps rolling down her arms.

With a fast, threatening movement, the tall lady stepped toward Cara and screamed a horrible, animalistic wail. Fear took over Cara and she stepped back, a scream escaping her chest. Then the golf club seemed to swing itself off of her shoulder and, a million miles per hour, hit the tall lady. The creature dropped to her knees. Pulling the golf club back for another hit, Cara swung again, connecting with the tall lady's face.

The golf club split in half, and she was left with a broken shaft that came to a sharp point. The tall lady wailed again and reached for Cara. This time, Cara was close enough that she could see the woman's sharp fingernails, ready to rip out her throat. Cara drove the shaft into the creature's chest.

But as soon as it penetrated her body, the lady transformed. She withered without a sound, until she was small, as small as her son... and shaped like him, too.

It was then she realized what she'd done. She reached out and grabbed the boy, falling to her knees and letting him lay in her lap, the golf club still protruding out of his chest.

At first, she tried to wake him. She shook him gently, "Wake up, honey, wake up. You're going to be alright. I'll just call an ambulance."

"I'm sorry," the voice came from the corner of the room. Then, looming and dark, a figure stepped into the light. The tall lady.

She crouched down. Her mouth, dried and cracked, moved oddly as she spoke. "You won' be callin' anyone." Her voice had no particular accent, but it sounded terribly old, like she'd lived two hundred years ago.

"What have you done?" Cara screamed, tears in her eyes and no longer afraid.

"What 'ave I done? Well, I reckon I've done nothin'."

"You made me kill him," she said, holding her son close to her.

A sound escaped the tall lady, the sort someone might make for a naïve child. "Oh, aren't you jus' the sweetest thing, thinking you just killed yer lil' boy."

"I didn't?" Cara asked, still on her knees, her son's blood on her hands.

"No, no, no, sweetie."

For a second, Cara was hopeful, feeling her heart beat in her chest with the possibilities. She wiped the tears from her eyes and looked up at the creature.

But all her hope went away when the tall lady spoke again. "He's been dead for hours. Look." The tall lady gestured to the body of her son in her hands. "You only killt him the first time. All these other times's just been 'is ghost. Surprised you din't realize. Him being so cold an' all. But off ya' go, we have more work to do. Gotta collect the whole lot of yer pain."

"What?" was all she could stammer through the tears.

"Here we are." The tall lady reached out with a talon-tipped finger. The point came to a sharp, black edge. Cara watched the lady's finger come closer and closer, but she didn't back away. Instead, she let the tall lady touch her on the forehead.

As soon as the finger made contact, Cara stood in a trance, discarding her son's body on the floor.

"So, dearie, up ye go. All the way to the top. Climb on into yer bed and sleep. And I shall see ye again in a few minutes."

With her son's blood still on her hands, Cara walked out of the basement and up to her bedroom. As soon as she climbed in bed, she awoke, reaching across the space to feel her son's warmth. But all she felt was something wet. She turned the light on, only to find that the sheets were covered in blood.

She hopped out of bed, searching the room for her son, wondering where he might be.

THE DYBBUK OF SPUTYN DUYVIL

J.S. KIERLAND

My favorite place for lunch is the zoo. A nice pea soup, a low-calorie salad, a table near the seals, and some herb tea is good enough for me. So when Selma *insisted* we meet at the Delmonico, just off Park Avenue, I got upset. There was no arguing with her. She wanted the super-deli where you gain ten pounds just reading the menu.

I got there early, grabbed a booth, and sat looking at a list of every blintz ever invented. I got down to raspberry-chocolate and felt her standing over me like a predatory bird about to strike. She heaved this long sigh, grabbed the menu right out of my hand, and said, "I'll do the ordering, Minnie."

It looked like she hadn't slept for a week. Mascara flaked down her cheeks, and her hair looked like a hamster had started living there. She had on the same green *schemata,* with the food stains. I wanted to scream, but when it's your only sister-in-law you sit there like a fool and wait for whatever comes. "Why don't we share a nice tuna salad?" I said.

"Order stuff like that in a place like this and they'll curse your family and throw you into the street," she said, lowering the monster menu. A gold tassel hung out of it like a waving tongue.

An old waiter with a combover hobbled to our table, toting an extra menu. Just so there wouldn't be any misunderstanding I came right out and asked, "Do you really want all these calories, Selma dear, or should we go somewhere less fattening?"

She didn't even look at me, and said to the waiter, "We'll split a knish."

I grunted an agreement, thinking that wasn't a bad choice. Then she looked the old guy straight in the eye and said, "One potato knish, a corn beef and pastrami on rye, extra pickles, coleslaw, side order of potato salad, and a Dr. Brown's Celery Tonic. For dessert I want *two* pieces of seven-layer cake (you can put them on the same plate) and black coffee."

I was stunned. Then the waiter looked over at me like nothing happened. "I'll have a white meat turkey on rye, Russian dressing on the side, and a cup of mint tea."

"Bring the potato knish right away," Selma added, handing the old man his three-hundred-pound menus. All of a sudden, eating with Selma felt like being strapped into one of those *machigonne* roller-coaster cars with a crazy person.

"I'm having an affair!" she said. When I didn't answer, she said it again, louder. "*I'm having an affair!*"

"I heard, I heard," I told her, glancing around to see if anyone else was interested in Selma's sex life. They weren't, but the *alter cocker* waiter was back with the potato knish, the Dr. Brown's, and my mint tea. Selma started cutting the knish before the man could even get it on the table. The stuffing oozed out as she shoved the smaller piece onto my plate.

The last thing I wanted to know was what my sister-in-law did with her spare time, but she wasn't about to leave it alone.

"Aren't you going to ask me how the affair started?" she asked, stuffing a hunk of knish into her mouth. "Go for a bus driver, maybe a dentist, but stay away from musicians."

"I'll try to remember that," I said. "I'd also like to point out that my dead brother, your loving husband, was none of the above."

"And worse," she went on, "If he's *Italian*, don't even stop to scratch."

"So now you're a love expert, Selma?"

"You think because your brother's been gone for ten years I haven't gotten laid in all that time?"

I really did think that, but mumbled something about her being a little light-headed.

"I suppose you think that water diet you talked me into is making me crazy, eh?"

"I didn't talk you into it, Selma. That water diet's the most popular thing in the whole country."

"And I'm not light-headed," she said. "I'm not light anything. I'm heavier than ever!"

"I never said you were—"

"*Feh!* But you think it. *Everybody* thinks it!"

"Selma, it's just a diet!" I said through clenched teeth. "Why do you keep saying I'm saying what I'm not saying?"

"You're *thinking* it!"

I could see the waiter shuffling towards us with our order, so I offered her a little quick philosophy. "There are certain things you should treasure and keep to yourself, darling."

"Like what?"

"Family matters, Selma. *Mishpocheh*. Private things."

"I'm in up to my *pubik* and you're giving with the social graces?" she wailed, just as the old man arrived with our food.

I thought I'd die right there in the booth, but the waiter just smiled and said, "Corned beef and pastrami, extra pickles, coleslaw, order of potato salad, and a Dr. Brown's. White breast on rye for you, my dear, with Russian on the side. Enjoy." He headed back to the kitchen.

Selma went at the corned beef and pastrami like a lion. "You wanna hear this, or what?" she asked, with a crust of rye bread sticking out of her mouth.

"Of course I want to hear," I said, but all I really wanted was to eat my turkey sandwich and listen to the Muzak.

"First time I saw this guy was at the Grand Central Oyster Bar," she told me. "He's wearing a white double-breasted suit, a black shirt, and a red silk scarf tucked in at the collar."

"It's called an ascot," I said.

"Ascot-schmascot," she yelled. "He's having clams on the half-shell and you'll never guess what he had under his arm."

"A violin?"

She stopped chewing and stared across the table at me like she couldn't believe what she'd just heard. Her eyes narrowed and her lip curled. "That's one helluva guess. You should be on a TV quiz show with a guess like that."

"You said he was a musician. He sounds dashing."

"In this town, if you're wearing a white double-breasted suit, a black shirt, and a red *ascot*, you're not dashing, you're Mafioso," she said.

"Selma, what happened in the Oyster Bar?"

"He was smiling at me over the cold fish display like he'd known me his entire life. My heart pounded like a squirrel on the run, and I could feel the sweats coming fast. I could hardly finish the clam chowder and the salty crackers."

"What about him?"

"He kept smiling at me through the pink lights while I'm paying for the soup. I'm so scared, I drop the change. Then I'm out the door and he's following me. I head for the subway and start looking for a transit cop."

"Forget about it."

"I actually found one hiding in back of a change booth. He's eating a brace of hotdogs with a *very* nice-looking relish. I tap him on the shoulder and point to the guy with the red ascot. Poof! The guy's gone. Just like that. But I tell the cop anyway so he can put it on the blotter. Make it official."

"Smart move."

"I tell him about the guy in the white suit, with the red ascot, ta-da, ta-da, ta-da. Meanwhile, this transit cop keeps eating and nodding. When I'm finished, he says, 'Lady, nobody dresses like that around here. It's against the law.' I feel like an idiot. I'm running away from some guy that looks like a movie star, and getting legal advice from a transit cop eating hotdogs. I tell the *schlumpf* to forget the whole thing because the stalker's gone," she said, pushing food in so fast I thought she'd choke.

"Thank God," was all I could squeeze in.

"Believe me, God had nothing to do with it. I get home and hear violin music coming from *inside* my apartment. I went into a panic. You live alone, you don't let *anyone* into your apartment."

"Not even the delivery boy," I said.

She gave me the thin-eyed stare again. "You wanna hear this, or what?"

"Of course I want to hear," I lied.

"I'm putting the last key into the lock when the violin music stops. You got any idea how frightening that is?"

"You should've called me," I told her. "We're family!"

"Who had time? Besides, when I open the door, the apartment is quiet like a tomb."

"It's supposed to be that way when you get home."

"I peek in. Give out with a 'Yoo-hoo, anyone there?' It's *mishegoss*. I'm standing in the hall yoo-hooing into my own apartment. Then I hear this Italian accent say, 'Come in, my darling, I've been waiting for you.' This time my heart starts beating like it belongs to a hummingbird."

"You should've called me, Selma."

"I got one foot in the door and the other foot in the hall. I don't know if this guy is a Dominican drug dealer, or the *monachem movis*!"

"Either way, you should've called."

"There wasn't time. The violin started in again."

"What was he playing?"

"A capricio. Da-da, de-da, de-da-de-dum—"

"La-la la-la de-da. I love that."

"I step inside and I'm dumbfounded. The whole place has been dusted and vacuumed, including the kitchen. Right away I figure I'm in the wrong apartment so I start backing out before anyone sees me. That's when the Italian accent says, 'Don't go, darling, I've made espresso.' And all the while he's playing this da-da, de-da, de-da-de-dum. Up and down he's sliding and plucking, and giving me that Oyster Bar smile."

"And that's when you got out of there?"

"Hell, no. I sat down on my clean couch and listened to this good-looking *gonif* play the violin. I was touched."

"He touched you?" I squealed, and got another one of those weirdo stares from her.

"He finishes playing, we drink the espresso, and he waltzes me into the bedroom."

"On the first date?"

She looks me straight in the eye, and says, "When a handsome guy cleans your apartment, makes a terrific cup of coffee, and plays a fantastic capriccio, you give a little."

"Please, Selma, you're talking to *mishpocheh* here."

"You think I'd tell this to just anyone?"

She had a point, so I asked, "What else?"

"In the bed, on the chair, against the wall. I lost count. Finally, he takes a break and goes back to playing the violin. So I staggered into the kitchen to make a little salad for two."

"And that's when he told you his name was Niccolo," I said.

She stopped in the middle of chewing and stared across the table at me. "You *know* him?"

"Slightly," I said, taking a bite out of my turkey sandwich. Not a muscle in her body moved. I gave with a big sigh, and said, "With me, he just showed up on special occasions. My birthday. Certain holidays—"

She bolted straight up in the booth, as if I'd slapped her. "MALTEDS… does *your* Niccolo drink malteds?" she asked. "My Niccolo loves malteds. Strawberry!"

"Does your Niccolo have a—" I began to stutter, trying to remember.

"A what?" she yelled, and the old waiter comes running with the black coffee and her two pieces of seven-layer cake.

"Selma, sit back," I said. "The waiter's coming—"

"Screw the waiter!"

A dead silence hit the deli. Everyone looked at the old guy as he put down the coffee, the layer cakes, and some forks. "Is that all, ladies?" he mumbled.

"Bring me an order of salami and eggs, and a toasted bialy. Cream cheese and lox on the side," she said, and this time the old man ran back to the kitchen.

"Where was I?" Selma asked, leaning over the dirty dishes.

"You were making a little salad for two."

"With leftover lettuce, a piece of challah, and a splash of Caesar that's been in my fridge since the year one."

"I hope he appreciated it."

"He cleaned the plate, I lit some candles, told him I was a Virgo, and he drags me into the bedroom again. We're on top of the bed, under the bed, on the dresser, across the floor. I got rug burns you wouldn't believe."

"Just tell me you didn't let him sleep over, Selma."

"I passed out," she said, starting to hyperventilate.

"What happened when you came out of it?"

"He was gone, I'm walking around like a cripple, and my whole apartment is dirty again."

"Selma," I said. "This guy preys on defenseless women. I know a few others that—"

"*Others*? What others? How many others?"

My mind started racing. "Lita Messer. She lives over on Kappock Street," I blurted. "She couldn't get rid of him so she introduced him to her best friend. Marion."

"Marion who?"

"Uber. From the Eastside Ubers," I said. "Married into money. Nice girl, but homely. Nobody knows how she managed to nail the Ubers. She left Spuyten Duyvil and lives in the Hudson View Gardens now and has—"

"Minnie, you're babbling!" she yelled, ramming the seven-layer cake into her mouth.

I waited for her to calm down but she kept glaring at me, so I said, "Niccolo isn't one of your average stay-at-home kind of guys. Know what I mean?"

"I can't believe this," she mumbled through a mouthful of chocolate icing.

"There are others," I said. "You want to know, or not?" She took a big swallow and gave with the nod. "Usually, Nicky goes after women that aren't getting enough action."

"You mean like you?"

"Think whatever you want, Selma, but when you go on these diets, start playing certain kinds of music, things happen. If you have to play music than play Bach or Mozart. Try Mahler, but stay away from Paganini."

"I'll kill him."

"He's just a ghost, Selma. A Dybbuk," I whispered.

"I'll kill him anyway!" she said.

I looked up and the waiter was standing over us with Selma's salami and eggs, the toasted bialy, and the cream cheese and lox on the side. He could barely fit it all on the table and when he accidentally touched what was left of Selma's seven-layer cake, she growled. The man pulled his hand away as if he'd been bitten and made a quick dash for the kitchen.

"Selma, darling," I said. "I think it'd be a good idea if you got off that water diet."

"I'm finished with all that *dreck*. Niccolo likes me just the way I am," she said, and shoveled into the salami and eggs. Then she stopped, gulped the coffee, and calmly asked, "Those other women you mentioned. Are they fat too?"

"Lita Messer isn't fat. She's an alcoholic."

She stared coldly at me and spread the cream cheese on her bialy. "And the other one? Uber. Is she a tubby?"

"She's a little *zaftig*," I said. "Trouble is, she can't stop shopping." I nibbled my turkey and watched her knock off the salami and eggs and start in on the lox.

She kept *fressing* and mumbling until I couldn't stand it anymore. I finally let out a groan and said, "Selma, you can't go on like this!"

"It's diabolic," she muttered, giving me the slits again.

"Selma, you're falling apart."

"I'm aware, Minnie," she said, and her eyes glowed. "Did you hear me use the word, Minnie?"

"I heard, Selma."

"Diabolic. How else do you get to play the violin like that?" she hissed across the table. "How else do you get to hang around and prey on innocent women? The bastard sold his soul! He's a monster!"

"But you said he cares?" I hissed back. Her eyes went wide like she was going to cry and I stopped nibbling, took a sip of the lukewarm tea, and prayed that the waiter would stay away so she wouldn't order the cherry cheesecake.

"He doesn't care about anyone but himself," she blubbered. "Now I see it. He encourages!"

"You got it," I said. "He kept Lita Messer drunk all the time. Bought her all kinds of liquor. With you it's malteds. With me it was ruggala." The tears began to stream down her cheeks and she dabbed at them with her napkin. I tried to calm her, but all I came up with was, "You think it's easy getting rid of that sonofabitch?" She stared back at me with a smirk on her face. "He's a curse!" I yelled.

Her eyes narrowed and she leaned toward me. "How did you do it, Minnie?"

"Do what?"

"Get rid of the sonofabitch!"

I looked straight back into her burning eyes and said, "You've got to *want* it, Selma."

"I want it, Minnie, I want it," she said, staring right through me like I was cellophane.

"I took away the one thing he can never do without."

"You made *him* suffer! Cut up his fancy white suit and he's finished."

"No, no! It's got nothing to do with the suit."

"The ascot!"

"You take away his Guarnieri and he turns into a *nafish*," I whispered. "The magic is gone!"

"What's a Guarnieri?"

"His violin!"

"Forget about that, it's never out of his sight."

"What about when he's bing-banging?"

She stopped chewing, and said, "You want me to grab his violin while he's *shtupping* me?"

"Not you. *I grab it!*"

"You mean, while he's... you're gonna grab his—"

"Guarnieri!"

"Wouldn't he be suspicious if we were all in the same room? Nicky and I get pretty noisy when we—"

"I'll be in the hall closet," I said.

She squinted in disbelief. I could feel her trying to back out. "How will you know when it's over?" she asked.

"All you have to do is make sure he leaves his fancy violin in the living room *before* he drags you into bed."

"That the way you did it?" she asked.

"I had to do it alone. It was terrible."

"Maybe I should just confront him with it."

"With what?"

"That if he wants to continue our relationship he can't go around screwing other women!"

"You think that's going to stop a guy like Niccolo?"

She started thinking again. "You're right," she said. "It's got to be his Guarnieri." A pained look came on her face as she clarified the plan. "You're in the closet. I make sure he leaves the violin in the living room. Then?"

"You take him into the bedroom for the last time."

She started nodding her head. A lot. Then she stopped and said, "Why don't we have something for the road while we're here? We could share some latkes, a piece of cheesecake—"

"You've got to start fighting now, Selma. Latkes and cheese cake will only work against you."

"All right, maybe just a half-order of ruggala to go?"

"Selma, you're trying to tempt me. Besides, you shouldn't have ruggala on your breath when you steal a man's Guarnieri!"

She wiped away her tears, reached over the pile of dirty dishes, and put her hand in mine. "I don't know what I'd do without you, Minnie," she said, and for the first time I felt like she meant it. We were a family again. *Mishpocheh*. Working together. Helping each other through terrible times.

The rest of the day I walked with her, talked with her, and took her to some stupid movie. All the while Selma kept repeating what she was supposed to do once we got to her apartment. It was machigonne Looney Tunes.

Finally the zero-hour arrived. We hit the building like commandos. Past the mailboxes, up the stairs, down the hall, and when we got to the door Selma started fumbling for her keys while this lilting capriccio came floating from the apartment. Then like some *yekl,* she threw herself against the door and yelled, "He's in there, waiting for me."

I grabbed her purse, took out the keys, and went at the locks. One by one they tumbled and the door wheezed open. I went straight for the hall closet, kicked a pair of galoshes out of the way, and settled in between a raincoat and a fancy fur collar jacket. Selma stood in the hallway like beef on the hoof. I had to come back out and push her towards the sound of the violin. She staggered toward it like a *golem*, and I climbed back into the closet.

It felt like I was in there for twenty years. I finally opened the door, moved down the dark hall, and slammed into the couch. Next thing I hit was the easy chair, then the TV, then the coffee table. That's when I saw Niccolo's beautiful violin lying on top of Selma's trashy magazines. I picked it up, cradled it in my arms, and accidentally struck one of the strings. The clear sound of it flew around the room. I ran down the hall, opened the door, and staggered out onto Independence Avenue, crying like a fool and running like a thief.

I hid in my apartment until I couldn't listen to another Sinatra record. It must've been two weeks before the knock came on the door. I waited. It came again. Then I hear, "I know you're in there, Minnie."

"What do you want?"

"You know what I want," he said.

"I don't have any more to give." I opened the peephole on the door. A liquid brown eye stared back at me.

"Please, Minnie, darling. I have to talk with you."

I hooked the chain across the door, grabbed the document off the counter, and opened the door just a crack.

"I've missed you," he said, pushing the door open a little more with his foot. "You've missed me too. I can tell."

"Take your foot out of the door, Nicky. We're through."

"Stealing one violin makes a statement, Minnie. Doing it twice is embarrassing."

"How did you know that I was the one—"

"As soon as I saw it missing, I knew. The others were only flings, Minnie, but you have such fire in your—"

"Enough!"

"If I had known that you were Selma's sister-in-law—"

"Go away, Nicky."

"Take the chain off and we'll have tea, darling. I brought some ruggala." He waved a pastry box so close I could smell the raspberry jam.

"Ohhhh, my God," I mumbled, trying to get my bearings.

"Please, Minnie. Open the door, you're hurting my foot."

"I'll give you back one of your violins, but you've got to sign this paper." I shoved the document through the crack. He grabbed it, pulling his foot out of the door at the same time. I watched him through the peephole.

"You even had it notarized," he said.

"Lita Messer is a notary."

"Ahhhh, Lita. Is she still drinking?"

"Sign it, Nicky!"

"You want me to leave Spuyten Duyvil? Where will I go?"

"I don't care. Try the Upper Westside or Brooklyn."

"Those territories are taken. It's getting crowded. Respighi just moved into Forest Hills."

"Not my problem. Leave us alone!"

"I can't believe you all ganged up on me like this. If I go, you'll have to give me my violins back."

"No! One violin. You come back and I'll smash the other one over your head." There was a long silence on the other side as I held back the tears.

"Do you know anyone in New Jersey that you could—"

"I'm not recommending, Nicky. Just sign it and get out."

The papers came sliding back through the crack in the door. I checked for his signature, grabbed the violin off the kitchen counter, and started shoving it through the crack in the door. It didn't fit.

"Don't break it, Minnie. Open the door," he said.

"No, no, no. Go outside, I'll throw it down to you."

"You know how much that violin is worth? It's a 1740 Cremona."

"Wait under my bedroom window," I said, slamming the door.

I grabbed the ball of used bakery string and tied the odd pieces around the violin. Nicky stood on the sidewalk three stories down, looking up at me with chocolate eyes. I lowered the violin inch by inch. It swung back and forth, spun in the air like a top, and I could hear it singing in the gentle breeze as it descended. Finally it stopped. When I looked down, he was holding it in his arms. I cut the string and watched it drift down over him. Then I shut the window, stepped back, and let the tears come.

Selma didn't call for almost a month. When she finally did, it was about meeting in our old haunt at the zoo. She was already there, hunched over her watery pea soup and tuna fish sandwich. She couldn't wait to tell me about her new diet and how she was going to lose fifteen pounds in ten days, blah, blah, blah, like nothing had happened.

When she finished her tuna fish she leaned over the graffiti-ridden table and asked, "So new?"

"So," I said with a shrug. "I made a deal." Her eyes widened. "I told him that if he didn't leave you alone I'd smash his Guarneri into little pieces and use them as tooth picks." Selma liked that. She settled back in the rickety iron chair to watch the seals catch the flying fish the children threw from the other side of the pool. Life is calmer when you don't know everything. Sometimes it's a *mitzvah* to let certain things just get dusty.

We take care of each other now. We're not living the high life, but we're not into the low life either. We're just family again. *Mishpocheh.*

THE TRAVELING SALESMAN AND THE FARMER'S DAUGHTER

STEPHEN NEWTON

He liked Morganville the moment he drove into town. Not because it was quaint, or at all attractive. Most of the buildings on Main Street were boarded up. Other than a few cars parked outside the only open restaurant, the streets were empty. Hard times were evident everywhere. Shop signs were so weathered and faded they had become unreadable hieroglyphics from better times. All of the windows of the derelict IGA grocery on the outskirts of town were broken. Despair hung over Morganville like a layer of smog. He thought it was perfect.

When he checked into the Mountaineer Motel a few miles outside the city limits, he was even more sure of his decision to spend the next few days prospecting the area. In addition to overnight rooms, the motel rented six fully furnished cabins situated respectfully apart in the pine woods, assuring guests of privacy and a pristine view of the mountains. He had his pick and chose cabin six, the most secluded, paying cash in advance for a week. He signed the register as M. Webster. When the desk clerk asked him why he was in town, he muttered, "Business."

It was one of the few rules he followed. Beyond the essential personal information one was required to provide in order to navigate the twenty-first century, he revealed little about himself. In all his years on the road, he came and went with little notice mostly because his appearance was unremarkable. He prided himself on being normal in nearly every way—another faceless road warrior among hundreds wearing wrinkle-free suits and toting sample cases. M. Webster cultivated his anonymity with discipline, like a body builder, feeding off the rush from the pursuit of total perfection.

On his second day in Morganville, he rose early, partook of the free breakfast at the motel, read the classified section of the local paper over his coffee, and then, sample case secured in the trunk of his car, drove off for a day of cold call prospecting.

Even more than the sale itself, he loved making cold calls. As was his nature, he likened prospecting to playing a lottery game of random house numbers. To win, you must play. And playing meant knocking on every door. He preferred remote, rundown farmhouses. That morning he had noticed two likely prospects in the classifieds—both family-owned farms in foreclosure forced to sell off their equipment and livestock.

The sunny fall morning suited him. He felt young and filled with energy as he drove through the open undeveloped countryside—a rare sight these days, when most of the available real estate was covered with sprawling gated communities, each one protected to the hilt by 24-hour security and "No Soliciting" signs.

His kind had become outcasts—not only were they barred from making a living, door to door sales people were denigrated as a public nuisance and often the target of crude jokes. Once the unheralded pioneer of the great consumer age, they peddled the world's goods to the doorsteps of rural families for generations. No more. His chosen vocation was already an endangered species years before online shopping changed everything, everywhere. The manageable analog world he knew and thrived in was gone. In its place, the invasive, all knowing internet, with its instant background checks, narcissistic virtual communities, and incessant demand for passwords, confounded and infuriated him. He was, without apology, a confirmed luddite. Loss of one's privacy, he believed, was too high a price for online global access. And in his precarious world, the loss of privacy came with serious consequences.

For the past year, he had been on top of his game—he was more ruthless, yes —but in every way that counted, more fulfilled. His collection of newspaper clippings about his successes had grown into quite a pile. He got a thrill out of openly reading about himself whenever he was in a crowded cafe or on the train.

Of course, it was reckless behavior, but there was a part of him longing to be recognized for his work. From time to time, his need was greater than his caution, but he only revealed his secrets to those he knew would take them to the grave.

That perfect fall morning, he felt optimistic as he drove along the quarter mile dirt road leading to the Harvey farmhouse: a faded, three-story Victorian that looked as if it had been deserted years ago. When he pulled up in front, a large black dog crawled from under the porch, stretched, and wagged its tail before wandering off. A friendly dog, he thought, as he got out of his car. Another good sign.

He removed his heavy aluminum sample case from the trunk and made his way to the front door. It promised to be a hot day. He was already perspiring, and it was just ten o'clock. After pushing it twice, he decided that the doorbell was out of order and was about to knock when the door opened to reveal a girl of about twelve. She was dressed in a white party dress and wore black leather Mary Janes with white socks. Her long black hair was tied back with a white ribbon.

He wasn't expecting a child. He said his name and proffered his business card. "Are your parents home?"

The girl peered at his card, but didn't take it. "You want to talk to Mr. and Mrs. Harvey?"

"If it's convenient," he said, beginning to feel less optimistic. "If not, I can stop by at a better time."

"They're not home," she said, sounding more adult than she looked. "If you like, you can wait in the parlor for them." She opened the door and he stepped inside. "It's the room at the end of the hall."

He hated waiting, but it would give him time to consider the best way to deal with the girl. He paused before entering the room and looked over his shoulder. She was still standing in the vestibule, her green eyes luminous in the darkness. After he dealt with the Harveys, he would have to kill her. He never left witnesses.

But when he walked into the parlor, the girl was sitting on a velvet love seat, as if she had been waiting there all along. He pretended her unexplained appearance was nothing unusual and took a seat in a straight back chair across from her, placing his sample case protectively between his knees.

"What do you have in that metal case?"

"The tools of my trade," he said, patting the case with one hand. "Where, exactly, are your parents? Will they be home soon?"

She shrugged. If she knew, she wasn't about to tell him. "I'll show you something you've never seen before, if you show me what's in your case."

He was immediately on his guard. Her explicit offer flummoxed him, while it stirred all that was unholy in him. There was something about her that was not at all childlike. He sensed danger. But what kind of danger, when he was the dangerous one? "You'll see everything when your parents arrive, and not before. I promise."

"Are you sure you want to wait, Mr. Webster?"

"For your parents?"

"No, silly." She moved over to make room for him. "Sit next to me, so you can get a good look."

Did she think he was a fool? His instincts, honed from years of survival, urged him to leave and never look back. "I have a lot of calls to make," he said, checking his wristwatch.

"Suit yourself," she said, looking disappointed.

That she didn't protest intrigued him. Perhaps he was being too paranoid. What difference did it make if he had some fun before he took care of business? The girl and her parents would not live to see the sun rise tomorrow anyway. Go with the flow, he told himself.

"Okay, young lady. You win. It's a deal."

She waited until he was seated next to her and then she removed her right shoe and sock. She lifted her bare foot so he could get a good look.

He leaned forward, not believing what he was seeing. Instead of a flat nail on her big toe, there was a long curved canine claw. He was certain it was a prosthetic, obviously some kind of joke toy, like plastic vomit. But the closer he looked, the more real it seemed.

Pleased with herself, she removed her other shoe and sock to reveal the same anomaly on her left toe. "You can touch if you like," she said, as she wiggled her toes in front of him.

Unable to resist, he touched one claw, and then another. They were authentic.

"That's not all," she said. She slipped off the loveseat and stood before him.

His heart raced with expectation as she placed her hands on his shoulders and gently pulled him closer, opening her mouth wide, to display her long canine teeth. Before he could react, she lunged forward and sank her fangs into his throat, piercing the carotid artery. He struggled, but her venomous bite paralyzed him. When he was still, she perched upon his chest like a bird of prey and tore at his throat, feasting until she was full.

The End

IN THE HOLLOW

BEKKI PATE

"I feel like I'm stepping on a town full of graves."

The sun barely shone through the empty eyes of buildings, where windows used to be. The bark of overrun trees glinted at us, almost in greeting. It was strange to hear birds chirping; because the place had such a tragic history and was now completely abandoned, it felt as though nothing should live here at all.

Anna and I and the rest of the small tour group took in our eerie surroundings. I'd seen photos, having been obsessed with the Chernobyl disaster ever since I'd heard about it, but nothing beats actually seeing it with your own eyes. Feeling the radioactive soil under your shoes, taking in the poisoned air. In some ways, it was beautiful. But mostly for me, it was a warning: how quickly it was possible to destroy our world. All it took was one mistake, and your life as you know it could grind to a halt.

Anna shivered next to me and I put my arm around her. Our tour guide was showing us some type of radioactive detector, how it flashed and screeched. He then handed them out. Others in the group began to test them, but I kept ours off. Too much noise in such a ghostly place—and I couldn't be sure what we might disturb if we were too noisy.

We followed the guide to the first place on our tour—an abandoned town. We stepped inside a school that still had desks, chairs, books, and lesson plans in the classrooms. It was a snapshot of history, an insight into the panic these people must have felt when they were told to evacuate. I watched Anna place a hand on the peeling walls.

"It's just so sad," she whispered. "Those poor people."

When we climbed back into the van, our tour guide informed us we were about to head for Pripyat. My stomach turned, a nervous knot wedging itself inside. Everyone else on the tour was quiet, solemn—all of us satisfying our morbid curiosity, but having the decency to be respectful about it. You could still feel the poignancy of this tragedy thirty-two years later. It would probably never go away. Anna leant into me as we looked out the window, watching buildings—falling apart now—come into view and disappear again. Although the buildings and streets of the area were left to crumble, trees and greenery flourished. Birds, foxes, and other wildlife were known to roam the area, seemingly unaffected by the high levels of radiation. It was fascinating.

Pripyat was depressing. It could have been so much more, given the chance. When we made our way past the amusement park, Anna gasped, tears forming in her eyes. The famous Ferris wheel loomed above us, haunting, ghostly. Everything had been left to rot.

Our last stop before returning to Kiev was the power plant itself. When we booked the tour, I was surprised that they'd open certain parts of it to the public, especially because we could only be in there a short amount of time before it became dangerous.

The driver pulled up and once again we all got out of the van. The building was grey against the bleak sky. The tour guide handed out bags containing protective gear, which everyone took gratefully. There were gloves and masks inside, as well as white protective suits, like an all-in-one raincoat. Behind us, the forest loomed. The trees stood tall and proud, as if to say: *we survived.*

I took Anna by the arm. "It's here. We should go now." I gestured to the trees.

She looked at me. I knew she was scared, but we hadn't come all the way here just to go on a tour.

"You sure?" she whispered. "Here?"

"Yes." We stood at the back of the crowd, and when everyone was preoccupied with putting on their protective clothing and listening to the tour guide's spiel about the new safe confinement, Anna and I slipped away into the forest.

I was almost certain that the tour guide had spotted us disappearing into the trees, but there were no shouts or yells for us to return to the group. The forest surrounded us. I looked around again, and when I saw that we were completely covered by the dense trees, I pulled out my camcorder and pressed *record.* I turned the camera to face myself.

"So, hi, everyone. This is Jake from TerrorFiles, and as always the lovely Anna White is here with me." I turned the camera to Anna and she curtsied. "We are finally in the exclusion zone, right near the power plant at Chernobyl. I have to tell you, it's fucking freaky being here. Eerie. As you can see..." I panned the camera around the forest. "We've managed to get into the forest. We've got our radiation detectors with us and our protective clothing. Anyone who is new to TerrorFiles, please check out the YouTube channel. There you can find other videos of us investigating rumors of all sorts of nasties. So, let's get to business."

Anna and I put on the clothing provided by the tour guide. We then walked deeper into the forest, and I narrated our journey.

"Some of you are already aware that we're here to check out the fabled creature of the hollow. *What the hell is the creature of the hollow?* you're asking. Well, boys and girls, let me tell you. You won't find this in any history book. The official explanation of the Chernobyl disaster is that on 26th April 1986, a routine simulation went wrong and a containment coolant system failed, rendering the uranium core radioactively unstable, causing a meltdown, deaths, cancer, and the evacuation of tens of thousands of people. We all know this.

"But there's a theory—one we're here to explore today—about a creature that the Ukrainian government used to fuel the power plants. This creature had a very high natural level of radiation. So they captured it and abused it. But somehow it escaped, and sought its revenge on the people who had kept it prisoner there, causing the meltdown. It is now thought to be hibernating in the red forest, its natural home for however many years. Some think the creature sleeps in one of the caves, or hollows, located in the area. Some think that the creature has since died. But considering the radiation levels around here, that may not be likely. Although high, the levels don't come close to what they would have been for the creature to have powered the nuclear plants in the first place.

"So where is the creature now? What does it look like? It is dangerous, or simply misunderstood? We're here to find out, guys. I hope we can give you all an answer, once and for all."

I stopped recording and turned the camera off to save the battery.

"Sheesh, Jake," Anna said. "Lay it on thick why don't you? *Once and for all?* Seriously?"

"I'm building tension," I replied. "They need all the facts before we discover anything new."

"There are no *facts*," Anna said. "Just theories."

"Okay, so let's look at the evidence," I said. We'd been over this multiple times, but it felt good to get it all straight in our heads. "The first piece of evidence is an actual photograph of inside the plant, before the accident. You can quite clearly see something non-human in the photo." I'd printed off all the evidence I'd had on file before we came on our trip, in case we needed to cross-check anything or provide live evidence to our viewers. All this evidence was already up on my website, but it felt good to carry hard-copies in my backpack. I pulled out a printout of the photo. It was a black and white of three men in uniforms, their features barely distinguishable due to the graininess of the photo. One of them had a clipboard in his hands. The other two were checking measurements and vitals of something that looked like an elongated skeleton. It was naked, around eight or nine feet tall. Its eyes were black, empty, face pinched and so taut that it resembled a skull. Its arms and legs were shackled to the wall. It looked scared.

"That's obviously a fake," Anna said. "Why would someone randomly post it online? You can't trace where it came from, or even who these men were."

"But…"

"Also, being that close to the creature would have killed them. *No one* would take a job like that."

"Maybe they figured a way to protect themselves. Or maybe they could concentrate the radiation levels to only be used for the nuclear plant, or something."

"Radiation doesn't work like that."

"Oh, I'm so sorry, Anna. I forgot that you have a degree in nuclear physics and technology."

She threw me a withering look.

"Plus, there's other evidence. Eyewitness accounts of people seeing the creature all over the area after the accident. Some photos of it, too."

I pulled one out. A color photo of a man standing at the edge of the red forest, smiling at the camera. In the background, a large, thin shape was visible, black eyes peeking out from behind a tree.

"Could be a bunch of twigs," Anna scoffed.

"Well when we find it, then you can tell me it's just a bunch of twigs."

"Wait."

"Don't grab me like that!"

"Shh!"

We both froze. I pulled my camera out and clicked it on. We heard a twig snap not too far from us, then another.

Someone was walking around just a few feet from us.

"Oh, shit, shit, shit," I whispered.

"Shut the fuck up."

The snapping twigs were now accompanied by a snuffling sound. Then we saw movement. My hands shook as I tried to keep the camera steady. Something was rustling in the bushes, something we couldn't see.

Anna put her hand to her mouth as the thing in the bushes came out of hiding. It was a fox. Small, skinny, almost the same color as the forest floor.

"Jesus Christ," I said. I followed the fox with the camera, and it walked straight past us, nuzzling the ground, before walking back to the forest.

"There we are, guys," I said. "A Chernobyl fox. Seems fine. No mutations. Looks all right. Okay, moving on."

We traipsed through the forest. I was thankful for the daylight, no matter how weak it was.

It wasn't long before we came across a sign, in Ukrainian, scratched into a tree.

"Look at that," Anna said. "Now *that's* creepy."

"Here, we've found some sort of carving or etching. Anna, would you translate that for us, please?"

"On it." Anna flipped out her phone, and began typing the letters into her translation app. "I can't read some of it, but it looks like a warning."

She pointed to each word for the camera as I filmed. "This word is definitely *stop*. Then the next part I can't make out. Then *beware* and *monster.* Sounds promising, right?"

"People must have come here before to try and locate the creature," I said to the faceless masses who would no doubt watch my video when I'd uploaded it to my channel. "I wonder what they found, what happened to them."

We carried on walking and found another sign on a tree, the same words. After that, the carvings turned into symbols.

They were scratched into the surface of the trees in an urgent, messy way, as if the writer was in a rush.

"Maybe a warning?" Anna offered.

"A warning!" I said to the camera. "Could it be the creature? Something else? Let's keep going."

Anna rolled her eyes at me again. I knew what she was thinking—*ham it up for the audience why don't you, Jake?* But that was the whole point.

After walking for another fifteen minutes, the trees and bushes around us began to look a bit dry, as though they weren't getting enough water. A little bit further in and the trees were bare, like in winter, stripped of all leaves and color. Carcasses of dead animals littered the floor, some of them half-eaten, some of them skeletons.

"Shit, I bet a bear lives around here," Anna said. "We need to be careful. If it sees us, it'll kill us for sure. I'm not dying out here in the wilderness."

For the first time, I felt nervous. But I couldn't let my viewers down. I couldn't come across like a wimp.

But was that worth dying for?

In a crazy flash of realization, I knew that it was. I would die for my fans, leave a legacy. I would be famous for something. I'd have millions of hits on my videos. I'd do it, if it meant everlasting fame.

The air suddenly changed. It became colder. There was a strange smell and I could spot a distinct line on the forest floor past which everything was dead. Trees, plants, grass. All dead. Withered. And in front of us was a clearing. A clearing of dead leaves. And in the middle of that clearing was an enormous, dead tree. It was little more than a husk, a shell.

"The hollow," Anna whispered. "The hollow is a dead tree."

"And the creature…"

We both saw movement in the darkness of the tree, something shifting, turning. Two black eyes opened and blinked at us.

My stomach dropped, and I almost let go of my bladder. My camera shook as I tried to keep filming. For my audience. For my fans.

"You two! I *knew* you'd be here!"

We whirled around. Anna actually screamed. Running after us, sweaty, his eyes flaming with rage, was our tour guide.

"Shit," Anna gasped.

"What do you think you're doing?!" he yelled. "Put that camera away!"

"No way," I said. "The public deserves to know the truth."

Rather than tackling us to the ground, as I expected, the tour guide ran straight past and up to the hollow tree. He stooped down against the opening and reached out his hand. "There, there, it's all right," he said. I kept filming, and when the creature's head came tentatively out of the hollow, I swallowed down a scream.

Its skin was white and stretched, eyes were black, nose nothing more than two holes in its face. It was spindly; the bones of its elbows and shoulders jutted out. Its teeth were razor-sharp. But it was docile; it let the tour guide pat its head and stroke its chin.

"Why can't you bloody tourists leave him be?" the tour guide asked. "He's never done anything to you. He was mistreated, that's all. Misunderstood."

"The public deserves to know the truth," I repeated. "We deserve to know the true cause of the meltdown."

"The true cause?" the tour guide seethed. "It was you. Your greed. Using this poor thing to fund your nuclear plants."

"But he's dangerous!" I yelled. I tried to keep the shake out of my voice, but couldn't. *Keep calm. Think about your fans. Think about your reputation.*

"No," he replied. "He's not. What's dangerous is greed. The selfishness, exploitative greed of rich people, wanting more and more. It was the best thing we ever did, releasing this creature from his prison."

"*You* released him? *You* caused the deaths of all those people?" Anna said. "You should be locked up!"

"Me and my colleagues, yes," he replied. "Years of watching him suffer, of them wanting more and more from him. They've burnt him out. His natural power is now gone. All that's left is what remains in the area. And that too will eventually vanish."

The creature closed its eyes and made a sick purring noise as the tour guide stroked its head.

Before I could reach out to stop him, the tour guide stood up quicker than I've ever seen anybody move, and threw something at Anna. It glinted in the sunlight before it lodged itself into her gut. She fell back and clutched her stomach. I saw it sticking out. A hunting knife.

"Anna!" I screamed, but before I could go to her aid, a sharp, blinding pain hit my side, slicing into my flesh. I went down, dropping my camera.

The tour guide pulled Anna closer to the creature. It sniffed the blood on her.

"No! You get away!" I yelled, and I tried to stand up. I fell back down into the blood-soaked dead grass as my blood pressure dropped, and tried to scramble towards them on my hands and knees. But the tour guide pulled the knife out of Anna's stomach and stabbed her again. Instead of a scream, Anna let out a whimper of agony.

"No!" *Anna*. My partner in crime, my best friend. She was too weak to react when the creature bit into her neck. A wet smack of flesh coming away from bone made me vomit.

That's it. We're dead. But I'll drag that bastard down with me.

I reached for my camcorder, lying on its side on the grass. With shaking fingers, I uploaded what I'd captured so far onto my phone. I then posted it as quickly as I could. No hashtags, no nothing. Just the video. Then I set my phone to livestream and positioned it against a dead bush, angling it to capture what was happening to Anna. The tour guide looked over at me, then stormed across to pick up my camcorder. He hadn't noticed my phone. He smashed the camcorder to bits before grabbing my legs and pulling me towards the creature.

I looked up at its black eyes. It sniffed my face, Anna's blood smearing against my cheek. Then it bit into my neck.

The pain was all-consuming. I felt the life spilling out of me with every beat of my heart. Blood streamed in massive gushes. I kept my eyes trained on Anna's beautiful face. She stared back at me. I could just about reach her cold hand.

The creature bit down again. Suddenly, I felt far away. So did the pain. I closed my eyes and smiled.

We did it, Anna. We found the creature.

Think of all those hits—we'll be famous.

GRANT

SAM HAYSOM

Back when I was in primary school, we had a teacher that everyone hated. Mr. Handscombe, his name was. He taught English.

Mr. Handscombe was probably about five foot five, with a ratty face and thick glasses. Fat little pot belly. Losing his hair on top. Pretty much every genetic disadvantage you could think of, all rolled into one arsehole.

Fuck, I hated him. I don't know if the power of being taller than thirty other human beings in one classroom went to the guy's head, but he treated us more like we were prisoners than his English students.

He yelled and screamed at kids. He humiliated them. He'd put you in detention for anything he could think of. He was a nasty, nasty piece of work.

He had his favorites, too. Not kids he liked, but kids he particularly liked to pick on. There was an overweight boy called John Pickard, for instance, and every time Handscombe took the register he'd call him "Pig-arse" and act like it was all a big mistake. Always made him read the part of Piggy when we studied *Lord of the Flies*. Then there was a girl called Mary Richards, who had a lisp. Whenever there were no volunteers to read out loud, he'd make Mary do it every time.

But the kid he loved picking on most of all was Grant.

Grant was a new kid who joined us at the start of Year 6. Mum told me he was a traveler, which meant he moved to lots of different places and lived in a caravan. Other kids at school had different names for him, but they'd never have said them to Grant's face. The kid was about a head taller than the rest of us, for one. Big boned and broad. He had this steely, don't-fuck-with-me look about him that meant the other kids left him well alone.

It didn't stop Mr. Handscombe, though. Not one bit. I don't know whether it was because Grant was almost as tall as he was, or because Grant's family were travelers, but Handscombe had him marked from day one. He hated Grant. You could just hear it in his voice, every time he spoke to him. He did not like the kid one bit.

Mr. Handscombe alternated between telling Grant off in front of everyone— this could be for literally anything, like sneezing while Handscombe was talking or having his shirt untucked—and trying his best to embarrass the kid. The first week he had Grant come up to the front of the class, then he berated him for ten minutes because his shoes weren't properly polished.

Another time, he told us we were going to practice synonyms, then wrote the word DIFFERENT in the middle of the blackboard. We had to take turns going up and writing words around it that meant something similar.

When we were done, Mr. Handscombe gave a thin smile.

"Now, we need someone well-versed in this subject to volunteer to read all these words out loud to the class," he said. "How about… you, Grant?"

I think he'd been expecting Grant to be a slow reader, but he was wrong. The kid might've looked like a thug, but boy, could he read. He rattled through those words with no problems at all, never giving any hint that the subject matter affected him. I could see Handscombe's smile slowly turning to a scowl the longer it went on.

Things carried on in the same vein for most of the autumn term. Handscombe needling, and Grant putting up with it as best he could. Then, come October, we had a special assignment. One for Halloween. The idea was to go away and write a scary story, so we could take turns reading them out loud in class on October 31st.

I don't remember many of the stories the other kids told that day. I barely even remember my own. I think it was something pretty generic about a monster in the cupboard of my room. But I remember Grant's. Even all these years later, I still remember it. The story Grant told was sort of a folk tale, and it had me hooked from the moment he began.

Here it is, in Grant's words, as best as I can remember it:

Once upon a time, there was a family of witches who lived in a cave. The witches kept to themselves, and most of the people and creatures in the nearby village left them well alone. But there was one exception.

A large, ugly troll terrorized the woods surrounding the village. The troll was eight feet tall, with a big green belly the size of a boulder. Hideous red boils and warts covered his face. He ate anything that was foolish enough to get in his way.

Now the troll thought he owned the woods, and he didn't like the fact the witches were living in a cave so close to them. He didn't like it at all.

But there wasn't much he could do about it. Whenever he'd see the witches, he'd give chase, but they'd always run back into the safety of their cave. They'd crawl back into the darkness between the rocks, and the troll was too big to follow them.

He'd stand at the mouth of the cave, and he'd bellow the same thing each day:

"Witches, hiding in the cracks,
Leave this land and don't come back!
If you refuse and choose to stay,
Know that I will make you pay."

Now, the witches were afraid of the troll—everyone was—but they didn't have anywhere else to go. So for a long time, they survived as best they could. They'd sneak out of the cave to get food, and to fetch the items they used to brew their spells, whenever the troll was out of sight. And whenever they saw him, they'd run back into the darkness.

The troll was never smart enough to catch them, and he got angrier and angrier. Soon, he started killing animals and leaving them to rot in the mouth of the cave. Badgers, foxes, birds—one day he even caught a child from the nearby village and left his tiny, broken body in the cave's entrance.

When the witches came out the next day and saw this, they were horrified. But they also spotted something else; something the troll would never have noticed. Stuck amongst the blood and broken remains of the child's body was one thick, black hair. A hair from the head of the troll. And when the witches saw this, they finally knew what to do.

They took the hair, and they gathered up some twigs from the forest, and they wove it all together into a miniature wooden doll. They made it tall and fat and ugly, so it looked as much like the troll as possible. Then they gathered around it in a circle to cast their spell.

And when they were finished with their magic? They got the doll and took turns sticking pins in it. Pin after pin after pin. By the time they were finished the thing had over one hundred sharp sticks of metal peppering its wooden body.

The next day, there was no dead animal outside their cave. There was no sign of the troll at all. The witches went looking for it in the forest, and soon enough they found some black troll's blood staining some ferns by the river. They followed the trail. The blood got thicker the further along they went, and the stains grew more and more frequent. Fresher.

Finally, in a clearing not far from the village, they found the troll itself. It was slumped in the shade of a giant oak tree, eyes closed. Pulling in shallow breath after shallow breath. And it was bleeding from a hundred tiny mouths that had been carved into its green flesh, its black blood leaching from it in the most slow and painful way imaginable—

I remember Mr. Handscombe stopping the story at this point.

He had a familiar scowl on his face as he gestured for the class to be silent. You could tell everyone had been into the story, because a bunch of kids groaned when Handscombe put a stop to it.

"Yes, yes, okay," he said, holding his hands up for quiet. "I think we've heard enough, Grant. That was… predictably unpleasant. I suppose you can take the boy out of the caravan, but you can never quite take the caravan out of the boy."

That wasn't the last day I saw Grant, but it must have been close; he left our school a couple of weeks later. Family moved away. I heard they went further south, but no one really knew for sure. All we knew was that one day Grant was in lessons, and the next his chair was empty. Gone, just like that.

And a few days later, so was Mr. Handscombe.

It started when a supply teacher appeared one morning to take his English class. We didn't think much of it at the time—just assumed he was sick or something. That was until we saw the front page of the next day's newspaper.

We never found out all the details. There was a talk from the headmaster and whispers in the playground, sure—but mainly just a lot of rumors. No one knew quite what to believe.

The one thing everyone could agree on was that Mr. Handscombe had been murdered. The police had no leads. And the details of his death were apparently too grim for the paper to print.

I don't know what it was that drove me to go looking for the spot where Grant's family had been camping.

Simple curiosity, perhaps. Maybe the fact I couldn't quite shake the memory of the story he'd told. Whatever it was, I spent the weeks after Handscombe's murder riding my bike around the local countryside after school and at weekends. Trying to track down their old campsite.

And eventually, I found it.

It was a man who worked in a newsagent on the edge of a nearby village that gave me the tip. Pointed me in the direction of some fields alongside a forest. Said the travelers had been staying somewhere over that way.

It didn't take me long to find the right field after that.

It was close to the edge of the woods, not that far from a river. Reminded me a bit of the setting in the story Grant had told. Just swap the cave for a field. I set my bike down and began looking around.

Grant's family has been gone a few weeks by then, but the signs were still there. Flattened patches of grass. A couple of rusted metal chairs. Cigarette butts. And, in what I guess must have been the middle of their campsite, a stone circle.

I don't know why, but I had a funny feeling in my stomach as I approached that circle. Butterflies, I suppose. Maybe a little fear.

The stone circle was empty but for one thing in the middle. A tiny shape, propped up against a rock. I think my mind knew what I was going to see a second before I got close enough to make it out in detail. I drew in a sharp breath.

The object leaning against the rock was a doll.

Wooden, painted. Carved out of some nearby tree, was my guess. The doll was small, but it had been decorated with careful detail. A little potbelly. Thinning hair. I recognized Mr. Handscombe almost immediately.

There was only one thing different—only one thing that separated the likeness of the doll from the image of Mr. Handscombe that had appeared in the local paper. Something subtly wrong with the face.

I leaned closer to get a better look, and felt a wave of nausea roll through my stomach.

Both the doll's eyes had been gouged out.

ARACHNE

N. M. BROWN

My feet leave the warm pocket of the comforter and meet the cold floor tiles. My body shivers in response. The ever increasing need to pee intensifies with each freezing step. I make it in time but forget to brace myself for the temperature of the plastic toilet seat. All I want is to return to the warmth of my bed.

The covers are pulled up to my chin as I shimmy back into the groove I'd created in my mattress from years of side sleeping. My teeth fight not to chatter as my head wiggles into my firmest pillow. My mind starts to float, along with my eyelids.

Then, out of the farthest reaches of my periphery I see movement. It's subtle at first, only a hint of shadow at the top corner of my wall. Sadly, years of living in the woods have taught me to identify shadows. This one was undeniably a spider.

With the slightest of movements, I reach to my bedside table for my television remote. The light of the screen illuminates my room enough for me to see my invader. This bastard is easily bigger than my hand. I'm not talking about one of those spiders with a tiny body and a huge leg-span. Its body was easily noticeable, along with the eyes... so many eyes.

My heart is pounding like horseshoes on a track at a race. If I hadn't just gotten back from the bathroom, I'm sure I'd have pissed myself. Tears sting the corners of my eyes like needles as I try to swallow against an invisible hand clutching my throat.

It's just the baby and I in the room. His crib is right against the wall that the spider's on. My husband won't be home for hours yet. I don't know how long I can keep my eyes on it before the baby wakes up from the light.

The creature and I are locked in a stare down, each waiting for the other to make the first move. There's no way I am willing to get close enough to this thing to kill it. At the same time, though, I should at least take the baby out of the room. I'll put him in his playpen in the living room until someone can produce a dead spider. Which means I'll have to take my eyes off its location.

I scoop up Dean and rush him out to his playpen. I grab a work boot and broom on the way back to my room and say a silent prayer before heading back into the battle zone.

The spider is still on the wall, about five inches lower than it was when I left the room. The crib agonizingly groans against the tiles as I slide it out of my way. There's nothing between us now, no stack of crafted wood to protect me from the path of this thing.

The broom is raised high with bated breath. A shoe fatally balances on the end of it. I'm about one foot away from hitting it when it skitters off to the left, barely out of reach. A piglet's squeal of a scream escapes from my throat. Who knows where this would have ended up if I hadn't woken up?!? Images of my three-month-old choking to death with spider legs flailing from his gagging mouth haunt my mind.

Once again, I'm about a foot away from smashing it when it moves. But this time, it *jumps*. The black mass of hairy legs and bright eyes sails towards my face. My body leans back just in time for it to miss its intended target, landing next to my left foot instead.

I take the boot off the of broomstick and bring it down as hard as I can with a banshee's wail of vindication. The invader falls limp and starts to curl its legs inward in a slow dance of death. I'm mainly relieved it didn't get stuck to the boot.

I am... horrified to see it twitch and jerk with movement. I lean down to look closer. Just as my face nears, its body bursts with life. What looked to be hundreds of the tiniest pinpricks erupt from its shredded cephalothorax.

My feet perform an uncoordinated tap dance in attempt to halt the miniscule spiders from spreading. I don't even want to imagine all the nooks and crannies they could make a new home out of. You hear about this type of thing often; you kill a pregnant mother spider and unintentionally release her babies. To me, though, it was only an urban legend until today. People hear stories of horrifying situations but never think it's going to happen to them.

Sleep doesn't come easily. My hands swat around my face due to nightmares of tiny spiders consuming my body. I'm pretty sure I even landed a few light blows on Grant's face during my most fitful periods. Sleep most likely hadn't come easily for my poor husband either. He didn't have to see that *thing* though. It literally stared me down, then leapt for my jugular. Whoever coined the phrase, *"it's more afraid of you than you are of it"* didn't see this eight-legged beast.

When I awake in the morning, Dean is gone. Laying in his crib is a doll, roughly the same size and shape, but with no face. The doll's fabric chest rises and falls as if its breathing. Tiny legs poke through various holes throughout its form. A living spider doll.

There's no time to worry about that now. I'll burn the crib after I find my son. I hear a skittering of legs from the living room. I just barely catch the figure out of the corner of my eye as it attempts to leave through the back door. I scream as I try to behold the living nightmare that is before my eyes.

A woman over eight feet tall is trying to leave with my baby. Only... she isn't a woman at all. Her hair is long and black, with winding tendrils that reach her waist. The... creature was bare breasted, and her lower half wasn't human. Not at all.

Tiny, barbed hairs cover every other inch of her lower half. Four sharpened legs support her black, bulbous frame on each side. All eight legs move in tandem effortlessly in a way that's horrifyingly mesmerizing. Dean's strapped to her chest in a woven sling of webbing, tightly nestled and sleeping.

Before I can reach her to attack, she unleashes a torrent of interwoven silk webbing. On her way out the door, she shouts something to me that I didn't recognize. Then they are gone, her legs carrying them faster than any human force could possibly match.

The police believe me when I say that someone took Dean. They don't question my grief or my assurances that I had nothing to do with his disappearance. What they don't believe is that he was taken by an eight-foot-tall evil spider queen. Even after finding traces of webbing all over the living room area of our home. Even after bagging the 'spider crib doll' for evidence.

The words the creature spoke haunt me for weeks. I become obsessed with learning all I can about them. I need to know what they meant. What she said to me. Maybe her words contain the key to getting my baby back.

The queen, I soon discover, spoke to me in Greek. When I finally learn the meaning of those words she spat at me as she took my baby out the door, I am horrified. They do not hold the hope I am looking for.

Πάρε το μωρό μου—*You take my babies, I take yours.*

IT LIVES IN THE MINESHAFT

E. SENECA

The people were beginning to come back. Human memory was short, Nan presumed. Twenty years was not, in the grand scheme of things, a long time, but rather, just long enough to forget.

She stood by the window and watched the smoke drifting into the air from the chimneys of the town, and even so far away, she could feel the occasional rumble passing through the ground from the excavators and the thud of beams and bricks settling into place. Although nobody had come this way yet, she knew it was only a matter of time, and then they would rediscover the mine shaft, and then... she exhaled slowly, trying to contain the instinctive tightening in her stomach. It would be fine. It had been fine for twenty years; she'd just continue making sure that things were fine.

And she couldn't stand there and keep watching for very much longer; it was almost lunchtime, and he was waiting. Nan turned away from the window just as her timer dinged, but the sense of foreboding remained as she pulled the pie from the oven and carefully placed it in the basket. She only hoped that nobody would come by while she was gone, as it was a bit of a walk until she reached the shaft. It didn't help that her joints were aching today, and the going would be slow.

She locked the door and set out, and after all these years, the path to the mine was clear, worn into the grass from daily footsteps. It wound deep, deep into the woods, where the felled trees and stumps had long since rotted away and new saplings had taken their place. Once, she had worried about animals lurking, but these woods were forever silent; the only sound as she walked, leaning on a trunk here and there, was that of her steps crunching on the grass. Not even the call of a bird broke the quiet, much less any stray wildlife. They had all learned, long ago, not to come here.

One thing that time had not changed, however, was the oppressive air. It was as heavy as it had ever been, as if weighed down by dust or moisture, an invisible miasma hanging from the trees that had never been dispelled even with all the new growth. Indeed, she didn't think it would ever be dispelled, not until death came over the valley. But she was sure that it would be a long time coming.

She walked on, heading ever downward, down and deeper into the forest, where the stunted trees grew tangled together and blocked out the light, until she reached a rocky clearing set into the side of the hill. Rusting tracks ran out of the mine's entrance, vanishing beneath the loose soil of the woods and deep into the darkness of the shaft. That darkness, too, was something that never changed, but remained forever thick and impenetrable despite the unimpeded sunlight blazing into the clearing.

The little structure beside the entrance had long since all but crumbled away under the elements, but a small, rusted roof remained, and within its dilapidated confines was an ancient chair, waiting for her. Nan approached the entrance to the mine and took out the pie, casting uneasy glances into the dark. There was a small ledge inside the cavernous entrance, and beyond, a straight vertical drop into what could have been only the void, for how intense and consuming the darkness was. She set the pie down, whisked off the cover, then tossed a pebble down the shaft and retreated into the shelter of the cabin and the embrace of the chair, where she had a clear view of the entrance.

She settled in for a wait, as this could take anywhere from five minutes to an hour.

But eventually, he came. He always did.

The darkness of the mouth moved, as if the darkness itself had come to life. Through the ancient walls of the cabin, she could hear the faintest scraping sound, nails rasping against rock. Sunlight broke through the cover of the trees, pushing forward just far enough to cast a beam into the entrance of the shaft.

For an instant, she caught a glimpse of his head, disfigured and deformed as the light passed over it, glinting off his eyes. Then he ducked back into the cover of twilight as if the exposure hurt him, and the rapid, savage clicking of teeth on glass was just barely audible.

As she watched, Nan wondered if he could taste it, if he knew what it was, if he remembered the flavor. At this point, she didn't believe it was possible, but she couldn't help but wonder.

The moment he finished, he dove back into the shaft, in the process knocking the dish off the ledge. With creaking bones, she pushed herself up, staggering out of the cabin and shuffling to the mine's entrance. It hurt to bend over and pick up the dish, but that pain meant little when she saw how it had been licked clean, and despite its numerous chips, it was still intact and bore no fatal cracks. She ran her fingers over the roughened rim for a moment, then turned and began the trudge home.

July 15th. That had been the day. Nan laid out the newspaper on the table, and although yellowed with age, she had kept it so carefully preserved that the front-page article was still clearly readable. Beside it, she had the latest paper detailing the renewed development of the valley. Having them side by side like that was surreal: on one side she had the cheerful story of the demolition and construction and all the opportunities; on the other, enormous letters screaming the utter catastrophe that had befallen the town, accompanied by black and white photographs of the hideous destruction. It was strange how memory was: she'd seen the scenes of the pictures with her own two eyes, but by now they had gone soft and foggy at the edges in her mind.

But even so, the photographs didn't do it justice. They didn't capture the parts that she'd never forget: the vivid orange of the snarling flames billowing from the mouth of the shaft; the pitch blackness of the spiraling clouds of smoke darkening the sky and the gray haze that had hung over the valley for months; the red of the bloodstained corpses they had managed to salvage from the wreckage, torn to pieces by the explosion. These were the things that nobody recorded or remembered, along with the names and faces of those who were gone and would never return.

Slowly she flipped through the paper from a few days' prior. It seemed the new town would be given a new name, as the old one had also been lost to time. So far, little mention was made of their intention to demolish the forest, but she knew it was only a matter of time. The trees would be torn down, and eventually, they would come upon the mine. And then... what then? She leaned heavily on the table, listening to the ticking of the clock filling the room. Soon it would be time to begin the lunchtime preparations and pay another visit.

For a moment, she thought about leaving the pie out in the middle of the gravel clearing and waiting there out in the open—but she knew that he wouldn't come out so long as she was there, she'd tried that before. The prospect of communicating with him, talking to him was slim, much less warning him or trying to get him to move away, if he could even comprehend her words at this point. The mine was his home now, and had been for twenty years, and this empty, dreary valley was hers—where could they possibly go? Where else could they possibly hide? There was nowhere nearby to escape where they could make it on foot during the cover of night; outside the valley, they'd be immediately spotted. That plan just wasn't viable.

But, well, of what interest would an old, abandoned mine shaft be to anyone? Even if they flattened the forest, the ground out here was unstable, unsuitable for building anything. The wreckage, abandoned in the wake of the accident, would have to be cleaned up from where it had settled into the environment. Maybe—maybe even the area was unsafe to be in: she'd certainly noticed the strange, fine dust that gathered on the windowsills and the plants following the accident, and the dark, warped colors that had stained the new grass around the entrance. Maybe they would notice that as soon as they arrived, and then maybe nothing would have to change. After all, they'd only just begun development. There was still time.

There was no reason to panic just yet.

The sound of voices outside the cottage made Nan's blood turn to ice. She hadn't heard voices outside for a long, long time—and it was early still, no later than eight o'clock, what was anyone doing here at this hour? She jolted out of bed and jerked the curtain aside, and her concern was only slightly alleviated by the fact that it was only a pair of children. They must've come out all this way to explore, or some other such childish motive. Well, she wasn't going to stand for that. This was no place to play.

She threw on a housecoat and tottered to the door as quickly as she could, her joints savagely protesting the sudden movement. The pain was particularly intense on her left side, stabbing viciously at her knees and her ankles and making her stumble against the door frame. Why was it always the left side when this sort of thing happened? She didn't have *time* for this! Ignoring the numbness of her left hand, she threw the door open with her right, staggering out into the blinding sunlight.

Immediately she spotted them, a few feet away from the walls. Her first instinct was to be at least a little polite, but the pain stole the words from her throat. At the sound of the door opening, they jumped and whirled, staring at her with blatant fear in their eyes, and she stared back, aware that she had to look like a complete madwoman with the way she was clutching the edge and breathing hard, but somehow she couldn't bring herself to care if she looked wild. No, if anything, that was *good*, it would scare them off if they believed for some reason that a crazy witch lived out in the middle of the woods.

"What are you doing out here?" she said curtly. "This isn't the place for children to be without supervision."

The older of the two boys glared at her, although he was pale. "We lost our ball. We're—we were just leaving."

"Then leave. It's dangerous here. This isn't a place to play, the woods aren't safe." She only just bit back a warning not to come back, taking a deep breath and pushing down her panic. "Be careful on your way home."

They didn't say anything, only hurriedly took the thin path leading back to the town between the trees. She watched them go, leaning heavily against the door, and she didn't go back inside until they were well and truly out of sight. Despite the fact that she must've waited at least fifteen minutes, the numbness in her leg did not fully disappear.

One by one, the trees at the far end of the valley were being felled. A cloud of dust hung over the forest, much as it had for the past few days. The boys, mercifully, had not come back, and neither had anyone else in the following weeks. But the march of progress had not halted. They were coming, they would get here eventually.

The ache in her knee had not gone away. If anything, it had only worsened, and the grip in her left hand had also weakened. Even as she limped into the depths of the silent woods towards the mine, dragging herself along step by step, resting the dish on her hip where her hand didn't shake, she could see it, and she could smell the sawdust where it carried on the wind, mingling with the scent of smoke, now ever-persistent, just like it had been for months following the explosion.

It was all so reminiscent of the initial event that she could scarcely stand it. She could hardly bear to draw the curtains aside, and it was only because this was her sacred duty that she had forced herself out. Nan hobbled onward, pain shooting down her rib cage and behind her watering left eye, her right fingers curled tight around the bottom of the dish as she leaned her left arm on the trees. It wasn't that much further, she told herself, gritting her teeth as she went. Just down the slope, she just had to be careful not to trip, just go carefully and easy, slowly. *Slowly.*

Her foot caught, and she hastily grabbed onto the nearest branch, stopping to catch her breath. It was fine, she would be fine. Just a moment, that was all she needed. She sucked in deep, heavy breaths, then pushed away from the trunk. She had to keep going, she couldn't stop here. He was waiting.

Somehow, she made it to the clearing, half-stumbling, and dragged her unwilling body to the mouth of the cave, still finding it in herself to set the dish carefully. It was rather more difficult to retreat back to the cabin even though the relief of the chair would be welcome. She managed to make it to a small rock at the edge of the woods, and sank heavily there to wait.

This time, he was a long time coming. Nan didn't doubt for a second it was because she was right there in plain sight, but she couldn't muster up the strength to make it to the cabin. He was going to have to come out while she was present. She leaned back against the nearest tree, and closed her eyes.

Eventually, she heard it. The scraping, the clawing, the guttural puffs and snorts of breath. There was a pause, a long one, then it was followed by the wet, animalistic sounds of sloppy eating.

As she listened, it crossed her mind to open her eyes, but she knew the moment she did that he would flee back into the shaft before she had a chance to say anything. And she was too far away, he wouldn't hear her. But she had to at least try, try to warn him.

"Trouble's coming," she said hoarsely.

Silence.

She opened one eye just a crack, and saw that he had nearly retreated back into the darkness, only the glint of his eyes to give him away. It was far; at least fifty feet, if not more. There was no way he'd heard, was there? But he'd stopped, at her very first movement.

Louder, she repeated. "*Trouble.*" What else could she say that would get to him? Something short, a matter of mere words, there was no time to explain. "Danger. We need to be careful."

His eyes blinked a several times, but he did not retreat immediately, causing a flicker of hope to flare at the bottom of her chest—then he vanished back into the gloom. The faint of sound of pebbles tumbling reached her, just barely audible, then that, too, stopped. Nan's hope withered as quickly as it came, and she couldn't quite find the will immediately to stand. She gazed up at trails of smoke clouding the sky, waiting for her energy to return.

She woke up, and she couldn't move.

One side of her body was utterly paralyzed and completely devoid of sensation. She tried to move her arm, to lift it above her head, but it didn't obey. She didn't think it was going to, either, and a sense of dread washed over her, cold as ice, the weight of it keeping her pinned beneath the covers. Even drawing breath was difficult, her lungs scarcely able to expand to take in the air, and as panic began to thud in her chest, a sensation of impending doom followed, suffusing her consciousness with its totality, bringing everything else into sharp clarity.

For a minute, she had no thoughts at all. She could feel the end creeping closer, inexorably with each passing moment, sure as she could feel the strength fading from her limbs. It was too late now, she realized; there was nothing she could do when she was so far away. Even if she could reach the phone, by the time anyone arrived, it would be too late. It was no use now.

I don't want to die, she thought dimly, staring up at the ceiling, unable to do much more. *I can't die…*

That thought stood out, clearer than anything else, bringing with it a sudden sense of urgency. All of her plans had revolved around the concept of outliving him, especially when it was nothing short of a miracle and a curse that he had lived this long. But there was no one else to take her place, who would even *understand*, much less perform the same duty day in and day out, nobody else who would care.

If she died, then who would take care of him? Who would bring him food so he wouldn't have to bother anyone, scare anyone? She *couldn't* die, she just couldn't, not yet, she'd promised him she wouldn't leave him alone…!

A shuffling sound reached her from beyond the walls, a heavy, shambling gait that made her blood turn to ice. She knew those footsteps, would know them anywhere. What was he doing here? It couldn't be—already? It had only been— no, she had no idea how long she'd been asleep for, how long she'd been resting. Long enough, that was the point, it had already been long enough for him to grow hungry. And desperate. Scarcely breathing, she waited for the inevitable.

A scraping on the door, and a broken voice whispering, "Help me…"

TWISTED BRANCHES

TARA A. DEVLIN

The cherry blossom tree at our school was cursed. That's what everyone said, anyway.

"Did you hear? Apparently they hired someone to cut the tree down again during spring break, but the moment his chainsaw touched the tree, it took on a life of its own!"

"A life of its own?"

"He was lucky to get out alive. I heard he lost his arm!"

"No way. We would have heard about it if something like that really happened."

I put my bag down beside my desk and settled in. The pale pink petals of cherry blossom trees stared back at me from the window, as if to say, "She's lying! It's not us! Look how beautiful we are!"

"Yeah, well, I don't plan to be the one who falls victim to its curse this year. You should watch yourself."

Two girls were standing by the classroom door, blocking the way in or out. Their names escaped me; our school was so big that you could go the entire three years without remembering everyone in the same grade. The joys of a big city school.

"Curse? You really believe that crap?"

"You can believe what you want. I want to graduate and get out of here in one piece, so superstition or not, you better believe I'm staying away from that tree."

A cursed tree. It was ridiculous, but it was the hot topic at the start of every year, particularly amongst the third graders. Who was it going to be this year? Every year for the past ten years, without fail, someone in the third grade died, and their body was usually found near the lone cherry blossom tree at the edge of school. "The third graders' curse," they called it. Everyone joked about it, but on our third day back after the start of a new school year, everyone suddenly felt differently. There was always that lingering doubt of "what if…?"

"Good morning, Takeru."

A cheerful voice brought me back from my musings.

"Oh, hey Rina."

Rina. The new girl from the class next door that all the boys fell over their own feet to befriend. I could feel them staring daggers into my back from the rear of the classroom.

"Do you have a moment?"

My heart skipped a beat.

"Of course." The crack in my voice betrayed my confidence.

"I was hoping you could help me with this math problem." She pulled a chair up in front of my desk and put her notebook down. "I spent hours on this last night, but I just don't understand it."

Math was not my strong point, but as I fumbled my way through an explanation, she smiled and made me feel like the most important man alive. Heat rose in my cheeks.

"All right, shitheads, to your seats."

Mr. Suzuki, our hometown teacher, slapped a lollipop out of the baseball captain's hand as he walked into the room. Bodies moved en masse to their desks in silence and Rina whispered "thank you" as she scurried out. I couldn't hide the grin on my face.

The supposed cursed tree loomed large as I entered the rear grounds for soccer practice. Its petals were darker than the trees lining the road into school. Almost red. That was evidence enough that the tree was cursed for many. To me, it just looked old and broken. Like it wanted to be put out of its misery.

"You sweet on Rina, huh?"

I turned around. Haruto, the goalkeeper, was putting his gloves on, a stony expression on his face.

"I'm sorry?"

"I get it, man. I really do. But watch yourself. You're not the only one."

He snapped his glove on and smiled.

"I'm not sure I'm following."

He clapped a few times, testing the feel of the padding, and then grabbed my shoulder.

"You're a good guy. I just don't want you to fall victim to any nasty accidents, you know? We're third graders now, after all. You know what they say."

"What do they say?" I attempted to make myself look larger. Squared my shoulders and puffed out my chest. My nervous swallow no doubt betrayed my true feelings.

Haruto looked over my shoulder at the tree. "Curses aren't the only things you need to worry about around here."

A group of boys were unloading soccer gear on the other side of the field. They looked in our direction and the vitriol was plain as day on their faces.

"Are you serious? She asked me to help her with her homework."

Haruto held his hands up in the air. "Hey man, what you do is your business. I just don't want to see anything happen that would mess with the team. This is our final year, you know? Our chance to make a name for ourselves!" Wind rustled through the trees and a cherry blossom petal fell at our feet. "Just watch yourself, hey?" Haruto clapped me on the shoulders a few times. He kept an eye on the petal and walked around it on his way back to the goal. I didn't know what was stupider: people's superstitions about the tree or everyone getting their panties in a bunch over me helping a girl with her homework. I shook my head and joined the rest of the team for practice.

The sun was well and truly gone by the time we were done, and judging by the look on the captain's face as he walked over, I could tell what words were coming next.

"Teruto, was it?"

"Takeru," I said, resisting the urge to punch the stupid grin off his face.

"Takeru, right. I knew it was something like that. My bad. Look, you don't mind cleaning all this stuff up for us, yeah? Me and the boys gotta run. Math homework, you know?"

The rest of the team were already walking away. Balls from training littered the ground.

"I knew we could count on you!" He slapped me on the arm before I could answer. "You're a good one, Teruto!"

"Takeru."

"Right. Sure." He jogged to catch up with his friends, their laughter carried away on the wind. I sighed. So, that was my role for the year set. I was the whipping dog. The team bitch. All because I was kind to the new girl.

"You shouldn't let them treat you like that."

I jumped. I turned around and Rina was leaning against the trunk of the cursed cherry blossom tree.

"Rina! How long have you... You shouldn't lean against... What are you doing here?" My mind wasn't sure of what to spit out first.

"I was just passing by." She pushed off the tree and picked up a soccer ball. "Just exploring the new neighborhood, you know?"

I smiled. "You should be careful, especially after dark. Tokyo isn't as nice as the countryside."

She put the ball in the bag and shrugged. "Maybe, but Tokyo has adventure, at least."

"I don't know if walking around late at night is the type of adventure you should be after."

She moved around me, brushing past my arm, and the scent of cherry blossoms was overwhelming.

"I can walk you home... if you want. I mean, I don't mean anything funny by it!" I held my hands up as she bent down to pick up another ball. Just once I didn't want to sound like a moron when I opened my mouth. "Just... Tokyo's dangerous, you know? You shouldn't be alone."

My cheeks turned red and I was glad for the darkness. *You shouldn't be alone.* I was as bad as the other guys and their passive aggressive threats.

Rina handed me another soccer ball. "Who says I'm alone?" Her grin sent my heart racing, and she laughed as I looked around. "Maybe you're the one who shouldn't be alone." She poked me in the chest and an uneasy grin formed on my lips.

"Well, I'm not… anymore…"

She smiled.

"So, what's the story with that tree?" Rina asked as we finished collecting the soccer balls and packed up the gear. Moonlight filtered on its pale red petals and it wasn't too difficult to see why people gossiped about it. A branch might reach out at any moment and suck us into its dark depths. Perhaps spit out a few bones for good measure, or just use them for nutrients to grow even larger and stronger.

"I dunno. People say that it's cursed, but no one knows why. Some people say that a boy hung himself there after a girl rejected him on graduation. Others say that it was actually a girl, and when her boyfriend found out she was pregnant, he rejected her. I've heard others say that a student failed to get into their university of choice, and others that it was a victim of bullying who couldn't take it anymore. The only things they have in common was that it was a third-grade student and they hung themselves from the tree."

"Huh, that's interesting." Rina circled the tree, running her hand around its trunk. "And do you believe that it's cursed?"

I threw the gear bag over my shoulder and walked underneath the red branches. "No."

Rina smiled as she walked around the tree. "You don't believe in ghosts?"

I shook my head.

"What if I'm a ghost?"

"You're not."

"How do you know?" She stopped directly in front of me and looked up.

I swallowed. "I wouldn't be able to touch you if you were." My heart was pounding like a jackhammer. I could barely get my tongue to form the words, and the moment they spilt out I regretted them.

"So, touch me."

I wanted nothing more. She was cute. She was funny. She was very much my type and everything I wanted in a girl. The wind rustled through the trees and a petal fluttered down into her hair. I reached out to grab it and then pulled back.

Watch yourself.

"We should get home. I mean your home. Then my home. Not together. I don't mean—"

Disappointment flitted across her face, but then she painted her best smile on again. "So you're not afraid of ghosts, huh? Just girls." She turned and walked away before I could say anything. I never wanted the tree to open up and swallow me into its dark depths more than at that very moment. I opened my mouth to reply, but I couldn't find any words. She was already down the street by the time I realized I still had to put the gear away. I sprinted as fast as my feet would take me and threw the bag into the shed, but when I returned, she was gone.

"Idiot. What is wrong with you?"

The cherry blossom rustled in response. "Yeah. What is wrong with you?"

Over the next few days I saw Rina sparingly. She didn't come to ask me for help on her homework, or say anything more than a cursory "good morning" when she entered the class. The other boys continued to shun me, and with Rina gone, I was truly alone.

"Did I do something wrong?" I stopped Rina by the shoe boxes after school one day. She looked up at me and smiled, her face a picture of innocence.

"No, why?"

"It feels like you've been avoiding me this past week."

"I was unaware that we were dating."

The words stung me more than I thought.

"No, just… Never mind."

I walked away, cursing my desire to push things further. I misread her signals, that was all. We were just classmates. Nothing more. It was silly of me to assume otherwise.

"Hey, Takeru." I stopped in my tracks. "Meet me by the tree tonight. Nine p.m." I turned around.

"The tree? Which one?"

"You know the one." She grinned. "The cursed one."

All I could do was nod. She put her shoes on and skipped out the door. I looked around to make sure no one else had heard, and then ran to grab my shoes as well. This was it. My last chance. I couldn't screw things up.

I waited by the tree in the darkness, the breeze sending a chill through my bones. It was spring, but the cold winds of winter lingered. I rubbed my arms and looked at my watch. It was 9:30. She was playing me for a fool. Again. Of course she didn't want to meet with me. I was a loser. I was too scared to make a move the first time and now she was standing somewhere nearby, watching me stand in the cold like an idiot.

"You're still here."

I jumped. "Rina! I didn't think you were coming."

"Did you really think I would stand you up?"

"No," I lied.

"Dad was late getting home from work today so I couldn't get out until just now, sorry."

"That's okay, I haven't been waiting here long anyway," I lied again. "Um, what did you want to talk about?"

Rina picked a flower from the tree and put it to her nose. "I need to ask you something."

"Okay."

"That boy, the captain of the team. What's his name?"

My heart dropped. Of course.

"Uh, Yuu. His name is Yuu."

She put the flower behind her ear. "Yuu. Huh. Nice name. I once knew a Yuu. Things didn't end very well between us though."

"I'm... sorry." I didn't know what to say and was feeling more and more awkward by the minute. She put her hand on the tree and started circling the trunk again.

"He was a liar. A womanizer. He told me that he loved me, but then he went behind my back and got my best friend pregnant."

I opened my mouth a few times, but words failed me. Why was she telling me this?

"My best friend. Do you know how that feels?"

"I... I don't have a best friend," I said.

She stopped before me. "I bet he treats you like shit, too."

I shook my head and shrugged my shoulders at the same time. "He's the captain."

"That's no excuse."

"I can't—"

"You shouldn't take that from him."

"I don't—"

"Don't you want to be free?"

"I'm not—"

"Be your own man. Do what you want without fear of repercussions."

"That's now how the—"

She leaned forward and kissed me. My protests were silenced and I melted into her. She was cold. I pulled her closer, and underneath the pale red flowers of the cursed cherry blossom tree, she kissed me. Deeply. Intimately. Passionately.

"Can I tell you a secret?" She broke away from me and looked up into my eyes. The moon itself sparkled within their depths.

"Of course."

"When I said I knew a Yuu in junior high school, I wasn't lying, and when I asked you about his name just now, I wasn't lying either. But I had to be sure. We were only thirteen at the time, and he's changed a lot."

My heart hammered in my chest. "You don't mean—"

"He's scum, Takeru. He got my best friend pregnant when she was only thirteen. When he found out, he beat her up so bad that... Well, he caused such a scandal that his parents had to move away and start fresh. I've been trying to find him all this time, but I never thought it would be here."

My mind was spinning. The star pupil and captain of the soccer team got a girl pregnant? And then he...

"I'm afraid that once he realizes who I am, and what I know... Well, his family has a lot of money and friends in high places, you know?"

"I won't let him hurt you." I had zero confidence in that statement, but at the same time, I believed it with all my heart.

"I don't think you have much say in that, Takeru. But that's sweet. You're sweet. I wish we could have had the chance to get to know each other under different circumstances."

"Wait, what? What are you saying?"

"I can't afford to change schools. Not now. I mean, the school year has only just started, and my parents had to pay a lot of money to get me into this school. And after all this time, I finally find Yuu again, but... the moment he realizes me, it's all over. I can't come back."

I tried wrapping my mind around what she was saying. I was missing something big. It was all too sudden.

"Rina, stop." I grabbed her by the shoulders and forced her to look at me. "What do you mean, you can't come back? The year just started. Whatever shitty thing Yuu did, I mean—"

"He killed her."

I stopped and stood up straight. "He what?"

"He didn't just beat her up and kill the baby. He killed her. He killed my best friend. He had sex with her behind my back, he got her pregnant, and when he found out, he beat her so badly that she died. He murdered her."

I didn't know what to say. It was all too much to take in. Sure, Yuu wasn't the nicest guy around, but a murderer? How would they even cover up something like that? And why?

"I wanted to check that it really was him. Now that I know that it is, I... I can't be here. I'll be next."

"If that's true, we need to go to the police. We should—"

She placed a finger on my lips and shook her head. "I already told you. His family knows people in high places. It's no good. I just don't want him to hurt anyone like he hurt my friend. I don't want to be next."

She took the cherry blossom flower from behind her ear and put it behind mine. She smiled a sad smile, and something blossomed within me. Something angry and full of rage. Something disgusted with the injustice of it all.

"I can't be here while he is," she repeated. "I can't be here until he's gone."

She gave me another kiss, this time on the cheek, and turned to walk away. Part of me told me that I should follow her, to make sure she was okay and to reassure her that everything would be all right. But another part of me, the blinding, red hot part, told me different. There was only one way to make sure she was safe. Only one way to make sure he could never hurt her again.

"Hey, can I talk to you for a moment?" I said to Yuu after soccer practice the next day. The sun was setting and a chill lingered in the air. The sweat on my arms turned cold the moment I stopped moving. Yuu wiped his brow and looked at me with disdain.

"What?"

"It's... a little awkward." I looked over his shoulder at the rest of the team. They were laughing and joking as they walked back to the club room, leaving me to pick up the balls as usual.

"Why would I care about that?"

I waited until they were out of sight and scratched the back of my neck. "It's about Rina."

"Who?"

"Rina. You know… the new girl?"

Yuu stared at me blankly. He really didn't recognize who she was. "There are lots of new girls. What do I care, and why do you need to talk to me about this?"

I picked up a scattered cherry blossom petal and squished it between my fingers. "I was told just a few days ago to watch my step." I looked pointedly at him. "That there would be trouble if I didn't."

Yuu held his hands out to the side and leaned forward, as though talking down to a moron. "Again, what the hell does that have to do with me?"

"You really don't remember her?"

"Who? Who am I supposed to be remembering?" His voice was testy. I didn't have much time before he got upset and walked away, and I couldn't have that.

"Rina. You knew her in junior high."

"I knew lots of girls in junior high! Are you a little slow or something? Get to the point!"

"You slept with her best friend. You… you…" You what? You got her pregnant and then killed her and your parents covered it up? Even if that were true, and I fully believed Rina when she said it, what would Yuu have to gain by admitting that to me? He would never say the words out loud. He didn't have to. The dirty act he committed long ago was already covered up and likely forgotten by everyone… everyone but Rina, and her best friend's family.

"Unless you got a point, Takuya, I gotta go. Clean up the balls, would you?"

"Takeru."

"What?"

"My name is Takeru."

"Whatever. Just clean up before you go, all right?"

It was too late. It was now or never. I reached into the gear bag and pulled out a rope. I closed the distance between us and looped it around Yuu's neck as he walked away. He let out a choke and I pulled back as hard as I could. His fingers grasped for the rope as his rear hit the ground, and his feet slid in the dirt as I pulled him towards the tree. My body knew what to do, and I wasn't going to argue with it. I slung the rope over the branch and yanked down as hard as I could. Yuu's feet dangled in the air as I pushed mine harder into the earth to get better footing. He struggled and kicked, his nails drawing blood as he clawed at the rope constricting his airway.

"What… are you…"

"What am I doing?" I asked for him. Warmth spread throughout my body as I watched his face change color and his kicks get weaker. "That's a good question. What am I doing? I stopping you from hurting anyone ever again. You're a murderer, Yuu. Not only that, but you're a real shitty captain and a real shitty person. I'm doing the world a favor. I'm removing you from it."

It was my voice, and they were my words, but it was as though my body was acting of its own accord. I didn't fight it; it felt right. This was how things were supposed to go down. The natural order. Fate. I never believed in fate, but in that moment it was hard to argue with.

In the distance I saw a shadow with long hair. It… she… smiled and disappeared back whence she came. Yuu stopped moving. His arms fell limp by his sides and his head tilted somewhat to the left. He was no longer Yuu. No longer the murderer that had taken a young woman's life, and that of her unborn baby. He was just a sack of lifeless flesh, floating in the air.

I tied the rope off and left him there. Someone would find him in the morning. They would fuss and pretend to care. There would be a school assembly and teachers would inform us with tears in their eyes of how he was such a good student, how he had such a promising future, how we all need to band together and talk to each other if we ever felt like things were getting out of our grasp. And then, in a few weeks, everything would return to normal. People would talk about what they watched on TV the night before, and Yuu's former friends would find a new leader to follow.

Perhaps, every now and then, someone might even bring up the curse of the cherry blossom tree. How it really was true. How they were glad it wasn't them.

"This is the second tragedy to befall us this year," the principal said at the hastily assembled assembly the next morning. "We, as a faculty and as people, want you to know that we are here for you, at any time. If the pressures of school get to be too much, or if you're struggling with things at home, we are here to help. There is no concern too big or small. It is our job to…"

Second tragedy? So the rumors about the janitor trying to cut down the tree were true? After all these years, why didn't they just leave the tree alone?

"Have you seen Rina?" I plucked up the courage to ask Naomi, one of the girls from class, as we walked back. She wasn't at school again.

"Who?"

"Rina."

"... Rina?"

I tilted my head. "Rina. You know? From next door."

"... Are you okay? Do you need to, like, see a teacher or something?"

She wasn't playing around. She didn't know who I was talking about. It was true, we were overcrowded and Rina was the new kid from next door, but...

"Never mind."

"Wasn't that the name of the new girl who suddenly disappeared?"

"What?" Both myself and Naomi responded in unison. It was her friend, Haruka.

"I don't know if it's true or not, but apparently they found the body of a girl hanging from the cursed cherry blossom tree a few days ago. A new girl. I didn't hear the details, but I overheard the teachers talking about it. 'The curse struck early,' they said. Officially, I think they said she transferred, but..."

My mind was spinning. It didn't make any sense. How could she be dead? She was in our class! She asked me to help her with her math homework! She...

And then it hit me. I never saw her speak to anyone else; not after that day. She wasn't just a quiet student, she... wasn't there to begin with. I was the only person who saw her. The only person she knew would help her. She was afraid of Yuu, of what he would do when he realized who she was. She must have... the tree must have...

It claimed her, like it had claimed many others over the years. It fed on her fears. The more lives it took, the more lives it wanted. It wasn't satisfied with just one anymore. It wanted more. It would keep wanting more, the spirits of those claimed by its branches growing stronger, angrier, and more vengeful. Its petals growing redder by the year, its branches thicker and more twisted.

I was a murderer. The tree didn't make me do that. It chose me because it knew that was already inside me. That I could help feed it.

I see Yuu standing by its thick, twisted trunk sometimes. I rarely see Rina, not when Yuu is around, anyway, and he's always there. His face twisted with rage like the branches of the tree, his eyes red like the petals that litter the ground. His lips open and close, repeating the same word, over and over. A word only I can hear, and a word only I can understand. He'll have his wish soon enough. The tree needs to be fed, and maybe if he's sated, he'll disappear long enough for me to see Rina again. I need to tell her that it's okay. Yuu can't hurt her now. Yuu can't hurt anyone now. And she doesn't need to be lonely for much longer. Her friends will be joining her soon.

Yuu's lips move, over and over. I smile and nod.

"More."

THE BOUND MAN OF THE HAUNTED MOUNT

MALINA DOUGLAS

I barely survived a trip to St. Michael's Mount. I haven't been the same since.

I pulled into a flat sandy carpark on the edge of the coast, stepped out of the car, and that's when I first caught sight of it. A mound of earth rising out of the sea, dark with foliage and crowned with a vast stone castle. I could see the dark maws of the long, pointed windows, several chimneys, and a flag, tiny and fluttering.

On the beach in the foreground, children skipped and splashed, and families defended wind shelters from being blown over. A few brave souls waded into the frigid water, despite the vast bulk of the grim drifting clouds.

Half the people passing by wore shorts and swimwear, the other half scarves and windbreakers, as if divided between those who faced the weather for what it was and those who blithely carried on as if it was different, determined to enjoy their beach holiday.

Wind like cold fingers accosted me and sought out every crevice in my clothes as it shoved me forward. It was as if the wind itself was pushing me towards the Mount.

The tide was out, exposing an ancient stone causeway stretching out from the mainland. If I waited too long, the waves would close over it.

I joined a procession of tourists: old couples in floppy hats and striped shirts, men in shorts that exposed their pale legs, families with children, leaping and shrieking, women who wore fluorescent cotton despite the sharp wind.

My mood was light and meandering. I'd taken time off work and most of it was still ahead of me, filled with the promise of sun-drenched days. I'd driven down to Cornwall on a whim, possessed of the vague notion that I would find something different here.

I would find something, and it would go beyond my wildest nightmares.

The sun came out. It glinted on distant water and brightened the stone walls of the village ahead.

I had no idea of the sinister forces afoot there. How could anyone?

The causeway was formed of rounded orange-brown stones specked with granite, slightly raised above the sea. It was lined with kelp, heaped in masses and covered with little round buoys.

A crowd had formed in the middle of the causeway. I wove my way through it, and discovered that part of the path was still partially submerged. I unlaced my shoes, peeled off my socks and joined the crowd wading through. I felt the chill water and rough stone beneath my feet as the sun was swallowed up again.

I came up to a village of stone houses and a harbor, where a handful of sailboats lay beached in the sand like abandoned toys. The sight was jarring. Shouldn't a harbor be deeper than that?

I walked along a row of old buildings and noticed a stone archway. I passed through into a narrow courtyard. Up a short flight of steps was a door set with a porthole. I peered in and saw a wooden wall mounted with a sculpture of fish, many small and silver, forming a ring. I pushed open the door and walked in.

I found myself in a long room, where windows set into rough walls of cream stone looked out over the grey wind-tossed sea.

My gaze drifted across a scattering of people to a man who was hunched over a table in the corner, dressed in clothes of faded black. He looked up as soon as I entered. I saw a rough, weathered face and piercing eyes that met mine. He beckoned.

I joined him.

"Lovely place, isn't it?" I said to make conversation.

"It's only lovely if you're able to leave."

The comment struck me as odd. "Why couldn't you?"

"I've seen things," he said. "Grim things best not put into words."

"Oh," I replied. Such things were furthest from my mind. I walked over to the bar and ordered a St. Austell Tribute. Then I returned to the table and sat down.

The man's name was Frank. "Let me tell you a story," he said.

I shrugged. "Sure." It seemed harmless enough. Stories were just entertainment for me back then.

Frank leaned back into his chair and cleared his throat. "Plenty of people know the legend of the giant who lived on this island, but there's more to it that nobody talks about... something darker."

The sun broke through the cloud and shone on the ocean through the window. People talked, laughed, clinked glasses. Anything dark seemed far beyond my imagining.

"I must've been around your age when I started to come here. Got a job as a hobbler on a boat—that's what people in these parts call a skipper. I rented a room on the mainland and ferried tourists back and forth, island children to school and staff to work. I'd heard about the family who live on the island but hadn't seen much of them. They tended to stick to themselves. I heard rumors that they were afraid of something." He took a sip of ale and leaned in closer.

"I heard that once dusk settled in, they would retreat to the castle and seal the doors. No one was allowed in or out. If they needed something, they'd send for it, and it was delivered by an underground tram that moved up through the mountain.

"I heard strange stories of unusually large bones dug up from the chapel. Of a ghost called the Lady in Grey who had thrown herself over the wall of the castle and haunted its gardens.

"Strangest of all is the legend of the Viscerine." He paused to take a sip of ale.

I watched him. Despite his slightly threatening appearance, with his thick beard and dark wavy hair, his words seemed earnest enough. "Oh yeah?"

"They are an ancient race that we thought had died out everywhere... except this island. I'm not exactly sure what they are, but you don't want to find out. I saw something I shouldn't have. And now I have been punished."

Curiosity prickled. "Well, what did you do?"

He took a long sip of ale and sighed. "I was foolish as you once, and thought I could impress a girl by taking her out for the night on the island. We hid from the wardens till the sun went down, hopped the gate to the castle gardens, spread a blanket in the moonlight…" He closed his eyes and shook his head slowly. "I'll never forget the sight of those dark shapes drifting over the lawn… They tried to take her but I fended them off. I was stronger then, more muscular. They attacked me. Their claws are something horrible. I was on my last legs when I started to bargain."

I sipped my beer and cocked my head. "You did?"

"They didn't want word to get out, you see. They knew they would be hunted to extinction.

In exchange for her life, I agreed to be bound. See?"

He showed me the ring. A thick band of iron, stamped with strange symbols and engraved with tiny writing I couldn't make out.

"They put it on me. It binds me to this place. If I start to walk across the causeway, it heats up. If I go further, it burns me."

I frowned. "Is that… some kind of new technology?"

Frank gave a short laugh. "Old technology. Some call it magic, which is really just a word for technology we don't understand."

"I see." I was starting to doubt the sanity of the speaker. "But couldn't you just take it off, toss it into the sea or something?"

"You can't just *take it off*." He shook his wild, hairy head. "They sentenced me to a hundred years on this island, which is the rest of my natural born life. For interfering." He leaned closer. "I shouldn't even be telling you this, but I can see an adventurous streak in you. I want to warn you. I don't want you to do something foolish, like I did."

"Oh, I'll be fine." I shrugged it off.

"Going up to the castle, are you?" He was brisk, somehow darker; a door in him had closed.

"Yeah," I said, expelling the word with a breath.

"You'd best be going to get back before the tide comes in."

"I can get the boat." I shrugged. I wasn't going to tell him my real intention.

"The evening boats are only for residents. Make sure you get across while you can. There's a reason people don't stay on the island overnight."

"What about the family who live in the castle?"

"They're all right. They have high walls to keep them out."

I sipped my beer. "But don't people live in the village?

"A few. Hardy people and broken people. Once they've taken something from them, they tend to leave them alone."

"What do they take?"

"Small children. Or a part of your soul."

"How can they only take *part* of a soul?"

He shook his head. "Oh, there are fates worse than death. Have you ever seen someone when the fire in their eyes has died out? The part of them that feels joy, curiosity, excitement in the world—that part of them has been stolen by the Viscerine."

"I think that you're just talking about depression. Come on, I really don't think that some *thing* comes and takes your soul around here. It sounds like a superstition to me."

Frank's face was solemn. "Think what you like. They come in at night. Through open windows."

"What happens when everyone seals their doors and windows?"

"They get hungry."

I scoffed. "I think you're just making this up."

With deliberate slowness, he rolled up the sleeves on each arm. Vertical streaks ran down both of his forearms, the skin white and withered.

I was silent a while.

"I'm going to… uh… go now," I said quietly.

"All right. See you around. Maybe."

"See you."

Although we both knew we weren't likely to see each other again.

My heaviness from the Sail Loft was soon dispelled.

I walked up a short flight up steps, past the kids clamoring around the ice cream booth, past a man in a small booth who took my ticket, past a stretch of lawn where a storyteller held kids in thrall—something about a giant stealing pasties. Then further, up the stone path that wound up to the castle.

Things like that don't happen to me.

I went to Bran Castle and didn't get attacked by a vampire. In fact, the sun came out to shine merrily on the rock hewn walls and in through slit windows to rooms airy and bright. Any lingering evil by then was long gone.

I didn't get attacked by the monster at Loch Ness. I even dangled my feet in. The Beast of Bodmin Moor never bothered me when I camped there. I believe in things that are solid, things I can feel with my hands. That's why I'm a carpenter. I can tell a type of wood by sight and the feel of the grain, but I can't tell you anything about ghosts. I've never seen one.

And I wasn't going to let some old folktales upend my plan.

Once I get an idea, it sticks to me like a barnacle.

Like cycling from Scotland to Lands' End in April. Even though my mum said "You'll catch a cold in that weather."

I wasn't going to let anything stop me, especially not someone else's opinion.

I'd heard curious things about the castle—of gardens where rare plants flourished in a microclimate created by granite walls, and gardeners who rappelled down the cliff face to root out weeds. That the castle contained a full suit of Samurai armor displayed in a glass case, and a detailed model built by the butler from corks saved from the family's daily champagne lunch.

I followed the crowds of stomping tourists through halls lined with swords, past the powder blue parlor where they hosted visiting queens, and into the war room where the Samurai armor stood with a furry fake moustache. I stalked the battlements and gazed out from turrets until the waning sun tilted toward the gleaming sea. I lingered around the cannons and scanned the sea for dolphins until wardens cleared the last of the tourists. Only then did I begin my descent.

I saw a heart-shaped stone on the path that was labeled as the Giant's Heart, and noticed when I passed the sealed trap door to the Giant's Well. Just stories, I thought.

Too late, I realized they were warnings.

A wooden plank stairway branched off the path. It led to a short trail that looped around with a bit of hedge in the middle. Supposedly a dead end—except it wasn't. I pushed through a gap in the hedge and found an opening, shaded by trees and partly walled by mossy hunks of rock. A bit uneven for sleeping, but possible. Then I noticed the tombstones.

Bill Rufus, one said. *Dearly Beloved.*

I looked around. There were more. Irregularly placed bits of rounded stone, some mossy. Strewn amongst ivy and fallen leaves. I was standing on a graveyard.

I felt slightly unnerved, but pressed on through the underbrush.

Once I was far enough away from the graveyard, I cleared the stones from a mostly flat place. I spread out my mat and sleeping bag beneath the overhanging pines and lay down to sleep.

I heard a creaking of rocks. I turned over. Then it came louder, as if the rocks were rising up around me. Nonsense.

But when I sat up, I saw a dark shape moving.

I didn't dare yell out for fear of attracting attention. It was taller than a man and coming towards me—then another, and another. I shrank into the shadows but I'd already been seen.

They were huge, towering over seven feet tall. Hoods hid their faces. They drifted over the ground without touching it.

The Viscerine.

One held my arm in an iron grip while another scratched the length of it with razor sharp claws. The third licked my blood. As he consumed, he grew more solid. A face emerged—a lad's face, deathly pale. I struggled to wrench my hand away, but it only tightened its grip. The second reached for my neck.

I jerked away from its touch, but the long-nailed fingers found me. They pierced my skin and slid underneath, a sharp, frozen presence in my throat. Then the entire hooded specter stepped *into* my body and an icy presence took over me. My thoughts slowed and grew hazy, pushed into the background by an unknown consciousness.

A sensation overtook me: of being ancient, dusty, worn out. The sensation was thirst, and I knew somehow that it could only be satisfied by the thick and pleasantly salty taste of blood. Propelled by this certainty, I felt my limbs moving forward, down the hill.

He looked into my eyes and he knew.

The man from the bar faced me. We stood in a shadowy courtyard at the end of the path to the castle.

I was ready to claw open windows, to tear the flesh from the warm bodies within, but he blocked my path.

"This might hurt," he warned. He withdrew something short and metallic from his pocket, pointed it at my feet and clicked it on.

The force that had overtaken me cringed, curling inwards, and began to creep back as the beam of light burned and blistered.

He shined the beam slowly up the length of my body, searing the edges of the entity inside me and forcing it to retreat.

I opened my mouth and a terrible, inhuman shriek came out.

The dark force continued to rise as the torch reached my eyes. They watered painfully, blinded.

A strange itch erupted at the top of my skull. All at once, I felt something leaving me, pouring out until I felt like a weakened, empty husk. My legs gave way and I toppled to the ground.

I opened my eyes.

My lips, when I licked them, were cracked and dry. I felt a terrible, desiccating thirst. I saw a glass on the floor beside me and seized it. Cold water coursed into my stomach like a torrent into a cavern, spilling over my lips and onto my chest.

Frank's voice startled me: "Feeling better?"

"Yes," I rasped, shocked at the hoarseness of my voice. "How long have I been here?"

"Two days."

I gasped. "I need to get home. I have work—" I moved to get out of the bed but a wave of dizziness overcame me. I fell back.

"Not so fast." Frank gave an unpleasant grimace. "The Viscerine are still at large and you're the only person who has been possessed by them and lived. I need your help to destroy them."

"So we'll go back, armed with torches—"

"Shining light on them will only scatter them around the island. We need something more."

"We can steal weapons from the War Room in the castle, fight them off…"

"Steel is powerless against them."

"Then what can we do?"

"I don't know."

My heart sank.

Frank looked to the window. "Hundreds of years ago, the Viscerine were hunted nearly to extinction. But all the records of their destruction have been lost."

"Do any other records mention them?"

"Yes. One was captured. His bones were discovered in a hidden cell in the chapel in the 1700s, during restoration work. They measure seven feet eight inches."

"I thought he was a hermit who lived in the cell there."

"That's what they want you to believe, but he was one of the Viscerine. The trouble is, their spirits still infest the place, and are capable of taking other forms."

I looked out the window, toward the dense slopes of forest and the castle that crouched, dark and somber, above it.

That was it; my life was bound to the man bound to the island. We would hunt apparitions with weapons of light. Scour rocks, woods, and crevices till every malevolent spirit had been routed.

I had the sense that I would be here for a very long time.

Now I'm the lone man who sits in the corner of the pub, nursing a pint of Korev and doling out warnings.

It was a dim windy day. The wind lashed at my back and pulled at my hair and I retreated to the upstairs of the Godolphin Arms.

The room was clean and bright, too airy for my mood.

Through a wall of windows, I looked over to the Mount. The path had been swallowed by the tide, as though it never was. Clouds turned the sea to a dull steely grey, and the large rock with stairs cut into it had become an island of its own.

A motorboat dotted with tiny figures moved across the wave-tops, ferrying passengers to the island. A half-dozen boats bobbed faintly in the harbor, and the stone houses lined with stone walls looked unchanged.

In one of those stone buildings, Frank was likely sitting, looking over the same stretch of water, living out his sentence. At the top was the castle like a hen brooding over her secrets.

I was lucky I'd escaped. We'd tried twice to fight the Viscerine with fire and light, and both times retreated, barely keeping our lives. I'd departed across the water to Marazion to recover and regain my strength.

A lad walked in. Rain jacket, backpack, hiking boots. He looked around. A newcomer. I saw the curiosity on his face, the foolish innocence.

I beckoned him.

He told me about his trip in a gush of words. First solo camping trip, drawn by some strange feeling to St. Michael's Mount.

"I'm going to walk across the causeway and stick up my tent in the underbrush. Ah, to spend a night on the island…" His eyes were as bright as mine were, once.

I'm more cynical than I used to be. I know that beautiful places can also be sinister. I look for the evil intentions beneath words, even when they are not there.

"I'm not sure that's really such a good idea…"

I could tell him that the rules were there for a reason, but I knew it wouldn't work.

I rolled up my shirtsleeves and showed him the lacerations on my arms.

He didn't balk. I saw something disturbing in the clear bright boldness on his face. I realized I was seeing myself in him.

I shrugged. "It's your life. Do as you wish."

He would thrill at the prospect of risking his life.

Secretly I knew the boy would be just what we needed.

To use as bait.

LIKE FLIES

TONY EVANS

"What about…"

Kevin closed his eyes and held out his hand, tracing his finger around a map pinned to the wall. He zigged and zagged, back and forth, and up and down to make sure there would be no way of knowing where he would stop.

"Really, Kevin? This is how we're deciding?" Tyler asked

He paused, eyes still shut. "Do you have any better ideas? We've been going around in circles trying to pick a place. This way, at least it'll be random. Right?"

Tyler sighed. "I guess."

Kevin jerked his finger to the right. "You interrupted my concentration," he joked. "Just one more move. It's gotta feel right, you know?" He slid his finger to the left, and then up. "Right there." He opened his eyes. "Southeastern Kentucky!"

"Kentucky?" Tyler scrunched his face. "Are you sure you don't just want to move a little further south and do the Smokey Mountains?"

"What's the matter, man? Where's your sense of adventure? Gatlinburg and Pigeon Forge are too touristy."

"Adventure? I have a sense of adventure, Kevin. Remember Colorado? Arizona? Remember that trip to Hawaii when we camped for a week deep in the forest and then couldn't find our way back? That was adventure."

"Oh yeah, I remember. That trip was a fucking blast."

"Hell yeah, it was. All of those trips were." Tyler glanced back to the map, face puckered. "But Kentucky? I'm just not sure there's any adventure to be had there. I mean, what's it got to offer? You never hear anything good about Kentucky. Especially the eastern part."

"Hillbillies?" Kevin responded.

"What?"

"You asked what it had to offer." Kevin laughed and punched his friend in the arm. "It's got hillbillies."

"That it does," he sighed, knowing the decision had been made regardless of his objection. "That it does. So, now that we know we're gonna be stuck in Hicktown, USA, it's time to find someplace to camp. Any public land or state parks down that way?"

Kevin opened his laptop and started searching. "There are a few, but most everything seems to be a regular campground. All the state parks are small and don't really offer backcountry camping."

Tyler's eyes widened slightly. Maybe there was hope after all. "Oh, well, I guess we may just have to change our destination after all then."

"But," Kevin continued, clicking on the mousepad. "There is a place down there called Pine Mountain. It's got some pretty remote areas, based on what I see here, and a partially completed trail that runs across the ridge."

"Oh, boy," Tyler said, enthusiasm lacking. "And here I was worried for a moment."

"I'll bet you were, buddy. But like always, I've saved the day again." He looked to Tyler and grinned. "Just think, a week in the Appalachian Mountains, and we probably won't see anybody at all."

"I guess that's true. A place like that probably is pretty secluded."

"Yeah, more so than that Hawaiian forest for sure."

Tyler thought about it for a moment, and he realized that Kevin was right. Seclusion and remoteness had always been the goal of these trips, and though all the places they'd visited before had been remote, they were still tourist destinations. There was no way in hell Pine Mountain, Kentucky was a tourist destination. Why would it be? It may just end up being the best annual camping trip yet. Even if it wasn't, it would the first time either of them had camped east of the Mississippi.

"You're right." A positive attitude often made all the difference in these situations. Hillbillies or no, he was going to make the best of it. "This will be a fun trip. Best one yet."

"Goddamn," Tyler said, bracing himself in the passenger's seat. "These roads are fucking horrible. I've never seen so many potholes in my life."

"Tell me about it. The narrowness doesn't bother me so much. I'm used to that. But these holes are ridiculous."

They'd just dropped down into a valley and rounded a curve when the largest pothole yet appeared out of nowhere. Kevin swerved to avoid it, but his reaction wasn't fast enough. The front tire skirted the edge of the hole, but the rear tire landed in the center, jolting them both. The truck fishtailed around the curve and a loud pop, followed by a hiss, erupted from the wheel area.

"Jesus, that was a big hole!" Tyler yelled, looking out the window to the back of the truck. "Looks like we got a flat, too."

"Yeah, I hear it, and feel it." Kevin slowed the vehicle to a crawl, looking for a wide spot on the edge of the road so he could pull off.

As they limped along, the total remoteness of the area became apparent. For as far as they could see in every direction, thick forest filled with oak and hickory trees covered the mountainous landscape. The tall canopy lurched over each side of the small road, covering it in a cascade of shadows.

"You know, we could probably change the damn thing here in the middle of the road. I haven't seen any other cars for a good while now." Tyler looked in the rearview mirror. Sure enough, there wasn't another vehicle in sight.

"Nah, we can stop right up there." Kevin pointed up the road. "Looks like a little gas station or convenience store. How... convenient."

"Ha, ha," Tyler said, sarcastically. "I wonder how many customers they get because of that same godforsaken hole?"

They parked around the side of the building. Other than a rundown, rusted-out truck that looked like it would crumble in a hard gust of wind, theirs was the only vehicle in the lot. Tyler stepped around to examine the flat tire while Kevin went to look at a map posted near the door.

"Nice! Looks like the trailhead is just up the road. At the top of the next hill, if I'm reading this map right."

"Oh yeah?" Tyler said. "That's good, because this thing is beyond repair. We could maybe put the spare on to get us to the nearest garage, but we'll need a new one before we head back home."

"Looks like y'all done went'n got a flat," a loud voice announced.

Startled, Tyler and Kevin turned to find a man standing in the doorway of the gas station. He was an older gentleman, beard full and scruffy. On top of his head was a faded University of Kentucky baseball cap.

"Well? What about it?" the man said.

"Oh," Tyler replied. "I'm sorry. I didn't think anyone was there. I apologize. Uh, yeah, got a flat."

"'Elp. I reckon you do." The man looked up the road and rubbed his belly. "Prolly come from that big ass goddamn hole in the middle of the goddamn road up 'er, didn't it?" He took off his cap to swat at a fly buzzing around his head.

The boys looked at each other, fighting mocking grins. "Well," Kevin started. "Actually... yeah, it did."

He put the cap back on and spit in the gravel. "'Elp. I've been onto 'em for years to fix 'at goddamn thang, but they keep ignorin' me." He looked up and slowly removed his cap again. "Goddamn flies. They's bad 'round here." He glanced to Kevin and Tyler, a strange look on his face. "specially this time-a-year." He returned his attention to the air and swung the cap wildly. "Almost like people just bring 'em in with'm. Ain't it?"

The boys stared at each other, confused. Was he talking about them? Was this some weird hillbilly way of saying they weren't welcome?

"Oh, well," the man continued. "This place is so far out in the middle of nowhere, though. Ain't no reason for 'em to do nothin' 'bout it, I guess."

"About... the flies?" Tyler asked.

He looked at the boys and grinned. "Naw. Not the flies. That problem'll take care of itself in due time. Always does."

"Oh."

"I'm talkin' 'bout the goddamn road, boy. Ain't you listenin'? Didn't your mamma teach ya no manners? If they don't fix it, sooner or later it's liable to get so deep it reaches all the way down into Hell." He chuckled, then spit again.

"Oh, the hole. Y-yeah. Sorry, sir."

"That'd be quite a hole," Kevin joked. "We were headed up to a trail on the top of Pine Mountain and it just jumped out of nowhere."

"Pine Mountain, huh?" The old man took his hat off once more, scratched his balding head. "What y'all lookin' to do up 'er, if ya don't mind me askin'?" He took another swing at a fly, this one larger than the other two. "Goddamn thangs."

"They're fast little buggers," Kevin stated.

The old man looked at him and cocked his head. "Do what?"

"The flies," Kevin replied. "They're fast. Hard to hit, you know?"

"I ain't tryin' to hit 'em," the man said, matter-of-factly. "Why would I wanna do that for?"

Kevin stared at him, unsure of what to say. As he looked at the man, he watched a fly land on his head, crawl around his face, and stop at his nose. "Oh, I just... I don't know." He mumbled. The fly made its way to the old man's nostril and crawled halfway inside causing Kevin to turn away in disgust.

"Now, as I was sayin', what y'all lookin' to do up 'er?"

Tyler replied, "We were gonna do a little camping."

"Campin'? Why, they's lots better places to camp than that, boys. That place gets awful rough." He eyed them up and down. "For city boys and people that ain't from these parts, that is. No offense. specially this time-a-year. You know, these goddamn flies and all."

"Well," Kevin said defensively, "I think we can handle a few flies. After all, they won't be so thick up on the mountain." He noticed two trash cans sitting to the side of the shop. "Once we get away from the trash, and all. No offense."

"Mhm. I see," the old man chuckled. He turned and looked into the thick forest. "'At's what they all say."

"Excuse me," Tyler said. "What's that supposed to mean?"

"Just these goddamn flies." He swatted at another. "They just get thicker 'n thicker till... well, till they just ain't no more."

"Yeah." Kevin tried and failed to keep the annoyance out of his voice. "Look, we'll get out of your way as soon as we can. Is there a garage or repair place close? Somewhere we can get this tire fixed?"

He looked over at the tire and snorted. "Garage? Naw, ain't nothin' like that in this place no more, boys. This town used to be pertty nice. Nobody really lives 'round here no more, though." He massaged his chin with one hand, squinting under the midday sun. "I'll tell ya what. How long you boys lookin' to be out campin'?"

"About a week or so."

"Mhm." He walked over and kicked the flat tire. "I can fix it for ya. Don't look too bad." He glanced at Kevin again. "For somebody 'at knows what they doin', anyway. Have it ready if… when y'all come out off the mountain. If ya want, that is."

"If?" Kevin started. "What do you mean i—"

"And how much is that gonna cost?" Tyler interrupted, expecting he would charge an arm and a leg for the meager fix.

The old man sighed. "Well, since I seem to've offended your bud over there… and the fact that these flies are only gonna get worse, how 'bout I do it for nothin'?"

"You mean, for free?"

"Well, unless you got another meanin' for the word nothin', I reckon that's what I meant. Hell, I'll even drive y'all up to the top of the hill if ya want. Long as ridin' in the back of that ol' rusty bugger over 'er don't bother ya."

"Look, uhm… I'm sorry, I didn't get your name."

"Jesse," he replied. "Jesse Moore."

"Ok then, Mr. Moore," Kevin said. "We appreciate that very much, and we'll take you up on the offer. But let us pay you for the trouble. I'm not sure I feel comfortable asking you to do this for free."

Jesse shuffled his feet. "Well, if you really wanna pay somethin', we can work it out when it's time, but I don't mind. Trust me, boy. It's the least I can do for all the trouble you're liable to run into."

"What kind of trouble are you talking about, Mr. Moore?" Tyler asked. "Thieves?"

"Look, boys. They ain't nobody up on that mountain 'cept for maybe a few other hikers comin' in from somewheres else, and I highly doubt that. You got nothin' to worry about from other… people. In fact, you prolly ain't even gonna see another human up there the whole time."

"Okay, well, if you're talking about animals… bears or something, then—"

"No, you ain't gonna have to be worried 'bout bears, neither. I mean, they're up 'er… but they won't bother ya. Ain't nothin' much gonna bother ya up 'er. Ain't nothin' wants anything to do with that place," Jesse said.

Kevin widened his eyes, an exaggerated look of impatience. "Look, man, I don't mean to be rude, but I'm a little tired of all these cryptic threats. Earlier, you said if we come out, and you keep talking about trouble we're probably going to run into, not to mention all the talk about the fucking flies. How about you just tell us straight up what you're talking about?"

Jesse arched his back, thrusting his chest out in an almost aggressive posture.

"The flies is only gonna get worse, and I can promise you both that you ain't gonna want any more trouble than that. Some folks thank it's just a story, but I've been 'round long enough to know different."

"What do you mean? Is there some kind of fly army in eastern Kentucky?" Kevin asked, patience wearing thin.

Jesse looked at him sternly, seriousness covering his face. "I know it sounds crazy, but like I said, I've been around here long enough to know. Hell, I'm 'bout the only one left. Folks up'n left after it all happened."

"After what happened?" Kevin asked.

"Yeah?" Tyler seconded. "What happened to make everybody leave?"

"Well, the way the story goes is that way back, a long time ago, they was a man come through 'ese parts lookin' to make a deal with Satan. Apparently, he'd heard tales 'bout how some of the ol' holler witches up here could talk to him. Everybody says they sold they souls and such, some for eternal life, others for riches."

"Satan, huh?" Tyler asked. "I see where this is going."

"'Elp. That ol' boy hunted and hunted till he came up on the cabin that ol' Molly Jenkins owned. Molly used to be known 'round these parts as the darkest of the witches. Nobody dared go near her. Stories of her stealin' babies and peelin' the skin off of 'em so she could fly are still told 'round here as a way to keep youngins mindin' they parents."

"So, it's just an old bedtime story, then? I see," Kevin shrugged. "I've heard a lot of those tales, Mr. Moore. Haven't come across one that's been real yet?"

"People say she could turn into a panther and that her eyes changed into pure fire under a full moon, but I now better 'n 'at. She was a dark witch, and she had ties to Satan, but she couldn't turn into no panther. That's just crazy talk."

"Oh," Kevin snarked. "A witch that talks to the devil is okay, but turning into a panther is just crazy? Yeah, I can see how that makes sense."

Jesse stared at him for a moment, then spit and wiped the saliva from his chin. "Everybody knows ain't never been no panthers 'round here."

"I see." Tyler smirked.

"Anyway, that ol' man lookin' for the devil found Molly and asked her if she could help him. Molly though, she didn't do nothin' for free, and let me tell ya, that boy paid a price." Jesse shook his head, a quiet chuckle under his breath. "See boys, the one thing you don't never wanna do is try to bargain with Satan or a dark witch. Why, they ain't got nothin' to lose, you see? Not just anybody can speak to ol' Satan in person, but like I said, Molly had powers, too."

"What did the man want?" Tyler asked.

"What's everybody want? To live forever. Damn, boy, ain't you been listenin'?"

"Yeah, dumbass," Kevin said, slapping Tyler's shoulder. "Listen."

"Molly told him that she could give him what he wanted, but he had to do somethin' for her first."

"Let me guess," Kevin said, "he had to give her his soul." Smugness crept onto his face. "It's the same old story everywhere. Sell your soul for riches and eternal life. Sorry, man. Not buying it."

"Nope," Jesse said. "Didn't have nothin' to do with no souls. Tell me, young man, what would a witch need a soul for?"

Kevin stared at him, mouth hanging open as if he'd just missed a million-dollar question on a gameshow. Tyler laughed and nudged him with his elbow.

"Uh… well, what then? What did she need from the man?" Kevin asked.

"What every witch needs. Innocent flesh. Too many people overlook that, you see? Witches ain't interested in no souls. Hell, they sell they own just to get they powers. They need flesh to live, though. To stay young. She told the man that if he went into town and collected ten babies for her, she'd grant him eternal life here on Earth."

"Innocent flesh, huh?" Kevin asked. "I don't understand. If she was a witch with all this dark power, why didn't she just take them herself?"

"Well," Tyler started. "It kind of makes sense, doesn't it? I mean, if she got caught herself, she'd be the one who died. If the man got caught, she'd be off free and clear."

"Nice try," Kevin replied. "She was a witch, remember? She lived forever."

"Not exactly," Jesse said. "You can kill a witch. Just gotta burn her alive. And trust me on this… people 'round here, specially back then, they didn't need many excuses to holler 'witch.' specially if they kids started goin' missin'."

"Interesting," Kevin said. "Interesting variation."

"Well, the man done just what she asked, and in return she gave him what he wanted."

"Yeah? Sounds like a win-win, then. Right?" Tyler said.

"Not quite. She gave him eternal life all right, but the feller still aged. See, he wanted to be young and attractive for all eternity. Turns out, he didn't specify that part."

"Okay," Kevin interrupted. "That's all well and good and everything, but what does this have to do with us? It's a good story. But it has absolutely nothing to do with us."

Tyler looked to Jesse, then shrugged his shoulders. "Yeah, what's it got to do with us?"

"You didn't let me finish." Jesse arched his back once more, his thumbs finding the bibs in his overalls. "Molly ended up gettin' burned a few years after all this happened, but before she did, she gave that man the ability to gain back his lost years. He just had to start doin' the same a witch would do."

"Eating flesh?" Tyler said.

"Absolutely. 'Cept it didn't have to be no innocent flesh. She was so mad at the town at that time for catchin' her that she turned that man loose with a reason to kill and eat anyone in sight. And he wanted to do it, since every single body he consumed gave him years back on his looks. Livin' forever sounds good, boys, but just imagine if you looked your age when you's five hundred years old! Be a mess, wouldn't it?" He chuckled.

"I guess it would," Tyler said, scrunching his face. "I guess it would."

"So, you see… this mountain is cursed. They say 'at man still roams 'round up 'er at night, lookin' for flesh." He swatted at another fly. "And they say that these goddamn flies follow him wherever he goes. Like I said, you can believe it or not, but I've been here long enough. I've seen hikers just like you not come back, and seems like every time they come the flies just get worse and worse."

"Mhm. I see, now," Kevin said. "Well, I can tell you this, Mr. Moore. I don't believe the story. In fact, it sounds crazy. Entertaining, but crazy. I think the flies are normal, and I also think my friend and I will be just fine."

"I agree, Mr. Moore," Tyler said. "This was a good story, but we've camped all over the west and almost every town has its own little scary tales."

"Suit yourself. Don't say I didn't warn y'all though. Tire'll still be fixed and ready for ya whether ya make it back or not." Jesse grinned and pointed to the rusted pickup. "Hop on in."

"Trust us, Mr. Moore, we'll be back. Hikers come and go in all parts of the world and, sometimes bad things happen, but none of them have to do with witches, and even less have to do with flies. It's just a story."

"'Elp," Jesse responded, grinning awkwardly. "They come and they go, all right... just like the flies."

As Tyler and Kevin started toward the trailhead, the old truck clanged and rattled back down the road and the smell of gas fumes lingered in the air.

"What a fucking weirdo," Tyler said, stepping into the forest. "Interesting story, though."

"Ha! I suppose. I've never seen anybody so obsessed with flies in my life. Did you see the way that one went up his nose? I bet he has a whole hoard of them in the back of that shop. Probably sleeps there with them, strokes their little heads every night. Hell, I bet he even has names for them... all of them."

Tyler laughed.

"You know it's true. Guy's a creep. We'll be lucky if he even knows how to fix a damn flat tire."

"Nah, he knows what he's doin'."

Kevin snorted. "What makes you so sure about that?"

Tyler looked around at the trees and inhaled deeply. "Because he's a fucking hillbilly. One thing they know how to do in these parts is fix their fucking trucks." He slapped Kevin on the arm playfully. "Well, two things I guess... that, and take care of their pet flies."

For nearly four hours, the boys pressed on down the trail, marveling at the beauty of the mountains. It wasn't quite what they'd expected—it was better, and they were enjoying it. The trees were large and the sounds of the outside world were oddly absent. It reminded them more of a legitimate wilderness area, one that you would find in the far reaches of Alaska or somewhere in the Amazon.

"See, I told you it'd be fun. Just look at this place!" Kevin jumped up on a large rock near the trail's edge, arms down and chest puffed out. "Just look! It's beautiful!" he yelled.

"It is." He looked around, inhaling and taking in the freshness of the air. "It most certainly is that. What time does the sun set around here? Do you remember?"

"Nope. Why? What time is it?"

"Coming up on seven thirty," Tyler said. "The way the sun looks now, I'd say we have another hour and a half, maybe."

"You're right," Kevin said, hopping off the rock. "Probably better find a place to set up camp for the night. We've covered a good distance already."

"Should we set up here on the ridge somewhere, or go down a bit?"

"Oh," Kevin said, climbing back up on the rock. Hand on his brow to block the light, he scanned the landscape. "I don't know. I guess it depends on the weath— Wait a second." He pointed down the hill. "Look at this, man. That looks perfect."

Tyler climbed up on the rock next to him and looked to where he was pointing. "Huh. Is that an old house?"

"Looks like it. An old house seat, anyway. The mountains are dotted with them, especially in and around these small towns. Mountain folk used to live way up in the middle of nowhere, remember?"

"I guess, yeah. Makes sense, anyway." Tyler plopped off the rock and started through the woods down the hill. He looked back to Kevin, who was still staring down, an odd look on his face. "What's the matter? You coming or not?"

Kevin's eyes grew large, his mouth hung open. In a dramatic voice, straining to mock the hill-folk accent to the best of his ability, he looked to Tyler and said, "Why, what if that's ol' Molly Jenkins' place?"

Tyler's eyes narrowed with annoyance. "Stop joking around and come on. We need to get our shit up and gather firewood before dark."

They set tents up in what looked to be an old front yard. The trees had been logged years prior, and the ground had since been coated with dead leaves and herbaceous vegetation allowing them minimal work to clear for camping. Large concrete blocks sat next to them, busted and broken from years of weathering and age, now covered with creeper and ivy growing from each and every crack.

"Man." Kevin tossed a branch into the fire. "We got lucky here, huh? This place is great."

Tyler held a small pot of boiling water and noodles over the fire. "Yeah, buddy. Minimal effort makes for easy camping."

"Sure does." He looked around, as if bracing himself for something to jump out at any minute. "And just think, we were lucky enough to get away from the flies!"

Tyler laughed. "Yeah, imagine that." He made a goofy face and attempted his best hillbilly accent. "Them gawddamn flie—" Suddenly, he slapped the back of his neck and let out a yelp. "Fuck!" He grasped at something, hurling it forward out of instinct. "That hurt like hell!"

"What is it?" Kevin asked, smirking.

"Shut up, asshole." He stood up and walked over next to the fire where whatever it was had landed. "Ha! Look at this shit!" He reached down and picked something up from the leaf litter. "Would you just look at this!"

"What is it?"

He held out his hand. In his palm lay a dead horsefly at least two inches in length.

"Holy shit, man," Kevin said. "It actually was a fly! That thing is huge!"

"Hell yeah, it is. Bit me on the neck, too." He reached back to feel the wound, which had already turned into a sizeable welt. "Damn, that hurts. Fucking fly."

Kevin burst out laughing uncontrollably. "Yeah, more like..." Again, he put on his accent. "Goddamn fly, huh?"

"Shut up, would you? That really hurt. I've never seen a fly that size in my life." He dug through his first aid kit and took out a stick of salve that was supposed to ease the pain of a bee sting. "Think this will help?"

Kevin snatched it from him and read the label. "Well, it says it's for bee stings, but I'd imagine it numbs the area. Probably the best thing you're gonna find in there. Where'd you put that thing? I've got to get a picture of it."

Tyler smeared the salve on his neck, wincing. "It's right there in front of you. Jesus, man, you can't miss it."

Kevin bent forward, camera in hand, and as he got close enough to get a picture, the fly rolled to its belly and flew away.

"What the fuck?" Tyler said, amazed. "I smacked the shit out of that thing, then squeezed it hard as I threw it. How did it live?"

"Super fly," Kevin said. "Get it? Like the—"

"Yeah, yeah. I get it. Very cute." He looked out into the night, head cocked to the side, eyes squinted.

"Thanks, I get that a—"

"Shh." Tyler put his hand out, gesturing Kevin to be quiet. "Do you hear that?"

Kevin looked to him, eyes growing in size. "Sounds like, a faint... buzz, maybe?"

"Yeah. But where's it coming from?"

Simultaneously, they looked up to the sky. The small opening in the canopy that had just moments before been a window to the stars was now dotted with small, black specks, plummeting toward them like little winged asteroids.

"What the fuck is that?" Tyler yelled.

"Get to the fucking tent!" Kevin screamed, lunging toward the opening as fast as possible. "Come on, get in!"

Tyler's stare jerked from the sky to the tent as he leaped inside. Kevin zipped the door closed just in time. One by one, the flies slammed into the fabric at full speed. Like little balls of ice coming from every direction during a hail storm, they crashed hard into all surfaces of the tent.

"Holy shit!" Kevin exclaimed. "What the fuck is going on? Were those all flies?"

"Sure looked and sounded like it. I don't know what's happening, but whatever it is, it isn't good!" He touched the bite on his neck again. "This fucking thing is throbbing. It feels like something is moving inside!"

Kevin fumbled around and shined his light on Tyler's neck. "What in the hell?"

"What is it?"

Kevin stared silently at the wound as the flies continued to slap into the tent. Their numbers seemed to grow with every passing second.

"What's wrong?" Tyler demanded.

"Flies have piercing mouthparts... for sucking blood, right? I mean, like mosquitos. They're just small flies, right?"

"So? What's that got to do with me?"

"This looks like a... a bite mark. Like an actual bite mark. You know, like a spider or snake bite. There are teeth marks, man. Puncture wounds. Lots of them."

In an instant, as quickly as the flies had descended, they were gone; the hammering of their insect bodies against the tent stopped.

Kevin and Tyler looked at each other, eyes filled with fear.

Outside, the sound of leaves crackling under footsteps sliced through the silence like fireworks exploding.

They turned their full attention to the door. The fire cast a silhouette onto the tent's fabric. Their hearts quickened in pace, the taste of metal splashing across their tongues.

"I-is that a-a-a person?" Kevin said, his hands shaking violently to match his voice.

"Shh," Tyler said, still grasping his bite wound. "Be quiet."

The shadow grew smaller as it approached them. "Now," a familiar voice said from outside, "do y'all believe me?"

Tyler reached over and clenched Kevin's wrist. "Is that—"

"Y'all know ya don't need to whisper? I can hear ya. Hell, I can hear y'alls hearts beatin'." He chuckled. "I can smell the stink of fear comin' off y'alls sweaty-ass bodies. Come on out."

The leaves crunched again as the man took another step toward them.

"I said, come on out!"

Tyler unzipped the flap and pulled it back to reveal Jesse, wearing the same old bibbed overalls. A sinister smile played across his face.

"Mr. Moore?" Tyler said. "What are you doing here?"

Kevin pulled Tyler back. "Don't. Something isn't right."

"What's the matter, boys? Y'all look scared as shit."

"I-it was the flies. They were everywhere. One bit me."

Jesse laughed. "Flies, huh? Tried to tell ya." He snorted, then gave a deep, hacking cough. "Say you got bit, huh?" He hacked again, snorted, and moved his tongue around before opening his mouth and sticking it out.

On it sat a huge horsefly.

Tyler gagged. Kevin reared back. "What the hell?"

Jesse held out his hand. The fly obediently flew from his tongue to his palm. "Told y'all they'd only get worse."

"I don't understand?" Kevin managed, just as Tyler began to vomit. "What's going on?"

"Ya don't understand? I thought y'all was s'posed to be some of them smart city boys?"

Kevin stood motionless. Tyler looked up and wiped his mouth.

"Ya see, way back then, I didn't really know what I's gettin' myself into, ol' Molly and all. I just wanted to live forever." He laughed and slowly walked toward them. "She gave me what I wanted, but I gotta eat ta stay pertty."

Kevin pulled Tyler to his feet. "You're him. That man."

"Ha! Finally got it, huh? Look atcha, catchin' up and shit." Jesse held his palm out and spoke a word of an unfamiliar language. The fly took flight, hovering as it faced Kevin and Tyler. "She also made it to where I didn't have to do the killin' and eatin' myself. Gets awful messy, all the blood and guts."

"Oh, no," Tyler said. "No… no."

Kevin looked to each of them, trying to figure out what was happening.

"I reckon your friend's done figured it out," Jesse said. "I always had a thing for flies, ya see. I like 'em. Most people think they's pests… disgustin' and such, but not me. I figured if there was a way that the flies could do the eatin', then just feed the on flesh to me, why not? And you know how witches have ties with Satan. He is called lord of the flies." He licked his lips, and continued. "Molly gave 'em some big ol' teeth for me… and me and them both is awful hungry."

He opened his mouth one last time as a million giant, starving flies erupted from his throat, ready to serve their master.

THE DAMNIT MAN

BY MARC FERRIS

Rufus taps Skip on the shoulder and whispers, "They're coming."

Skip covers his nose and mouth with his hands to keep from laughing. Two teenage boys scale the fence of the storage yard behind the Phillips 66 station on Wentworth Road, and duck behind a doorless 1980 Toyota Corolla. A lone head rises to check if the coast is clear, and now Rufus is the one trying not to laugh. The boys stand and head to the crumpled 1985 Chrysler LeBaron which rests in the middle of the yard, waiting to be picked up by one of the guys from Peterson Salvage on Monday. One of the boys freezes ten feet away from the wreck. The other boy cajoles him, but he refuses to get any closer. They flip each other off, and the other boy continues to the car where he bends down to look inside.

The steering wheel is gone. It now rests in the back seat now, U-shaped from where the late driver's head impacted and bent it to the horn from the force of the head-on collision with a Peterbilt hauling sand. The dashboard has been cut away by the firefighters who responded to the accident out on Fuller Road. The car is just a year old, and while the backseat looks brand new, the front looks like a modern art sculpture from hell.

Skip wonders if the kid realizes he can smell the blood on the floorboards.

Rufus turns the valve on the compressed air tank. A loud hiss comes from the near side of the Chrysler. The two boys start hopping in place. A black shape rises from behind the car.

Skip yells, "I can see you! I-Can-See-You!"

The boys are screaming. Holding onto the fence seems impossible while they scamper over, and one wets his pants halfway across.

"You're hosing that off," Rufus says.

Skip opens the back door of the mechanic's shop. "Worth it."

While he hoses the piss off the fence, Rufus unhooks the Halloween decoration from the air hose and rolls it up to be returned to its box in the storeroom next to the Christmas decorations.

Back in the office, Skip notes the time on the wall clock while he pours a cup of coffee. His shift ends at six in the morning. Four hours to go. The room is large enough for one desk, and that belongs to Rufus. Skip gets a chair in the corner. The station is open twenty-four hours, but in the eight months he's worked here he's never filled a tank of gas after 11:00 P.M. The other gas station in town got rid of their mechanics, and replaced their shop with something called a Mini-Mart. While the 66 station is closer to the highway, the other station gets all the business. Rufus owns the place, and Rufus sees no reason to change.

"Cars are still going to break down and need towing. Soft drinks and potato chips ain't no help," Rufus told him once.

He doesn't mind the eight hours of quiet darkness. His kids are at school by the time he gets home, and this allows him time to sleep until the afternoon. His wife gets home in the evening, and after dinner they trade off when he leaves for work at ten. Not perfect, but it works for now, and the money he makes working here is all going into the bank to pay for his last semester at McPherson College, starting next January.

Rufus swaggers into the office and plants himself at his desk where he kicks his feet up. "The Damnit Man strikes again!"

"How often do you pull that stunt?"

"Every full moon, and nights like tonight make it all worthwhile—best show in town."

"They never catch on?"

"Buddy, it's free advertising. Those two turd-brains will tell all their friends about how they saw Damnit Man, and their days are numbered."

"What do you mean, 'days are numbered?'"

Rufus frowns and rolls his eyes. "Oh shit, that's right, you ain't from around here."

That's apparent from the lack of callouses on my knuckles, Skip thinks.

"Okay, the story goes the Damnit Man is a spirit that roams the earth looking for souls. The problem is he can't take them unless someone sees him, and that's a bigger problem since he's invisible. So he feeds on energy left in new car wrecks left by dying people. Something about the sudden shock and agony makes the energy sweeter. Anyway, the story says that he can only been seen on full moons, but only at the freshest wreck."

Skip refills his coffee cup. "You ever seen him?"

"Son, do I look like I believe in that bullshit?"

"Why is the back-door window boarded up?"

Rufus shoots a glance to the back door and shrugs. "It just is."

Skip opens his mouth to say something else, but the color in his boss's cheeks makes him change his mind. He needs the job.

The phone on Rufus's desk rings.

Rufus pulls a clipboard off the wall and starts writing. "Highway Twelve, mile past Dillinger Road. On our way." He gets up. "Grab your coat and gloves, you're coming too."

Skip slips into his coat on the way to the truck. "What if someone needs gas?"

"Not our problem. This is a two-hundred-fifty-dollar county tow."

The 1980 Chevy Rollback 350 growls to life and Rufus drives the six blocks to Highway 12. Ten minutes later, the flashing red and blue lights mark the spot.

A State Trooper waves his flashlight and the truck stops. "Just pull in in front of the second Pumper and wait. They're still getting the bodies out."

Skip leans forward. "How bad?"

"Family of four."

Rufus rolls past the scene. Portable flood lights illuminate the smoldering wreck of a 1982 Ford LTD Country Squire station wagon. Two plastic yellow tarps have been folded over the human remains, while firefighters work to free two blackened skeletal children from the back seat. Their bodies are frozen with the arms up and hands flat where the palms banged on the unyielding windows.

Skip closes his eyes hard enough to scrunch his face. "Jesus, I didn't need to see that."

"You'll need to get used to this. It's part of the job, son."

"I'll never get used to that."

Rufus laughs. "Maybe that's a good thing. I used to be all philosophical about it, you know, how fragile life really is. But now I just think it's just one less idiot on the road not paying attention."

"Even with a family and kids in the car?"

"Son, I don't know what happened here, but if the rest of the people in that car meant anything to the driver, they'd still be alive."

"Accidents do happen."

"Not as often as you'd think. Stupid is a crime punishable by death on the highway."

The truck is parked and they wait in the cab. Skip is willing to suffer through one of Rufus's unfiltered Camel cigarettes rather than wait near the back of the truck. A Sheriff's Deputy taps on the driver-side window.

Rufus rolls it down. "What's the word, Clem?"

"Looks like the front tire blew out and the car shot into the other lane. Nailed that Semi parked over by the fence."

"Who's towing that beast?"

Clem points to the headlights crossing the median. "Big Art."

The massive red Peterbilt tow rig thunders past them at five miles per hour. Big Art sticks out his tongue.

"Better him than me." Rufus pumps his hollow fist in return.

Clem's face breaks into a grin. "Word is the Damnit Man put in an appearance at your lot tonight."

"Is that so?" Rufus bites his lip.

"Dick Powell says his son, Dirk, came home with soggy drawers, crying about how he's doomed."

"Tell Dick that's what happens when punk kids trespass on my property, and I won't press charges."

"As much as I admire your commitment to setting kids onto the path of right-eousness, I can't imagine it's good for business. Dick will get the word around."

"Dick can kiss my ass. This is my real business, and even Dick will need a tow sometime."

Clem slaps the roof of the truck. "You're right about that. I'd have paid good money to see that kid wet himself. Anyway, they'll have the bodies out in twenty minutes."

Skip watches the deputy walk back to the wreck in the side mirror. "Word gets around fast."

"Small town."

"Dick Powell is my wife's boss at the pharmacy."

"If he gives her trouble, you let me know. I'll straighten him out."

A whistle comes from behind the truck and Rufus sees one of the firefighters waving him back. He puts the truck in reverse and they get out. He has Skip grab the jack to lift the rear of the car, and once it's up, he crawls under to hook the chain to the rear axle. The firefighters help unstick the melted tires from the pavement with shovels until the wreck slides free, and Rufus runs the winch until it is on the back of the truck. Once the bed is flat, he and Skip strap the hulk to the bed and ratchet the chains tight. Skip gets back in the cab while his boss gets the proper signatures on the billing paperwork. He can't get the image of the burned kids out of his head. Each time he tries, it only gets worse until the faces of the dead are replaced with those of his own children. He bolts from the cab and vomits on the side of the road. The more he pukes, the more he needs to puke.

Once he's done he looks back to see Rufus, and the deputy, and most of the firefighters, and the two State Police officers looking at him.

"Must be the new guy."

Skip can't tell who said it, but knows it's what they're all thinking. He gets back in the truck and rolls down the window.

Big Art honks his horn. "Whoohoo! Damn, Rufus, pickins must be slim. Some fine help you got there, boy."

Rufus climbs behind the wheel and slams his door. "You told me when I hired you that you could take this kind of thing."

"I thought I could."

"I can't have a driver who pukes at every crash."

The truck makes a U-turn across the grassy median back toward town. Neither man speaks, but both have red faces. When they reach the station, Skip gets out and unlocks the gate to the back lot. Rufus backs in. The wreck is unstrapped, the bed is tilted, and the winch lowers its cargo onto the gravel. Skip eases the truck forward until Rufus yells to stop. The car is jacked up, and the chain unhooked and reeled back into place.

"Come on." Rufus waves him to the back door.

When he gets to the office, he sees his boss working the adding machine. "What's up?"

Rufus unlocks the smack floor safe, and pulls out some cash. "You're fired."

"Because I blew chunks? That was my first wreck."

"You lied to me, son, I need a guy with an iron stomach for this job." He hands Skip one hundred and twenty-five dollars, and walks back out into the back lot to lock the gate.

Skip isn't sure how he feels about losing this job, but he knows this is the worst night of his life. Not many options for work, and with Rufus's stunt upsetting his wife's boss things will only get worse. How long will he have to put off that last semester now?

Rufus yells from outside. "Boy, I'm losing my sense of humor."

Skip stuffs the cash in his pocket and goes to the back door to see what the old man is running his mouth about. Rufus is standing between the truck and the gate. Something is moving inside the burned-out Ford.

"Boy, I ain't gonna waste time calling the cops. I'll beat your ass myself." Rufus rolls up his sleeves and stomps to the car.

He yanks open the rear door and then sees Skip standing in the back door of the garage looking at him. "Oh, mother of God."

A long black hairy arm grabs his shirt. The gleaming black claws tear through the fabric like razors. Rufus grabs the arm and pushes back. His shirt rips open as he falls backward. The thing in the car emerges into the early morning air and stands up. Skip guesses it is seven feet tall, but its narrow shoulders make it look taller. The bony black face fades into cone-shaped, earless head covered in short hair. Rufus gets to his feet. The thing hisses like a snake.

The Damnit Man, Skip's brain screams. If he sees you, he takes you.

Rufus sidesteps toward the back door. Skip backs in and locks the door behind him before his ex-boss can get there.

Rufus bangs on the door. "Open up, kid. You'll get your job back. Please. Please."

Skip hides in the restroom as Rufus screams.

He stays there cowering on the toilet until he sees sunlight beam in through the small smoked glass window near the ceiling. He opens the restroom door, moving in slow motion, listening after every step. Running out the front door is the smart move, but he has to know for sure. He turns the knob and pushes the back door open. The wreck looks smaller in the morning light. The gravel crunches under his shoes, which makes sneaking around impossible. There are no drag marks on the ground. The far side of the wrecked Ford is clear. Rufus is nowhere in sight.

Back in the office, he calls the police to report his boss missing. A short time later a patrolman arrives, and they both search the back lot a second time. Skip tells him that Rufus never came back into the office after they'd unhooked the wreck, which was the easier truth.

He continues to work at the 66 until state probate laws kicked in. The property is claimed by the city eight weeks later due to the lack of an heir.

On that last day, Dick Powell drives in to fill his tank. Skip apologizes for helping to scare his son.

Dick nods and grins. "No worries. In a way, I should thank you. The boy is home and in bed by nine every night. Me and the wife haven't slept this good since he was twelve."

"I still feel bad about it."

"That's because you're a standup guy. Besides, I told my son he had the story all wrong."

"How so?"

"Sure, the Damnit Man drinks from new fatal wrecks. But on those full moons when you can see him, he doesn't take just anybody, only the ones whose souls are already damned."

Skip hands him his change. "He never told me that part."

Dick points to the back door. "Why do you think he had that window boarded up?"

Skip smiles for the first time in weeks. "I guess so."

"Good luck next year in college. Keep doing it right."

Later that day some lady from the city comes, and he locks the place up for the last time and hands her the keys. On his walk home he feels lighter the further away from the station he gets, until he is almost floating down the sidewalk. A loud diesel engine overtakes him at a corner two blocks from his house. A big green tow truck rumbles to a stop. Big Art's Heavy-Duty Tow Service is written in yellow block letters on the door. The guy in the passenger seat rolls down his window and sticks his finger down his throat while making gagging noises. Skip hears two men laughing as the truck drives away.

He wonders if either of them know there's a full moon this weekend, and if they remember they're now the only towing game in town.

HELLHOLE FISHING

STANLEY B. WEBB

Pat Tinker backed his pickup truck onto the boat ramp at Herschel's Bait-n-Break on the shore of Oneida Lake in Constantia, New York. Pat's white-oak skiff overhung the tailgate, with a red rag tied on the boat's bow. He dragged the boat out of the truck, and it hit the ground with a bang.

"Watch it, Tinker," he spoke to himself. "She leaks enough already."

He dragged the boat down the muddy ramp, pushed it in until the bow floated, then returned to the truck for his fishing pole, flashlight, and oars. He left them in the boat and took his empty thermos into Herschel's.

"Evening, Hersh!"

"Hello, Tink," replied the fat bald man behind the counter. "Bull-heading tonight?"

"Oh, yes, I finished the mess of them that I caught last week. I had bullhead for breakfast, dinner, and supper for seven days straight. I had to dig a hole this deep to bury all the bones." Tinker leveled a hand at waist height.

Herschel grinned and said, "It's amazing you could fit that many fish in your galvanized pail." He leveled his hand one foot above his counter's top.

"I filled that bucket fifteen times!"

Herschel laughed. "What can I get you?"

"Two ham on ryes, a thermos of black coffee, and a can of nightcrawlers."

A gaunt man entered the Bait-n-Break.

"Evening, Stosh," said Herschel. "Having your usual?"

Stosh nodded. "Egg sandwich and apple pie to go."

Herschel disappeared into the kitchen.

Tinker silently considered how to tease Stosh. He finally asked, "You going out to look for Hellhole tonight?"

Stosh nodded.

"In your little old canoe?"

Another nod.

"You have your camera?"

Stosh closed his eyes and nodded.

"You know, I think I found Hellhole once," said Tinker. "I was out bull-heading, like I'm going tonight, and I found a place where my anchor never touched bottom. I've got a two-hundred-foot line on that anchor, you know?"

"No, I didn't."

"Anyway, I knew I couldn't catch any bullhead there because there wasn't any bottom for them to feed on, but I just thought I'd drop my line anyway and see if I could hook something."

Stosh rolled his eyes.

"I hooked something," said Tinker. "But I couldn't reel it in. Whatever it was, it kept pulling my line out. So, I set the drag on high, and then the thing started to tow me! I think it got me going twenty, twenty-five miles an hour. I was afraid it would swamp my boat, so I cut the line. Whatever it was, it had pulled me so far out it took me two hours to row back."

Herschel reappeared with their orders.

Stosh said to Tinker, "You're not the first man to make fun of me, nor the best."

"Aw, Stosh, don't you have a sense of humor?"

"Not after listening to guys like you for forty years. I still dream about that night. I was just a kid, out bull-heading on the lake, and it happened like you said: I found a place where my anchor didn't hit bottom. Then the thing rose beside my boat. The moon was dark so I could hardly see it, but I'll never forget its smell: just as if the bottom of the lake had risen."

"Seriously," said Tinker. "It was probably just a waterlogged old stump that rose to the surface full of decay gas."

"It was alive. Someday, I'll get its picture. Maybe tonight! Then you'll see, you'll all see!"

Stosh paid for his order, and left.

"You shouldn't fun him," said Herschel.

Tinker gestured broadly. "How can I resist? You know as well as I do that there's no monster in this lake. There's no Hellhole, either. Oneida Lake never gets much deeper than fifty feet."

"Have you dropped anchor on every square foot of that lakebed?"

"Well, most of them."

"Oneida Lake is old. It's a remnant of prehistoric Lake Iroquois, which once covered most of New York State. I'll reserve judgment on what might be down there."

"Maybe you should help Stosh hunt his monster."

Herschel shivered. "No, thanks."

Tinker chuckled all the way out to his skiff. Evening had become night. He sat in his boat's middle plank seat, locked in his oars, and put his gear on the stern seat before him. His feet splashed on the bottom boards. "An inch of water already," he said. He set his bailing can between his feet. "When that floats, I'll bail out."

He rowed toward the middle of the lake. He was about half a mile from shore when the Bait-n-Break's lights went off.

"Herschel's closed up and gone home. I feel kind of lonely now." Tinker raised his voice. "Can you hear me, Stosh?"

A silent minute passed, then a faint echo returned.

"I guess Stosh ain't close by, or he don't want to talk to me. I'll catch a fish to keep me company."

Tinker checked the knot at the bow, then played out twenty feet of anchor line until the grapnel hook caught the bottom. He bailed out his bilge, crammed a struggling worm onto his hook and dropped his line to the bottom of the lake.

Then Tinker lay the pole aside, humming as he poured himself a cup of coffee. He took a cautious sip just as the tip of his pole sagged. He put his cup down, took up the pole, felt the weight at the end of the line, and gave a jerk to set the hook. The fish tried to run. Tinker laughed as he reeled it in. "You're a good one!"

The bullhead was a black, slimy fish with whiskers around its mouth and stinging spines on its fins. Tinker avoided the spines as he removed the hook, and dropped the fish into his bucket. Then he examined his bait.

"You're still wiggling; I think you're good for another go."

He sank the worm, and resumed his coffee. Some while later, he reeled in his line and cast to another direction.

Tinker finished his coffee, poured another cup, and opened one of his sandwiches. When the sandwich was gone, he reeled in again and studied the limp bait.

"I guess there's not enough left of you."

He pulled the dead worm from the hook and threw its fragments into the lake.

"I'm feeling restless. I think I'll try another spot."

He bailed, then rowed for a while and let down fifty feet of anchor line.

"The bottom seems steep in this direction."

Tinker baited his hook, then looked at the glittering stars.

"The dark of the moon," he said, then looked around. "Stosh! Are you nearby? I ain't going to tease you anymore."

Twenty seconds passed quietly before his echo returned, clear and distant. Tinker smiled.

"I'll have a sing-a-long! 'Was a farmer had a dog, and Bingo was his name-oh!'"

The seconds passed, and his echo sang back to him.

Tinker sang the next line.

"'B-I-N-G-O, B-I-N-G-O, B-I-N-G-O! And, Bingo was his name-oh!'"

He tapped his foot when the song returned, then continued.

"'Was a farmer had a dog, and Bingo was his name-oh!'"

When he sang the following line, Tinker dropped the first letter from the dog's name.

"'… -I-N-G-O,… -I-N-G-O,… -I-N-G-O! And, Ingo was his name-oh!'"

The sing-a-long continued in that manner until the final verse, when Bingo's name was silence.

A close and heavy splash broke that silence. Tinker's echo returned, followed by the echo of the splash.

"What in hell was that?" he asked softly.

A single wave passed under the boat. He drew a quivering breath, then reeled in his line.

"I'm going to call it a night."

He stowed his pole, pulled the anchor up, unshipped his oars, and turned the boat around.

Tinker paused. "As much as I'd like to run away, I'd never be able to tease Stosh again. That was probably just a sturgeon; they grow pretty big. I'll just row in that direction and have a look around."

Tinker sat at the oars for a long time.

"Damn it, I owe it to Stosh."

He bailed, then rowed toward the splash. Tinker shipped his oars, and lowered all two hundred feet of his anchor line, which hung vertically in the lake. Tinker bounced the anchor a few times in the hopes that he could find the bottom.

"If Stosh was right about Hellhole…"

He pulled the anchor in, seized the oars, and stopped.

"No, I invited this, so I might as well see if I can catch anything."

He baited his hook, paused, and pinched a ball sinker onto the line. Then he swung the tip of the pole over the water and released the reel. The line dropped into the lake and sank. His expression turned increasingly gloomy as the line spooled out until it reached its end. Tinker bounced the sinker.

"Bottomless."

He let the line hang there for a while.

"Well, there's nothing here. I might as well go home after all."

Tinker tried to turn the reel, but the line would not come.

"Snagged. I must have hit bottom after all."

He strained against the snag, until his pole bent double.

"It's snagged good."

Then, he noticed that the line was slowly traversing around the boat. Tinker went still. The line circled the boat, then went slack. Tinker reeled in the broken end.

"There's something down there, all right. Stosh, you've been a true man all along, and I'll tell you as soon as I'm ashore."

Tinker put the oars in the lake, then hesitated.

"If I was a true man, I'd catch that monster. Well. I did try, didn't I? But it broke my line."

His eyes fell upon the anchor, and he sighed.

"Lord, I've not always been a good man, but I don't think I've been bad. Mischievous, I'd say, but if you see things differently, I pray that you'll be forgiving, and protect me tonight."

Tinker opened his last sandwich, baited the anchor's prongs with ham, and let it sink. He sipped another cup of coffee as he waited.

The anchor line suddenly pulled. The bow dipped. Tinker dropped his cup, and clutched the gunnels.

"Easy, now!"

Tinker eased forward and took ahold of the line. Great power vibrated from the depths. He took a deep breath and set the hook. The line jerked out of his hand.

"Ouch!"

The bow tipped. Cold water poured in.

"No, No, No, this old bobber has too much float in her! Let up!"

The bow rose again.

"Thank you, Lord."

The boat lunged ahead. Tinker fell backward off his seat. He scrambled up, and gripped the sides. Rooster-tails of water rose from the bow as his catch towed him. The boat cut to the left, then to the right, then made tight circles. Frightening sounds came from the old oak planks.

"Please hold together!"

The boat stopped, wallowing in its own wake. The line went slack. Tinker crouched.

"You're coming up now to see who's caught you."

Fetid bubbles rose alongside. The smell was deep and old. The water broke with a sigh. Tinker could see nothing. He found his light, and flashed the beam. An armored hump floated beside him, ten feet long by three feet high. A serrated ridge ran down its middle. Huge crawfish swarmed upon it.

Tinker felt relieved. "You're just an overgrown turtle! Wait until I tell Stosh."

The monster raised its long neck from under the water.

Tinker's heart froze. "Dear God!"

The head resembled a crocodile's more than a turtle's. Much larger than a horse's head, with narrow jaws that bristled with teeth. Its eyes stared like twin moons. The anchor hung from its jaws.

"I'm sorry. I hope I didn't hurt you. Surely, I couldn't hurt such a big fellow. I'll just unhook you, then maybe we'll let bygones be bygones?"

Tinker lifted reached out with an oar blade, and poked beneath the anchor's prong. The anchor came free and dropped back into the lake.

The monster regarded him for another minute, then sank. An oily slick whirled in its wake.

Tink cried for a time. Then he noticed that the water in the boat had risen above his ankles. He bailed desperately.

"I do not want to go swimming here, no sir!"

Dawn was near when he returned to the Bait-n-Break. He loaded his boat and gear into his truck, then went inside. Stosh was among the breakfast crowd. Tinker joined him.

"I didn't go out last night," said Stosh.

"No?"

Stosh shook his head. "I'm tired of being a fool."

"Well," said Tinker. "There are fools, and there are fools. I've been a bit of a fool myself, and I'd like to make amends. It would be a shame for you to give up the lake. Suppose we go fishing together tomorrow night?"

Stosh looked suspiciously at him. "What's the joke?"

"No joke. I'm just tired of fishing alone. I need someone to talk to, keep me from talking to myself."

Stosh considered, then shrugged. "Why not?"

"Remember to bring your camera. A fisherman never knows when he might catch something that's worthy of a photograph!"

"I want you to believe. To believe in things that you cannot."

FOLK-LORE

DAVID CLÉMENCEAU

I

For the head of the small Presque Isle congregation, it was a dreaded ritual seeing young Danny Birch coming to question him after every Sunday mass, about yet another metaphysical issue he had encountered while exploring popular culture. The questions the boy carried to him usually bordered on blasphemy and Reverend Bartholomew Furlong thought it important to provide competent advice—and, possibly, salvation.

Sure enough, as everyone else flocked out of church, Reverend Furlong saw the freckled little red-head trotting towards him with a look on his face that said Danny had begun his weekly interrogation long before mass was over.

"Hello, Reverend. I was wondering if you could help me with something." Danny opened the conversation with a casual icebreaker.

Reverend Furlong took it to heart to equitably divide his care and attention between each member of his congregation. And sometimes, there was the need for a little more care than usual; often because one of the more curious souls had developed a tendency to stray from the path, and could fall prey to temptation if not watched over—or listened to.

In principle, he saw no harm in a sound amount of criticism to better understand and thus embrace the Holy Book. But the Birch kid was a tough nut; his interest in the fantastic variations of the after-life was disturbing. He might become a black sheep, one that could poison the rest of the herd. Reverend Furlong thought that there must be some reason why God should send him this somehow cumbersome seven-year-old with his inquisition. Perhaps he had done something to deserve more penance than expected, something he had forgotten long ago. Then again, he also knew that no one was perfect and that even Jesus Christ had had his trials to face. The best everyone could do was to be faithfully true to the Book, and repent when necessary.

"Sure, Danny," he said, walking towards his car. "How can I help you on this beautiful Sunday?" It was a bright April morning. The air was still fresh but the warmer rays of the sun promised a lovely afternoon with barbecues.

Strolling by the Reverend, Danny accepted the invitation for an enlightening chat.

"You know, I've seen that movie about a bunch of teenagers who're dead and alive at the same time with my sister and her friends. Well, actually our mum told her to let me watch it with them, Sally didn't want me with her friends but she had to and well…"

The Reverend began rolling his eyeballs and instantly cast a silent prayer into the light blue sky as Danny continued.

"And I was wondering, it's supposed to be very romantic and stuff, I got that and all, but I thought it was really boring and apparently there's four sequels but I don't think I want to see the other flicks and so, I was wondering where God stands about that kind of stuff, with creation and all that."

"Well, as you know, there is the resurrection of Christ and one or two others, too. But usually, it's God's will to have His children in one state or the other, not both at the same time. The only possibility for such an aberration to somehow occur would be in Hell. Were they in Hell?"

"Yeah, no, okay. That's what my granma said too, something like that," Danny conceded. "But have you ever thought about Jesus being a living dead?"

Reverend Furlong winced at the question, as if he'd just walked barefoot into a tack. Secretly he wished for a ball to roll by, to divert the boy's attention—or perhaps a puppy. Yes, a puppy would be better.

"I mean, he died on the cross, right, speared and all." Danny seemed to be making a point. "And then, he came back a couple of days later, stronger than before and immortal. I mean, it just made me think of Castlevania."

They were approaching the Reverend's white '98 Ford Escort, so the

Reverend had to cut Danny's exposé short until next Sunday, when the boy would be back next week with yet another question. Last week it was Frankenstein's creature, the week before, some alphabetical plan from outer space. He could not possibly imagine what it would be next Sunday—mummies perhaps.

He wanted to sound resolute without scolding Danny for his curiosity. "For the hundredth time—and this is not only in the Bible—what's alive can't be dead and what's dead can't be alive. The rest is God's will and part of His plan for each of us. Now if you'll excuse me, I need to be somewhere else. We can talk again next week." The Reverend got into his car and said, "Take care and see you next Sunday."

"Alright, thanks anyway," Danny said. "See you next week, Reverend!"

II

Lyra and her parents went to her Grandmother's house for lunch and spent the afternoon there. The little family came each Sunday to Grandma Siggie's house, a handful of miles west of Presque Isle. They shared a nice Sunday meal together, spoke of family life and work and all the free time one has in retirement, and often went for a walk after coffee and cake.

That Sunday, Lyra's parents had fallen asleep on the couch. It was a warm, late September afternoon; the sun shone gently through the living room windows, creating a warm and cozy atmosphere. The little girl was playing with her granny's American Alsatian, Kooyo, outside the large colonial house she enjoyed so much. It used to be a farm, with all the machinery, tractors and tools required to grow several acres of potatoes. But after Siggie's husband had a heart attack at age sixty-eight, they decided to sell most of the property, keeping only the large parcel of land on which the house sat.

When Lyra came back inside, the seventy-five-year-old dame intercepted her to keep her from waking her parents, and lured her into the kitchen with the promise of hot cocoa. The washed-out blue jeans and tucked-in red plaid shirt somehow looked tasteful on the old lady as she prepared the beverage. Although her face had, of course, wrinkles and her hair had faded from amber blonde to white, Granma Siggie retained a youthful glow that always surprised anyone meeting her for the first time. And no wonder; in Lyra's experience, grandparents did not look like that—at least not her classmates' grand-parents. Despite many years of hard work on the potato farm, Granma Siggie did not have a curved back, nor did she walk with a cane. Rather, she stood proudly upright with her shoulders back, giving the impression of a marine standing to attention.

As Lyra watched her grandmother bring two cups of cocoa to the table, she wondered if she, too, would be as vivid when she was her granny's age. Her pride had something admirable, Lyra thought.

After exchanging a few bits of news about Kooyo being a great dog, although not always cooperative from the perspective of a ten-year-old, Lyra mentioned next week's big homework assignment: an original story.

"What kind of story?" her grandmother inquired.

"Well, it's a creative writing assignment and I've already started something but I'm really not sure if that's what Mrs. Delmore expects."

"Uhum." Siggie nodded sympathetically.

"Mrs. Delmore said about this year's first assignment that our creative writing was so realistic that she was worried our imaginations were completely atrophied. I had to look that word up in a dictionary."

Siggie's heart sank. But this was the sort of opening she'd been waiting for. After all, the girl had to know at some point. Now that he was back and she was old, Lyra was the only suitable candidate. She'd been about the same age when her grandfather had begun telling her. But Siggie knew from experience that it was better to feed the information piece by piece, rather than all at once. Lyra was still young and Siggie had still a few years left, so there was no need to bear it all on the little girl now. Her son Henry and his wife Maud were too busy living in the city, working at the office and going along with the tech age. They did not have time for tradition. Or at least, not that one; even though it was far more than a relic from ancient times, that tradition was about more than their own little family. It was about selflessness and responsibility for others.

"Your father must have told you that our family has been here in New England for over a century."

Her granddaughter looked unsure. "I guess so, yes."

"Back in the old world…" Siggie began.

"That's Europe, right?"

"Yes, in Europe. A long time ago one of our ancestors once had a vision. In this vision a voice told him to gather his family, leave their home and seek a man who can't die. He would have to travel, searching far and wide. When he finally found the undying man, he was not to lose him ever, even if that man went away travelling himself."

"What for?" Lyra wanted to know.

"To guide and advise him on his quest to regain his soul."

III

The local gazette reported that the graveyard had been vandalized the night before. Well, not the entire graveyard; more precisely, one grave had been the target of vandalism. Early Monday morning, a villager walking his dog discovered it wide open. The stone lay flat, but the grave itself looked as if two giant hands had reached down from the skies to rip the earth open, almost like someone digging a trench for planting crops. The coffin was still six feet below, as one would expect.

It was not, however, closed.

More intriguing elements of the possible crime scene included the existence —or rather the absence—of any conclusive evidence that a crime had occurred. There were no signs pointing toward the use of a shovel for removing the soil or a crow bar to lift the coffin's missing lid, pieces of which were found in the coffin and scattered around the grave. Another aspect that caused the inspector to light his first cigarette several hours before he normally would was that all the nails used to fasten the lid remained in the coffin's side boards. Most of them were where they were supposed to be, but a few were found among the splintered wood.

At 8:42 am, the inspector decided that the grave and the coffin had somehow been opened from the inside.

The dig was otherwise inconclusive.

IV

After three days of investigation, the mayor declared that in the absence of a reasonable explanation or even evidence of an actual crime, the grave had to be filled with earth and the stone erected again.

Soon after, the case of the open grave was officially closed.

＊ ＊ ＊

V

On Thursday, two grave diggers arrived at 7:30 am to close and restore the grave. As they shoveled damp earth laboriously back into the ground, elderly George found a potato. He held a shovel in his right hand and the potato in his left and stood there in his dark blue sailor's coat, a corduroy flat cap on his grey head and his rubber boots ankle deep in mud. His small, blue-grey eyes seemed to be carved into his face somehow, along with the wrinkles warning of how life could be less than gentle. The old man had worked the earth for the better part of his life, growing crops after he had left the army until he lost his wife to tuberculosis. He had sold the house and rented a smaller one close to the graveyard, for him and his only daughter.

People rarely plan to work in the funeral business or in graveyards. Often it is because no one else wants to do the job, which makes for an easy hire. Sometimes it is because their life has lost its meaning. A combination of the two seemed to be the case for George; the previous gravedigger left abruptly to start a new life in the flower business, leaving a job that needed doing. So George took it. It allowed him to provide a home for his child until she was old enough to marry. A few years after that, he offered his son-in-law a partnership in his business.

He held the potato out to his youthful ward and said, "Can you believe it? I just found a potato!"

Twenty-three-year-old Hank took the opportunity for a break. He wiped his forehead and long brown bangs with a dirty cloth, leaning against a nearby walnut tree. The air was damp from a stubborn, intermittent drizzle. It was not the best day for shoveling earth. With both eyebrows raised in mild bewilderment, he looked at his father-in-law. "If you find a handful more, I'll ask Henrietta to fix us mashed potatoes with cheese and lard tomorrow. Siggie will be happy to have you around."

VI

Hank met Henrietta on a summer dance in Gamlin six years ago. They had fallen in love at first sight and got married the same year. She became pregnant soon after. Hank, who did not know his parents, had fled the orphanage at ten and found work as a stable boy a few miles downstream from Gamlin. The childless farmer couple adopted the young boy when he appeared on their doorstep asking for work and a place to sleep.

They were kind-hearted people used to country life, which was harsh but rewarding. What they did not have in wealth and education, they made up for in kindness and knowledge about the land. So Hank learned everything there was to know about livestock: how to pay attention to the needs of all the beasts at the farm, from the chickens to the horses—and to live by the seasons. The small salary he received taught him the value of money well-earned. The work at the farm strengthened his hands and broadened his shoulders.

By the time he turned seventeen, he was not a boy anymore. His innocent-looking eyes and brown hair contrasted with his rough build. Henrietta later told Siggie that when he smiled, his eyes glowed, and his entire face became younger, more radiant.

It was when she first saw him smile that she decided to go talk to him at the summer dance.

VII

Hank invited his father-in-law to share a meal at their house on the outskirts of Gamlin. After lunch, the four of them went for a walk through the village. It was an early October Sunday, mid-afternoon. The clouds were moving fast. Rays of sun shone through, warm and comforting despite the chill wind rattling the leaves of the walnut trees. George had fallen a little behind the others, while Siggie was well ahead, singing to trees, crows, squirrels, walnuts, and of course to her parents.

At some point, Henrietta turned around to check on her father. Hank enjoyed watching her amber blonde hair fly in the wind as she moved. George used to say she looked every little bit like her mother, with the same pale blue eyes and thin long lips. But he'd always put her southern temperament on his wife's parents' account. In his family, naturally, everybody had wonderful tempers.

He told them not to wait for him; he would catch up later. But Siggie ran back to join him anyway, long golden hair flying in the wind and shining in the warm autumn sun.

The moment she reached him, she told George everything she'd experienced during the last two days—which of course seemed like two weeks from the perspective of a six-year-old—without him asking and without her minding that he had not asked. She enjoyed talking to her grandfather. To her, he was like an old hero with glorious tales and adventures to tell. Even better, George always listened to what Siggie told him: inquiring if that was really so, always asking what happened next. The round soft lines of her face brightened with every question.

As he listened, George thought she was like a mountain river: full of energy, tireless, sometimes a little rash.

VIII

When they arrived at the abandoned house, George paused to take out his pipe. As he stuffed the pipe, Siggie thought he seemed distracted, particularly by the dark, empty windows of the house. But she waited patiently until he had lit the tobacco and taken a puff to ask what he was looking at. "What is it, Grampa?"

George told Siggie that this was one of the oldest houses in the village and that it had once belonged to a nobleman of foreign origin called Mr. Twigg. He was rumored to be very pale, and whenever he went out he always wore wide brim hats and long crimson coats. When George had been a boy, he heard stories about how Mr. Twigg bought up all the land in the area and made a fortune cultivating the potatoes he'd brought from his home country. That was after the great famine, so everybody was happy to have such wonderful potatoes. So successful was Mr. Twigg's enterprise that many people came to work and live in the village.

"Why potatoes?" Siggie wanted to know.

"They grow easily around these parts. You can have several harvests between spring and the first frost and you can feed the pigs with them, too. While there's enough potatoes to eat and still more growing, you can farm other crops in the meantime and focus on livestock. And there are lots of different ways to cook them."

Siggie seemed satisfied with that answer, so he continued.

IX

But George did not know the whole story; how, a few centuries ago, the village was barely larger than a handful of wooden huts. How one day a hunter came, built a hut of his own and never left, thus becoming the first permanent inhabitant of the valley. When more hunters came along to hunt deer, bears and wolves in the forests nearby, they found a wooden sign in front of the hunter's house with one word written upon it in coal: Gamlin.

Gamlin turned out to be the hunter's name. The other hunters who went to the cities in the valley to trade their loot henceforth called the place Gamlin.

There were plenty of wild animals to hunt in Gamlin, so eventually others came and built more huts. However, it remained a hunter outpost; most people did not stay more than a few months before returning downstream, loaded with pelts for the markets in the lower valleys.

Then the plague struck.

The harsh winter finished all those who lingered on the threshold between life and death. In the end, only a few survived and Gamlin nearly became a ghost village. Folklore had it the place was cursed. Some people even said that the handful of plague survivors who stayed there were not human; if they were, they would have died like everybody else.

A few years later, a stranger appeared on the dirt road along the river. It was clear he was an outsider. He wore a crimson red brim hat and a coat of the same color. With him, he had a small bag full of potatoes. He gave one to every inhabitant, along with instructions to plant them as soon as winter was over. They did. Those potatoes grew faster and had better yield than local species. Life was harsh in those days, and the promise of a trustworthy crop raised hopes.

At first, Mr. Twigg lived in an inn in Two Rivers, about five miles downstream. But he came to Gamlin frequently to visit the people. He gave money freely, and soon the hunters considered him a friend and a benefactor. In the months before the first planting season, Mr. Twigg acquired all the land in the area: from the mountain gorge to the north, along either side of the valley, to the fields of Two Springs, including that on which the hunters built their huts.

The first year, the harvest yielded so much that the first inhabitants of Gamlin took up potato farming in addition to hunting. Within two short years the harvest grew so large that every resident had enough to eat, feed their pigs and use a full third of the potatoes to plant the following season. Three years after Mr. Twigg's arrival, the farmers had enough to sell at the markets of villages and cities close by. Word of the miraculous crop and cheap land spread around the region and attracted more people. To show their gratitude, the inhabitants of slowly growing Gamlin built Mr. Twigg a manor house and elected him mayor of their small community. From that time on he stayed in the manor house, coming out only occasionally. His public appearances decreased as the population increased. By the fourth year, he required a secretary who acted in his name in village matters: Mr. Plough.

Mr. Plough was a lean, not yet middle-aged man, tall and literate. He came from the countryside but preferred to pursue an intellectual career before he met Mr. Twigg. His future employer and patron noticed that Plough was good with people. Very good. And indeed, Plough knew how to deal with communal matters, financial matters, neighbor and property issues and, until the arrival of a clergyman who built a chapel next to the small graveyard, he even performed weddings and burials.

Within ten years the hunter outpost grew into a prosperous little town with over forty families of framers and traders who had food, livestock, commerce, and a fair amount of prosperity. The only issues they faced were neighborly disputes and sporadic disappearances of livestock: chickens, a goat, even a pig from time to time. Such minor incidents were usually attributed to human negligence or to the intrusion of foxes.

When it came to more trying incidents, wild beasts were blamed. When a little girl was found dead near the forest, her corpse was so terribly ruined that the townsfolk concluded she'd fallen victim to wolves or perhaps a bear.

The people of Gamlin found little satisfaction when two hunters brought returned from the forest with the corpse of an enormous wolf beast and exposed it on the market place. Although such gruesome incidents occurred very rarely, they caused great grief in the community. Each time the people grew closer together.

Whenever such things happened, the mayor was conspicuously absent. His failure to appear incited growing resentment. Although the townspeople had everything they needed, many began to feel that there was something they did not have. Most were content with their lives, but the invisibility of the town's highest authority in times of crisis was a stark reminder that they did not own the land upon which they worked so hard.

Greed, already plaguing the hearts of a few, began to spread. The villagers became convinced that it was inequitable that the mayor alone owned everything, while they—the very people who worked the land—were expected to content themselves with renting pieces of it. The chief of the Town's Watch, Ron Boot, soon emerged as the leader of a growing group of villagers who thought that the mayor should be replaced.

The following spring and summer, disaster struck. The season yielded more rain than usual, and the crops rotted in the ground, winding the townsfolk's angst to a fever pitch.

One late September evening, the town council gathered at The Shepherd's Dog tavern to discuss the future. Heavy rains already caused the loss of the May and August crops, leaving little hope for the last harvest. The mayor offered no compensation for the lost crops.

"That would be the least he could do," the tavern owner, a frog-faced old lady, said bitterly.

As a murmur of assent swept the room, Old Mrs. Boot hid a triumphant smile. She was very much looking forward to seeing her son as the new mayor. He would combine the two most influential functions in Gamlin—head of the Watch and mayor—into one position. She, of course, would devote herself to advising and counselling to her son. "Mr. Twigg's helped many of us, no question," she said carefully. "But it seems to me he's outlived his competence."

More agreeing murmurs. When the frog-faced old lady asked if anybody knew why Twigg hadn't sold the lands to each family who worked on it, nobody knew the answer. "I know," she bawled. "Because he wants to keep it all to himself."

Had they each owned their pieces of land, she continued, they could have sold some off to make up for the dismal harvest. But because Mr. Twigg kept it all for himself, they had no choice.

Soon everyone present was furiously vociferating that they had had enough and they would not stand for any more of the mayor's abuse.

With great satisfaction, Mrs. Boot observed the effect of the meeting on her audience. Her son, Ron, and the shorter-tempered men under his command prepared to storm the mayor's manor.

When Mr. Twigg saw the angry mob gathering in his front yard, burning torches and farming tools ready, he knew they hadn't come to talk. Despair rose inside him. He had failed again. For a moment, he considered negotiating with Mrs. Boot. But he quickly dismissed the notion. He knew from experience that once people reach the point where poking a pitch fork into their leader seems a reasonable solution, communication isn't possible.

As he watched the mob swell, Mr. Twigg's despair turned into anger... and into wrath. He could kill them all—slaughter them like the Vandals slaughtered the Romans; tear their bodies apart like freshly-baked bread. He wanted to rain fire on them, to drown them in a sea of their own blood. Any resistance would be futile. And then he could feed; at long last he could have a feast, his first in ages. The mob would not know that they would be up against a force of Nature: one of Her most destructive mutations. Once a Vampire sets his mind on a goal, there is no deterring him.

For a moment, Twigg considered waiting until they all went to sleep, then strategically smothering the leaders in their beds. No one would ever prove what had happened. But all would understand the message: do not bite the hand that gave you everything.

But this possibility did not feel satisfactory to Mr. Twigg. Experience had shown that whether he showed his true nature or not, the cooperation of the people of Gamlin had reached an end.

A broad smile appeared on his pale, cold face. The anticipation of fresh, warm blood was so vivid in his mind that he could already taste it.

He called down to the mob from the window of his study. He said he understood their plea, and that he would address it first thing in the morning by calling a counsel to elect his successor. He assured them that they had nothing to fear in him, nothing to distrust.

Mrs. Boot was content with this public announcement. She would have enjoyed a demonstration of force, but this was satisfactory. There was no doubt in her mind that the townsfolk would elect her son as the next mayor.

The following day, the people of Gamlin awoke to three deaths. Ron Boot was found face down near the forest, limbs and face terribly maimed. It seemed he had been attacked by a wild animal during his evening walk. There was no reason to believe otherwise.

His mother, Gerda Boot, appeared to have been the victim of a snakebite. Gamlin's snakes weren't known to be venomous, but the bite marks on her throat left no other explanation. The town's medic concluded that the snake bite had caused a stroke, which, in turn, had caused her death.

The discovery of the first two bodies led the townsfolk to be suspicious of things no one would openly admit. But they sensed that the mayor had something to do with it… until his inert body was discovered in his bed.

He appeared to be sleeping, but nothing could wake him. After the initial uproar, they found a small empty vial on his bedside table with a note pinned underneath.

Mr. Plough appeared to have left town during the night; the room he occupied in Mr. Twigg's manor was empty.

X

"And then, the poor man had died," George said.

Siggie frowned. "That's sad. He was living there all alone and then he died?"

"Yes," George said. "That's what everybody thought."

"Who wrote the note?"

"No one knows. Rumor had it might've been the postman, who was the first to see the corpse and feared being accused of murdering Mr. Twigg."

"That's... unlikely," she said, eyebrows wrinkled in disbelief.

"Indeed. But there's something else."

The sun was leaning to the west, the shadows growing longer towards the east and Siggie wanted to know what it was. "Are you going to tell me what it is?"

George gave her an understanding smile; she was a swift-minded little girl; of course she wanted to know. He looked the house's dark windows. For a moment he thought he caught a glimpse of something moving within. But no one had lived there in decades. Perhaps a cat, hunting for rats?

"I hadn't thought about it until now," he finally continued, "but around here we often plant walnut trees in the potato fields, a kind of corner stones to limit our plots, you know. Some of them must be more than a hundred years old."

Siggie's big eyes widened expectantly. "Aaaand...?"

"And there hasn't always been a graveyard where it is today. Back in the early days of Gamlin, families buried their dead behind their houses. The chapel and the graveyard came later, when more people moved to Gamlin to grow crops. They planted most of those walnut trees around that time. It just struck me that there's one right next to the grave that we fixed up with your father last week. And that the grave was Mr. Twigg's."

XI

Granma Siggie and Lyra were just finishing their cocoa. The girl had listened carefully to Granma's story, and was now considering its potential for next week's writing assignment. Lyra concluded that some of it was probably just folklore, but altogether Granma Siggie provided a solid basis for her story.

While Siggie put the cocoa mugs into the dish washer, Lyra glanced past the entrance into the living room and saw that her parents had woken from their nap. The sun had turned; the warmth of the afternoon was slowly making way for the cold of the night. She considered playing one last round with Kooyo in the front yard before they left.

"You see," Siggie said, "Viktor has known our family for a long time."

"Viktor..." Lyra frowned. "That's your neighbor, right?"

"Yes, it is."

"Known how? Do you mean like more than just neighbors?"

"Yes, like friends. Like neighbors, too. But we never invite each other over for tea or lunch."

Lyra tilted her head, trying to understand. From the expression on her granddaughter's face, Siggie intuited the need for clarity.

"It's more like travel companions. Wayfarers, sharing a piece of the road together while keeping a respectful distance, never too close or too far away. It can be comforting to know that you're not alone, that someone's nearby when you need them. They're either a short distance ahead or behind. And sometimes you can meet to share impressions or ask for advice."

Lyra's parents entered the kitchen, bringing a swift end to the conversation.

Later, while she waved goodbye as her son, daughter-in-law and granddaughter started back to Presque Isle, Siggie silently hoped that her neighbor would stay put until Lyra was ready to take her place.

XII

Siggie went out on the porch to watch the sunset from a rocking chair. Autumn had turned the leaves from genuine green to yellow, orange and vermillion. Her next-door neighbor was also on his porch, sitting comfortably in a wooden arm chair, dressed in a dark red morning gown, large brim hat and sunglasses. He could have been an actor from the 1930s, resting backstage. He seemed to be always alone, quite to himself. He noticed her and raised a very pale hand in greeting.

"Good afternoon, Mrs. Plough."

"Good afternoon to you, neighbor."

They listened in silence to the wind in the walnut trees.

Eventually he asked, "Have you ever met Him?"

"No, we only do His bidding."

"I met Him once in the shape of a little girl. He fooled me."

"At least you could talk to Him."

"Indeed. And what a talk to remember. I haven't forgotten the day when I mocked His creation and His ridiculous humans. The little blonde asked if I thought I could do better than He and I said sure. Then He offered me a bargain at the end of which He'd renounce Heaven to make me ruler of all realms—of this life and the next—if I succeed. Eternal life always has that shine to it in the first place, like all new things. But if you can't really choose, it gets less fun over time."

"What do you mean, choose?"

"I told you, He fooled me. He gave me eternal life, but the little vixen didn't tell me that to sustain it—and so have a chance at succeeding—I'd have to feed on human blood."

That's almost ungodly, Siggie thought. Out loud she said, "Seems rather ironic to me."

"You can say that again. I knew He had a sense of humor as soon as he gave brains to mankind. But I didn't know He was a cynic, too. Of course that was before I realized that I had been misled."

"At least I'm here to watch over you."

Mr. Twigg remained silent for a while. Eventually he said, "It's good to have someone to talk to."

Both looked out across the fields of white flowers, signals that the time for the year's last harvest was near.

When the disk met the mountain line, gleaming, red-golden light flushed the entirety of Aroostook County, from the Appalachians, over the border, and to the sea.

The sudden stench of sulfur and rotting flesh assaulted Twigg's nose. He was back. Returned to check on his victim without warning, as He so often did, always by taking control of the closest human being.

Twigg asked, "What I don't understand is why did you do it? Why me?"

"Well, He doesn't like people questioning His work; I know that from experience." His neighbor's eyeballs rolled back in her sockets. "And I so enjoy a good bargain. Since I was at the right place at the right time, I couldn't resist. Being a bit slower to react than yours truly, He tried to even it out and therefore sent an entire dynasty to assist you."

After the lady regained possession of her body, the stench lingered silently in the air until a cool evening breeze replaced it with the scent of flowers and earth.

At a crossroads in the middle of the fields, not far from the two cottages, was a man wearing a suit and a hat, sitting on a trunk under a road sign, picking his guitar.

XIII

Ages ago.

A merchant travelling with his mule, laden with goods to sell, along a dirt road through a canyon. The merchant plans on spending the night at an inn, in a real bed. He is neither old nor young, but his youth was stolen by wars for Christendom and freedom more than a decade ago, when he fought alongside Prince Bethlen of Transylvania against the Emperor.

The country he is crossing is called Crna Gora in a local language. On hearing what it means, it makes him think of another faraway place he remembers well: a huge dark forest with a strange blackness to it. This region was called the black mountain.

It takes half a day's walk to cross the canyon and reach the village. On a map shown to him in Zabljak, he saw that upon crossing the Piva river, he could follow the road to the south and west which would take him to Dubrovnik in about one week. But it has been ten days since he left the Piva river, and he does not know where he is; only that the last road sign said something about a village close by. He hopes to arrive before nightfall.

As the merchant walks with his mule, they pass the rotting corpse of a horse on the side of the road. It looks as if it has been attacked by wolves but it has not been there long. Crows have barely begun to gather around it. The mule becomes restless. The merchant tries to soothe it, but he sees the panic rising in its eyes. It takes some time before he notices that the stench of foulness and burnt wood surrounds them. Swarms of flies seem to grow with every step he takes toward the village.

Soon he spots a thick column of smoke a short distance ahead, climbing into the sky. Maybe an accident, he thinks. Perhaps the smithy caught fire. Or maybe a lamp tipped over and fell into the straw in the stables. Surely people are taking care of it. It is probably already under control. Hopefully no one was harmed, the merchant thinks, as he walks onward. The air is filled with flies.

XIV

Seen from the top of the canyon, the village bears resemblance to a snake that has swallowed a hare. It is a good place to enforce taxes on merchandise, as there are only two roads leading to and from it. There are no other ways to this place.

The mule grows increasingly nervous, pulling continually on the rope between its neck and the merchant's hand, leaving no doubt that it wishes to turn around and go back the way they came. The smell of decomposing flesh saturates the air. Thick smoke columns rise against the setting sun. Everything else seems to be covered in flies. He should be hearing voices and village noises by now, but all he hears are his steps, the hooves of his mule, the buzzing of flies, and as they reach the gates the crackle of burning, wooden architecture.

The merchant sees nothing but ruins and death. He shivers in terror. No building is unburnt, no being left alive. Everything is destroyed. Corpses scatter the ground. Whatever happened here, no one escaped. He remembers the dead horse, and wishes he'd turned around when he saw it.

The merchant struggles to hold onto his senses and keep fear at bay. It is only a short way through the rest of the village. In a few moments he will be past it, able to forget all he has seen.

As his overloading senses threaten to fail him, he throws up his modest meal. Afterward, he pulls the rope closer and walks on with his mule. Death must have been here in person, and he does not intend to be around if Death comes back.

As the traveling merchant makes his way through the ruins, he sees a silhouette walking through the smoke and flies. He believes it to be a survivor. But instead of lessening, the terror he feels in every fiber of his body increases. The silhouette is tall, wearing a large brim hat and a wide coat.

The merchant stops as the stranger steadily approaches. Too late, he realizes that it is not a person. With dark, glowing, wrathful eyes, the creature looks at him from under its hat. Out of an unnaturally pale, cold face its monstrous mouth shows long fangs. An ancient voice growls, "This is what happens when you bite the hand that's given you everything."

IN THE DARK AND SECRET SHADOWS

GINA EASTON

In my heart of hearts it wasn't that I didn't believe these things could happen. I simply had an overpowering need *not* to believe Gilly when she told me. Of course it's tempting to hide behind excuses, to try to wash away guilt in the cleansing waters of rationality, to attribute all of it to a child's frenetic imagination. Which is what I did, after first checking Gilly's story to the best of my ability and finding nothing to substantiate her claims. Or so I thought. I merely told her to avoid the alley-way. Strange, looking back on it now, that I should have been so naive, so blind to my own demons.

It all began when my seven-year-old daughter asked me if I would walk her to school the next day. I was puzzled by this request, as Gilly was an independent and adventurous child. I thought maybe she'd quarreled with one of her friends and was avoiding the walk to school with her usual circle of pals.

"Why, Gilly?" I asked.

Her small face clouded over, a pinched look marring her features. "Because of the Shadow-Man."

"The… what man?"

She glanced at me but quickly dropped her gaze, as though ashamed of demonstrating vulnerability. "The Shadow-Man in the alley."

I felt the first quickening of alarm. Gilly and her friends used the alleyway at the end of our street as a shortcut to school. "There's a man in the alley?" I struggled to keep my voice calm and even.

Gilly nodded, her face flushed. She began to fidget as she stood before me, increasingly uncomfortable.

"What does the man do? Does he talk to you?"

We'd had the "talk" of course, the one about strangers approaching with credible stories about lost puppies, medical emergencies, any kind of pretense designed to lure vulnerable young girls. I liked to think that Gilly was sufficiently "street-smart" to avoid the pitfalls of any would-be predator.

Gilly shook her head. "No, he doesn't say anything. He just stands at the end of the alley and he watches."

"Is he there every time?"

"At first, he wasn't. He was only there sometimes. But now it's more often. Soon he'll be there every day. Watching. Waiting for me."

Something about the way Gilly uttered those words sent a frisson of dread down my spine. A blast of arctic wind shivered through me, carrying a sharp stab of fear. "What does he look like?"

Gilly's voice had a defiant edge to it, as though she suspected I might not believe her. "He's all dark."

I was puzzled by her description. "He's black?"

Gilly shook her head impatiently. "No, Mommy. He's DARK. He's all the same color—-his clothes, his hair, his face. He looks kind of like a shadow, but shaped into a person." A frustrated frown cramped her features as she struggled for the words her limited vocabulary dangled just beyond her reach. Then she took a deep breath and said firmly, "All black. Except for his eyes. They're red."

"Red?" My mind scrambled for a reasonable explanation. "Maybe he wears tinted sunglasses?"

Gilly shook her head again. "They're not sunglasses. They're his eyes, glowing like blood-drops. He watches me with those eyes. Even after I leave the alley I feel his eyes, like they're burning holes into me. He's evil, Mommy. He wants to kill me." She delivered those last words quietly, calmly. And for that reason fear spread in me, taking root in my spine and sending creeping tendrils through the rest of my body.

"Why would you say that, Gilly?" My mouth was dry, but I managed to keep my voice from trembling. "He's never come near you? Never threatened you?"

"No."

I peered closely at my daughter's pinched little face. "Gilly, you would tell me, wouldn't you? You know you can tell me anything."

"No, Mommy. He doesn't talk. He doesn't move. He only stands there."

"Well…" I wasn't quite sure how to proceed. It was clear Gilly feared this person, albeit in the absence of an overt threat. "What about the other kids? Are they afraid, too?"

Gilly hung her head momentarily before looking at me once more. Her eyes were troubled and cloudy again. "The other kids don't see him."

I gaped at her. "What do you mean?"

"They don't see him," she repeated. "I asked them what they thought of him and they just looked at me like I was crazy. They walk right by him like he's not even there. So now, I act like I don't see him, too. I thought maybe he'd go away if I pretended I couldn't see. But it didn't work. He's still there."

"But, Gilly…" I trailed off, confusion apparent in my tone.

The cloudy look flashed into a stormy one. "You don't believe me!" she accused, voice shrill. "I knew you wouldn't. You think I made it up. But I didn't! The Shadow-Man is real!" She was gone in a pounding of feet up the stairs. A moment later, I heard her bedroom door slam shut.

The next day, I walked with Gilly from our house to the alleyway. She was still angry with me, silent and sullen as she trudged beside me. I found myself tensing as we approached the alley, my muscles stiffening in response to a subconscious warning.

I saw no sign of Gilly's friends. This wasn't unexpected, as we'd deliberately left early so we could walk to school alone. The alley seemed empty as we entered. My head swiveled from side to side, eyes sweeping every visible inch of the alleyway, inwardly daring anyone or anything to jump out at me. *Now why did I think that?* I asked myself. Because Gilly's description was of no ordinary man. Even though I wasn't yet sure what was going on, I knew that it was something singularly disturbing. Men weren't the color of shadows and they didn't have piercing red eyes…

Silence, heavy as mist, enshrouded the alley. The noise of nearby traffic was oddly muted, as though coming from a much farther distance. Even the sound of my shoes against the pavement seemed distorted, a hollow ring echoing in my ears. It was cold, too, several degrees colder than the sunlit street behind us, a street that now seemed so far away it could have belonged to another world.

Where had the cold come from? No wind disturbed the eerie stillness of the alley; a multitude of trash and debris huddled in the corners, motionless. No animals trespassed here, no stalking alley cats or mangy mongrels slinking in the shadowed recesses. No living thing. Uneasiness tingled through me. This was a forbidden place. A dead place.

"Do you see him?" I whispered tensely.

Gilly shook her head. Relief flooded me, so intense it surprised me. I relaxed my grip on her hand. A dejected look clung to Gilly's face; disappointed that she'd failed to prove the Shadow-Man's existence.

"He's not here," she said miserably. "I knew he wouldn't be. Not with you here."

"Do you think he's afraid of me?" I asked.

"Of course not, Mommy, "she said scornfully. "The Shadow-Man isn't afraid of grownups. He's just hiding 'cause he wants to. He could kill you if he wanted to," she added matter-of-factly.

We walked through the alley as quickly as we could. Gilly pointed to an area about two-thirds of the way down the alley. "There. That's where he always stands."

"Beside that rubbish bin in the corner?"

She nodded, lips pursed. I stared at the dumpster as we passed. It was a large contraption, perhaps four feet high and as many wide. *Big enough to hide in*, I thought uneasily. It was painted a dark hunter green, with rusty patches showing through. My intestines contracted in fascinated fear. There was something deeply disturbing and sinister about this bin. And something vaguely familiar.

"That's where he lives," Gilly whispered.

Her voice startled me back to the present, summoning my thoughts from nether regions of half-remembered nightmares and shadow memories.

I grabbed Gilly's hand tightly once more. "Come on. Let's get out of here."

I dropped Gilly off at school, promising to pick her up at the end of the day. It was my day off from the art gallery where I worked. The weather was fair, a sunny and mild autumn day and so I decided to go for a walk before returning home. My enjoyment of the day was marred, however, by Gilly's story.

Gilly had always been a highly imaginative child, loving stories of fairies and magic. She'd gone through a phase of being afraid of the dark, like most children, I assume, but a nightlight solved that problem. This was the first time she had conjured up such a disturbing and menacing figure. No matter how I tried to dismiss the Shadow-Man as the product of childish fantasy, apprehension gnawed at me, persistent as a throbbing toothache.

When I was pregnant with Gilly, I'd seriously considered having an abortion. I was barely twenty years old and on my own, a promising art student. My boyfriend ran off the moment he learned of the pregnancy. I was torn by indecision, beset by doubts. By the time I'd made up my mind to go ahead with the abortion it was too late; the pregnancy was too far advanced.

Being a single mother hasn't come easily or naturally to me. There have been sacrifices –the loss of my freedom, and hardest of all, the dissipation of my cherished goal of becoming a successful artist. That dream was shelved in favor of more practical employment to support my daughter and myself; the art degree I had so proudly earned enabled me to obtain the job at the art gallery. I thought I'd dealt with that disappointment, but the job was a constant reminder of my crushed hopes and obliterated dreams. I'd never allowed myself to really face the pain, to mourn those losses. I now realize that all I did was bury the anger.

I was nearing home, my walk almost complete. But a kind of compulsion drew me away; though I'd had every intention of continuing along the street and bypassing the shortcut, hounded by an irresistible urge to return via the alley.

As I turned the corner from sunlight into shadow it felt like entering another world, a nether region, a bridge between this world and another. I've heard that certain places in this world serve as portals between dimensions or parallel universes. Places where time and the very fabric of reality itself are distorted, causing disturbing sensations and disorienting experiences. That alley was such a place. Though I didn't believe it then, I do now. And even then, I think the belief was there, lurking in the deep layers of my subconscious.

My heart sped up as I walked down the alley, mingled anticipation and dread building as I approached the garbage bin. A sensation tugged at me, pulling me back to childhood's lost domain. This feeling, similar to my first ride on a roller-coaster: the breathless, dizzy thrill, an electric tingle through my body—excitement, yes, but a sharp pang of fear, too, knowing that I was only an angel's breath from death itself.

I recognized this churning, pounding fear. Familiar, a fragment rescued from the shipwrecked seas of memory's limitless depths. But when had I felt it before?

I stopped in front of the dumpster. Dizziness swept over me, causing me to reach out and hold onto the bin for support. The paint was gritty, flaking away beneath my fingers, some of the tiny pieces embedding themselves in my sweaty palm.

I pulled my hand away, shuddering in revulsion. An overwhelming urge to get away from the alley and that sinister bin seized me, but I knew I couldn't leave without looking inside the dumpster. Maybe I would surprise Gilly's Shadow-Man, a harmless vagrant snatching in slumber a brief respite from the harsh realities of life.

Forcing my trepidation aside, I once again reached for the bin and slowly lifted the lid.

It was empty.

I threw the lid back, courage returning. Odd bits of scrap and trash clung to the corners of the dumpster, but that was all. Or not quite—an oily black residue covered the bottom, and from this substance a peculiar smell emanated. It was pungent and noxious in the extreme, excrement and blood mixed with graveyard dirt. As it penetrated my nostrils, recognition jolted through my gut and up to my brain.

I was catapulted back to childhood, to nights of sublime terror as I waited for the evil to take form from the black depths of the shadows in my room. Darkest shapeshifter, snatching the molecules from the air and drawing them to itself, human form like a cutout against the back-drop of night. Shadow-Man, yes, his eyes blazing scarlet hunger, ready to pounce and sink razor fangs into my flesh, biting through muscle and tendon, crunching through bone. Down to the tender morsel of quivering soul, the essence of me.

My panicked cries for help, sobbing into the arms of my mother, comfort and assurances that it was only a nightmare, all children had them. Just my active imagination working overtime. Unable, in my child's inarticulate misery, to tell her, of course he's real, he's the Shadow-Man.

And in the morning, golden relief as the sun streamed through the window, banishing the chill that had wrapped icy fingers around my soul. Light and happiness filling me with hope once more, causing me to expand, chasing the fear that had shriveled me to a mummified husk in the night.

Until I ran to my bedroom window and looked down into the backyard and the adjacent alley where the garbage dumpster loomed like an ominous sentinel. Lair of the Shadow-Man, the monster who preyed on the hopeless and the lost. Like the transient man who was found mangled and mutilated in the alley shortly after my eighth birthday...

Body sprawled brokenly, neck bent at a hideous angle, a huge gaping slash in his abdomen, and stuff leaking out: slimy and grey and viscous, mixing with the foul black sludge that surrounded the corpse. Empty eye sockets, windows to an absent soul, eyeballs wrenched out, but no sign of them anywhere. Blood in congealed pools, no longer fresh, a mosaic of dark stains in the rough pavement of the alley. Mouth agape, jaws strained, throat tendons bulging with the pressure of a scream that was never released—no time to scream, muscles frozen in paralyzed terror...

I leaned over and vomited into the alley, gut-wrenching spasms that forced the sour, scalding stream from me. I heaved until my stomach muscles throbbed and my throat was raw. Then came the tears, wracking sobs erupting deep within as the memory dam collapsed and the flood-tide of feelings deluged me. I was once again that eight-year-old child who'd witnessed that scene of carnage.

I don't know how long I knelt there, immobilized by terror. But gradually, the iron vise loosened, the pressure around my heart and other organs ceased, and I was able to straighten up. My knees shook and so I rose slowly, feeling fragile and brittle as a sun-damaged statue. it took me a while to remember where I was, and who I was. No longer a terrified child, but a twenty-eight-year-old woman who had just experienced a close encounter with a shadow demon too long hidden in memory's labyrinth.

I left the alley and returned to the sunlit street, sanctuary from fear and insanity. Somnambulistically, feet dragging on sidewalk, body on autopilot, I headed home. My mind was hazy, caught in a monstrous cobweb. Echoes of thoughts swirled nebulously in the haze. I made no effort to sort them out. Only one thing stood out in stark clarity; I knew Gilly's Shadow-Man, had experienced the terror of him when I was her age, then forgot he'd ever existed. I'd wiped from my conscious mind every memory of him and the horrific murder whose aftermath I'd stumbled upon.

That much I understood and on a certain level would probably come to accept. But how was it possible that Gilly was seeing him now, some twenty years later? If the Shadow-Man was indeed a figment of my own childish imagination, how was it that Gilly's mind had conjured up the exact image? It seemed preposterous to call it a coincidence. The only other possibility was equally incredible—that the Shadow-Man was real, existing in, but not of, our reality, slipping between worlds at will like water through cracks. But how could my adult rational mind accept this? I felt like my psyche had been violently ripped in half, laying bare both the logical, reasoning side and the other. The side that was mostly hidden, subsumed in the mature adult mind. The side prone to flights of imagination, where magic cavorted alongside its darker twin, a twin born of evil and corruption, seeking not to delight, but to destroy.

The next few hours passed in a daze, until it was time to collect Gilly from school. I still didn't know how I was going to handle the subject of the Shadow-Man with her. I hadn't yet processed the afternoon's events and was still fragile and shell-shocked. I would just have to make sure we didn't use the alleyway anymore, under any circumstance.

The schoolyard was deserted, but several people were gathered around the front doors. A firetruck was parked on the street in front of the school. My heart beat faster as I approached the steps. I saw adults only, no sign of children anywhere.

The school principal, Mr. Nolan, was talking to a fireman. I hurried over to him. "Excuse me, Mr. Nolan?"

He turned, a polite, slightly harried look on his face. "Yes?"

"I'm Nadine Burnsfield. My daughter, Gilly, is in Mrs. Rainer's class."

"Ah, yes, Mrs. Burnsfield. How may I help you?"

"What's going on?" I asked. "Where are the children?"

"We had a small fire in the cafeteria just after lunch. No one was in any danger," he hastily assured me, "but the fire department recommended we close the school for the remainder of the day so they could check out the electrical wiring. Just as a precaution, you understand."

I tried to keep the anxiety from my voice. "What time did you let the kids out?"

"A bit after one o'clock. The children behaved marvelously, just like we practiced in the fire drill." He beamed proudly, then noticed the stricken look on my face. "Is something wrong, Mrs. Burnsfield?"

I looked at my watch with a sick feeling, like a worm burrowing in my gut. A quarter past three. Two hours since Gilly got out of school. She should have been home a long time ago. Gilly didn't have a cell phone. I'd been holding off until she was a little older. It was only a twenty-minute walk to school. She should've arrived at the house before I set off to meet her. My daughter was an obedient child and always came straight home from school with her friends, heeding my command to never walk home alone. She knew I'd be coming to meet her today. She would've stayed around the building, playing in the schoolyard.

Unless she decided to walk home with her friends. After all, there was safety in numbers. The evil couldn't get you if you were with your friends. Unless it was the Shadow-Man and he managed somehow to get you alone...

I fled, racing back along the way I'd come, knowing I had to enter the alley again. Praying that I wasn't too late, fighting the sick despair and raw panic threatening to consume me in nauseating waves.

I hesitated when I reached the alley, gathering my courage about me like a frayed mantle, then plunged forward. My eyes saw but did not want to register the black oozing substance that lay in scattered droplets about the pavement near the dumpster.

In a corner, caught in the dark puddle, a glistening of silver. I ran toward it. A great tearing sob shook my body as I recognized the sterling fairy pendant I'd given Gilly for her birthday last year. I threw myself to my knees, prying the trinket from the stinking slime and clasping it to me, tears flowing in a caustic torrent.

Gilly's body was never found, though the police searched diligently. Despite the ensuing press and publicity, it remained just one more unsolved case, a missing child who disappeared without a trace. Except for a pendant and an oily residue, clues which frustrated the investigating officers. No DNA or other forensic evidence. They couldn't put the pieces together. And I couldn't tell them.

It's been ten years since Gilly's disappearance. For a long time I hid away, hugging my misery, clinging it to it like some perverse lifeline. Then I met Jack, who quite literally saved me from my spiraling despair. He loves me despite my flaws, despite my failure to protect my daughter. Unlike me, he doesn't understand that I'm responsible for Gilly's death. We have a good life together, with beautiful four-year old twins, a boy and girl. I am vigilant, watching over them day and night.

I will always carry the sorrow and the pain, unrelieved by any solace or illusory words of comfort. Gilly died because of me. It was the Shadow-Man, *my* Shadow-Man who took her. If only I'd been stronger, able to face my bitterness and fear all those years ago. Instead those feelings festered like some monstrous tumor in the sun-starved regions of my subconscious.

My fear and anger summoned the Shadow-Man from the other realm to which he'd been banished after I outgrew my childish fears. He became the dark avenger of my dead and withered dreams. And the object of its rage was my beautiful and innocent child. The tears I cry can never bring her back from death. And I will never be free from the guilt... or the fear.

The Shadow-Man is under lock and key now. But I ask myself how long it will be before he escapes again?

And who will he come for this time?

THE FAERIES OF ESMY - A TALE OF THE BAJAZID

KENNETH BYKERK

"How much farther?" Esmerelda's voice was tired, bordering on cranky. She walked in unconquered darkness.

No reply other than her footfalls, sure as a cat in the night.

"I'm getting tired, that's why."

Her step was not natural. It did not falter, did not seek purchase in the pitch, but stepped with the ease of a garden stroll.

"I don't know what you mean?"

Flowers did not grow on the path she strode, only sharp stones.

"But I don't know anything about faeries. I just know what you told me."

Only sharp stones and old, moldy bones littered the path she walked.

"Yes, Guqon, I do want to be a faerie."

The sun had never seen these stones, these old, moldy bones. Her step was not once disturbed by this debris, this litter of stones and bones and picks and shovels and old iron rails.

"I have to piss."

She stepped with enchanted grace as if her path were blessed, untainted by the world about.

"Do faeries piss? I don't want to have to piss no more."

Esmerelda Kearns, Esmy as the Family called her, was growing tired with the beautiful garden. She was growing tired of the journey and she did have to piss.

She was also starting to get hungry, but she didn't want to mention that to Guqon because she didn't want the faerie to think she was a spoilt child like everyone else did. As pretty as this path was, it was taking too long and Esmy wanted to see the Faerie King like Guqon promised her before she had to go to bed.

She stopped. A burst of fear flushed her. If she wasn't found in her bed in the morning or if Mama Elena looked in or if Millie woke up or if Billy snuck in... she was going to be in trouble. She tried to turn, to hurry back, the fear was that strong. She tried but her face held forth, unable to even turn her gaze. She pulled with all her might but in vain, her body held by invisible bonds.

"Guqon, I don't wanna be in trouble! If they find out..."

Her struggles ebbed, her body calming. Her nose glowed ever so faintly in the stygian black about.

"But..."

Except for the odd angle of her head, she stood with body relaxed. Her fingers no longer dug deep into the faceless sack-doll in her hand.

"Faeries don't look back? Why?"

Invisible to her, beneath her feet, children of the earth crawled through grim remains long stripped.

"Oh..." Esmy's tone was low, contrite.

Guqon, to Esmy's relief, let go of her face and fluttered backwards. It, for what gender is a faerie, fluttered before her with coruscating waves of rainbows flowing across its pretty little body, faint and lithe with slender limbs and stardust sparkling in its hair. The other faeries, the ones who had come out to help hold Esmy tight, fluttered back into the vines and flowers that enclosed the garden path.

No light pierced the canopy above, neither stars nor the moon Esmy knew was full this night. The path was lit in glory though, for the flowers and even the leaves and vines that filled it gave off their own warm and inviting luminance. Then there were the dust dancers. Esmy didn't know what else to call the tiny specks of light, pin-pricks in the air, that floated about like fireflies and cast the path with their glow.

Guqon fluttered, beckoning Esmy and Esmy, enchanted, followed. Into the distance ahead, the tunnel of bright vines and petals wove a path that at times ran straight, at times twisted and turned, but always the way was clear, always free of obstruction. It had not begun so. At first it was dark and terrifying, the only thing keeping Esmy from crying was Guqon assuring her it was going to be all right. The tunnel was frightening, a black maw in the mountain leading to the bad place, the place the Family stood vigil. Ever since Esmy could remember, she had been told it led to Baird's Holler and the very threshold of Hell on the other side of the ridge.

Guqon assured her, with pretty lights and smells and promises, that the way to the Faerie King was hidden beyond and beside and underneath Baird's Holler, that nasty old place. Esmy didn't understand but Guqon swore on the Faerie King himself that the tunnel would lead to a secret path and from there, to the Land of Faeries. Guqon called her a brave little girl and gave her a kiss on the nose that made it glow and tickle. Since Esmy knew that faeries never lie... Guqon had told her so... she made herself brave and she followed. She liked it when Guqon kissed her nose.

Guqon was her favorite. There were other faeries that played with her, but none had she formed such a deep friendship with. The others were often afraid to come out, fearing Mama Deidre and Father and the other grown-ups. The faeries especially didn't like her grandpapa, but that was all right for she didn't like him either. He scared her more than all the stories of the Devil and of Mama Death and the Strawman combined. She believed in the Devil and she believed in Mama Death and the Strawman. They were not just stories Billy told her to scare her; Grandpapa spoke of them too and Grandpapa spoke for God. Besides, she knew Mama Death was real. Everyone knew Mama Death was real. Mama Death took Gamma Jane, so she had to be real. She knew her grandpapa was real as well, and her grandpapa scared her even more than Mama Death did.

Down the idyllic lane she strode, that tunnel of vines and flowers, with Guqon ever beckoning, ever keeping her gaze forward through trick and guile. Not much longer, she was assured, not much longer. So she followed, her step innocent to what lay beneath the cobbled road she trod; the detritus of nightmares long spent. She followed for she trusted Guqon. Ever since Esmy had entered the old tunnel, the one that led to Baird's Holler and to Hell, she had trusted the faerie. She held true that truth known by children before they forget, that magic truly does exist. Guqon was her magic. Guqon was helping her escape her home, what she knew in her heart was a very bad place.

They had to be careful, Guqon and her, for she was forbidden to play with Guqon or any of her friends. She was only four when Guqon first kissed her nose and she got a beating when she told Mama Deidre and again when Mama Deidre told Father. Mama Elena argued with Father that Esmy only had an active imagination but Mama Diedre said she was sinning, that she was playing with demons and faeries and threatened to take her to Grandpapa. Mama Elena got mad and hit Mama Deidre and Mama Deidre hit Mama Elena back. They only stopped hitting each other because Father hit them both and told Esmy she would go see Grandpapa if she talked with demons again.

That is how Esmy first heard the word faerie. It was a full month before she would let Guqon know she saw it as it tried over and again to get her attention. Esmy was afraid of Grandpapa, as well she should be. Esmy's cousin, the pretty one with the black hair and the yellow ribbon, the one that played with her, she was sent to see Grandpapa and Esmy never saw her again. So she ignored Guqon, fearing fates imagined as only a child could, fearing her cousin was eaten up like the Innocents. She didn't want to be eaten up. Esmy knew what the Innocents were and she often wished she'd been born one, or not born at all. Esmy didn't really understand. She just knew the Innocents never woke up to the world. Esmy heard everything, heard but understood very little. There were entire concepts she couldn't understand, but she formed impressions from context. Grandpapa ate her pretty cousin with the black hair and the bright bow to keep the Devil of the Bajazid, as Grandpapa called it, from coming through the mountain to Bezer.

Guqon told her faeries weren't demons nor were they devils. They were just faeries and they found out sad little boys and girls, for faeries loved nothing more than to find sad little girls and boys and make them happy. That is why Guqon found her out. That is why it first kissed her nose and that is why Guqon kept insisting its attentions until it kissed her on the nose again. Esmy's heart melted in that moment. No one had ever shown her such warmth, not even Mama Elena. Esmy's soul was sold for the price of a kiss promised forever and again. Their friendship sealed, she and Guqon kept their play a secret so as not to incur the wrath of Grandpapa. Faeries need sad children without love just as children without love need faeries.

When Guqon first found her, Esmy was a very sad little girl. She was sad because she had been beaten and her doll, who she was forbidden to name, was taken from her. She had marked two eyes upon its blank burlap face with charcoal. Her big brother and sister, Billy and Millie, teased her loss and she ran to hide in the crawlspace beneath the house. It was then that Guqon first found her and kissed her nose. Billy and Millie had picked on her, teased her about her doll and called her ugly because she had dark skin and hair like Mama Elena and they had light hair like Mama Deidre and Mama Deidre was nice to them. Esmy didn't know what that meant, but she thought that was a good thing. She liked Mama Elena more. Mama Deidre was mean.

Esmy was delighted when they first came upon this pretty path. When Guqon snuck her from bed and out past the tunnel gate, he could only give her a little light. The tunnel ran through the mountain and she knew that in the old times, they sent gold from Baird's Holler through it out into the sinful world. Nobody came through the tunnel anymore because nobody lived in Baird's Holler anymore. Uncle Warren called it a ghost town. Esmy didn't know what that was but she was very aware of the old iron rails for they tripped her often. When Guqon showed her the faerie sign shining faint in the earthen wall, it sang and the wall of the old tunnel opened up to this road she now trod. The enchantment she felt when first stepping through that gate from that dark and scary tunnel and onto those yellow cobble-stones had long worn its course. Now she was just tired, hungry and needing to piss. Now she wanted to rest.

In the absence of her doll, Esmy quietly played with her new friends. Guqon would always hide when grownups were around and Esmy would pretend she wasn't talking to faeries by singing softly what she could remember of the Sunday hymns. It took her time to learn this trick and over the year was caught out quite often and beaten each time. Sometimes Mama Deidre would beat her just to beat her.

It was Mama Deidre who told Grandpapa. Esmy cried and was scolded by Grandpapa but he didn't eat her or even spank her. Esmy was thankful for that but Grandpapa still scared her. The Family prayed for her and Gamma Rosie and Gamma Jane made a nasty, stinky paste that they put all over her. Esmy did not like that. She also didn't like Grandpapa standing over her in church and telling all the Family that she was in sin. All were made to pray over her, to touch her hand to chase the demonic stain of the faeries away. None of her cousins would play with her after that because their mamas wouldn't let them. Mama Elena told her it was because she wasn't clean yet but when she was, her cousins would be allowed to play with her again. Esmy was alone and Esmy was sad and would often crawl under the house where Guqon would come and kiss her nose and make the sad go away if even for a little while.

Shadows are cast only where needed. She could not smell the musty decay about nor feel the bones beneath her feet roll. She could not hear the soft, shuffled steps behind. She could see only the beautiful trail ahead. She had no desire to look back. Faeries do not look back, so Guqon had told her. Fear of discovery and the beating it would bring when her bed was discovered no longer disturbed her. She had but to keep her step for Guqon assured her she need never go home, never have to feel Billy touching her again. She knew she wouldn't have to turn six. She was afraid of being six. Millie turned six the year before and she had to go see Grandpapa for help to start growing up. Millie cried and cried after, so much that Esmy pitied her and tried to comfort her. Millie had angrily pushed her away and reminded her that it was her turn at being six next. That made Esmy cry. Esmy didn't want to be six.

Despair at what her birthday would bring sent Esmy into a deep gloom, one beyond where even Guqon could draw her. Kisses to her nose would just bring forth soft, warm tears and even hugs from Mama Elena weren't welcome. A gloom came down upon Esmy, one impervious to such magics as motherly hugs and faerie kisses. Even Father noticed Esmy's state and a great fuss was made over her. Mama Deidre insisted loudly that Esmy was taken and should go, that the Devil had stripped her of her soul and that is why Esmy no longer laughed or played. Then Mama Elena went to Grandpapa to pray and to beg and when Mama Elena sat by Esmy's bed the next morning, her face covered by a veil, she held forth Esmy's doll for her. She would have to cede the doll on her sixth birthday, as all little girls in the Family must, but she would be allowed it until then as long as she didn't draw eyes upon its blank and empty face.

Esmy was still a sad little girl but she learned to hide it. Mama Elena wore her veil long enough for Esmy to get used to it. Esmy knew Mama Elena had to wear it for her face was hurt, shamed as Mama Deidre put it. Esmy was slapped hard for saying she'd seen Mama Deidre's face shamed a lot and in truth, Esmy had. Father hit Mama Deidre often. Mama Elena's shames were worse though, worse than Esmy had seen either mother wear before; bad enough to need a veil. So Esmy tried, for Mama Elena's sake, to pretend at being a happy child. Shunned still by her cousins, she played quietly with her doll and ignored the pretty lights Guqon would cast her way. She did her chores stoically and put up with Billy and sometimes her cousins Jeff and Teddy coming into the room late at night to touch her and Millie. She bore her trials patiently, waiting and dreading that day when she would turn six and would have to give up her doll forever along with things she only faintly understood.

As that fateful day loomed ever nearer, Millie began to take an ever-greater joy at the anticipation of Esmy's fate. What would Grandpapa do? Oh, Millie knew! Millie knew but she wasn't going to say. Millie knew, and her own disgust was pronounced in how hopeful she was Esmy would suffer at least as much as she. Millie teased her, hinting at far darker things than what Esmy feared. Millie teased that Billy's antics were nothing for what was coming and Esmy's dark imaginings took hold. What would Grandpapa do? Would he eat her like he did her cousin with the pretty black hair and yellow ribbon? Would she become ugly and mean like Millie? Dread sank Esmy's heart, crushed her spirit but she remained ever faithful to the mask of pretense she wore to still Mama Elena's fears. Guqon was not fooled by Esmy's mask. It could see her true heart, her true sadness and lurked ever on the periphery of her sight, ever trying to catch her attentions, ever ignored for fear of punishment and the security of a doll to hold.

It was less than a week before her birthday and Esmy was afraid. Mama Deidre had bathed her that day. She was to get a bath each day until her birthday and Esmy did not like that. Mama Elena had bathed her the day before and she used water warmed by the fire and was gentle, sobbing silently as she washed Esmy. Not so with Mama Deidre. Not only was the water too cold, but Esmy could tell Mama Deidre took pleasure in scrubbing her as hard as she could. All day, as with the day before, Millie teased her and offered dark portents and hints of what was to come to frighten her. Billy as well sneered and leered at her and promised her what the night would bring, to remind her of what was coming. Esmy was distraught and lay curled that night in her bed, fearful and waiting.

It was with a kiss that Guqon woke her in the darkest hours of the night. A soft wind was brushing the hollow wind-chimes outside her window, something every window in Bezer had to help hide any songs Mama Death might sing from beyond the palisade. Aside from the gentle chatter of the chimes, not a sound stirred in the rest of the house.

"Go away! If they catch you, I'll be in trouble!" Esmy whispered.

But Guqon had something to say, something to propose and didn't go. Guqon insisted Esmy hear it out, listen to what it had to say. Guqon knew as well what was coming and it feared for Esmy, feared Esmy would be taken from the world of children and would be made to grow up too early and then Guqon would never be able to kiss her on the nose again. This Guqon feared and reminded Esmy the stories it had told her of the Land of the Faeries and of the great Faerie King. Esmy pleaded, begged to be left alone but Guqon persisted, weaving pictures of sound only she could see and songs of gardens only she could hear until at last Esmy relented and a faint smile crawled across her lips. From there it was no great feat for Guqon to seduce Esmy to its plan, to reveal to Esmy the secrets of the Faeries so that Esmy didn't have to turn six and be like Millie.

Esmy listened to Guqon there in the dark of the small room she shared with Millie. Her sister was sleeping, snoring soundly in her bed and Guqon assured Esmy that Millie wouldn't wake. Guqon had given her some sleeping dust, powerful faerie magic that would keep Millie sleeping all through the night but Esmy, still fearing, whispered quietly her responses to the faerie.

"What about Billy? What if he comes in?" Esmy asked fearfully.

Worry not, Guqon had assured her. Guqon said it put a marble in the back of Billy's mouth to help his breathing sleep and that the boy wouldn't wake to disturb her anymore. Esmy felt safe in the moment, her excited and frightened mind not thinking more into what Guqon promised. Knowledge that Billy would not molest her this night was enough.

Enchanted, Esmy rose from her bed and followed Guqon from her room. It was locked from beyond, as was her and Millie's room each night, but Guqon fooled the latch and out they went. Through the silent halls of the house and out again through a door released by Guqon, for all the outside doors in all the houses in Bezer were locked each evening. Into the night and under the bright, shining moon, Guqon led her to the great wooden wall that kept Bezer safe from the Strawman and from Mama Death. Through a hole beneath the fence Guqon led her. She had to crawl through grass and spider webs to get through, but she did with Guqon enticing her with kisses promised to her nose. Then to the forbidden tunnel where two men from the Family nodded in a shack meant to guard the tunnel and bar any man or demon who sought passage. Esmy could see the two men, Uncle Warren and another, one of Mr. Heng's sons, through the thicket of long, sharpened stakes affixed all about the shack and especially at the doors and the open window. She saw that they were sound asleep within as she snuck past, Guqon leading her quickly and quietly into the tunnel itself.

Now Esmy just wished, as she clenched hard on her bladder, that the wait would soon be over. The garden tunnel had lost its luster. It still shone as beautiful as ever, but Esmy no longer cared. She needed to piss and she needed to eat and she wanted to lay down, but she also really wanted to meet the Faerie King. She also thought she had been hearing something behind her but every time she tried to turn, to see what it was, Guqon held her face fast. Soon, soon, it would promise, but Esmy was getting tired and soon was too far away. And then, it wasn't.

The tunnel had wound down a thinner and thinner path until it came to a close, the end of the path a wall of flowers nodding gently in the absence of any breeze. From beyond that wall of flowers, light, warm and friendly, peeked through the gaps in the leaves. Guqon flew through the leafy wall like a ghost, its slender limbs disappearing as it beckoned Esmy follow. Hesitantly she reached out to brush the flowers aside, but they moved from her hand of their own accord and beyond… beyond Esmy saw the Land of Faeries.

It was beautiful, more so than she dared hope. A small gasp escaped her lips as she took in the sight through the portal of flowers parted before her. It was an underground kingdom, a cave of immense proportions with great, fantastic columns and curtains of stone carved in fashions delicate and grand. Gardens stretched throughout, hanging from the very towers with weird trees and giant mushrooms of all colors growing everywhere. Back, beyond where her eye could see, these gardens stretched deeper and deeper, their paths leading ever downward. Faeries of all colors beautiful fluttered about, and dust dancers filled the air. It was the grandest of sights.

Guqon fluttered there before her, before all that grandeur, and beckoned her follow. As she stepped through the curtain of flowers, they swept shut behind her. She did not see them close, did not see them whither and fade. She did not see them, dried, dead things, flowers and vines, shriveling and crumbling and falling in a silent shower of dust. She did not see the shadows gathered behind the disintegration of that fantasy nor the dull, dry bones at their feet. Shadows are cast only where needed.

Excited at the prospect of Guqon's promise fulfilled, Esmy let her feet carry her in a light skip behind the faerie. A wave of happiness greater than any she'd known buoyed her spirits. Joy was hers as she raced down that fantastic trail, joy at the thought of never having to be six and never having to know what horrors awaited her in Grandpapa's room. Never again would Billy touch her where she didn't want him to and never again would Millie pull her hair and tease her. And never, never ever again would Mama Deidre beat her to the delight of Billy and Millie. She was free. She was to forever be a faerie, free from the abuses she had suffered and free from ever having to be six. Mama Elena never crossed her thoughts.

The way to the Faerie King was not long though the path twisted through gardens of wondrous stone and columns of beautiful design. Just when Esmy was set to complain, her bladder now a painful issue, Guqon led her around a great carved stone and there he was, sitting upon his resplendent throne in all his mundane glory. Esmy expected a creature of magical design, of beauty unbearable. What she saw was a Chinaman in dirty work clothes sitting cross-legged on that throne, that magnificent seat meant for a king. He sat with his hands folded in his lap, something small covered by his palms. Esmy knew he was a Chinaman because he looked like Mr. Heng and his family and she knew Mr. Heng was a Chinaman, but why here? Why was the Faerie King a Chinaman?

Esmy looked to Guqon for answers and it told her to shut up and be patient. Esmy was taken aback. Guqon had never been short with her before. She flashed Guqon a sharp glance, one that wilted upon seeing on the faerie. It looked different somehow, changed. Those slender limbs, they looked waxy and hard and its eyes, they were bigger, bulging, not the wide, friendly things she knew.

Again Guqon admonished her and told her to pay attention. Again Esmy was startled for Guqon's voice did not ring out sweet and beautiful as it would, but with a stuttering, chittering rasp. For the first time, doubt crept into Esmy's heart. She did as she was told and turned her attentions to the man with the long ponytail slung over his shoulder.

"Mr. Faerie King?" Esmy ventured, hesitant but hopeful. "Can I be a faerie now? I have to piss."

The Faerie King said nothing. His only motion was to slowly raise one of his hands to his mouth and in that hand was a pipe. Esmy recognized it as such for all the men in Bezer smoked pipes but this one looked different, looked funny. The bowl of the pipe glowed and the Chinaman took a deep draw. A sickly-sweet perfume washed over Esmy as the smoke from the pipe wafted around her. Then, as the Chinaman exhaled, that cloud turned quick to an acrid, burnt stench, foul and rotten; a breath without life.

Esmy coughed, choking, her eyes watering in defense. Her first hope had been ascent, that the Fairy King was beginning his magic. When the cloud of rotten air, rank and putrid, reached her, she fretted the nature of that spell. Her eyes confirmed her concern and dread froze her breath. The Chinaman was returning his hand to his lap, but as he did so, as the smoke billowed around him, he began to change. Over the flesh of his face, a crust began to form, a hard mask of frozen fungus. The Chinaman had returned to his posture of rest, his hands calcified claws crusted together.

Esmy gasped and stepped back. The colors around were fading. The glorious gardens all about fell to darkness as the dust dancers began fading out and all the glory crumbled to dust in a rush. What remained were dark and gloomy caverns with great sheets of sinister stone curtains and columns of nightmarish design disappearing into the quick descending gloom.

The change was too quick, too fast for Esmy to understand. One moment everything was beautiful and then, then she was in a lonely, dark place, a cave deeper than the tunnel to Baird's Holler ever was supposed to go. She was afraid. She longed all at once for Mama Elena's warm, encompassing arms. She turned around, trying to find her bearings, where she was. She did not recognize the world around her in the deepening gloom. She did not recognize the host gathered behind her when she turned.

Guqon squealed in delight at Esmy's confusion. It darted and dashed in flight, not the graceful flutter she knew. Guqon's laughter, a sharp, chittering screech, echoed from the ancient walls of the cavern as Esmy stared with growing understanding at the crowd before her. Most were men dressed in the rotting remains of work clothes, but a few stood out. A man finely dressed held the hand of a woman in nightclothes. There was a woman in a once elegant green dress. A child, a little girl no taller than she stood in a stained gown, her face hidden beneath a blank, cracked mask. They stood, silent sentinels corrupted in fungal protrusions and stared at her with eyes long dead.

As the last light faded, leaving only a faint noxious glow about Guqon, the faerie hovered before Esmy and admonished her to silence. Then it landed on her nose and made to kiss it. Esmy was horrified, scared silent at the giant, repellent insect her betrayer had become. Then the demon jammed an inch-long stinger, a thick, vile drop at its tip, into her nose before flying off, laughing, into the darkness.

Esmy stood in stygian silence, lost in the heart of a mountain accursed. About her, a grim host waited, watching as she rubbed her abused nose with one hand and held tightly her faceless doll with the other. She held her tongue, fearful of Guqon's final warning, but her bladder failed her and a tear, doomed to congeal, rolled down her cheek.

THE END

THE PALE LADY

K. M. BENNETT

A dust storm.

An earth-molder.

A spirit.

The sprite of the forest was all of these things. She changed her physical appearance at will, and used the perfect camouflage of nature to become invisible when she chose.

But most days, she appeared as a small, brown humanoid creature, reminiscent of an elf. In this form she used her delicate, translucent wings to flutter about the forest, where she spent her days helping woodland creatures and collecting favors.

She assisted the moles with their digging, the beavers with their dams, and the birds with their nests. She threw dust in the eyes of hunters, then danced in the cloud as they rubbed their red eyes. She went deep into the ground and guided the blind cave animals to the best homes. No creature left her wood without meeting her, and no creature left untouched by her kindness.

She could do just about anything she pleased, but for one limitation: she could use her powers only three times in a day. If she used them a fourth, she would transform her into a mortal and lose her powers forever.

One day, as the sprite danced and darted among the trees, she saw a human lady. The sprite transformed herself into the bark of a tree to watch unnoticed.

Her brown eyes danced with excitement, for it had been years since she'd last seen a human in her wood.

At the bottom of a steep ravine as deep as a wrinkle on a great god's face, the lady slouched. She was completely drained of color. The sprite thought it might have been a trick of the light, but even the ground and plants around the lady seemed grayer than everything else in the woods. Her eyes were the color of winter clouds, and the sprite had difficulty distinguishing her irises from the bloodshot whites. Even the lady's hair was pale, almost white in the sun. Her shoulders quivered with sobs.

The sprite, ever helpful, materialized.

"I am far from home, and I'm in this ravine," the lady said. "My blessings have been taken from me."

"Not all of them; you are blessed, indeed. For I will take you home upon my own back." The sprite puffed out her translucent, amber chest.

"Even if you could take me, I'll never escape this ravine." The woman gestured up the steep incline.

"Truly, I am able," said the sprite, turning a shade redder. "And I will get you out."

The lady sighed. "Leave me to die. You'll only be brought down with me. This is your only warning."

The sprite twirled, blazing orange as a candle flame, and took flight. She considered the ways in which a traumatized human could be brought back to their senses. Soon, an idea surface. The sprite knew from experience humans were particularly unreasonable when they lacked adequate rest.

So she called to the birds with her dulcet voice. The ravine clamored with birds of brown, blue, red, yellow, white, and black. Within a few minutes, a human-sized nest appeared amid a flurry of straw and feathers.

The pale lady only hung her head between her knees, staring at her feet.

That was the first of the sprite's three powers used for the day. Her head ached, the first indication of just how deeply her powers cost her. The birds departed in pairs and triplets, leaving the nest and the lady and the sprite.

The sprite had used one power already to create the soft straw bed, but lady steadfastly ignored it. *Then it is better to use two and accomplish my ends*, the sprite thought. She studied the pale woman carefully, and soon decided that something truly beautiful might return her to her senses.

So the sprite used her hands to split the earth and recreate the famous human works of art she had seen. She carved them into the rock walls of the ravine, turning the earth molten with her fingertips. Her magic carved smoothly and left a shimmer of sparkling embers as a finishing touch. In the evening light, they shone like rubies.

That was the second power used.

The ache in the sprite's acorn-shaped head was now a throbbing hammer on her magical brain. Her fine, jewel-sized heart began to burn. The sprite looked down at her hands, which had paled considerably: a soft beige now, instead of her usual rich brown. The sprite wondered absently just how long it had been since she'd used two powers in a day.

The woman glanced at the artwork, but rather than smile, she wailed. "Oh, how I once loved beautiful things. If only I could return to that time again." Her weeping faded slowly into tearful deep moans and sighs. Finally she sat silent again, fresh tears still streaming down her face. "If I could only go back to that time," she whimpered. Her eyes stared blankly, staring at something in the past despite the breathtaking view of the present.

The sprite, with an aching, paling body, finally considered leaving the woman to die in the ravine. She'd done all she could. Nobody would blame her. Not the foxes. Not the birds. Not even the humans who would eventually find the pale lady's forsaken corpse.

But I would blame myself if she died at my second power, thought the sprite. She looked down and noticed that she could see through her own hands; she'd lost almost all of her corporeal form. It was now a monumental effort to simply flicker into view.

She groaned with effort, creating swirling dust devils, but failed to make herself solid. She tried a second time and managed to force a foot back into existence for just a moment before being thrown back to the invisible plane with a snap.

She was terribly weak. But she'd already invested so much. This was her great challenge, and it would all go to waste if she didn't succeed in helping the woman.

With enormous effort, she gathered a final reserve deep within herself to appear before the woman again. She was now more wisp than sprite, and white-hot pain consumed her entire being. The sprite then remembered another thing about humans: their pride. *Maybe the woman wants a way to save herself*, she thought. And so she gave the woman a way to do just that.

The earth sprite enchanted the lady's eyes to weep tiny pebbles created from her sadness, rather than tears. As the woman's sadness escalated once more, she wept stones, and finally boulders.

"The stones are your staircase! Build your way to freedom!" cried the exhausted wisp as she faded. That was the third power gone, diminishing her to a pair of glowing, tormented eyes, a small creature bearing enough pain for the entire world.

The pale woman, stones and pebbles still cascading from her eyes, turned toward the tortured whimpers of the sprite. A malevolent grin spread between her cheekbones as rocks continued to fall. She extended a hand, and the earth sprite became solid.

At that moment, the earth sprite felt her immortality slip off like shed skin.

"Of course, your blood would be renewable if I kept you alive," the pale lady said. "But I can't risk anyone finding out we can do that. The market is supply and demand, you know. And I've got to keep this stuff in high demand. It's been a long time since I've found one of you, and I need as much money as I can get right now." She pulled an ornate, ceremonial knife from the folds of her dress.

The earth sprite screamed and thrashed. "I have never hurt you. Why would you do this to me?"

The pale lady pinched the earth sprite's cheek and gave her a dark grin. "And I never hurt you. Not yet, anyway. You did this all by yourself. You sprites never know when to stop."

Inhuman cries careened through the forest. Every root of every tree and every blade of grass shivered as the blade pierced the now-mortal earth sprite's stomach. The pale lady yanked the blade out with a flourish. The sprite watched her own blood, once green, trickle away red and sticky.

The woman produced a pail from the folds of her long dress, then slashed the blade across the earth sprite's throat. She smiled as blood gushed over the sprite's skin and sluiced the base of the metal pail.

When the flow finally slowed, the pale lady turned the sprite over and shook the last few drops from the dead creature as though she were a dirty rag.

When she finished, the lady wiped the sweat from her brow and braided her long blonde hair. Her hands were still wet with blood and left red streaks in her strands. So she went down to the river and plunged her hands in among river weeds and frightened minnows. The blood washed from her hands and blossomed in the water, red and murky.

EVERGLADES REST STOP

DOUGLAS FORD

It shouldn't matter how you found the rest stop. Maybe Bobby telling all those stories got into your head. Maybe when he died, you took his wishes a little too literally. "Just dump my ashes down in the Glades somewhere," he said. "Just let the wind scatter them wherever. I was happiest when I lived that way—letting the road take me wherever it wanted me to go." A deep breath before he added, "That's how I found that rest stop I told you about."

You never could get a clear mental image of that rest stop from Bobby's description. Maybe his memory began to fade as the cancer ate up his insides, or maybe Bobby kept things deliberately vague because he wanted it to stay concealed. Like he wanted to hide it in plain sight.

If so, you shouldn't judge him harshly. He lost Megan on one of those Everglades trips. Details remained scant—something about an airboat accident, and the fact that no one ever recovered her remains didn't seem so strange. You remember hearing something about airplanes going missing in the swamp all the time, often never turning up, or perhaps revealed decades later thanks to brush fire. When that happens, no one finds human remains—the swamp and its inhabitants claim everything. So no surprise if Megan's remains went unrecovered.

She never left the Glades then, and for that reason alone, you would've followed Bobby's instructions about what to do with his ashes. That way they could spend eternity together. And all that.

Besides, maybe Bobby wanted you to stumble on the rest stop the same way he did, coming up on it out of nowhere, sometime near the end of his trek to find the "Lost City," or some such shit. "Out of historical interest," he explained. "It's not marked on the maps, and the roads don't lead to it, but certain locals will help you get there." Calling it a "city" just lays the groundwork for disappointment, it turns out—more like an old Confederate camp, according to Bobby, and later the site of a distillery run by prohibition-era bootleggers, possibly Al Capone himself. Before that, it supposedly housed a village for Tequesta Indians, though they abandoned the settlement over a thousand years ago for reasons unknown. Assuming some truth to these stories, it all boils down to the way things get repurposed in the Glades.

That's the real story of the Glades, Bobby told you. Repurposing.

And that includes this fabled rest stop.

Bobby said it used to house some kind of obscure religious sect, or maybe just a splinter group of extreme Pentecostals who once belonged to the hollow earth settlement in nearby Estero. Apparently, once that movement fell apart, a group of them moved deeper into the Glades, looking for divine truth by turning to snake-handling rituals. "A snake cult, basically," Bobby explained, one located off the beaten path, though by the late 50s and early 60s their descendants gave up the mumbo jumbo, but kept the snakes and established a roadside attraction. "Of course, a roadside attraction needs a fucking road that people will actually use," Bobby said, "so that didn't work out. But like I said, the Glades is all about repurposing, so the structure went on sitting there, even if it got a little rundown. But the plumbing kept working. So now it's just a rest stop."

Where to take Bobby's ashes, then? You don't know the Everglades like he did. You don't hunt, and you barely know which end of fish hook to put the worm on. You couldn't tell the difference between a gator and a crocodile, though you have a vague recollection that it's mostly the former that you'll find down there. You suppose—you hope—that you can just put Bobby's urn in the seat next to you and drive down there and ask the first local you see how to find that Lost City of Bobby's.

Nothing prepares you for the miles of nothing you see on Alligator Alley, the lonely stretch of highway that cuts through the swamp, and when you finally come to Exit 49, you take it without hesitation and find yourself on Snake Road. The hour has grown late, and you pull into the first gas station you see. The sign outside advertises souvenirs. You go inside before filling up, and you walk right into an argument in progress.

A paunchy middle-aged man leans across the store counter, insisting that the attendant on duty—an Indian by the looks of him—tell him where he can find the casino. "The good one," says the man. "Because I didn't come all this way to lose my shirt."

The man's female companion bears a paunch similar to his, and her eyes go to you as you approach the counter, as if she's counting on you to join their side of the argument. Probably because you don't look like an Indian. You recognize these as the sort of folks who believe that white people always stick together.

"You believe this?" says the woman. "We're on a reservation, and he says no casino. Not even slots."

"Typical bullshit," the man says. "We let them keep all this money, tax free, and this is the thanks we get."

Behind the counter, the attendant's eyes shift from the man to you and then to the woman. His face grows a shade darker, but his eyes widen as if he has just realized something. "Oh, you want slots. Well, why didn't you say so?" In front of him a white piece of paper materializes, and with a pencil he begins sketching lines and circles that it turns out represent a series of complex directions.

"To the casino?" the man says. He smells like canned anchovies, like something used to lure a sick cat out of a gutter.

"Well, not an official casino. But lots of slots."

"That's what we want," the man says. "That's exactly what we want. That's more like it."

The woman continues to regard you, snapping her gum, as the man takes the directions and pays for gas. You return her gaze and she smiles as if to say, *That's how it's done. That's how you play to win.*

They shuffle past you, the woman's eyes locked with your own for as long as possible, and make their way to an SUV parked outside. The attendant looks at you and says, "What about you? You want to know where the secret magical casino is, too?"

You don't answer right away. To affirm your worth as a customer, you pretend to browse through a selection of walking sticks stocked in a dirty rain barrel. FOR THE TRUE GLADESMAN, the sign on the barrel says. An unduplicated carving marks each stick: a bear, a panther, an alligator, a snake. You choose the snake and place the walking stick on the counter, begin digging out a credit card. "Cash only," says the attendant, but you swear you saw Mr. Casino pay with plastic. You shrug and pull out a folded stack of bills, the fruits of Bobby's life insurance, proffered to you as the beneficiary. The bills catch the attention of the attendant, and you return them to your pocket with deliberate slowness as you pop the question:

"You know where I can find the Lost City?"

No answer right away, but the faint trace of a smile appears on the attendant's lips, and he maintains eye contact even when the door opens and Mr. Casino rushes back inside. "Bathroom," says the man, clearly in dire need.

"Paying customers only," says attendant, as if paying for fuel doesn't count, but the man doesn't break stride, and after two wrong turns, he manages to find the john on his own.

"The Lost City?" the attendant says after the door to the men's room closes.

You nod. The attendant produces another piece of paper, as if he keeps a whole storehouse for clueless white people, and he begins scratching out more lines and circles. When he turns it toward you, tracing the path with his pencil, you wonder if they match what he just gave Mr. Casino.

You say, "I thought roads don't lead to it."

"Sometimes you got to make your own road. Go here," and he draws a star that appears upside down from your perspective, "and the rest of the way is easy."

You nod, thank the man, and add a tip when you pay for gas.

"Don't forget your stick," says the attendant after you've turned to leave. He holds it with the carved snake's fangs extended in your direction. You don't like to imagine what it would feel like if the thing could really bite. "You might need it where you're going."

Outside, you find Mrs. Casino leaning against your car, smoking a cigarette. Her shorts barely contain her hips, but she has undeniable appeal. You recognize frustrated libido in the look she gives you. You've seen it before from this kind of woman, and you know how to respond to it favorably. Not now though, not when you have someplace to go.

Besides, it doesn't seem right with Bobby's ashes on the other side of the window she leans against. If she turns, she'll see the urn sitting there on the passenger seat. She might ask about it, like *who's that? Who's the stiff?* Or maybe you shouldn't feel this way. Maybe Bobby is watching from the Great Beyond, waiting for this lady to notice him, anxious to enjoy her attention. Maybe he would notice some likeness between his own Megan and this lady, perhaps in the way they carry themselves, and who knows, maybe this counts as part of the journey he wanted you to take. Maybe you're even supposed to see if Mrs. Casino here wants to get in the backseat for a quick one before her husband comes back.

"What's that for?"

A beat passes before you make sense of her question. She means your walking stick.

You lean it against the car so you can start the gas pump. Without waiting for permission, she picks it up and uses her cigarette hand to fondle the snake's neck in a way that couldn't be more obvious. Her grin suggests she finds your silence more amusing than off-putting.

"You take this into the casino," she says, "and they'll crown you the King of the Glades."

You laugh even though that means taking her bait. You say, "I'm not king of anything. I'm just passing through."

"I bet it's good luck."

"I just thought it looked interesting. I don't know anything about luck. I know even less about the Everglades."

"Well, you know it's full of snakes, don't you? Dennis tells me people in Miami flush baby pythons down their toilets, and they make their way down here to the swamp and grow into monsters. Dennis says that the pythons out there grow big enough to slurp down a gator." She draws on the cigarette and stifles a burp. "Dennis showed me a picture off the Internet of a python that blew apart from trying to swallow a gator." She pauses to consider the sun, hanging by a thread over the western horizon. "Wouldn't want to be caught out there after dark." She turns her gaze back to you as she breathes smoke through her nostrils. When she speaks again, her voice sounds different, lower in timbre, as if all those things she said before constitute an act she puts on for certain men, and in just a short span of time she has judged you as different somehow. "This is where men take their wives to kill them. Some place remote and unpopulated and full of snakes." She extends the snake staff in a manner that conveys disgust, as if you made her touch it. Like a hornet nest you insisted she fondle.

With perfect timing and a lighter step, Mr. Casino returns from the men's room. You accept the return of the walking stick, realizing that, like an idiot, you forgot to finish pumping the gas. "Be well," you say, but too late for her to hear, as she has already made it back to the SUV. You watch as it pulls out of the gas station and heads south.

The staff feels wrong now, tainted, and a monumental waste of cash. Fueled up, you return to get your money back, but the attendant frowns and points to a NO REFUNDS sign you swear didn't exist ten minutes ago. "Indian magic," says the attendant. "Besides, you say you want to find the Lost City?" You nod in reply. "Well," he says, "think of that stick as a totem. It'll ward away the creepy-crawlies and make you a true Gladesman. Just like the sign says. Indian signs don't lie."

You feel like nothing of the sort as you travel south, the mythic river of grass surrounding you, the road being the sole monument to civilization. A crow stands on the edge of the concrete and dares you to run over him. Instead of flying away, he caws with laughter as you pass him untouched. You think of Mrs. Casino, and of husbands who murder their wives. Increasingly, she reminds you of Bobby's wife, Megan, and you consider things you'd prefer to leave unremembered, especially with Bobby's ashes riding next to you. Like that time you found yourself alone with Megan. Bobby never found out, she wouldn't tell him, and besides, it all amounted to just a friendly grope on the back porch one evening when Bobby had to take a leak. No way would Bobby have found out, and maybe it didn't happen the way you remember, what with all the beer, the whole thing a bit fuzzy.

Just a sloppy grope that Bobby wouldn't know about, and maybe a quick kiss that went with it, nothing serious, everything consensual. And how many years passed between that and the day that Megan didn't come home? Or maybe it was only months. You can't remember.

The sun falls a few more ticks, but not the heat. Due east, lightning flashes and storm clouds loom, black as oil. You think of downed aircrafts swallowed beneath reptilian-backed water, this strange landscape, neither land nor sea, ruled by equally strange gods. The attendant's directions prove surprisingly easy to follow, even as the road grows narrower, signs of neglect increasing with its remoteness. Instead of becoming more frequent, signs of wildlife begin to wane, as if they have withdrawn to make way for something else. The Lost City feels close.

Unconsciously, you touch the snake staff next to you. Alive, it could have bitten you, but you wouldn't have noticed because of what appears in the fading sunlight.

The head of a giant cobra looming over the sawgrass.

You might have seen it further back if not for it getting lost in the storm clouds. Once revealed, it announces itself as one of those gods you sensed, the one who lords over missing villages and bootleggers escaping justice, the protector of missing planes and murdered wives. Now it has found you.

But then the building comes into view, squat and desiccated and absurd under the majesty of the snake head, which you now recognize as a cheesy gimmick sculpted to attract passing motorists. The long-gone proprietors anticipated a hub of tourism and hoped to attract those wanting a chance to get close to nature— hold a snake, feel its scaly texture, watch its venom get drained. All this promised by a molded, rain-rotted sign. Only nature has encroached, and like everything else in its path, it has repurposed the structure. Someone has tacked an additional sign to the wooden post, this one handwritten on a piece of cardboard: FACILITIES ~~UN~~AVAILABLE.

You have found Bobby's rest stop.

Events unfold like something dreamed by the sulfurous wetlands surrounding you, itself an organic creature in the middle of a restless sleep. You park next to an SUV which looks an awful lot like the vehicle that spirited away Mr. and Mrs. Casino. When you see the figure beckoning to you from the building's north corner, you begin to wonder if maybe you really have fallen asleep, and you hope you'll awake before you crash into the swamp. Because that beckoning figure looks an awful lot like Bobby, poor dead Bobby. You shouldn't exit the vehicle, but you do and answer the shadow-Bobby's summons. Head bowed as if in supplication, he gestures toward a door-less entry, one that leads to a room of flickering light.

It's an old men's room lined with browning urinals and wet floors. The flickering lights come from tea candles, rows and rows of them laid out on the floor, forming a path between toilet stalls. That path takes you to a cream-colored wall of crumbling plaster with a hastily-made wood panel in the center, just at eye level. Written in lettering similar to what adorns the sign outside:

Pik up and behold the lost sittee

Some joker has penciled in an "h" between the "s" and the "i." A hinge holds the sign against the wall, so you follow the instructions and lift.

Underneath, you find a crudely formed hole about the size of your face, big enough to peer into. More flickering light comes from yet another room beyond. You look and see.

At first, you just notice the shoes. So many shoes. Hundreds of them, different styles and sizes, from old loafers to sandals to sneakers, covering the floor of what looks like an old, enclosed courtyard. Then your eyes catch movement, what you first mistake for an effect of the flickering light created by yet more candles.

You realize, finally, that the ground is moving.

Snakes, slithering scores of them, ranging from a few of modest length to pythons of astonishing size, crawling around the littered shoes.

The shoes. Where did they come from?

An answer presents itself in the form of a gigantic serpent, one with a girth that would accommodate an adult alligator easily. A person even, you realize.

Because that's a leg you see sticking out of its mouth. A sandal dangling off the shoe of a limp foot, the big toe angled wrong and crooked.

You close the wooden panel and feel the desire to get as far away as possible.

But the shadow figure stands behind you, blocking the path out.

You start to beg Bobby's forgiveness, plead with him to call off whatever awful revenge he intended by leading you out here.

A good look at the man quiets your blubbering. This is not Bobby. This is some old Gladesman, his face covered in what looks like coal dust produced by hell's flames.

He says something you need repeated.

"I said you didn't pay. Back there at the door I said you gotta pay. Paying customers only."

You ask how much but find yourself handing over an assortment of bills without hearing the answer. He seems more than satisfied, and you leave him counting as you go back outside.

The SUV is gone, and your front passenger door hangs open. As your eyes scan the road in both directions, seeing nothing, you consider who that leg belonged to, the one in the snake's mouth. You think of what the woman said about husbands murdering their wives and decide that yes, that fits.

Only your car tells a different story. Through the open passenger door you see the urn containing bobby's ashes tilted upside down, the ashes, or what's left of them, blowing in the breeze. A closer look tells you the rest of the story: the snake staff is gone. Stolen. Mr. Casino wouldn't do that—but Mrs. Casino might.

To let you know she's okay, that those legs sticking out of the snake's mouth don't belong to her. But Mr. Casino's? Possibly.

No point going further. Bobby said he liked to just let the road take him wherever it wanted him to go, but now his ashes swirl at the mercy of the wind. A heap of them has formed near your car. As you drive away, you don't see them disperse.

THE DEVIL'S DOORSTEP

CARYS CROSSEN

EXCERPT FROM THE MANSFIELD RECORDER, 14TH MARCH:

DISUSED WELL DISCOVERED NEXT TO CHURCH

A disused well has been discovered outside St. Gall's Church.

The well was found by accident. A visitor to the churchyard stepped on the cover, which had rotted and gave way beneath his foot. Luckily the vicar, Father Paul Hattersley, heard the man's cries for help and managed to pull him free.

'It's fortunate I was there. There could have been a very nasty accident otherwise,' said Father Paul. 'I will be ensuring the hole is blocked up as soon as possible. We get a lot of children in the churchyard and the well is very unsafe. In the meantime, I advise all our visitors to steer clear of that section of churchyard.'

The well's existence was unknown before the incident and the Mansfield Historical Society have expressed an interest in finding out who constructed it and why...

* * *

EXCERPT FROM DIARY OF PAUL HATTERSLEY, VICAR OF ST. GALL'S, 15TH MARCH:

It's been a crazy few days. The newspaper report about the well has sent dozens of new visitors to our churchyard and the doorbell has been ringing nonstop. I've had to write this week's sermon in the library. I'm glad the council has put up a barrier around the well, but I worry that some child or teenager might have more curiosity than sense. The sooner it gets boarded over the better.

Not seen the man who put his foot through the old cover again. He said he was an amateur historian. Bit surprising—he was so keen on tracing the history of the well he was badgering me not to report it, didn't want anyone stealing his thunder. Of course I couldn't do that, but it's a bit odd in retrospect, I shouldn't think there'd be much interest in disused wells...

* * *

TEXT MESSAGES, 15TH MARCH:

JC: You total idiot. I never should have sent you. How do you plan to fix this?

MS: It would have been fine except for that bloody vicar! Leave it, the fuss will die down in a few days.

* * *

E-MAILS, 16TH MARCH:

From: naomi.lewis36@gmail.com
To: danny_boygolding@gmail.com

Hi Danny,

Been through the records at the town hall and haven't found anything about a well on church property, so it looks like we're out of luck for next week's meeting of the Mansfield Historical Society! According to the British Geological Foundation this isn't unusual—prior to the 20th century wells weren't usually marked on maps and sometimes not even then. The archivist thought I might have better luck with church records so will have a quick chat with the vicar tomorrow and see if he has access to anything.

Cheers,

Naomi

* * *

EXCERPT FROM 999 CALL MADE AT 2.08 AM, 17TH MARCH:

Operator: 999, what's your emergency?
Caller: Oh, God, you have to send someone! There's screaming, someone's screaming and I can hear the most horrible (inaudible), awful sounds...
Operator: There's screaming? Where, inside your home?
Caller: No, outside, in the churchyard! Just across the road! Please come, it's just horrible... (sobs)
Operator: Hang on, love, we'll get police out right away. What's your address?
Caller: Twenty... twenty-three Church Street. It's in St. Gall's churchyard... Oh, God...
Operator: Stay on the line, love. I'm sending someone right now...

* * *

EXCERPT OF ARTICLE ON WEBSITE OF MANSFIELD AND BRISCOMBE ORGANISER, 17TH MARCH:

TERROR IN THE NIGHT: LOCAL RESIDENTS REPORT SCREAMS COMING FROM CHURCHYARD IN THE EARLY HOURS

Police were called at 2 am last night to Church Street in Mansfield after multiple residents rang police, stating that there were screams and 'awful noises' coming from St. Gall's churchyard.

'It was terrifying,' said resident Robert Beach, 42. 'My wife and I were woken in the small hours by shrieks and what sounded like a lion roaring. The whole street was disturbed. We all ran outside but no-one dared go and look.'

The noise quietened by the time police arrived, but they conducted a search of the churchyard before advising residents to go back inside and go to bed. A police spokesperson said they are 'keeping an open mind' about what might have caused the disturbance. Anyone with information is asked to call Crimestoppers on...

* * *

EMAIL FROM 17TH MARCH:

From: Hattersley@COE.co.uk
To: Wharton@COE.co.uk

Dear Eric,

Thanks for your message, and I'm happy to report I'm absolutely fine, if a bit unnerved by all the goings-on. Honestly, I never heard a thing last night and only woke when the police came banging on my door at 4 am. It's strange, given there was enough noise to wake the whole of Church Street. I know the vicarage is on the other side of the church, but even so, I thought I would have heard something.

Thanks for the offer but I'll stay where I am, my parishioners are understandably unsettled and need their vicar close. If I went scurrying off it would only make matters worse. I'd be more than happy to borrow Winston for a few days though; it's been weird here lately and I'd feel better having a dog in the house, even your soppy mutt!

Take care,

Paul

* * *

TEXT MESSAGES, 17TH MARCH:

JC: Fix this. NOW!
MH: Leave it with me, pet. I know how to pacify it.

* * *

EXCERPT FROM 'THE SUMMONINGS ACCORDING TO THE MOST ENLIGHTENED TEACHINGS OF JOHN DEE' BY DEBORAH KELLY (OUT OF PRINT):

A violent spirit must either be contained or pacified. If left to rampage unchecked, it's power will grow until it will no longer be receptive to the will of the necromancer...

* * *

E-MAILS, 17TH MARCH:

From: danny_boygolding@gmail.com
To: naomi.lewis36@gmail.com

Hi Naomi,

Bloody hell, did you read the news reports?? My mate Rowan lives on Church Street, he was really rattled by what went on last night. I wonder if our disused well has something to do with it? Okay, probably not, but it's a funny coincidence.

I'm e-mailing because all the palaver reminded me of a local legend, called 'The Devil's Doorstep.' Apparently sometime in the 16th century a local man made a deal with the Devil for wealth and power. In return, he had to dig a tunnel down to Hell so the Devil could escape and come and claim his victims. Can you guess what the tunnel was disguised as? Yes, a well! This went on for a bit until a priest battled the Devil one night as he emerged and actually stole one of his horns. The priest won, and boarded the well over. The legend has been around for yonks and most people have forgotten it by now, but it's creepy how much it tallies with what's been happening lately.

Let me know what you think,

Danny

From: naomi.lewis36@gmail.com
To: danny_boygolding@gmail.com

Hi Danny,

Thanks loads for the e-mail! You're right, that is creepy. Can you send me a link to a copy of the legend or the library reference? I'm going to the library later for research so would be a good chance to look it up.

Thanks,

Naomi

From: danny_boygolding@gmail.com
To: naomi.lewis36@gmail.com

Naomi,

Sorry mate, but I've never seen the legend written down. My Gran used to tell it to me when I was being a pain and she wanted to scare me into good behaviour. The Devil would come and get me if I didn't stop dressing her cat up and so forth. Not that it ever worked... I'll have a word with my Mum and see if she remembers anything else.

Danny

From: naomi.lewis36@gmail.com
To: danny_boygolding@gmail.com

Dressing the cat up?! I demand the particulars!

* * *

INVOICE DELIVERED FROM POWELL'S BUILDERS TO ST. GALL'S VICARAGE, 17TH MARCH, WITH HANDWRITTEN NOTE ADDED:

- Inspection fee: £25

Dear Vicar, there's a couple of things we could do about the hole. An iron grating would be the easiest option. Bricking it over will take longer but is doable. Let us know what you think, from Dave Powell.

PS: sorry we left in such a hurry, my lad came over all funny and I had to drive him home. I'll pick up my bucket later.

* * *

EXCERPT FROM TWITTER THREAD, BEGUN 3.08AM 18TH MARCH:

Gaz1992 @FHMReader

Satanic ritual going on in the graveyard in Mansfield!!!

SarahLouKayak @manipedipro

Okay how many pints gaz???

Gaz1992 @FHMReader

7 pints but theres dead animals all over!!

AshFlynn @F&FFan3000

WTF?? Send us a pic!

Gaz1992 @FHMReader

Sending it to your fone got banned last time i tweeted dead stuff

AshFlynn @F&FFan3000

That's horrible mate. Ring the bloody police!

SarahLouKayak @manipedipro

Its disgusting ring 999 NOW!

Roger Gale @galeforceforever

That's sick, mate. Call for help.

AshFlynn @F&FFan3000

Gaz you still there? Answer your bloody phone!

EXCERPT OF ARTICLE ON WEBSITE OF MANSFIELD AND
BRISCOMBE ORGANISER, 18TH MARCH:

SATANIC RITUALS SUSPECTED IN CHURCHYARD MUTILATIONS

Several dead animals have been found skinned and mutilated in St. Gall's churchyard.

The gruesome discovery was made early this morning by the church's vicar and reported to police. It follows a night of terror for local residents after screams and terrifying noises were reported coming from the churchyard.

A witness, who did not want to be identified, said 'it was awful, absolutely revolting. There was blood all over and the animals lying around. It was definitely the work of some psycho. It looked like someone had been worshipping the devil.'

The police have not released a statement regarding the incident and are said to be keeping an open mind regarding the motives, but local residents are convinced a Satanic cult is behind the killings and the recent disturbances. Church Street resident Annie Wharton, 55, says 'this is too nasty to be kids playing about. It's got to be a cult of some kind. The area has declined in recent years. Community spirit has been lost and this is the result.'

St. Gall's vicar, Paul Hattersley, when contacted declined to comment on recent events and said only church services will continue as normal, but he recommends keeping out of the churchyard after dark for the time being.

Police are appealing for witnesses and anyone with any information is urged to contact officers by phone or by e-mail...

* * *

EXCERPT FROM DIARY OF PAUL HATTERSLEY, VICAR OF ST. GALL'S, 18TH MARCH:

I haven't been able to write for quite a while, I'm just snatching a few minutes in the Scout Hut to scribble this. The whole world seems to have gone berserk these past few days, first reports of screams in the night and now these poor dead animals strewn all over. The phone's been ringing nonstop with local journalists, even had a call off the Daily Mail (I haven't responded to it). Luckily the council sent someone out right away to gather up the corpses – I don't think they want any more bad publicity.

It's getting beyond weird and is becoming very frightening. I'm praying for guidance every spare moment. Later I'm going to drive over to Eric's and pick up Winston. He's only a scruffy little dog but he's brave, according to his owner. I'll feel much better having him around. And I'm going to get that damned well bricked up ASAP. All the trouble started since it was uncovered, wonder if that legend old Mrs Phelps mentioned at the WI meeting is true?

Sorry, not helping. Off to do the afternoon service. Church attendance has skyrocketed since all this started. Silver linings—though the cloud is a very dark one and shows no sign of lifting...

* * *

EMAILS, 18TH MARCH:

From: naomi.lewis36@gmail.com
To: danny_boygolding@gmail.com

Hi Danny,

Have you read the latest news? This is getting really scary, I keep thinking about that legend you told me. Okay, maybe it's not the devil but there's some psycho hanging around and it's freaking me out. Maybe we shouldn't investigate the well until all this has died down. Let me know what you reckon.

Naomi

From: danny_boygolding@gmail.com
To: naomi.lewis36@gmail.com

Hi Naomi,

I agree, it's creepy but I think we'll be fine if we stick to investigating the history of the site and don't go wandering around the churchyard at midnight. Why not come round to mine tonight and we'll go over those old newspaper articles you mentioned over the phone yesterday?

Danny

From: naomi.lewis36@gmail.com
To: danny_boygolding@gmail.com

Hi Dan,

It's giving me the heebie-jeebies but I know better than to try and talk you out of it. Is seven okay for you? I'll bring photocopies of what I found. The librarian was really helpful, she remembered back in the seventies there was a spate of animal mutilations and vandalism similar to what's happening now and she located all sorts for me.

See you later,

Naomi

* * *

EXCERPT FROM MISSING PERSONS REPORT, RECORDED AT MANSFIELD POLICE STATION, 18TH MARCH:

Time and date of report: 18th March, 6.52 pm.
Name of missing: Gareth Lee Rawlings
Age: 27
Height: 5' 9"
Appearance: dark brown hair, brown eyes, stocky build. Was wearing jeans, a grey hoodie and Nike trainers when last seen.
Distinguishing features: has a tattoo of a dragon on his left bicep.
Last confirmed sighting: approx. 11.40 pm on the night of 17th March. Mr Rawlings left the Black Bull pub, and according to witnesses Eleanor Tomkins and Matthew Appleton, said he was going home owing to having work the next day. They have

suggested he continued drinking in another establishment, but this has not been verified.

Further details: although there are no confirmed sightings of Mr Rawlings after 11.40 pm, witnesses have confirmed he was active on Twitter in the early hours of 18th March, commenting on suspicious events in the churchyard of St. Gall's Church. Mr Rawlings did not answer his mobile when a friend rang him, and it was presumed he had gone home.

Mr Rawlings did not turn up for work (place of work: Shepherd's Electricals) on the 18th although he was due to work a full shift and did not respond to calls from his boss or workmates. According to his colleague Roger Gale, Mr Rawlings has missed shifts without notice on several occasions so this behaviour did not prompt any concern.

Alarm was raised by Mr Gale when he visited Mr Rawlings's house and discovered he was not at home. His mother, Linda Rawlings, confirmed he had not been home all night and she had assumed he spent the night with a friend, which again was not unusual behaviour. After ringing round Mr Rawlings's friends, it was established that no-one had seen or heard from him since approx. 3 am on 18th March...

* * *

TEXT MESSAGES, 18TH MARCH:

MH: I know its bad but will get it sorted by tonight. Trust me.
JC: TRUST YOU?! After last night? YOU WERE SEEN!
MH: I took care of it!
JC: Forget it, I'm coming down there. Don't bother protesting. I'm going to take charge. This ends TONIGHT.

* * *

EXCERPT FROM 'THE SUMMONINGS ACCORDING TO THE MOST ENLIGHTENED TEACHINGS OF JOHN DEE' BY DEBORAH KELLY (OUT OF PRINT):

Although the power possessed by spirits is gargantuan, they can be repelled by substances such as silver and the wood of the rowan tree. Animals are the eternal enemies of all spirits, and a summoning should not be attempted in the presence of a familiar or any mortal beast...

* * *

TEXT MESSAGES, 18TH MARCH:

NL: Hi Dan, can we make it 8 rather than 7? Have found something out at the library. Naomi.
DG: Hi Naomi, no worries, 8 is fine, was going to order pizza anyway. What have you got?
NL: Did some research on those events in the seventies and found when they happened repair work was being done on the church's foundations.
DG: Bloody hell.
NL: I'm beginning to think it is just that.
DG: Come over ASAP. This is BIG.

EXCERPT FROM DIARY OF PAUL HATTERSLEY, VICAR OF ST. GALL'S, 18-19TH MARCH:

It's now quarter to eleven and all is peaceful. I gave Winston his evening walk in the park and he's settled down to sleep. He had a barking fit a little earlier at something, but when I looked out of the window I couldn't see anything. A fox or cat, probably. Hopefully.

No further strange goings on! That I know of, at least. Had a young man named Roger at the vicarage door this evening to see if I'd seen his mate 'Gaz' but could honestly say no, I hadn't. From what Roger said, Gaz is a young man who prefers pubs and parties to church, so I'm rather bemused as to why Roger thought I might have seen him.

Off to bed now. Praying for a peaceful night.

19th March, 6.15 am:

Shaking as I write. Must get this down before I forget!

Got woken by Winston at round about 3am. He was barking ferociously, so I went to the window and saw people moving about in the churchyard, or rather saw the beams from their torches. Like an idiot, instead of ringing the police, I threw my shoes and coat on and went to investigate. Why didn't I ring? Didn't want to cause a fuss, I suppose.

I went outside, Winston at my heels (he'd gone silent as we left the house. Only just realised it). I was creeping along the west side of the church when I saw two people up ahead, peering round the corner. They weren't the ones with torches, they were crouched in the dark by the corner of the building. Nearly jumped out of their skins when I tapped them on their shoulders. Winston wagged his tail at both of them, so I was fairly certain they didn't intend any harm. Whispered introductions all round.

They're called Danny and Naomi, and I vaguely recognised the names (they're members of the local historical society). They'd been up till stupid o'clock discussing the events of recent days and Danny was walking Naomi home when they'd spotted the torches in the churchyard.

We all peeked round the corner to see what was going on. There were two people there, both in long dark cloaks with cowls that looked like monks' robes. They were standing by the well and were chanting something in Latin (I'm rusty but I recognise omnia bella. It's usually translated as 'all beautiful things,' but another interpretation is 'all wars...') Winston started snarling when he heard it.

And then—

Having a hard time describing it. It was human-shaped, but not human. Humans are not supposed to have big leathery bat wings, or that red light in their eyes, or claws, or—never mind. It emerged from the well, and I stood there like a statue. All three of us were shocked stupid.

It was the Devil. It couldn't be anything else. How? Why?

If I was frozen, Winston wasn't. He surged forward barking like mad, and suddenly we had two people and a devil staring at us.

The next few minutes are blurry. None of us knew what to do. Except Winston. He ran forward and bit the big demon-thing right on its leg. It shrieked. I think it cracked some of the stained glass in the church windows.

I ran forward too—or rather, I got dragged forward by Danny and Naomi as they charged after Winston. The two people in cowls fell on them, hitting and kicking. Which left me to back up Winston.

I vaguely remember Naomi yelling at me to say something from the Bible. I think I said 'Christ!' which probably wasn't what she meant. But then something clicked into place inside and I started quoting Revelation. Blessed is he that readeth, and they that hear the words of this prophecy, and keep those things which are written therein: for the time is at hand...

I kept speaking and reciting, and the thing emerging from the well actually retreated a little... though that could've been Winston. He'd torn a big chunk out of the thing's leg and was worrying a wing. The demon kept swiping at him but Winston was good at keeping out of its reach, thank the Lord.

Meanwhile, Naomi had managed to fend off the person attacking her and jumped on the back of the one hitting Danny. I then had the fabulous idea of running and fetching the holy water from the font, only to find of course the door was locked. The only thing around was the bucket the builders had left. Full of water. I uttered a hasty blessing over it, hauled it over and threw it over the thing.

If the earlier shrieking was bad, then what followed—I can't describe it. I don't want to. Moving on.

Winston tore a piece out of the creature's wing, and next thing I knew it was vanishing back down the well. Naomi and Danny managed to overcome the second cowl person—at least, when I looked, they were both standing while the cowl person was lying on the ground—and they came and we all peered down the well.

It was dark, and quiet. Nothing moved down there. No sounds emerged.

We three covered it up with whatever we could find. Wooden planks, a marquee left over from the church fete, a few bricks to weigh everything down. I called the police to report the two robed people. I said they'd attacked two of my congregation, which was true enough, and the police came out right away and took them off, robes and all. First thing tomorrow I'll get the well bricked up.

Then I'll go about my business. My faith.

Except it isn't faith really. Not now I have proof. Have seen the Devil with my own two God-given eyes.

Note: buy Winston a steak to say thank you.

* * *

EXCERPT FROM ARTICLE ON THE WEBSITE OF THE MANSFIELD RECORDER, 19TH MARCH:

ARRESTS AT ST. GALL'S FOLLOWING ATTACK

Two people have been arrested in connection with an assault in St. Gall's churchyard.

Police were called early in the morning after two people were attacked in St. Gall's churchyard. Police have arrested a man and a woman, neither of whom have been identified. It has not been confirmed whether or not the assault was related to the recent alarming events that have taken place around the church.

Police are appealing for witnesses and request that anyone with relevant information contact them on...

* * *

INVOICE DELIVERED FROM POWELL'S BUILDERS TO ST. GALL'S VICARAGE, 19TH MARCH, WITH HANDWRITTEN NOTE ADDED:

- Bricks: £300
- Mortar: £100
- Iron Grating: £300
- Labour: £250
- Total: £950

Hi vicar, all sorted. Good thing we had that cancellation and could get the well filled in. Hope this makes you feel better, you sounded rough on the phone this morning. From Dave Powell

* * *

EMAIL, 23RD MARCH:

From: major_majorie@gmail.com
To: naomi.lewis36@gmail.com

Hi Naomi,

I got your message. So sorry you and Danny had to go through a mugging, of all things! Still, I don't quite see why you think we should do a history of the Mansfield WI instead of talking about the well. I think it would be thrilling, given all the spooky goings on! Let me know if you change your minds.

Best,

Marjorie

* * *

EXCERPT OF ARTICLE IN MANSFIELD AND BRISCOMBE ORGANISER, 30TH MARCH:

POLICE RENEW APPEAL FOR HELP IN CASE OF MISSING MAN

Police are requesting help in locating local resident Gareth 'Gaz' Rawlings. Mr Rawlings was last seen on 17th March at the Black Bull pub, but has not been heard off since. He was reported missing after failing to turn up for work the next day. Police have emphasised there are no suspicious circumstances surrounding Mr Rawlings's disappearance, but his family are anxious for him to get in touch...

* * *

TEXT MESSAGES, 30TH MARCH:

NL: Hi Dan! Swung past the churchyard last night, all is quiet still.
DG: Good to hear. Let's keeping checking for a while, just to make sure.
NL: Yes, good plan. By the way, Paul's asked us round to the vicarage
tonight for dinner.
DG: Great, we can surprise him with the puppy! He's looked low since
Winston went back.
NL: Are you sure he wants a dog?
DG: Positive!
NL: On your head be it!

* * *

EMAILS, 31ST MARCH:

From: Wharton@COE.co.uk
To: Hattersley@COE.co.uk

Hi Paul,

Got your message! I knew you wouldn't be able to manage without a dog
after Winston. I know it must have been quite a surprise, but dogs are
wonderful creatures. I'll bring some supplies over later. You'll do brilliantly.

Did you see the news about the people who carried out the mugging in the
churchyard a couple of weeks ago? It was all over the BBC this morning,
they've been linked to a series of desecrations carried out in London last
year and they're being questioned in connection with a murder. I think your
parishioners had a very lucky escape.

One more thing – what happened to Winston when he was staying with you?
His muzzle has turned black! I thought it was just dirt at first but it looks as
though he's been singed. Have you got any idea what happened?

Best wishes,

Eric

* * *

TEXT MESSAGES, 30TH MARCH

    JC: You got the message out?
    MH: Done. They're on their way.
    JC: DON'T screw up again.
    MH: Not to worry. There's always Plan B.

END

DARK LAKE

DAWN NAPIER

Tammy sat at the edge of the lake and looked out over the water. It was early fall, so the beach was officially closed, but all that meant was that there was no lifeguard on duty. That was all right. In fact, it was perfect. What Tammy needed today was time alone.

There were a few boats out on the water, toward the middle where they could zip around and kick up waves without pissing off the residents who lived on the water's edge. Tammy watched the bright dots zoom around like water bugs and listened to the faint shouts of the boaters. At this distance, the cacophony was almost soothing.

It beat the hell out of listening to a colicky baby scream in her ear for hours, anyway.

She looked up at the trees overhead, the wide oak leaves just turning from green to yellow. Soon they'd be orange and red and dropping into the water, covering the shallows and hiding the fish as they settled into the muck to sleep away the winter.

Tammy looked back at the empty stroller behind her. Sleep sounded good. She wanted to go home and sleep for days.

Maybe if she could sleep, this sick, heavy feeling in her guts would disappear.

Tammy got up and wandered back over to the little pier. It was barely big enough to launch a canoe, but the water was mucky and full of weeds, which made the pier an attractive fishing spot. Kids usually sat here and dangled their feet in the water or threw stones.

The view from here was so calm and pretty. Tammy could see houses and piers on the other side, beautiful homes surrounded by wreaths of yellow and green. The boats were leaving, and the water was still. The afternoon was turning to evening, and the cool autumn breeze was kicking up. Tammy closed her eyes and breathed deeply of the peace.

She looked down at her reflection in the dark water, and practiced her 911 call.

I was holding her in my lap, and I was showing her the water. She must have slipped out of my arms. I don't know how it happened. Oh God, I'm so sorry.

She said the words out loud, quietly. They sounded dry and mechanical. She needed to cry. They wouldn't believe her if she didn't cry.

But how could she cry, with this sick lump in her stomach and throat? Tammy felt bad, even remorseful, but she wasn't hysterical. She was too calm to cry.

She frowned at her reflection.

It smiled back at her.

Tammy jumped and let out a little scream, but her reflection's smile did not move.

Tammy's frown became a scowl, but the other Tammy's smile only widened. She touched her own face, and the sick feeling in her stomach now felt cold and tight with fear. Her life had changed today, and now somehow the laws of the universe had changed as well.

Her reflection changed as it broke the surface of the lake. Dyed blonde hair became black, and her smile was young and elfin. "Hello, woman," it said in a childlike voice. "Why have you brought me this gift?"

Tammy blinked and stepped away. In the shallow water below the pier was a tiny woman with black hair and bright green eyes. Her ears were pointed, and so were her teeth. She appeared to be nude, but all Tammy could see of her was above her bare, white shoulders.

"What gift?" Tammy asked. Maybe she'd fallen asleep on the beach, and she was dreaming.

"This." The tiny woman rose a few inches and looked down at the tiny blue baby suckling at her breast. Its wrinkled fist waved and clutched at the woman's bare skin.

"Nobody has sacrificed to me in centuries," said the woman in the lake. "I owe you a boon for this gift. She's such a delight."

"She was never a delight to me," Tammy said. "She was born six weeks early, she was sick all the time, we racked up thousands of dollars in debt trying to get her the therapy she needed. Then Mike started banging that slut he worked with… but I guess it all worked out, if she's happy with you."

The woman's smile faded. "This wasn't a gift?" Her voice was puzzled. "You —discarded your child? In my lake?"

"I didn't know it was yours." Tammy's voice sounded feeble, and her vision blurred. *I must be hallucinating*, she thought distantly. *This is that postpartum psychosis I read about. I'm not just tired. I'm actually crazy.*

When the police came they wouldn't treat her like a bereaved mother. They'd treat her like a crazy criminal. They'd lock her up. That fear lurked behind this one, like a shadow behind a screen. Tammy almost hoped that this was real. As strange and frightening as it was, it felt less real than police, a trial, iron bars.

The woman in the lake stared at her. Her green eyes were dark, like a stormy sea. Then she grinned, showing all of her pointed, silvery teeth. "It's all right," she said. "I will give her all the love you never could. What's your name, woman?"

"Tammy," she whispered. As soon as she spoke the dizziness got worse, and the heavy pit of fear in her gut thickened. She felt off-balance, as though she might collapse in any direction. "Tammy Jane Maher."

The sky overhead was clouding over, and the boats on the lake were gone. A chill wind ruffled Tammy's hair.

"Give me your hand, Tammy Jane Maher." The woman's voice was deeper, deep as the middle of the lake. "I want to thank you for this gift."

Tammy tried to back away, run away down the pier and never come back. But she couldn't move. She could only watch helplessly as her hand moved of its own accord and reached into the water towards the tiny woman who was not a woman.

The spirit of the lake seized her hand in a cold, rubbery grip. Her nails were needle-sharp, and her fingers were webbed. Tammy cried out as the creature's claws pierced her flesh, and her blood dripped down her arm and into the water.

"Thank you," the creature hissed. "Today I have been given two gifts. A baby to love—and a fresh meal to make her strong."

With a sharp yank Tammy was dragged into the lake and beneath the surface. She kicked out, but her feet found no purchase though the lake was only four feet deep here at the pier. She tried to pull her arm free, but the creature of the lake had her in a deadly tight grip, fingers digging deeper and deeper into her flesh. She couldn't find the bottom of the lake, or the cement pier, or anything at all solid to touch. All she could feel were those claws dragging her down further and further.

The last thing Tammy saw was a ring of needle-thin teeth rushing through the water at her throat.

And the last thing she felt was a tiny toothless mouth, suckling at the pouring blood.

Mike's friends and parents told him that it wasn't his fault. Postpartum depression was an insidious condition, hard to predict. How could he have known that Tammy could drown her own baby and then herself? She'd seemed stable enough, maybe a little tired and overwhelmed after Mike moved in with Megan. But still, nobody could have predicted what she did. And it wasn't Mike's fault.

It was a blessing in disguise, they said privately, *that the baby's body was never found*. Tammy had been horribly mutilated and partially devoured by the fish and other critters living in the lake. To think of finding one's child in such a condition was unthinkable.

Mike himself could almost believe it. Megan couldn't; she kicked him out three days after the funeral, saying she could barely live with herself and sure as hell couldn't live with him. But during the day, when the sun was bright and the autumn leaves pretty on the trees, he could almost convince himself that his wife's psychotic break was just a crazy fluke, the neurological equivalent of winning a jackpot. It couldn't have been predicted, and it wasn't his fault.

During the day he could believe it. But at night his dreams were full of terror and guilt and autumn leaves falling into dark water.

And in the water, rows of shining, needle-sharp teeth.

BLAME THE WIND

PETER NINNES

Ethan slammed the gate, wiped his nose on his sleeve, and stomped out into a wall of rain. His face was full of snot, the Friday afternoon staff meeting had dragged into the evening, he had a hundred assignments to mark, and his umbrella leaked. Seven more days, he reminded himself, and you'll be on that big jet plane back home and done with this dreadful country. His decongestants had worn off. A long-delayed sneeze dispatched a droplet swarm into battle against the downpour. He spat a gob of mucus toward the drain. The wind caught the sputum, flinging it against a small stone fox statue planted in the roadside grass. Illuminated by a street light's anxious glow, Ethan watched the goo trickle over the fox's pointy nose and onto the cloth flapping around its shoulders.

Who the hell worships a fox with a Superman cape anyway? He'd never understood religion, let alone the strange spiritual salmagundi he'd stumbled upon in this backwater. There were gods and goblins everywhere: in a large tree; an oddly shaped stone; even a piece of rope. Probably in that piece of chewing gum squashed on the pavement. The whole place spooked him.

A bolt of lightning hit a tree not far ahead. Ethan jumped. A clap of thunder rattled his bones. The wind swept down the road and thrashed his umbrella into an inscrutable wire sculpture. His scalp crawled as if infested with static electricity. He threw the umbrella in the road and dashed through the doors of the familiar 24-hour convenience store that he passed every day going to and from work.

Ethan didn't recognize the man at the counter, who looked at him with blank, preoccupied eyes. He scowled when Ethan gave him the exact change. Ethan grabbed his six-pack and hurried out the sliding doors. The rain had eased, leaving a malcontent dampness in the air. Ethan snuffled his way home, took some more cold pills, and heated leftovers for dinner. By the time he'd graded his assignments, the clock hands had found their way to the midnight hour. Six empty cans loitered like abandoned souls on the table. He stretched out on the couch in his boxers. Grading students' work always overstimulated his mind, and he needed to relax before bed.

But his body felt as taut as a mad dog's chain. An eerie suspicion lurked in the dimmer recesses of his brain. The air in the room felt thick, like a hand on a victim's throat. The curtains waved madly. The breeze stumbled in the window, unsure of itself. Dankness eked out of the wallpaper, as if his apartment sat in a swamp.

Ethan's nose was running. He fumbled with the blister pack, then swallowed a couple of night-time tablets. Sweat ran down his neck. He turned his head and spied the beer cans on the table. That's what I need. Why don't they make a seven-pack? Time for another beer run. As he pulled on his shorts, he recalled the strange man who'd served him earlier. A shiver percolated through his spine. He didn't want to encounter that fellow again. But the shop attendants usually change shift at 11 pm. With a little luck, it'll be that nice young woman with the warm, toothy smile, the skin tanned slightly more than usual, and the big, fake eyelashes. She'd visited him in his fantasies, but he'd barely spoken to her in real life. He was convinced that one day he would ask her on a date, if he ever found the nerve. At any rate, the thought of her pushed him off the couch.

He grabbed his wallet and keys and walked along the deserted street to the convenience store. The clouds had slunk away over the mountains. The moon, full as a plum, turned every shadow into impenetrable darkness.

He exhaled deeply in the gaudy brightness of the store. She's here! The young woman had her back to him, stacking a shelf. He admired her uniform for a moment, letting his eyes wander from the pale green pleated shirt tucked in at the waist, to the black trousers tight on her narrow hips. He tore himself away, to the less alluring refrigerators at the back of the store. He chose a beer brand he hadn't tried before.

He put the cans on the counter as the woman appeared beside the register.

"Three thousand bijus, please," she said, blinking her long lashes. He handed over a four-thousand biju note, his heart beating a little faster as he anticipated her smile. She broke into a grin. The corners of her mouth stretched behind her ears. Ethan's throat constricted. He stared at her teeth, much longer and sharper than he remembered, and at her exposed crimson gums, like raw meat in a butcher's shop. Her nose, too, appeared to be changing, stretching out towards him. She grabbed his hand and pressed his change into it. Her fingers were cold, as if the skin had thickened into pads on her fingertips.

Ethan yelped, grabbed his beer and tried to make for the door. He was halted by her preternatural grip on his other hand. Her fingernails dug into his palm. She pulled herself over the counter and knocked the six-pack out of his hands. One can burst, sending the amber liquid under his sneakers. The spilled beer immediately froze, pinning him to the floor.

Ethan's nose started to itch.

The woman stared at his face. "Let me help." She plunged her free hand into the hot water tray next to the cash register, grabbed a mini frankfurter and, before he could stop her, shoved it up his nostril.

Nathan shrieked. The woman opened her mouth as if to laugh, but instead, leaned both hands on the counter, tilted back her head, and emitted a lycanthropic howl.

The sneeze exploded. The sausage shot out and landed in the newspaper rack. Ethan wrenched his shoes free of the frozen beer and ran for the door, but the woman reached it first.

"Get out of the way, you bindlestiff!" Ethan dodged around her and crashed into the glass, hitting his head, stunning himself. He spun around, trying to locate the emergency release knob.

"Have you ever seen one of these?" she asked, pulling up her shirt.

Ethan pressed back against the door, gawking at the knife handle tattooed across her midriff. The blade appeared to be embedded in her flesh.

A police siren wailed nearby. Thank God. The cops! The woman put her hand on the tattoo and pulled the knife from her belly. Ethan watched it, sweat pouring down his face. She waved the blade under his nose, then laughed and backed away, shooting him a glare. She's going to charge me! He chanced a quick glance out the door. The police officer was right there.

"I'm saved!" Ethan cried.

The police officer walked through the door without it opening.

"What? Officer?" Ethan gasped, backing down the aisle next to the ice cream freezer as the cop came straight at him. Ethan held out his hands, as if to ward him off. "No! Stop!"

The cop whipped out his cuffs and snapped one on Ethan's wrist. Then he locked the other end of the cuffs to a shelf.

"That'll teach you," the cop said. Teach me what? For God's sake, you're all insane!

"Nice one," the women said to the cop. She lifted up Ethan's shirt and ran the back of her knife along his skin, poking his tummy flab with the pointy end. "Maybe you'd like a hot dog? Or some sushi?" She nodded at the food on a distant shelf.

"I'm not hungry! Let me go!" Ethan yelled, following her gaze. A long sushi roll, clear plastic encasing its outer layer of seaweed, rose into the air, drifted over, and landed a meter from Ethan's feet. The tape holding the plastic peeled off, and the plastic unrolled. The rice and cucumber sticks slid out from their seaweed sheath. Every hair on Ethan's body stood on end. Two more rolls flew over and deconstructed themselves on the floor.

The cucumber pieces piled together. Before Ethan's startled eyes, they formed themselves back into a long, green, knobby cucumber. He felt a number of frightened sphincters contract as two wings sprouted from the cucumber's body. It rose into the air, and flew towards Ethan. He swiped wildly at it, but it dodged to the side, flew up and poked him hard in the eye with such force, Ethan thought his eyeball would pop. He tried again to grab it with his free hand, but it jumped out of the way. Now it hurtled at his groin, striking him a nauseating blow. The woman laughed. Spittle dripped off her canines and down her chin. The cucumber jabbed Ethan hard in the solar plexus, and the wind went out of him.

The cop was on his knees, licking the rice off the floor with a pink, sandpapery tongue. Smacking his lips, he jumped up and grabbed Ethan's free hand. Then the cucumber dived down the back of Ethan's shorts, intent on serious harm. Ethan reflexively scrunched his bum muscles, catching the cucurbit between his cheeks. Got you, you little bastard! He slammed his backside into the shelf behind him, eliciting a satisfying crunch. Two halves of cucumber fell at his feet, splashing into the beer, which had begun to melt.

The hum of the automatic doors made them turn. In the doorway stood a fox, all orange fur, pointy ears, sharp teeth and dress-ups. He—and Ethan could tell it was a male fox because it was standing upright on its hind legs, and there was a significant bulge in the fox's blue underpants—was at least six feet tall. He sported a blue t-shirt embroidered with a large letter F and a red cape, the ends of which flapped in the violent breeze whipping through the door. A black patch covered his right eye.

The cop let go of Ethan's hand and curled up on the floor, his eyes closed, his breath making faint whirring sounds as he inhaled and exhaled. The woman hopped up on the counter and crossed her trousered legs. She removed a hot lemon drink from the case to her left, unscrewed the lid and took a sip, casting a casual glance over the scene as if watching a golf tournament.

The fox marched up to Ethan. Ethan's knees sagged and the cuffs cut into his wrist. The fox drew himself up to his full height. His one good eye cast an accusatory stare at Ethan's head. Ethan caught a damp, sordid smell, like the dog he'd had as a child that his mother had to remind him to bathe. Nothing happened. The store was still and quiet, except for the cop's breathing. Eventually, Ethan looked up at the white fur under the fox's chin. The whole scene stoked a vague memory that struggled to surface in Ethan's mind.

The fox's mouth hung open. A long dribble of saliva stretched down toward the floor. Ethan stared at the fox's sharp, yellow fangs. All the better to tear me to pieces with.

The giant fox opened his mouth wider and took a deep breath. This is it. He's going to bite my face off. Or sink his chompers into my cranium.

Ethan heard a noise like a bicycle pump's plunger, then a large, amoebic blob shot out of the fox's mouth. It hit Ethan in the eye, stung like a jelly fish, and slid down his cheek. The fox turned with a flourish of his cape and walked out the door.

A penny dropped in Ethan's brain. His anger began to mount and he shouted into the dark. "It wasn't my fault! Blame the wind for blowing the gob onto the stone fox god!"

The store lights came on. The glass flew back into the windows.

The cop stood up and stretched. "Well, that's that, then," he said, unlocking the cuffs.

"Grab another six-pack on your way out," the woman said, smiling normally and tucking in her shirt.

Ethan didn't bother about the beer. White-hot rage overtook his fear and kidnapped his common sense. He sped out the door and dashed across the road. He gave the stone fox a mighty kick. It broke off at the base and fell in the grass. "Take that, you stupid dumb rock god Superman fox prick!"

Ethan ran back to his apartment. He called a taxi and threw his few possessions in a suitcase. He wasn't staying in this diabolical town a minute longer. He'd sleep in the airport if necessary. The main thing is to get away before that fox shows up again.

When the cab arrived, Ethan didn't wait for the driver to get out and help him. He heaved the case into the trunk himself. Then he slumped in the back seat, his head in his hands, his chest pounding from the effort.

"Where to, sir?" asked the driver.

Ethan looked up and screamed. The driver flashed a yellow-toothed grin. The moonlight sparkled on his svelte, orange fur. A fox driving a taxi? Before he could move, a paw flew at Ethan. Claws dug into his neck, sealing off his lungs and aborting a cry. A supernatural force pulled him between the front seats and his head crashed into the dashboard. The passenger door swung open of its own volition, and Ethan's unconscious body was ejected onto the soggy curb. Moments later, his suitcase crashed to the ground beside him and spilled its contents in the mud.

The fox drove back to the convenience store and slipped inside.

"He probably won't be leering at you anymore," the fox said, unclipping his cape.

"Thank you. You're my hero," replied the young vixen behind the counter. She scribbled the word "Closed" on a piece of paper and taped it to the door.

"You deserve a reward," she said, switching off half the lights.

"I believe I do." He reached out and gently stroked the fur on her cheek.

She took the fox's other paw and led him to the back room. A drunk arrived and started banging on the front doors, but the pair were oblivious, locked in a fervent, canine embrace.

STAGNANT MAY

R. H. BERRY

The little town of Moulder Valley was sinking. It was a landlocked little spit nestled between sparse forests and cattle farms, the sort of place no one chose to live in but that no one ever left. Every house had a porch, every window had shutters, every resident had a slow and easy demeanor. Family hired family hired family, an insular community that rarely saw the need to reach out to the rest of the world. They were self-sufficient. They didn't need anything an outsider could possibly offer, no sir, thank you kindly.

But it was sinking, and no one really knew why.

It was no Venice; they hadn't paved their streets atop a lagoon. For reasons no one had yet explained, the sloping freeways grew incrementally steeper with every passing year. Gravity worked on Moulder Valley just that much harder, gouging a concave pocket into the surface of the Earth like it, too, didn't want to see May Leeman leave home. It was a literal uphill climb, getting out of Moulder Valley.

But she was going to do it. Nobody had managed it yet, but that was because nobody else was like May.

She'd always been brainy. Not just clever, but imaginative. She received a new notebook for every birthday and Christmas, bartered routinely with her brother John and sister Carrie for their allotted computer time. She wrote, and she wrote constantly. The notebooks were full of ideas, poetry, bits of folklore and facts about worlds that didn't exist anywhere outside her head. Her private file folder on the family desktop was full of drafts upon drafts of novels, most of which were unfinished.

May was going to be a novelist. World-famous, a household name. Nothing was going to stop her. She was seventeen years old when she finished high school, and hadn't been out of classes for a whole day when she sat her parents down to tell them she wouldn't be working in the family business.

The Leeman family lived and breathed automotive repair. They were the best in the business, and the only garage around for miles. They didn't even advertise. They didn't need to. It was a good business, a solid one, and both John and Carrie were shaping up to take the reins once their parents retired. They didn't need May. Her skills weren't applicable, anyway, for she'd always had too busy of a head to pay attention to cars.

More importantly, her dreams weren't here. Not at Leeman's Garage, not in Moulder Valley. She was going to write something great and use her first book advance to move to a city. Somewhere big and inspiring, like New York or Toronto. She told her parents all about it, and waited with bated breath for a reaction.

They hemmed. They hawed. They warned her, maybe learn a thing or two about cars in the meantime, maybe work a day job while chasing her fancy dreams, but May insisted. She was going to be a novelist. She'd write fantasy and romance and action. They relented and said she'd have a place under their roof, if nothing else.

That was when May was seventeen.

May Leeman still received a notebook every birthday and Christmas, but they weren't all in use. A good portion of them were collecting dust on her bookshelf, disjointed notes taking up only the first couple of pages. She was twenty years old now, sitting in front of her family's rundown desktop computer, typing away at a brand-new story.

She had a lot of writing under her belt, but nothing to show for it yet. Not one of her manuscripts had been picked up for publication. She wasn't honestly ready to try yet, was the thing—she'd only ever finished one story, and she knew damn well it needed polish. A few revisions, for sure, and maybe a section or two could be rewritten.

Moulder Valley had fallen even further towards the center of the Earth. That spring, a construction crew had been rounded up to work on the crumbling sections of road leading into the town proper. It'd sunk enough to stretch the asphalt thin enough to break.

May wasn't concerned with that. She still had fictional worlds to get on paper. Gingerly hitting the space bar over and over again, May stared at the document she was working on with glazed eyes: she'd written three pages and wasn't sure she liked a single word. With a soft sigh, she rolled her chair back with a bit of difficulty and rubbed at her sore temples.

She paid little attention to the soupy fingers wiggling up through the floorboards. They weren't any more than gooey, peeling flesh over brittle bones, but they caught at her feet and held her firm in front of her computer, a foot away from the keyboard. May absentmindedly kicked, but the fingers found purchase against her bare soles. They dug into her flesh. She winced.

Maybe she just needed to do more brainstorming. She'd pick up one of her more-often used notebooks and take a look at the groundwork she'd laid. Something was bound to inspire her.

She wrenched her feet off the floor with a dry gasp. Something had gouged dirty holes into her heels. With a whimper, May loped to the bathroom instead, leaving spots of blood and her notions of reading behind. She had to clean up her feet.

That was when May was twenty.

That old computer died eventually. They managed to salvage some of the information off the hard drive, but not all. May lived off her parents' money and refused to occupy precious writing time with other work, so she'd had to bargain for a personal laptop. Her computer was a present that encapsulated several years' worth of birthdays and Christmases, but it was well worth it. May didn't need any new notebooks, anyway. She hadn't used one for at least…

Was it three years, now? Four? May was twenty-nine years old and hadn't even picked up one of her notebooks in ages. She'd decided a while back to dedicate herself to one great novel instead of several mediocre ones, and she knew every facet of the story she wanted to write now. It was all written out in her head, she told John, whenever he asked how the writing was going. She just had to adjust it here and there, she told Carrie. It was just such a chore: sloughing through the editing process, finding an agent willing to represent her, going back over the story with rejection notes from the publishers. May often needed the perfect venue to sit down and get some real work done, and home just wasn't doing it for her anymore.

There was a little coffee shop that she liked. It was an uphill trek, but it was still high enough up the slanted street that you could appreciate the view of the trees down a ways. May walked with her laptop in a bag slung across her shoulders, and with clammy hands grasping at her feet with every step.

They had bloated palms and a sallow tint to the oozing, muddied skin. One would sprout from the grout between cobblestone bricks and clutch at May's sneaker while two others dragged their way out of the ground to wrap around her ankle. The nails on these hands were grimy, sharp, ragged. They were caked with disease, something corrosive and repugnant, and every touch, every scratch, made May's skin sizzle and blister.

But she was used to this, and so ignored it. She made the trek to the coffee shop, ordered herself an iced cappuccino, and sat down to write yet another draft of her magnum opus.

Sadly, the walk had taken a lot out of her. She sat there, drinking coffee and letting her mind wander until she came to the conclusion that she just wasn't going to get any writing done today. By the heavy orange light of sundown, May trudged back home—the rotting hands actively attempting to hold her in place all the way.

That was when May was twenty-nine.

Getting out of the house took gargantuan effort, but sitting down with her laptop took even more. There was just so much around to distract and depress her. She was supposed to have been published by now, be *famous*. Writing was the only thing she had in her wheelhouse, and the fact that she hadn't succeeded with it could only mean she was a failure.

It was hard to find the motivation to do *anything*, let alone offer herself up for more defeat. She'd managed to finish a couple of books now, but even independent publishers didn't seem to care for the stories. The characters felt two-dimensional; the settings were confusing; the dialogue felt forced. Eventually, she put them online for anyone to read, only to receive absolutely no feedback. No one was buying, no one was reading.

May gazed at her laptop. It was sitting on the desk across the room, a document still open. Carefully, she placed a hand on the bedpost and attempted to haul herself upright.

Gooey strings of flesh tore like plasticine. Her eroding ankle bone jutted through the remnants of muscle poorly trying to keep her feet attached. The moment she touched the ground, those oozing hands came up through the soggy floorboards and groped for her, as usual. May ignored them as much as she could. The touch seared, bacteria feasting on raw tissue.

Her laptop screen glowered. May steeled herself, and limped.

She only made it halfway across the room before she buckled. Her kneecaps bruised upon their impact with the floor, and she cried out, catching herself just well enough to avoid breaking her neck. Hungry hands began clawing through her pant legs, scratching up her shins and finding purchase in her fleshy calves. Her face screwed up in desperate concentration, and she tried to drag herself towards her desk.

The hands did not let go. They scratched through her exposed nerves and she screamed, sobbed. But she didn't give up, *couldn't* give up, this was *all she had left –*

So May pulled. And *pulled.*

The tendons ripped. Blood sprayed the floorboards and bedspread, began to rapidly pool underneath her. The hands utterly destroyed the flimsy bone, weakened by years of corrosion, and rent her feet from her body.

May hauled herself the last little way and reached up the desk, using the remainder of her strength. She closed the laptop lid.

She gave up, and bled out on the floor of her bedroom.

That was when May was thirty-five.

Moulder Valley sank a little lower. It's still sinking, but no one who lives there really minds. They're not going anywhere.

No one in their right mind wants to leave Moulder Valley, because they have everything they need right there.

A DINGO ALMOST ATE HIS BABY

ALANNA ROBERTSON-WEBB

I don't have any official, hoity-toity medical training, but I'm the closest thing to an EMT that we've got out here. When someone breaks a leg, gets in a fist fight, or gets bitten by something, I can usually get to them hours before the nearest police or ambulance can. As such, they actually give me medical supplies to keep in Ol' Bessie, my beater truck, just in case of an emergency. I've been doing this for years and years, and I've seen some crazy things go down. Nothing, however, can top the experience I had two years ago in the northern part of the Outback.

I was at Dennis Fargo's place in the heat of summer, and I was splinting his broken leg. The idjit had tried to avoid getting bit by a croc, which he did manage to do just before he tripped over a rock and tumbled face-first down a small cliff. He wasn't in too bad of shape, but he wouldn't be walking fast for a while either. I had just finished drying the last layer of his cast when we heard a gut-wrenching scream, and I nearly broke my neck whipping it around as fast as I did. The scream had come from where Mic and Lindsey Chambers, his nearest neighbors, lived. Their ranch was about two miles away, and without hesitating I made sure my shotgun was loaded, hopped into ol' Bessie, and sped towards them.

My drive, which would normally have taken me about ten minutes, took barely five. I pumped the brakes, Bessie screeching to a halt in front of their porch.

"Mic, you here!? What's wrong!?"

Mic stumbled out of the house, his shirt covered splattered with blood. He nearly fell down the steps, but I managed to catch him before he could land on the scorching earth.

"Dingo... took my baby..."

Lindsey had pretty recently popped out little tyke number five, and I don't think it was more than a year old. Red flags were immediately waving around in my head though, because dingoes didn't often frequent this area. Even if they did, they weren't exactly keen on eating human offspring, and how would he have gotten so much blood on him? A wild dog shouldn't have attacked a grown man without its pack by its side, and I was praying to anyone listening that Mic hadn't killed his kid and tried to make it look like an animal attack.

"Slow down buddy! Take a deep breath and tell me what the heck happened here."

I made him sit him down on the steps so that he wouldn't fall, but he was trying to stand up again within seconds. He had his pistol in his hand, and looked like he was ready to shoot me if I got in his way.

"No time, Jenny, gotta rescue Arlia! That mongrel has her, and she's still alive!"

"Where's Lindsey and the other kids? Are they okay?"

"Yeah, not even here. She took 'em to town to get our weekly rations. Now come on!"

"Mic, stay here. I'll get her back. Take my shotgun and give me the pistol, I'll be faster that way."

"Damn it, Jenny, no! I gotta fight for her. You think I'm just goin' to waltz up to the police and say, 'Sorry officer, a dingo ate my baby so I can't prove I'm innocent. Oops.'? I don't think so!"

I didn't argue. I knew how stubborn Mic was, and it would be a waste of time. Before I could turn around, he gripped my sleeve, practically dragging me past my truck. He was pointing his gun towards a trail of bloody paw prints, and they were so fresh that I could see them glistening in the sunset.

"If we go fast, we can catch it. Be careful though, it's gotta be rabid because it attacked me to get to my girl."

He lifted his shirt, and I was shocked to see huge gouges down his right side.

I had seen plenty of animal-based wounds, and that was definitely claw marks. We began trotting alongside the trail, and even though my instincts were shouting at me to sprint, I knew Mic couldn't handle that. We were heading straight into the wild of the Outback, and it wasn't a fun place to be in the dark. I shoved my fear deep inside, trying to distract myself instead of worrying.

"So what happened? It just came in through the back door, attacked you and took the kid?"

"Front door, but yeah. It didn't look normal either, kinda look like someone ran over it or something. Pretty messed up."

Mic was wheezing, and I couldn't stand to see him stressing his wounds this badly. I reached out and grabbed his sleeve, forcing him to stop.

"Mic, we gotta run after the trail, but one of us needs to stay here in case it doubles back with her. Can you do that? The boulder over there would make a good lookout spot."

He hesitated so long that I thought he'd say no, but then reached for my gun. He took it, handing me the pistol, then he slowly limped to the boulder. He hauled himself up as quickly as he could, standing with one hand shielding his eyes in true scout fashion. He glanced down at me, trying not to show signs of his pain.

"Go on, bring her back. Please... that's my little girl out there."

I nodded, breaking into a sprint. I was a decent enough tracker, and with a trail this obvious it didn't take me long to lose sight of the house. A few minutes later Mic was out of sight too, though I felt better knowing he was at least sitting down. He might pass out from blood loss, but that would be easier to fix than a dead kid. The trail had begun weaving in and out of some rocky outcroppings, and I for a moment I thought I could hear the baby crying. I kept a steady course, and I was so focused that I didn't realize just how quickly I was losing daylight.

Thirty minutes from the house the trail began drying up, the bloody prints becoming drier and less frequent. I only had a little time left before I was in pitch black without a light source, and I didn't relish the thought of a rabid dog getting the jump on me. I've known men to accidentally shoot themselves when they were firing off in the dark, and I wasn't about to become one of my own EMT stories. I pressed on, my heart hammering painfully as I made sure to avoid the rough terrain. I was nearing the point of giving up when I heard a thin, exhausted-sounding wail. I doubled my pace, breaking into an all-out run.

Screw the rattlers, scorpions. and everything else that tries to kill you on this damned continent. When I found out the kid was alive, I wasn't stopping for anything, not even death. I barreled around a corner of one of the rocky outcroppings, skidding to a halt just in time to avoid colliding with the kid. She was bloody, and I could see that the dingo had taken a few chunks out of one of her legs, but she was alive. She reached her pudgy little arms out to me, hysteria clear in her wail. I was relieved that her father wasn't the bad guy, and I gathered her into my arms.

"Come on, kid, stick with me and I'll get ya home."

She was still too small to talk, but she looked at me with big, teary eyes. I could have sworn that she understood me, and she clung to me as I began to jog back the way I had come. I hadn't spotted so much as a hair from the dingo, and I was hoping that it would stay that way. If I was really lucky it would have died from heat stroke or something, and we could put this whole thing behind us. When was I ever that lucky, though? Never, that's when.

I was making my way carefully through one of the dried-out gullies when I heard a howl, and it wasn't far off. I froze, closing my eyes like I could shoo the animal away with sheer willpower. As I stood there with my eyes shut, I listened, waiting to hear if anything approached us. After a moment I caught the muffled sound of movement, and I swung around to face whatever was sneaking up on us. I had the pistol ready to fire, and I clutched the little tyke close to my side. I couldn't see much in the moonlight, but it would be enough to show me where to point.

"Back off! I'm locked and loaded, so don't try anything stupid. I like shooting first and questioning later."

I didn't actually think my bravado would help me against a rabid dingo, but it did make me feel better. I heard the kid whimper, and I turned my head to her. She was fixated on the darkness, her chubby finger pointing at something I couldn't see. I tried to follow her line of sight, and for a moment I thought I caught a glimpse of a person darting behind a large rock.

"Mic, ya damned fool, I told you to stay at the boulder! Come on, stop sneaking around now. I've got Arlia."

I expected to hear Mic's wheezy voice, but only silence greeted me. This was getting damned creepy. No one in their right mind would be out here without a light, not even people like drug dealers who were trying to remain undetected. I had run into my fair share of scumbags, such as poachers and human traffickers out in these wastelands, but even the ones wearing night-vision goggles could be identified when the metal glinted in the moonlight. This person didn't seem to be equipped with anything like that, and I kept my eyes peeled as I slowly backed away from where they were hiding.

"Give me back the child."

I nearly jumped, the silence-breaking shocking me. It was such a quiet whisper that I barely heard it, but something about it made me wince. It was too sharp, like every word was a needle jabbing the listener.

"I don't know who you think you are, but you're not gettin' her."

"Give her to me, or die."

I still couldn't get a good look at the speaker. They were cloaked in darkness, and the only thing I could make out was that their long hair seemed to be standing almost upright. That, or they were in a damned weird costume to be traversing the Outback in. The voice sounded vaguely masculine, and as the figure slinked closer to me I could see that it had large, bulbous eyes. The glint of fang-like teeth drew my attention, and for the first time I felt a tremble run through my pistol-holding hand. The more I observed this thing the more convinced I was that it wasn't entirely human, but that made no sense.

I had been continuously backing away from it, and to my relief I recognized the halfway point between where I found Arlia and the boulder where I had left her dad. The poor little tyke was beginning to cry in earnest now, and the being trailing us kept hissing that I should hand her over. I didn't respond to it, instead focusing my energy on safely navigating the harsh terrain. I may not be a mother, but my instinct to protect the kid was still stronger than my desire to drop her and flee. I had taken my eyes off of the thing for a moment, and in that time my back slammed against something solid. I jolted, nearly dropping Arlia.

It was the creature. Even with the semi-inky night surrounding us I was able to see it just a little better, and it was something that shouldn't exist. My mind raced back to the stories I had heard growing up, which were the only knowledge I had about what I was dealing with. The natives call these things the Mamu, and they're a type of spirit or monster with sharp, fang-like teeth capable of stripping the flesh off of their still-living victims. They're human-like shape-shifters, and the legends say they can change into birds and wild dogs.

If the stories were accurate, and I was starting to think that they were, then the Mamu typically resided underground and were weak until their first taste of blood. They only came up every few decades to feed, and I figured that Arlia must be looking like a high-class cheeseburger to them right about now.

"Give us the child!"

I quickly twisted my body, maneuvering us around the creature. We did a semi-tango, it trying to block me as I tried to move past it without making contact. I quickly got tired of that though, and as it went to step towards me I did a tuck-and-roll, curling my body around Arlia as I somersaulted past the creature. I scrambled up, my aging joints creaking in protest as I darted off towards the house. I heard its thunderous footfalls close behind us, but I had a terrain advantage. I knew where I was going, and used the boulders and trenches to slow it down.

My energy was depleting fast though, and at one point I didn't think I was going to make it. I was nearing the bouldering where I had left Mic, and without realizing it I had begun screaming for him. I lost focus for just a moment, and that was all it took. I inadvertently slowed down while scanning for Mic, and that gave the creature an attack of opportunity. It lashed out with razor-like claws, and I felt the skin of my leg part like warm butter under a knife. My agonized cry rang out, but it was partially covered by the sound of a gunshot. Mic was in front of us, the shotgun smoking in his hands. The thing behind me let out a roar, and I limped away as fast as I could.

I remember Mic grabbing onto me and leading us back to the house, but the pain was starting to make my vision swim. I could hear us being followed, but the Mamu stayed well out of sight. Arlia, who had remained almost completely silent, began to cry and reach for her dad. I didn't hand her over, though; my grip on the child remained unwavering even when I collapsed into a heap on their porch. I blacked out, and woke sometime the next day in a crisp, starched hospital bed. I was alone, and it took me awhile to focus on my surroundings.

The first thing I noticed was the TV above my bed. It was on my local news channel, and even though the volume was muted I was able to tell what the breaking news story was by reading the scrolling banner at the bottom of the screen.

RABID DINGO STOLE CHILD FROM HOME, LOCAL WOMAN FOUGHT DINGO AND SAVED CHILD. CHILD RETURNED SAFELY TO PARENTS, WOMAN PLACED IN NEARBY HOSPITAL IN CRITICAL CONDITION. UPDATES COMING SOON.

It was absurd, but as close to the truth as the news would ever get. When

Doctor Lee Martin, a man I had known for years, came in later he congratulated me. He informed me that I had been bit by a rattlesnake, and that I had several broken ribs. Doc Martin said that I had been talking about monsters in my sleep, and I was having feverish dreams about creatures trying to take Arlia from me. I began to protest, but he just shushed me and said that Arlia was fine, and that the Chambers family wanted to take me out to dinner when I recovered.

I once again tried to explain what happened, but he wouldn't listen. I got more agitated, and before I knew it Doc Martin was pinning me down and calling for backup. A sedative was soon coursing through my system, and as my body started to relax I began to wonder if, just maybe, my whole experience really was just a hallucination. Before long I was sleeping, and I can't recall dreaming at all. I awoke sometime later, and I was alone that time.

I started checking my body, my hands being careful to avoid my ribs. Within minutes I could feel my eyelids getting heavier again, and at points I would lose focus for a moment or two, but before I fully lost consciousness I was able to check myself. I had cuts and scrapes, broken bones and lacerations, but I couldn't find a puncture wound.

THROUGH THE LENS OF ST. VINCENT'S

CHARLOTTE PLATT

"We're going to a haunted house?" Lucy asked, hands on her hips and brows raked high.

"Haunted warehouse."

"Simon, why on earth are you taking me to something so grim?" she huffed, plonking herself down on the overstuffed sofa. A puff of dust rose up about her, making her grimace. Their "office" was Simon's basement and while it was better than nothing, it still left a lot to be desired.

"Because it's interesting, and we'll get views—the bigger the numbers the bigger the fee, eventually. If we don't get demonetized."

"You make it so vulgar. It's not going to be some *Most Haunted* shit, is it? I can't take screaming at the camera whenever there's an echo. Unless there's a rat: I might scream at that." She pulled a face at the thought, slipping her phone out to catch a picture.

"Where's Brett?" Simon asked, tugging his headphones off and wrapping them up to go into his pocket. He was never without wires, with something always blinking at him from a pocket.

"Loading his car, then he'll be over," she said, applying a suitable filter. "Can we even get in this place, or is it going to be like that last one?"

"It's not open to the public, but I know a way in," Simon said with a wink.

"What have you been up to?" she asked, uploading the selfie to her sites.

She'd been instrumental in growing the channel, and while she bemoaned being used as eye candy just as much as a host, it helped the "brand."

"Nothing. A little bit of breaking and entering. They'd boarded it up but nothing serious. I broke the wood down in like three kicks."

"I didn't know you had it in you!" She laughed, scandalized.

"It takes a lot of muscle to be hefting equipment around all day you know," Simon said, laughing with her. "It's been boarded up since the company canned the expansion. It's hardly been touched inside. Lots of rusted old equipment and the like."

"Okay—and what's spooky about it?"

"It's old school ghost hunting—we get to show people the inside of some-where they won't have seen, and there's a few rumors about it."

"Like?" She twisted round on the cushions to face him.

"The town says a serial killer buried all his bodies there."

"This place is nothing like interesting enough to have a serial killer. There's not even a McDonalds." A fact she had been bemoaning since moving here after college. Her job was decent, it would get her the credentials she needed, but holy crap was it a two-horse town down eight hooves.

"They say he took people travelling through and hid the bodies in the ware-house scrubland. There's lots of disappeared people around here, not making it to where they meant to go." Simon waggled his eyebrows at her.

"But no bodies."

"Not a one."

"And why haven't I heard of this?" she asked, watching him pack his laptop and other bits into his carry case.

"Because it's a rumor and no one's been able to prove anything. Just local knowledge."

"We're going body hunting then?"

"Nah, just to see if we can spot any ghosts. Maybe get some EVP or something."

"What now?"

"Electronic voice phenomenon. Hearing ghosts on a video."

"Well, that sounds terrifying," Lucy said.

"It'll look really good on the channel."

"Let's see how it goes. I draw the line at digging anything up."

"Not entirely unreasonable. We didn't take you on for manual labour." He nodded, tapping over his body to check he had everything on him.

A car horn blared and they scrambled up, scooping bags as they went. Brett sat waiting for them, blowing smoke out of the window as his music thumped low against the evening chatter. They slipped into their seats and buckled up, Simon poking a hand through with directions.

"What's the story?" Brett asked, squinting at the scrawl of Simon's writing.

"It's the abandoned warehouse up at St. Vincent Street, by the railway."

"That place you were scoping out the other day? You were weird as hell when you came out of there."

"The very same."

"You seemed pretty shook up, dude. The lighting up there is going to be awful at this time of day, too." Brett sighed, glancing at the sky.

"We have the light fitting on the camera and I brought flashlights. You can check the quality between shots."

"All right. You ready to go, baby girl?" He grinned at Lucy and she slapped his shoulder, rolling her eyes at his charms. Brett was cute, six foot and change, gorgeous dark skin and hair so soft Lucy wanted to sink her hands into it.

It didn't do to mix business and pleasure, though.

"Simon was telling me about your alleged serial killer."

"That theory's been kicking around for a while, but they never got anything to stick. There's not been anyone go missing for a bit either," Brett said.

"Maybe he died, if he existed," Lucy said, checking her makeup—it had to be good for the video, or that would be the first two hundred comments.

"Maybe we'll find his body and we can get a full news story out of it."

"Simon, dial back the weird. First sign of something like that and I'm gone, I ain't getting messed up in any bodies." Brett laughed.

"I'm just saying." Simon shrugged, back on his tablet within the instant.

"Seriously though, you think any of this is too much just let me know, I'm happy to stop when you are." Brett gave Lucy a sideways glance.

"It's fine. If it gets too bad, I'm running."

The warehouse was worse than Lucy had imagined: damp rippled up the walls in bubbles of peeling, corrugated paint, and the constant drip of water beat a staccato rhythm at the back of their skulls.

"Simon, this is disgusting." She grimaced at the white scuffs on her jeans. It was cold here, too; the chill crept off the walls in waves.

"I know, isn't it perfect? The damp will give a really eerie light and the sound levels should be brilliant, minus the echo."

"Says you," Brett grumbled, hefting his pack higher.

"How long are we going to be in here? I don't even have a phone signal. What if there's an emergency?" Lucy said, swaying her phone in different directions to see if she could at least catch some 4G.

"Just an hour. If there's a problem, someone can go get help," Simon said, waving away her concerns with one broad hand.

"I didn't see any danger pay in my contract," Brett said, camera now at the ready.

"Well Lucy's the one in the real danger. She's the frontwoman." Simon laughed and Lucy stuck her tongue out at him. "Anything for the story, right?"

Lucy ran a hand through her hair. It came away with flecks of damp plaster and she shuddered. "Let's just get on with it—where are we starting?"

"Upstairs, there's these great spooky rooms and the sounds are all distorted from the size. Perfect ghost hunting territory." Simon nodded to a set of broad concrete steps.

"Doesn't seem like a good spot to bury people," Lucy muttered under her breath, arching an eyebrow at Brett. He gave a shrug as she followed Simon, trying to avoid the worst of the slick green growth on the steps. "So gross."

He led them over a broad concrete platform, a third of the size of the cavernous center room, with the rusted teeth of railings jutting out of the far end. It curled around the space, giving access to three squat rooms along the far wall.

"You were up here on your own?" Brett asked, panning over the edge of the platform.

"Yeah, just for scouting about," Simon called back.

"Not safe, dude. What if there'd been a soft spot?"

"You would've gotten worried about me eventually." Simon dropped his bag in front of the closest doorway. It was pitch black inside; none of the murky natural light from downstairs pierced the shadows.

"That's a hard pass from me, Simon. You expect me to walk into that?" Lucy asked, staring between the darkened room and the man knelt before his bundle of tech.

"I'll be in there, too. I want to try and get some readings."

"Brett?" Lucy asked, looking to the light of the camera.

"I won't fit with the gear, not enough room."

"That's not what I meant, you git." She shook her head. "You're going in first."

"Of course. I want to get a reading with no interference." Simon ducked into the gloom.

"Boy's crazy," Brett said with a grin.

"True that," Lucy sighed, following. Her torch made a short beam into the dark, solidifying the shadow around Simon into something thicker.

"So Simon, you were telling me that there's rumors about a killer round here?" she prompted, glancing back at the camera. Brett's shape filled the doorway, blocking what little light filtered in.

"The theories never materialized into anything solid, but local legend says there's a psychopath that's been picking off travelers. He's meant to take them whenever suits him, no long-term pattern, but then if he's targeting traveling people, then it'd be difficult to pinpoint who exactly is his type. So many young people go missing, and you know how often the police like to say they're runaways. Dude would have the perfect cover."

"Like truck stop killers," Lucy said with a choked laugh. "So you're trying to see if you can get any EVP did you say?"

"Yeah, see if there's anything here that wants to speak to us and if so, what it wants to say."

"Like any murder victims that were buried here, or the spirit of the killer if he's passed on. We are of course assuming he's a he."

"Statistically speaking, probably a he—mass murderers are almost always male overachievers," Simon said. Lucy looked to camera, snorting a laugh when Brett shrugged again.

"Okay, do we need to be silent for this part or what happens? I've never done this before."

"It would be better, yeah," Simon said with a nod. "We're looking for anyone that wants to contact us, to tell us any message they have." His voice was loud in the cramped space.

Lucy put a hand to her mouth, trying not to hear anything other than the tapping of the water throughout the building. But something low and repetitive was hissing in the distance, a dull clacking that could have been a door or window swinging in the wind if there'd been a breath of air in the dull October evening.

"What's that?" Brett whispered.

Lucy jumped, and Simon shoot him a withering look.

"Seriously, you don't hear that noise?"

Lucy nodded.

"It's probably a train." Simon glanced at the concrete walls around them.

"That we can hear up here?" Brett asked, eyeballing Simon over the camera.

"Shut up, I might be able to get a reading," Simon looked to Lucy. "What do you think it is?"

"I don't know. It *is* kind of like a train, but I thought you said they'd given up with that here?" Lucy said.

"They gave up on the expansion, but the line's still active sometimes."

"Sometimes?"

"They're usually later at night, cargo hauls." Brett looked over his shoulder. The noise was louder now, rattling Lucy's teeth as it sounded all around them. A piercing shriek engulfed the building. Lucy's hands went up around her ears, against the echo bouncing back off the cement walls, and Brett pivoted out of the room. Simon looked to be laughing, squinting at the screen in front of him with no regard for the cacophony around them.

It died away, the repetitive clanking fading as suddenly as it had begun, and Brett's figure came to the door again. Lucy brought her hands down, ears still ringing, and glared at him.

"Where'd you go?" she asked, waggling her jaw to try and shift the noise in her head.

"Had to duck out. The echo in here was throwing the levels way off. That footage is gonna be useless sound-wise," he huffed. "Why the hell would a train be sounding a whistle now?"

"Maybe something on the line?" Simon asked, hands flopping down to his sides. "We should go to another room, maybe the over the far side of the gap."

"Will that strip take three people's weight?" Brett leaned out of the room to glance over the open space. The remains of railings stood at the far end, dirty brown with the rust that had eaten everything else.

"It took me just fine," Simon said with a shrug.

"Are we not checking the recording?" Lucy asked. "We should get our reactions on camera for that, too."

"The stuff on here's going to be total rubbish." Brett screwed his face up. "I could check it with my headphones in while you to listen to what's on that thing? That way we can skip to the usable bits and save me from editing a bunch of useless shit."

"Sounds good. Lucy, get your phone out. You can record it while I play it back." Simon waved her over. She moved toward him, turning on her LED case so she could get the best light for their close ups.

"Do you think you got anything over that train?" she asked as she tapped to the recording options.

"I don't know. The reverb was pretty intense. May as well check though. So this is us listening to the recording we just made to see if we have anyone in this room." He clicked play, holding it close to keep them both in the shot.

Then the noise started again, slow at first and scratchy as a briar. It started to grow layers, tripping over itself with the echo and beginning to sound like voices, words slapping together like waves.

"Do you hear something in that?" Lucy asked, leaning in closer.

Simon shook his head. "I thought I was getting snatches of voices, but nothing really discernible."

"It sounds like words over and over." Vexed at the jumble, Lucy turned her head so she could focus on the sound. The scream came through suddenly, so sharp that she jumped and dropped her phone. "Fucking hell!"

"Sorry, I wasn't thinking about that." Simon stepped back as she picked it up and checked the screen. "Is it okay?"

"Yeah, no cracks. This case is great for that," she said with a laugh, trying to calm herself down. Her heart was in her throat, and her face burned from the sudden rush of fear.

"You should keep that bit. People will love hearing you freak out." Simon laughed, rolling his eyes at her glare. "Let's see what Brett's got." He moved past her and out the door, leaving her in the darkness. It pressed up against her for a beat and she bolted, shaking her head at her own silliness. No one liked being in spooky old rooms alone; she was just letting it get to her.

"What's the verdict?" she called out. The two men stood beside each other, heads bowed together.

"I swear I can hear voices in this shit." Brett looked up, eyes wider than made her comfortable. "That whistle? Sounds a lot like a scream. I'm sure there's something talking. I don't like this."

"Come on, man, we've seen weirder than this. It's just distortion." Simon rolled his neck and glanced back along the platform. "Quit being a pussy. Let's get footage of the other rooms. I want us to go to that bottom one; it's going to have the best view over the two floors."

"He's right," Lucy said, holding her phone up again. "You can get a great shot of the creepy staircase and the old machinery down there. It'll look like some videogame stills."

"Yeah, that'll be awesome! They can play it on the news while they're reporting us missing." Brett said with a sigh.

"Come on, you'll love the visuals—if you're really scared once you've got the footage, then we can get some more mood shots and go downstairs," Simon said, leaning against the slick wall.

"It'll look so good," Lucy wheedled, holding her phone up to capture the frown on Brett's face.

"Fucking fine, but we're going as soon as we've got that."

They walked along the thinner strip of the floor, towards the long rectangle of the furthest room.

"Were you not worried about falling off this bit?" Lucy peered at the rusted railings.

"Not really. I wasn't shoving myself off the edge of it." Simon shrugged. "Anyway, what I found in here was way too interesting."

"What do you mean?" Lucy asked. He was a few steps ahead of her, eyes on the dark doorway.

"You'll see," he said over his shoulder. "Hey Brett, speed it up."

"I'm getting your damn creep shots, dude," Brett called back.

"I want this room on camera. It's going to be the star of the show," Simon said, pausing for Brett to catch up with them.

"What are you talking about?" Lucy looked at him sharply.

"Trust me, it's going to be awesome." Simon winked, stepping forward once Brett was with them.

"You okay, Lucy?" Brett asked in a low murmur, glancing up from the camera to check in with her.

"This is pretty ropey." She kicked a stone off the edge.

"We'll be done soon. It's not gonna be more than twenty minutes." Brett gave her a smile that didn't match his eyes.

"It might be fine. Let's see what's got him so excited." Lucy dragged her own smile up to match.

They reached Simon, who stood with his hands on either side of the doorway. He leaned in ever so slightly, with a rough shaking to his chest that set Lucy's teeth on edge.

"Hey man, you okay?" Brett asked.

Simon looked back over his shoulder with a wicked grin. "I'm good."

"I don't like this," Brett said. "I was listening to the audio again. I swear I can hear something being said."

"You're just letting yourself get spooked, it's no big deal." Simon pulled himself up and turning to face them. "Lucy, come look at this with me."

"What's in there?"

"It'll blow your mind, I promise." He held his hand out to her, pouting.

She glanced at Brett, then took Simon's hand and moved toward the dark door.

"Trust me?" Simon asked.

"What sort of question is that?" She snorted a laugh. "Of course. I wouldn't go scrambling through creepy buildings if I didn't."

"Good." He gave her hand a squeeze.

Then he yanked her forward, shoving her into the room with a vicious flick of his arm. She barreled into something huge in the darkness and cool to the touch. It bounced back into her, touches skirting her flank, then falling back. She shrieked, the sound choking off as the stench of stale sweat hit her. She stumbled back into a wall, flicking her light on to see what was in there with her.

The beam landed on a body hanging from the ceiling by a hook through the shoulder, swinging from her collision with it. Flicking the light up she started to scream again. The sound forced its way out of her throat like a wild thing—the face was Simon, slack jawed and glass eyed.

"What the fuck?" she screamed, skittered along the wall, seeking a corner to press herself into, the wetness a cold strength at her back. Something glowed in the back, a single point of light blinking in and out as the body swung to a stop.

"What did you do?" she heard Brett shout. Something hit the other side of the wall. The impact shook the room as an ugly laugh echoed around her.

"It's just a prank. That footage is going to be worth thousands of views," Simon said, a cruel edge to his voice that Lucy felt right down her spine.

"Cut that shit out, this isn't you!" Brett yelled. Lucy heard him punch the wall.

"Look, I'll show it to you. Just go in," Simon said. Lucy would have punched him if she could extricate herself from the corner in which her body stubbornly stayed wedged.

"You okay, baby girl?" Brett called.

She squeaked, hating herself for it, then shook herself and looked away from the body. "I'm in the corner. This is really fucked up." She forced herself to peel off the wall. "Where the hell did you find this stuff, Simon?"

"Isn't it great?" Simon's head popped into view, grinning like a feral thing.

"It's a shitty thing to do to a co-host, but it is impressive," she said, glaring at him. "You set this all up yourself?"

"I think Brett's far too sweet on you to help out with something like this, hmm?" Simon moved toward the body, flicking his own light to illuminate his face from underneath. "Great likeness, don't you think?" He pouted for a moment before letting his head loll to the side, sticking his tongue out to match the ghoulish hanging body.

"It's fucking horrific." She turned her head away.

"Don't sulk because I got one over on you." Simon huffed.

She rolled her eyes, turning to look for Brett. He stood at the side of the doorway, frowning as he checked something over "Did you not even get footage of that?"

"Oh, I saw all of it," Simon promised as she went to tug Brett's arm. He flinched away.

"You okay?" she asked as he took his headphones off.

"This is some shit. It's not right. I'm not staying for this." Brett shook his head. "That recording sounds like chanting or something."

"It's just a prank," Simon called, voice distorted by the room's echo.

"He has a camera or something back there. I saw the light of it when I was freaking out." Lucy leaned away so Brett could see inside. "It's pretty realistic."

"I don't care. If it's a prank then it's a shitty thing to do to your team, and I'm bouncing the fuck out. You coming?"

"I don't think we should. The reveal's such an important part of the video. Plus, you should see how realistic the body in there is. I was having a full on freak over it." Lucy glanced back to the room. Simon's light had gone off but she could still see the red dot in there, blinking now and then.

"Fuck that—you want the footage, you record it. This isn't safe and he isn't acting normal." Brett handed her the camera. "You can come find me later. I'll be in the car."

"Don't sulk." Simon's voice echoed, with a scratchy tone to it now. "Just because I got here first."

"You deal with him." Brett walked off as Lucy rolled her eyes.

"Right, Simon, thanks to whatever's got into you, Brett's now in a sulk and we're down a crewman. I now have the camera, and you'd better start explaining what you just did." She walked back into the room. The camera's light was a pinprick, barely piercing the dark.

"Come in deeper, and I'll show you," Simon said with a bubbling giggle.

"Can you flick your torch on or something? I can't see shit." She huffed a breath as she tried to juggle the camera, her phone, and the flashlight. "I'm going to switch to the infrared. That'll look cool." She fiddled with the settings, breathing out curses as she flicked between the filters. Finally, she landed on the dull green glow.

"You done?" Simon's voice bounced around the room.

"I think so." She brought the lens up. The room was suddenly flooded with detail, the light from outside creeping in as fingers of lime across the mossy backdrop. She panned over the room until she saw the swinging body in the middle and Simon's dark shape beside it. "Something's wrong with the levels."

"Why do you say that?"

"Well, I can see the light from outside showing up, but you're showing up cold, no heat coming off you." She chewed her lip as she fiddled with the settings.

"Put your hand in front of it, see if that helps." Simon leaned around the body to stare at her.

"I mean, I suppose that might make it refocus." She gripped her flashlight between her thighs and waggled one hand in front of the camera. It trailed a neon line over the screen, skin blazing white.

"Any luck?" Simon asked, still moving about behind the body.

"It worked on my hand, so it should be okay." She grabbed the flashlight again and looked back at him. "Stand next to it like you did before. It'll look great."

Simon did as instructed, moving beside the doppelganger and leaning his head to the side again. Lucy laughed, shaking her head as she pulled the camera up and began to speak.

"Simon here is about to explain how he managed this horrifying prank, which, as you've probably seen in this episode, took me totally by surprise and spooked Brett so badly that he left. So, aside from being a total dick move, tell me what inspired you to do this?"

"Well, Lucy, I thought to myself, 'what would be the best lure to get some gullible idiots to a dangerous and obviously hostile environment?' Everyone likes a puzzle to solve, and what better than a murder mystery? Nothing like a bit of death to get the blood pumping." He looped an arm around the body.

"All right, don't be such an ass about it." She shook her head, tucked her phone away and tried to finish getting herself camera-ready. "So you set this up and decided you'd lure us here? Well done, it worked. How did you shift such a heavy prop, and what camera have you got back there?"

"The body was easy; once you whisper enough to some people, they just want to jump into the dark," Simon said, his voice reverberating off the walls.

"What's going on with the sound? It's not another train, is it?" Lucy asked, looking up from her finishing touches.

"Doubt it. Barely any trains go past here now." Simon laughed, leaning forward and almost hanging off the body. She started to roll her eyes then stopped, gaze catching the camera.

"Simon?" she asked, looking up at him.

"Yes, Lucy?" he asked back, batting his lashes at her.

"Why don't you show up on the infrared?"

"Neat trick, huh?" he said, and she saw the mouth on the body was moving too, the lips forming soundless words in tandem with the Simon in front of her.

"How are you doing that?" she choked out, hands shaking as she moved the camera aside.

"It started off just like I said. How do you lure idiots into a trap? You use good bait. People just love to think they're smarter than everyone else, it's not hard to see the weaknesses. An inferiority complex about being second on his precious show and a thirst to prove himself? Too easy."

"What do you mean?" Lucy asked, stepping back as Simon stalked forward.

"It's the same old trick. All I had to do was get him on the hook, and there was a free body to knock around in. People are nothing like as cautious as they used to be, you know. Sure, some of them used to break in for a place to sleep and they were easy pickings, but having a fresh, young man? It's delicious." He was still coming at her, his steps shadowing her own retreat onto the platform.

"Simon, you're scaring me." She dropped the camera with a jolt as she felt the railings brush up against her back.

"Good—it should. Though there's no point in calling me Simon, he's not here," he said, standing tall in front of her. "It's so tricky to get a good body here, the waifs and strays rot down so quickly."

"If something happened, if you're afraid, you can tell me, Simon." She tried to glance around him to see if the camera in the room was still running.

"Told you, he's not here anymore. You're a smart girl, Lucy, surely you can put this together? Look in the room, what do you see?" He curled away from the doorway so she could see into the room again. A dull glow was coming from in there now, the whole room dusted with a blue gleam that flickered and waved like flames.

"Fire?" she whispered, voice small in her throat.

"And?" he asked, exaggerated and long.

"The body's not there anymore." The blue glow grew stronger.

"Well done! And what could make a body vanish?"

"I don't know! If this is some extension of the prank, it's a fucking joke!" She shoved her hands in his chest and walked off from him, towards the other side of the platform.

"Not so fast," he called, somehow both in front of her and coming from the larger side of the platform.

"What the fuck?" she whined, backing into the wall as both Simons walk towards her, the one from behind laughing that high-pitched giggle that set her teeth on edge.

"Think, Lucy," the new one said, grinning wide.

"You have a twin? If so, at least you're matching dicks," she said, inching towards the platform.

"No, but a good guess," said the giggling one, coming to a stop a pace or so away from her. The other Simon walked towards him, spiking a brow up as he passed Lucy only to spin round, falling into his double the way he would sit on a couch. With a blink of the blue light they merged together, a faint sizzling sound rasping up from below them. "Possession's such an easy trick when you get them scared enough. They panic, and they beg, and then when you're in control they scream and cry and yell at the others to run."

"The whistle?" she asked, stepping off the wall and walking backwards, into the space of the upper story. She could make it to the stairs if she got closer, could get out of arms reach of whatever this was.

"The scream was a bit dramatic, but he's such a feisty one. The old regulars, they're the 'train'—get out, get out, over and over they say it, and it means nothing!" He cackled, suddenly shooting forward so that he was in front of her and grabbing her shoulders. "It's so boring to have them screaming at you all the time, but when I have something fresh and new like you, Lucy, how could I be mad at them?"

She shrieked, jolting a knee up into his crotch and ripping herself away. She ran, tripping over her feet then righting herself as she stumbled along the grimy concrete. She was near the first room now, if she could make it past there and onto the expanse of the platform, she could reach the stairs. His breath was in her ear behind her before a ripple of laughter loomed from in front, forcing her to come up short. He barreled into her, crashing them both into the wall. Her head rang with the impact, vision skewing to the side. She scrabbled to right herself.

He gripped her, dragging her up the wall and pinning her shoulders with his hands, silhouetted in the void of the doorway. Blood ran down her cheek, a gash on her head pulsing with pain that ran in tandem with her adrenaline.

"Leaving so soon?" he asked, that vicious smile back on his face. The blue light in the other room was stronger now, licking out of the door and over the platform.

"What are you?" she asked. The words sounded far off against the clattering inside her skull.

"The old folks used to call me a demon, though I've been playing this game so long I can't remember if that's what I started out as." He licked a stripe along her cheek. "You taste scared, but not enough. Not enough to beg. What else do I have to do to spook you?"

"Try this, chuckle-fuck," came a voice from within the room, before a solid crack, like a branch snapping, echoed around them. Simon let go of her as he crumpled to the ground. Lucy started to slump before an arm snagged her, pulling her towards a solid figure. Brett.

"I thought you were in the car?" she slurred, blinking away the blood in her eye.

"Honestly, I was just hiding in here to give Simon a fright when you guys were done, pay back for that asshole prank," Brett said, wincing at the sight of her. "Let's get the fuck out of here."

"Shouldn't we do something about him?" Lucy's head lolled to indicate Simon.

"Girl, that's how you get killed. We get out of here, then we make a plan." Brett said rolled his eyes as he scooped a hand round her waist. "Come on."

"What about the camera?" she asked, limping along with him as they made for the exit.

"We'll come back for it."

"Really?"

"Hell no, we're writing it off and never coming back!"

"He'll come after us, I think," she said, leaning on the rail as they raced down the slick stairs.

"Let him. By that time, we'll have reported this shit to a priest and be the hell out of town." Brett helped her hop the last few steps and together, they ran for the car. They heard the shriek of Simon's laugh behind them as they fled the building, and as Brett bundled her into the car, Lucy saw the blue flames take hold. They arced up like a bird, racing along the roof and flooding the night in azure.

"Is that real?" she asked, turning to watch it as they drove off.

"Don't know, darlin, and don't plan to find out. You need to go to hospital for that head wound and then we need to get gone for a while, all right?"

"All right," she agreed, slumping back into her seat and putting a hand to her wound. A headache was blossoming now, the beat of her pulse echoing the train she swore was coming in the night, and she giggled to herself at the idea of it.

THE MÓRRIGÁN

GRANT HINTON

"You're too close," Mary warned as the dirt under my hand started to slip.

"Just a little further," I begged lightly, stretching my hand further into the hole. Mary pulled at the bottom of my shirt.

"Be careful, Sam. You might fall."

A hint of a smile crossed my lips. "Why? You scared?"

Just as the words left my lips the ground beneath me moved, and I tumbled over the edge onto the wooden coffin with a hollow thud.

"Now you've done it, stupid." Mary's half-smile played on her lips as she tucked a strand of auburn hair behind one ear. But—even though she was at that moment breathtakingly beautiful—the hollow thud of the coffin held my attention. I didn't know what sound a coffin should make, but that empty noise wasn't it.

"Why this one anyway? It's like, ancient." I squinted up at Mary in the twilight, her slender frame outlined by a backdrop of stars through the trees of the cemetery.

She chewed her lip and looked away when she turned back her eyes burnt with something I couldn't detect. "It's this one, trust me," she said.

I could taste the nervous tension between us; it came perilously close to fear. It crept up my neck and gripped my throat as I sat up and moved the dirt off a brass label on the coffin lid.

"What's a Mórrígan?

"Don't worry about that, just open the lid." The tension in her voice lay thick in the night air. Thankfully no one was around to catch us, as I'm sure grave digging wouldn't be looked upon too fondly in this neck of woods.

I shifted my position, gripped the side of the coffin lid and pulled. I was expecting some resistance, but when it opened as easily as a regular door, I fell against the dirt wall. Mary scrambled over the edge just as I righted myself. A glow diffused over her face, lighting it from below.

"Wow, the Mórrígan sure is bright." My chuckle died in my throat as Mary disappeared into the coffin.

"Mórrígan isn't a what," she called, "it's a who." I glanced inside the lid to see Mary descending metals steps to an illuminated dirt tunnel. "Are you coming or just gonna stand up there catching flies?"

The hollow earth was cold, far colder than I would have thought. Tree roots broke the side of the walls and poked through like skeletal fingers feeding off our fear. Something wasn't right. I knew that the moment I opened the coffin. I didn't realize it fully until my foot touched the tunnel floor, but I knew it now watching the slight rise of Mary's shoulders as we rounded a corner.

"What is it?" I hissed.

"Shhh." She motioned me to look and turned sideways.

The tunnel opened up into a stone crypt. Moss and lichen clung to the walls between the stones, and in the center of the tomb stood a mound of rocks and boulders. The thick sides piled up and levelled out to an opening; whatever had been in there before wasn't any more.

"W-what…" I began.

"Shh!" Mary pointed to a part of the wall that bunched out. I didn't see what she meant, and waved my hands to signal, *huh*?

Then it moved.

It wasn't a quick movement, but a slow, debilitating, earth-moving change. My hackles rose as the grating of stone on stone assaulted my ears. Mary stepped fully into the crypt, and the movement of the wall quickened.

The mound turned, shifted, and metamorphosed. Three figures now stood where the mound had been, all women. The first of the ladies was breathtakingly beautiful, with strawberry blond hair that flew back in luscious waves, as though caught in a ghostly breeze. A shimmering white cloth draped over her ample frame. As my gaze slid to her legs, I noticed that one was conjoined with the other ladies at the shin.

My eyes shifted and went up another leg, wrinkled with time. Blemishes puckered the skin below the knee. My gaze traversed the moth-ridden cloth and continued up over breasts that sagged like deflated balloons, up a flabby throat to an equally saggy face. Eyes with a depth I couldn't fathom look upon us, like time itself poured from them—or more precisely, was sucked into them.

A cracking noise made me turn to the third woman. She was more skeleton than person. Stooped and crooked, her skin clung to bones in clumps of dried, sinewy muscle, and parts of her grey skull showed through jagged holes in her face. The line of partial teeth chattered as she looked at me with sightless eyes clouded by greens and blues.

As I followed the ragged cloth down her skeletal frame, her right leg ended, joined with the middle crone in a burst of gangrenous skin: the three Mórrígans interlocked in an eternal four-legged race.

Mary moved once again and bowed before the crones three.

"Badb, Macha, Nemain, you know why I've come."

"One," spoke the first.

"For," continued the second.

"One," finished the last.

Even though the voices were the same, each aged like their host until the third's scratchy whisper, which I felt more felt than heard. Mary glanced at me in the doorway, bit her lip again, then nodded.

"So be it," she said.

"Speak."

"Thy."

"Name."

"Matthew Hendershot," Mary said, then bowed.

My voice caught in my throat. Mary's dad had died two years ago. I knew she missed him terribly, and his battle with cancer had been a hard pill to swallow, but I thought Mary had come to terms with it.

"One."

"For."

"One."

Suddenly the walls shook. Flakes of dirt crumbled from the walls. Mary fell flat on the floor. I dropped to my knees. Something was happening. Not only in the room, but in me. I felt weak, weaker than I had ever felt, and thirsty. Like no amount of water would ever quell my thirst. Pain coursed up my spine as it cracked and twisted, forcing my body to stoop. I watched as my hands withered. Blemishes like the crone's popped into existence on the backs and wrinkles sagged the skin between my knuckles. The crones were draining my life.

The first crone sucked at the air, and my genitals blazed with fire as my fertility was drawn from my body in violet rays. *One.*

The second crone eagerly lapped at the air through cracked-yellow teeth. My mind and memories poured from my head to mingle and twist with the violet mist coursing toward her cracked lips. *For.*

The third—although she had no lips upon her face—gulped at the yellow vapor that streamed from my mouth and deteriorated my body. *One.*

Through milky eyes, I saw a man's outline on the dirt wall, faint like a pencil drawing. Then thicker, more pronounced. Until the lines bulged, and a person in a black suit and greying hair stepped through. Mary rose from the floor as the crones twisted back and became part of the tomb once again.

She sprang up as the man looked at his hands, then touched his face. Mary flew at his chest and hugged him tightly. Matthew Hendershot looked at his daughter in shock, then hugged her back.

"Mary? What am I doing here? Why aren't we in Saint Phillips?"

"It's okay, Dad. You're back now." Tears dripped down her cheeks and splashed on the dusty floor. She took his arm and turned to leave, then spotted me.

The heaviness hung between us. I didn't need to see Mary's reaction to know that I had changed. I felt it in my bones. One for one, a tribute to each for the life of another. My memories, my fertility, my life.

"Oh, Sam, I'm sorry. I had to." She steered her father around me. I reached out and grabbed her arm. Forced her to look into my cataractous eyes.

"She's taken more than…" My breath caught, and Mary took the advantage to peel my gnarly fingers from her wrist.

"One part for each crone, Sam. That was the price." She smiled at me with a pitying look and left me in the crypt.

I lay there for some time, fading as my life slowly drained, listening to the earth shift, and talk, not knowing if I could move. My old legs, more bone than skin. Could they bear my weight? I shifted around, back to the pile of rocks, to the crones at the far wall. Maybe a deal could be brokered. I forced the words passed my parched throat.

"Mórrígan?"

The shift of the wall answered my call, and soon the crones three looked upon me with their eternal gaze.

"You."

"Have."

"Nothing."

"No, but I can give more."

I dragged myself forward. Determined for them to see that I wanted to live. Revenge proved a powerful motive.

"Speak."

"Thy."

"Plea."

I made it to the mound, and pulled myself up over, scraping my skin, drawing blood that smeared the ancient stones.

"Give me back my strength, and I will bring one person for each of you."

I didn't hear them as I fell forwards into the deep hole of the mound. A grave, their grave. I don't know how long my dreams were plagued with their memories, but when I came to, I moved more freely. The blemishes and puckered skin had faded somewhat from my hands and face, and my strength had returned.

I climbed from the hole, one purpose burning in my mind as I bowed before the crones three. Then turned and walked back to the grave and the outside world.

Mary was my first; I dragged her back screaming. She didn't know who I was, not with my deteriorated skin. But she did recognize the old guy pulling her by the hair when we reached the gravesite. She begged all the way to the Mórrígan, and I enjoyed watching her beg for another deal.

"One," spoke the first.

"For," continued the second.

"One," finished the last.

"What… I don't understand?" Mary's scared face looked around at me, and I smiled wide. I knew.

"One deal for one person, Mary. That means you've had your one and only deal."

The Mórrígan sucked at the air with lips, teeth, and bone, and soon Mary was no more. With my youth back I went for Matthew. Again, an easy choice; he had had his time. It was remarkably simple to get him to the grave as well.

"Mr. Hendershot, it's Mary! She's fallen into a hole at the cemetery!"

He even drove us there in his old family car. The crones exchanged my memories for his body, and I felt whole again. I covered the grave after I climbed out of the coffin, and carved the unmarked tombstone with a small x. Just one thing remains for me to collect. My fertility. But I'm young. Why would I waste that on a frivolous victim?

I think I'll keep that one, for now.

DREAMCATCHER TUNNEL

R. C. BOWMAN

This is a long, ugly story, and I guess it starts with Mercy Rowland.

Mercy was a drug-addicted vagrant with no past worth remembering and no future to speak of. I'd go so far as to say that Mercy was the kind of person who never had a future in the first place.

Everyone in town hated her. It was horrible, but that's often the way of quaint little towns. In our cultural imagination, small towns are all like Mayberry or Willoughby. But our cultural imagination is wrong. Most of the time, small towns are rotten microcosms of social cruelty, miniature universes where one wrong step can kill you.

Mercy had made many wrong steps, and had had several more made for her. One of the wrongest was her appearance. Mercy had the kind of withered face that might've been thirty or eighty. Long ago, an old boyfriend beat her up badly, breaking her nose and cheeks in the process. Doctors hadn't bothered to set the bones correctly, so her face healed in strange, unsettling ways that made her look like she'd just started to melt. Her few remaining teeth were broken and yellow. She had small, cataract-clouded eyes and stubbly gray hair that grew in patches.

Mercy always slept in the local park. My dad, who was the caretaker at the time, didn't really have the heart to chase her off. He tried anyway because he had to: Mercy was an active drug user, after all, and occasionally left her used needles around the trees.

I knew all this because I spent all my free time at that park. It was a beautiful place: all old-growth trees and grassy hillocks, dotted with memorials and elaborate war monuments. Through it all the river wound, rushing in the cold months and babbling agreeable through spring and summer.

I loved it. I was a painfully shy child, but living beside the park gave me an advantage. I knew all the secrets that children covet, you see; I knew where the squirrels lived, which of the feral cats liked to be pet, where to find the wild strawberries.

Best of all, I knew how to sneak into the sunflower fields.

Now, there used to be this old man in town. I don't know his real name, but everyone called him Boba. Boba lived on five acres along the northeastern border of the park. Every year, year in and year out, he seeded those five acres with sunflowers.

They were magnificent: over six feet tall, with enormous blossoms bigger than my father's head. They were as good as a forest, especially to little kids. I wasn't supposed to trespass and for the longest time I resisted the temptation… until I found a secret entrance.

On the border of the park, right next to Boba's property line, was a playground. In the northernmost corner of the playground was a low warren of painted concrete tunnels. The tunnel exit overshot the boundary of the park by several feet, and thus emptied straight into old man Boba's sunflowers.

It was the perfect way to smuggle myself in. Everyone in town avoided these tunnels like the plague. This was partly due to the fact that they were incredibly ugly. Ancient and covered with graffiti, they predated the playground itself by at least fifteen years, and they looked it: they were cracked, chipped, and tucked away at the edge of the playground, perpetually cast in the sunflowers' strange, quivering shadows.

But this mass avoidance was triggered by local legends, too. Boy, did we have some stories. According to one, a child killer used to wait within those tunnels for an unsuspecting child to pass, timing his strikes with a predator's precision. He'd been a fussy little man with a lipless mouth and small round eyes the color of riverweeds.

This man pulled children in the tunnels, assaulted them, and dragged them back to his cottage on the river's edge, where he cut them open, pulled their guts out, stuffed them with sawdust, and dunked them in lacquer to preserve the skin. Then he'd paint and dress them until they looked like giant porcelain dolls. He stored all the bodies in his attic, which was how he'd finally got caught. Because of this, we called him the Doll Man.

Doll Man was my favorite story, but there were others. Another legend claimed that the tunnels had been built atop a mass grave of Chinese railroad workers. Another claimed the site had once been occupied by a witch who ate pregnant women. Yet another claimed that if you slept in the tunnel on exactly the right night, all your dreams would come true.

It was enough to scare any normal, self-respecting child. Unfortunately, I was neither normal nor self-respecting. My bad influence eventually leached into the other children. Before I knew it, we were all crawling through the tunnels on a daily basis to enter Boba's sunflowers.

Of course, we had to be very careful. For one thing, Boba didn't like trespassers and we had no idea what he might do if he caught us. For another, vagrants and addicts frequently took cover in the fields. Nothing ruined our sunflower treks like stumbling across a drooling junkie nodding off in a puddle of their own piss.

When it came to that sort of thing, Mercy Rowland was far and away the worst offender.

We saw her in the sunflowers nearly every day. She looked worse and worse every time: patchy hair, flaking bald spots, cloudy eyes, sunken mouth, weathered skin riddled with sores, and of course her crooked, broken face. She looked like a witch, or perhaps a goblin: small and mean and barely human. She was the kind of person everyone wants to forget.

As we explored the flowers one chilly spring morning, we found Mercy propped up against a tangle of stalks. She looked... wrong. Wrong enough that I told the younger kids to cover their eyes.

I approached carefully. My heart thudded, heavy and sick like a war drum. Mercy's fingers twisted at terrible angles. Her mouth dribbling blood. Her head lolled against her shoulder, and she was so horrifically thin, like a scarecrow missing half its stuffing.

For several awful seconds, I thought she was dead. What would I do? I couldn't leave her like this. But then I'd have to admit I trespassed in the flowers. Worse, I'd have to admit that I'd talked all my friends into trespassing, too.

Then Mercy's dull eyes rolled and met mine. "Be careful, honey," she croaked. "This is what happens when you pick a mean john."

I was so frightened, and she looked so dead, that I burst into tears. Mercy watched me for a moment, frowning as though deeply confused.

And then she laughed.

She laughed and laughed. Her ruined mouth stretched across her face, a gaping, hypnotic hole. Revulsion filled me. She was so ugly. So ruined. And she was laughing at me. This homeless, jobless, useless, worthless bitch, laughing at me.

I'd had enough. "What are you laughing about, you idiot?"

She kept laughing. The eyes of my friends bored into my head like cold drills. I couldn't stand it. I drew myself up and shrieked, "Why are you laughing? You're stupid! You're useless! You need to stop doing drugs and you need to get a job!"

Mercy giggled savagely. "All kinds of things I need and don't get. If you aren't lucky, you might be just the same."

I stared at her, struggling to process an utterly alien sense of mounting horror. Mercy stared back, smiling in the dappled sunlight of a beautiful morning. But she was the antithesis of beautiful: ravaged skin, broken face, with the withered agelessness of a human ruin. And in that instant, I had my first grownup thought, felt my first adult fear:

Was she right?

Was it possible that I—I, with my wonderful dad and nice teachers and pretty house in the mountains—could turn into an ugly, forgotten vagrant like Mercy?

A single tear spilled from Mercy's clouded, watery eye even as her smile widened. "I have wishes, you know. Wishes and dreams, just like all you kids. Know what I wish for?"

I shook my head.

Her terrible smile crumpled into a quivering moue. "I wish for pretty blue eyes and nice white teeth and long hair the color of old man Boba's sunflowers, and nice expensive makeup to put on my face. That way, spoiled little shits like you won't look at me no more. Now run back to your daddy. He don't bother me, so why do you?"

Disgust and hate welled up and erupted. Before I could even think, I picked up a rock and threw it at her. It hit her cheek with a meaty little thwap. Mercy flinched, then smiled again. "When your nice little life falls apart, come find me here," she said. "I'll be waiting for you."

Then she staggered to her feet and sloped away. The sunflower stalks rattled behind her.

A sense of humiliation quickly subsumed my disgust. What had I done? I couldn't even breathe for shame. The thought of turning around and facing my friends seemed impossible.

Then—

"What a crazy creep she is." The speaker was a girl named Marilou. She was a year older than me, but so tiny that she looked much younger.

"Yeah." This was Grant. He was the new kid in school, and desperate to fit in. "Nasty old bitch."

"Grant!" Marilou gasped, even as the younger kids tittered.

"Come on, let's get out of here." This was Angela. I didn't know much about her, except that she had an older brother named Wallace who was both crazy and a genius. I'd never met Wallace, but *boy* had I heard of him. "People like her are all over the place today."

They weren't fazed, I realized. They didn't care that I'd hurt Mercy. It was nothing to them. *She* was nothing to them. Like I said... small towns.

Small, cruel, shitty little towns.

Obviously we were done for the day; after that confrontation with Mercy, the idea of wandering through the sunflowers had soured. So I led everybody back. I herded them through the tunnel one by one, timing them—one every three minutes. That way we wouldn't draw attention from others in the park.

Once the last kid left the tunnels, I looked around. Green stalks in every direction; enormous blossoms staring down at me like judgmental eyes. I shuddered and looked down.

And I saw something that hadn't been there before.

Freshly etched into the top of the tunnel was a huge, intricate carving of a dreamcatcher. Scratched beneath were the words:

dreamcatcher's tunnel

It stood out among years and layers of graffiti like the moon against the night sky. There was no missing it. So how had I missed it before?

I touched it and immediately yelped: an electric *zing* tore through my fingertip and bored into the bone. I wrenched away with such force that I nearly fell. I stared at it for the longest time, equal parts frightened and fascinated. It was beautiful, probably the most beautiful thing anyone had ever etched into the tunnels. But what the hell? How had it shocked me?

After that, I didn't have the guts to crawl back through the tunnels. Instead, I sat down and gazed up at the sunflowers. Their scent enveloped me, dry and bitterly green and strangely warm. Sunflowers always seem warm, even on cold days.

I really did love those flowers.

The next day, my dad dropped me at the playground before shuffling off to his tiny little office across the park. I wandered around for a little while, drinking in the crisp, bright coolness of the morning.

After half an hour—plenty of time for my father to immerse himself in his caretaking duties—I ambled over to the playground. It was empty. Too early in the day for anybody else to be there. I was glad; the solitude would be a relief.

I glanced around surreptitiously. Nothing, no one. Silence except for the wind rustling the sunflowers. I hurried toward the tunnel and crouched down, preparing to crawl through.

And I froze.

There was a face in there, peering out of the tunnel's dark opening. A weathered face with deep lines and bright, terrified eyes. "Sorry," it whispered.

No, not *it*, I realized: *She.*

I watched, stunned, as a withered lady in filthy clothes crawled out. A tangled mat of yellow hair swung around her face, which was coated in makeup so thick it reminded me of a ventriloquist dummy.

"Sorry," she repeated. "I sleep in there on cold nights." A small, trembling smile broke over her face. "You going to tell your dad on me?"

"No," I croaked. Who was this lady? How did she know my dad?

Her face broke into a smile. She had beautiful teeth: even and blazing white, the self-satisfied possum grin of a movie star. "Thanks. You like my teeth?"

"Yeah," I said.

She tapped them with her dirty fingertips, then ran her saliva-damp fingers through her hair. "You like my hair?"

"It's very pretty."

"Isn't it?" The lady patted the tunnel rim. Her smile widened. Her teeth glistened brightly. "I got it all in here. This place really does make your dreams come true."

I stared at her for what felt a long time. There was something familiar about her, something I couldn't quite place. I don't know how to describe it; it was as if something had swapped out the features of a person I knew, leaving the face behind.

Her smile widened briefly—snowy square teeth arranged neatly along a discolored gumline. My stomach churned unpleasantly. Then the lady snaked out, dragging a black trash bag behind her.

I couldn't look away. I'd seen homeless folks before. I'd seen a bunch of them. But something about this withered, lost lady with eyes like stars and hair like sunflowers disturbed me profoundly.

"Sweetheart," she said. "Don't be embarrassed. People have done a lot worse to me than throw rocks."

It was like I'd been hit over the head with a rocking chair.

Mercy.

This scary, starry-eyed lady with insane yellow hair and a celebrity's smile was Mercy Rowland.

I could see it now: the broken planes of her cheeks, now disguised by a pretty smile, prettier eyes, and thick makeup. The pointed chin, the thin eyebrows, the curiously skinny neck. It was Mercy.

But how?

Yesterday she'd been broken, beaten, nearly bald and toothless, with eyes full of cataracts. But now... *now*—

Mercy patted the tunnel affectionately. Her hair cascaded over her shoulders, a thick sheet the precise hue of Boba's sunflowers. "This place is good for dreams."

Then she giggled, swung the bag over her shoulder, and slithered back into the tunnel.

I watched her go, paralyzed. Everything in me seemed to hurt. Seemed to zing, like electricity was coursing through me. I thought of the dreamcatcher etching, bright and detailed and beautiful.

My paralysis broke. I broke into a run, stopping only when I reached the other end of the playground. I looked back. Across the expanse of sand and swings and metal slides, I saw the sunflowers through Boba's wire fence. They nodded serenely. Petals rippled gently in the breeze.

Then I saw her standing among them: blue-eyed with that inhuman, blossom-yellow hair, peering at me through the sunflowers with a wide grin.

I ran again. This time I didn't stop until I reached my dad's office all the way on the other end of the park.

I stayed out of the sunflower field after that. I still loved them—their dry dustiness, the bitter green, the almost alien beauty of them—but I couldn't bring myself to venture within. I couldn't risk seeing Mercy. And I couldn't risk seeing that dreamcatcher etching, either.

Spring slowly gave way to summer. Before I knew it, it was vacation. Half the kids in town spent all their time at that park. And of course, they all wanted me to take them into the sunflowers.

They were disappointed—and often quite cruel—when I refused.

"Well, aren't you just a damn baby," Grant snapped.

This was a sentiment shared by most of the others. In fact, Angela was the only one who made an effort to be my friend.

"Don't worry about it," she said. "The flowers are full of needles and druggies. Even if it wasn't, well... it's not like we're supposed to trespass, anyway. "

Angela and I became quite close that summer. We bonded over school, movies, scary stories, and urban legends.

I told her every story I knew, delighting in her reaction to the *Doll Man* tale. It terrified her. She claimed it gave her nightmares. Even so, she couldn't hear enough of it. It was as if hearing about it diminished the power it held over her.

I told her the other stories—about the railroad workers and the witch who ate pregnant girls, and even the one about how the tunnels make your wishes come true. But she didn't care about any of those the way she cared about Doll Man.

Over time, our superficial interests forged a deeper bond. Soon we were discussing our parents—she was missing her father, I my mother—and her brother, Wallace.

"I don't know what to do," she always said. "He's smart. He's so smart, you know? But he's..." She broke off, frustrated, clearly searching for the right word. "He's special, too. And not really the right kind of special."

It was hard for me to understand what she was saying. From what I parsed, Wallace truly was a genius. But that intellect was essentially wasted; he was mentally ill and developmentally disabled, like a perpetual eleven-year-old with an awe-inspiring intellect tempered by constant hallucinations.

"He's totally screwed," Angela vented. "It's a joke. He's a genius who's too crazy to ever actually be smart. I'll have to take care of him for the rest of my life. That's what my mom says. I don't get a choice." A small smile, halfway between sad and mean, curled her mouth. "I'm about ready to see if that crazy old lady is right."

"What do you mean?" I asked.

Angela kicked a stone. It skittered across the grass and hit a nearby tree. "You know. That stupid story? How if you sleep in the tunnels, your dreams come true?"

I thought of Mercy—*this place is good for dreams*—and shuddered. "Oh. Yeah. So... if it was true, what would you wish for?"

She kicked another rock. "To not have to take care of Wallace."

I didn't know what to say.

One golden morning toward the end of summer, I went to the playground to wait for Angela. It was our ritual: meet at the park with sack lunches and library books, claim a picnic table, and while away the day with *Henry Huggins*, peanut butter sandwiches, and Chocodiles.

Golden haze covered the playground that morning, a twinkling aura that reminded me of mist. The elongated shadows of swing sets and slides stretched across the sand like the legs of a huge, incomprehensible insect. Across the playground, the sunflowers rustled and nodded agreeably. They looked alive. Strange, sentient things nudging each other and murmuring amongst themselves.

The dazzling haze left dark, copper-tinged shadows pooled at the mouth of the tunnels. Something about them made me uneasy, so I looked up at the sunflowers instead.

There, among the bright, nodding blossoms, was a head.

I stopped.

It was a familiar head, a familiar face. Prematurely lined and painted with so much makeup it looked like a ventriloquist dummy. Mats of long yellow hair cascaded down either side, so bright they blended with the nodding sunflowers.

Mercy.

Those sunflowers were six feet tall or more. Mercy wasn't any taller than me.

Yet there she was, of a height with these giant flowers, smiling serenely at the morning sun.

"Mercy?" I whispered.

She opened her eyes. They blazed yellow, a violently cheerful shade of spoiled gold just a shade darker than the sunflowers. Then she descended, slipping down among the stalks as smoothly as a mermaid sinking beneath the waves.

Panic threatened to overtake me. I looked over my shoulder, hoping to see someone—adult, child, stranger, friend, it didn't matter, just someone—but there was nothing. Just the empty playground, and beyond that an uninterrupted expanse of rolling green spread to the street beyond.

I was alone.

Except for Mercy. Creepy old Mercy with her nasty hair and broken face. But maybe she wasn't being creepy on purpose. Maybe she needed help. And since I was the only person in the park, I had to check on her. So I steeled myself and strode forward. The sunflowers seemed to watch me from over the fence; unreadable sentinels forming a living wall.

I reached the concrete tunnels. Something caught my eye. Something bright and intricate and blazing white, like a star. I looked down. There, etched cleanly over the top of the entrance, was the dreamcatcher.

I slowed to a halt as my foot sank into a congealing puddle. I looked down, disgusted. What I'd taken for shadows at the mouth of the tunnel was a pool.

A thick, sticky, terribly red pool.

Just a few yards away, the sunflowers whispered and rattled.

It can't be, I thought. *It can't be.*

It couldn't be. So I knelt down to look inside.

Two crumpled, bloodstained faces peered from the tunnel shadows. Mercy's starry blue eyes stared back at me, bright and blank. Wedged beside hers like a second head was a small, mutilated, horrifically familiar face.

Angela.

The sun rose. Sunlight spilled into the tunnel like golden syrup, glancing off those dead, broken faces. Unable to look away, I scooted backward on all fours. My hands splashed in the blood puddle. It was thick and cold and stank like rusting iron.

Something shifted in the darkness behind them. Soft grunts met my ears, like someone forcing an overlarge body through a small space. That shapeless shadow moved forward and slowly resolved into the form of a man. The sunlight brightened, spilling farther into the hole and illuminating a third face: fleshy and round, with a lipless mouth and eyes the color of water weeds.

He watched me curiously, eyes glittering. "Well. Good morning." He buried one hand in Mercy's sunflower-yellow mats, and the other in Angela's blood-soaked hair. He gave each head a shake. "Pick a doll, what do you say? A pretty doll for a pretty girl?"

I tried to scream, but my breath issued in a shrill whisper.

He burst out laughing: low, meaty peals that echoed through the park.

The sound broke my paralysis. I kicked away, climbed to my feet and ran. I found my father quickly. He took one look at me—weeping and quivering, hands soaked in blood—and called the police.

They found Mercy and Angela right away, then closed the park down and launched a manhunt for the killer. That dough-faced, fussy little killer with a lipless mouth and murky green eyes. Doll Man, who'd scared Angela so.

Doll Man, who'd given her so many bad dreams.

Several days later, authorities pulled the wet, decomposed corpse of an over-weight man out of the river. According to the news, he couldn't be the killer because the coroner estimated that he'd been dead for at least three weeks.

They never identified him. And they never found the killer. In the absence of a culprit, public opinion changed and over time, everyone decided that Mercy—crazy, tiny, feather-light Mercy—had killed Angela, and I'd merely hallucinated the Doll Man.

Small towns. Small, cruel little towns filled with small-minded, cruel little people. Too cruel and too little to take note of the nightmarish miracle in their midst. But I suppose that's for the best. Sometimes, I imagine what would happen if those people knew that they lived on top of a tunnel that literally makes dreams come true. I imagine what they might dream of, what they might do.

And I shiver.

MORE FROM SOTEIRA PRESS

VISIT SOTEIRAPRESS.COM TO JOIN OUR MAILING LIST

THE MONSTERS WE FORGOT

VOLUME I

HORROR USA

CALIFORNIA

AN ANTHOLOGY OF HORROR FROM THE GOLDEN STATE

The first in a series of terrifying anthologies showcasing horror in every state, "Horror USA: California" is all about the terrors, horrors, creeps, and shrieks unique to the Golden State.

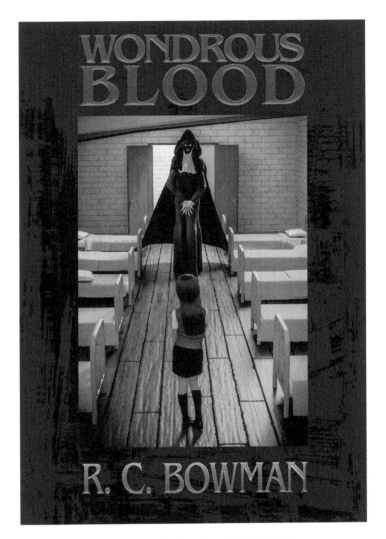

A new horror anthology from R. C. Bowman.

SLATED FOR RELEASE IN EARLY 2020.

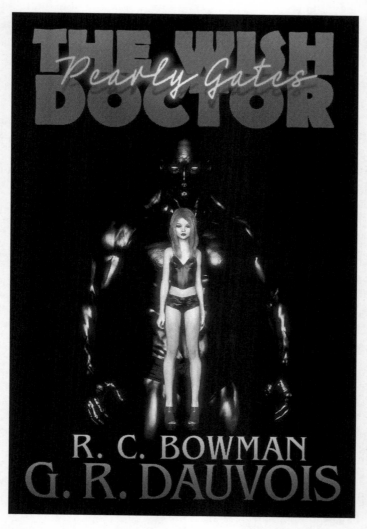

Driven by the relentless impulse to grant intriguing wishes, an amoral killer suddenly finds himself trapped into playing guardian to a street child.

SLATED FOR RELEASE IN EARLY 2020.

HOARDER HOUSE

A NOVELLA BY R. C. BOWMAN

IN THE UNLIKELIEST OF PLACES, A HAZMAT CLEANER FINDS A HIDDEN WORLD. IT'S ETHEREAL, DREAMLIKE, EXQUISITELY BEAUTIFUL… AND FULL OF MONSTERS WHO WANT OUT. Originally posted to Reddit's Nosleep community where it met with immense success, this edition of R.C. Bowman's popular horror series is revised, edited, and best of all, features 10,000 words of new content!

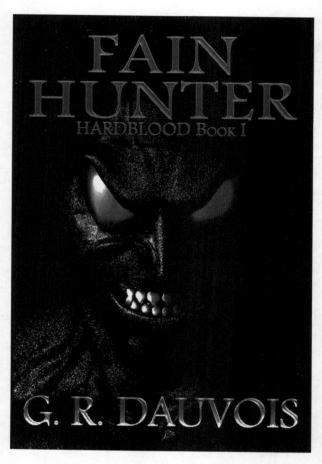

FAIN HUNTER

HARDBLOOD Book I

G. R. DAUVOIS

Euthain Kürowin doesn't belong. A high-born elf of extraordinary beauty, he has every advantage in his Utopian enclave of gentle immortals; and yet, unlike his gentle kinfolk, Euthain constantly quells a storm of such violent impulses that even hunting—the most barbaric of sports in his peaceful society—barely satisfies him. Finally he accepts that the darkness in his heart is inescapable. He decides to exile himself in order to protect his deeply empathetic people from the rage within. But when a barbaric force invades the realm of the Wood Nymphs, Euthain seems to have found his place. In a terrible twist of fate, he must decide whether that place is fighting for his people... or serving at the side of their greatest enemy. FAIN HUNTER is the first book in the HARDBLOOD grimdark trilogy, which comprises the first part of the epic IMMEMORIAL saga spanning centuries and worlds.

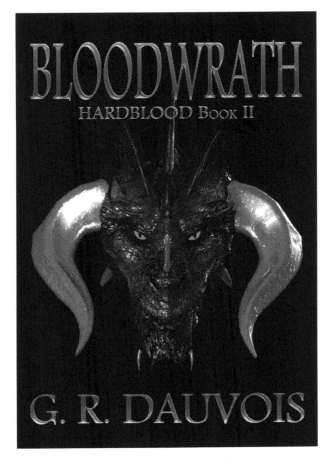

BLOODWRATH

HARDBLOOD BOOK II

G. R. DAUVOIS

Euthain Kürowin—pariah to his people, and lone champion of the gentle *Sylvain*—has traveled to the Black Mountain to confront the mysterious Molder whose monstrous minions have brought untold terror to the Nymphs of the Sylva. What he discovers within those caverns threatens to unravel all he has been led to believe about his people, and his place among them. Learning that he has been afflicted by the *Bloodwrath*—a soldier impulse that emerges whenever the Elvean race comes under cataclysmic threat—Euthain finds himself in greater conflict with his aberrant nature than ever before: Will he answer the call of his blood, and avenge the Molder's crimes, or will he surrender his outcast heart to the Molder's beautiful daughter Zhavelle, and thereby betray all he intended to defend? BLOODWRATH is the second book in the *HARDBLOOD* dark fantasy trilogy, which comprises the first part of the epic IMMEMORIAL saga.

RAVENSAGE

HARDBLOOD Book III

G. R. DAUVOIS

Having set out in the company of the nymphet Kyji to
investigate rumors of a new threat to his home province of
Haven Dale, the outcast Euthain Kürowin finds himself in the
Gelid Plains, a vast desert of snow and ice. Starved for truth
and desperate to justify his many questionable actions so far,
he drives on despite the suspicion that the Molder has tricked
him into a fool's errand. When starving predators render his
dragon flightless, Euthain is forced to decide whether to push
on with his mission, or start the long trek home, if only to
ensure that the little Nymph in his company survives her
ordeal. Meanwhile, unbeknownst to them, an ancient menace
far greater than the one they have been hunting—a menace
that will decide the fate of not only the Elvean race, but the
entire world—is amassing its forces. Will Euthain's desire to
elevate himself from pariah to champion of the Elveni prove
meaningless in the face of such overwhelming odds, or will he
finally find redemption?

Made in the USA
Middletown, DE
23 December 2019

81828205R00229